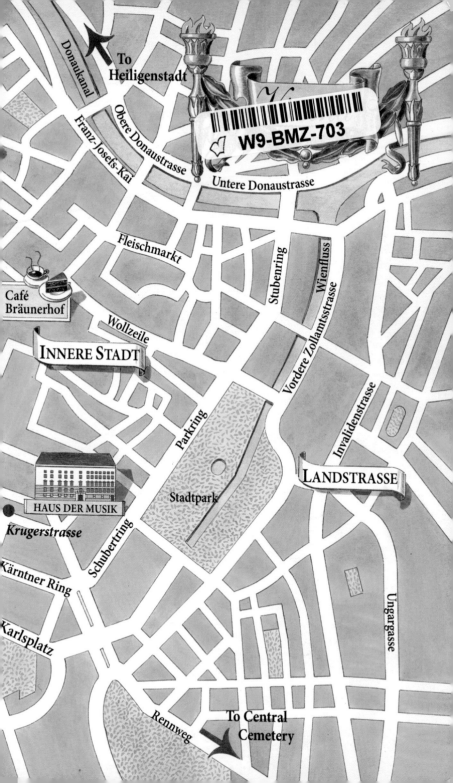

CITY of LOST DREAMS

A Novel

MAGNUS FLYTE

PENGUIN BOOKS

PENGUIN BOOKS

Published by the Penguin Group
Penguin Group (USA) LLC
375 Hudson Street
New York, New York 10014

USA | Canada | UK | Ireland | Australia | New Zealand | India | South Africa | China
penguin.com
A Penguin Random House Company

First published in Penguin Books 2013

LIBRARY OF CONGRESS CATALOGING-IN-PUBLICATION DATA
Flyte, Magnus.
City of lost dreams : a novel / Magnus Flyte.
pages cm
ISBN 978-0-14-312327-9
I. Title.
PS3606.L98C58 2013
813'.6—dc23
2013031311

Printed in the United States of America
1 3 5 7 9 10 8 6 4 2

Set in Minion Pro • Designed by Elke Sigal
Endpaper Illustration by Rodica Prato

2/10/14

History allows us to realize the tragedy of human existence in its entirety. Knowing the truth means exiting space and time. All movement is searching. The essence of art lies in thinking and giving shape to visions. This is what changes the world.

—RUDOLF LEITNER-GRÜNDBERG

That's a nice girl, that. But she ought to go careful in Vienna. Everybody ought to go careful in a city like this.

—GRAHAM GREENE, *The Third Man*

Early Praise for *Ci*

"A magical mystery tour that pic[ks] you've never been before but is exactly where you want to be. Sexy, suspenseful, historical—an absolute page-turner."

—M. J. Rose, international bestselling author of *Seduction*

Praise for *City of Dark Magic*

A *New York Times* Bestseller
A *USA Today* "New and Noteworthy" Pick

"This deliciously madcap novel has it all: murder in Prague, time travel, a misanthropic Beethoven, tantric sex, and a dwarf with attitude. I salute you, Magnus Flyte!" —Conan O'Brien

"A comical, rollicking and sexy thriller." —*Huffington Post*

"An entertaining mix of magic, mystery, and romance, it's one of the most original novels released this year." —CNN.com

"Never fails to shimmer exotically, erotically, on the page."

—*Slate*

"The most wickedly enchanting novel I've ever read and also the funniest. A Champagne magnum of intrigue and wit, this book sparkles from beginning to end."

—Anne Fortier, bestselling author of *Juliet*

"I was sold on newcomer Magnus Flyte's recent novel when I looked at the clock and realized that I'd been reading for four hours without pause. . . . Smart, sexy, and self-aware." —Tor.com

"Sometimes you want a book that simply entertains, and *City of Dark Magic* does just that. There's a bit of everything, and when one scene seems impossible, know that the next will top it. Go with it. It's a good ride and a great way to escape reality for a bit."

—Bookreporter.com

"The darkly charming and twisted streets of Prague provide the deliciously dramatic backdrop for this paranormal romp that fires on all cylinders, masquerading by turns as a romance, a time-travel thriller, and a tongue-in-cheek mystery." —*Booklist*

"A story that abounds in mysterious portents, wild coincidences, violent death, and furtive but lusty sex . . . [this novel] cleverly combines time travel, murder, history, and musical lore."

—*Publishers Weekly*

PENGUIN BOOKS

CITY of LOST DREAMS

After the uproar over the publication of his first novel, *City of Dark Magic*, Magnus Flyte retreated to his dacha in the Urals, where he enjoys exploring underground tributaries of the Ufa, observing the mating habits of the spotted nutcracker, and smelting.

Mr. Flyte is currently at work on a half-hour television comedy about sixteenth-century ethnographer Sigismund von Herberstein, entitled *Ural I Love*.

Acknowledgments

Magnus Flyte would like to acknowledge the many people who have aided and abetted him during this project: Eva-Maria Berger for her generosity, advice, and good company in Vienna; Charlotte Sommer and Bruce Walker, for ongoing ground support of every kind in Prague; Renato Marena for wonderful hosting and the finest samosas in all of London; Nina Viswanathan for being the best virtual dinner guest ever; Matteo, Berta, and Sabine Tamanini for joining Magnus for a mad dash through Schloss Ambras; Kathleen McCleary for being the first reader; John and Jennifer Brancato for fueling Magnus with moral support and mortadella; Betty Luceigh for unveiling the wonders of nanotechnology; Claudia Cross and Sally Brady for knowing when to send in either the cavalry or the caviar and champagne; Carolyn Carlson, Ramona Demme, and all of Team Penguin for taking a leap of faith (twice); Lindsay Prevette and Laura Abbott for putting Magnus up in style; man-in-the-field Brian Wilson for buoying all things Magnus; Nick Sherman and Adam Dannheisser for guerrilla-style video-making; Patrick Tully for five musical notes on a winter evening; and a special thank-you to all those gorgeous, brilliant, sexy people working at bookstores across the land. You know who you are.

Editor's Note

Because Magnus Flyte can be quite elusive and shuns the public eye, we would like to thank Mr. Flyte's representatives for their cooperation in the publication of this book:

Meg Howrey is the author of *Blind Sight* and *The Cranes Dance*.

Christina Lynch is a television writer and journalist.

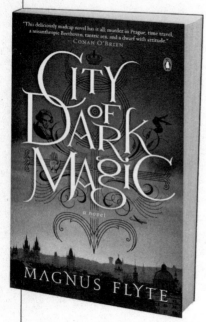

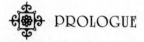 PROLOGUE

Even the local tourism board had to admit the church attracted a rather unusual crop of visitors. Some came for the novelty, others out of a hazy respect for their fellow man, and some came for more sinister reasons. The last group often turned up after hours, when the gates were locked, the laminated information cards in six languages neatly replaced in their color-coded folders, and the ticket takers safely home in their beds.

About fifty miles east of Prague, the town of Kutná Hora was best reached by a series of country highways pleasantly dotted with fruit stands and artisans selling a patriotic symbol that had been banned under communism: the garden gnome. And in case the Czech place-names with their tongue-twisting traffic jams of consonants proved difficult to decipher for nervous travelers in rental cars, handmade signs in English announcing *Bone Church* at every intersection provided easy clues for navigation.

Kutná Hora was just another parish in Bohemia until it got the ultimate status bump when a local abbot returned from the Holy Land and sprinkled authentic Golgothan dirt in the abbey's cemetery. Word got out that being buried in such sacred ground was a shortcut to Heaven. A chapel was constructed on the site, and those who felt death's cold embrace traveled from far and wide to get last rites and be buried in the cemetery. By the mid-1400s, Kutná Hora was *the* place to die.

It didn't take long for the gravediggers to be overwhelmed, their real estate being, as is true of tony enclaves everywhere, in limited supply. Graves were dug deep into the hallowed ground, coffins stacked up like shoe boxes in a fetishist's closet, but still they ran out of room. Soon it was time to put out the No Vacancy sign and hang up their shovels.

But, since people paid good money to be buried at Kutná Hora and no one in the hardscrabble area wanted to lose a revenue stream, a solution was quickly found. Older bodies, those from centuries past whose families were no longer around to protest, were exhumed. Treated with the utmost respect, of course, the skeletons were rehoused downstairs in a specially dug crypt, dubbed the Sedlec Ossuary.

As one might expect, eventually the crypt, too, filled up, and due to some annoying geological restrictions it wasn't safe to tunnel farther. And still people showed up and died. The piles of bones became quite large and prone to toppling over. For a holy place, it became something of an unholy mess.

But eventually the vogue of being buried at Kutná Hora passed. Though the bones remained, they were out of sight and out of mind, and Kutná Hora was once again just a nice little place to stop and have a beer and a plate of *palachinki* on the way to market.

In the late nineteenth century a local woodsman was hired to be the caretaker of the church. The woodsman pondered the rather spare main rooms of his beloved little house of God. He had heard of cathedrals in far-off cities bedecked with statues and cornices and sculpted arabesques. It saddened him that his parish of simple farmers and miners wouldn't spring for a little sprucing up, a little face-lift for their place of worship. And the woodsman was horrified by the chaos he found in the basement. So he immediately began to neaten and tidy what he found there. Like the trees he hewed and chopped into manageable lengths, skeletons were untangled and bones were separated by size and shape. Soon there were pyramids of skulls, towers of tibias, and hives of hips. There was symmetry, there was order, and there was beauty. It was a shame, really, that the fruits of his slightly OCD labor were hidden in the basement, while the austere church upstairs was such a poor reflection of the glory of God in the highest.

The woodsman got to work. He created a chandelier composed of every single bone in the human body. He strung phalanges into strings and then threaded them with popcorn garlands of skulls that gracefully arched from nave to apse. He fanned out scapulae like decks of cards to make the bases of monstrous monstrances topped with more skulls. Skulls and crossbones snaked up from floor to ceiling, delineating archways and barrel vaults.

Perhaps the crowning achievement was the holy cross itself, crafted out of skulls and leg bones, with slender arm bones representing the gentle rays of celestial glory. Beneath it the woodsman signed his name. In bones, naturally.

At first the inhabitants, though awestruck by his initiative and undeniable creativity, were wary of having somehow offended God or their fellow man. These were, they reminded each other, *actual* bones of actual *people*. Long dead, yes, but still children of the same Lord and due a certain respect. And yet . . . were not the woodsman's displays a form of veneration? Had he not given forebears and strangers alike a sort of eternal, beautiful life for their remains, while their souls safely resided with the angels in Heaven?

Also, people came from far and wide and paid good money to see the thing.

And so the church of bones became one of the Czech nation's most visited destinations.

And if, now and then, a car arrived with a rather serious, scholarly woman at the wheel, and a new skull, or set of ribs, or pair of tibias were discreetly, after hours, added to the neatly arranged piles, who noticed?

No one.

ONE

$\mathcal{S}$arah Weston heard the splash just as Nico got to the part in the story about the gorilla.

Her plane from Boston was meant to arrive in Prague in the morning, but a series of delays and a missed connecting flight in Heathrow had made her late, which was upsetting as she was on a very particular mission. Hoping to at least get a little background on the situation in Prague, Sarah decided to call upon a master thief and repository of secrets great and small. Nicolas Pertusato suggested she join him at Barbora a Kateřina, a chic new restaurant on the banks of the Vltava River.

"We will sit outside and have a good gossip," Nico said when she arrived. "It is unseasonably warm for late October. You can admire the view and I can admire you. It's been too long since I've seen you. I intend to bask."

In a sand-colored cashmere suit and polka-dot silk tie, Nicolas was easily the best-dressed man in the restaurant. He was also the shortest, being a dwarf, a term he preferred to the more politically correct "little person."

Barbora a Kateřina had evidently taken its name from the saints Barbara and Catherine, whose images appeared on the restaurant walls and the menus, where the two saints appeared to be somewhat critically eyeing each other's jewels. (Babs had the nicer brooch, Cathy the prettier tiara.) The setting was exquisite, with the Charles Bridge throwing golden shadows across the river, and Prague Castle on its hill, dramatically lit in emerald green, but Sarah's mind was on other things.

"Is it a good sign or a bad sign that Pols is in bed by eight?" Sarah asked as she began her interrogation. "How is her energy? Is she eating?"

"You will see Pollina tomorrow." Nico reached over and patted her hand.

"Yes, but I'm leaving for Vienna in the afternoon," Sarah reminded him. "I just want to get as clear a picture as possible of how she's responding to the last round of medications so I can make a convincing case to Dr. Müller."

Pollina Rutherford, a thirteen-year-old blind musical prodigy of astounding talent, had moved to Prague from Boston a year earlier. The girl had never been of vigorous health and had lately been plagued by a series of lung infections. In the past several months, these had become much more serious. Sarah had frantically researched everything related to Pols's illness, a rare autoimmune disorder that seemed to be caused by a malfunction on chromosome 20. When she heard about a nanobiologist at the University of Vienna who was developing a promising new drug targeting mutations in chromosome 20, she had contacted her about enrolling Pols in a trial. And when Dr. Müller had turned them down, Sarah had dropped everything to make this trip to Vienna to change the woman's mind.

It wasn't easy for Sarah to explain her emotions where Pollina was concerned. She had begun tutoring her when she was in high school and Pols was only four, though it was clear from the beginning that in many ways it was the younger girl who was the older soul. Their backgrounds were entirely different. Sarah had grown up in working-class South Boston, had lost her dad when she was nine, had blazed through high school, college, and grad school, all the way to, at age twenty-five, a PhD in neuromusicology on a mixture of ambition and passion. Before coming to Prague, Pollina had spent most of her young life inside a Back Bay mansion, cared for by a devoted but eccentric Mexican housekeeper and left largely to her own devices by her wealthy dilettante parents. But music had erased the disparity of their ages and their experiences. Music, and a sort of kindred fierceness they recognized in each other.

Cocktails arrived at the table. Sarah's came garnished with a large wheel of orange slice, and the olive in Nico's glass was pierced with a giant plastic sword.

"I ordered you the Catheratini," Nico explained. "The orange is meant to symbolize the wheel that the unfortunate Saint Catherine was tortured upon, though this is not explained on the menu and perhaps the symbolism is lost on some. My Barbatini, you may note, contains a sword."

"I'm going to go out on a limb here and guess that Barbara was decapitated."

"By her own father, poor dear. Admit. Impiety tastes delicious. I'm glad you like it, as I own a share in this place. A side venture of mine. I thought it would be amusing, but I fear that, like everything else, it will end by being either a bore or a heartbreak."

Sarah put down her Catheratini. She had been so caught up in her concern over seeing Pols that she was only now noticing that the little man didn't look particularly well himself.

But Nico waved off her questions with a hand, attributing his low spirits to the modern climate of political correctness that inhibited flirtation with the miniskirted female waitstaff, and ordered a bottle of Roudnice red.

"And so, you go to Vienna tomorrow," he continued. "To bully the nanobiologist into helping our Pollina?"

"I think this Dr. Müller is just being cautious"—Sarah leaned forward—"because Pols's immune system is very compromised. Maybe she doesn't want to take a risk and potentially skew her results."

"And you have never taken no for an answer."

"I am not leaving Vienna until that bitch says yes." Sarah smiled. Nico raised his glass to her.

"Oksana, too, thinks targeting the chromosome itself might be helpful." Nico sighed. Nico's wife, Oksana, a nurse, was overseeing Pols's care. "But these are all drugs of the future, and, as you know, I have much more experience with drugs of the past. I, too, want to make an experiment."

"Are we talking alchemy here?" Sarah raised an eyebrow. "I am not letting you give Pols ground-up narwhal horn."

"Nonsense." Nico poured himself another glass of wine. "I haven't been able to get my hands on that for two centuries."

Though he appeared to be in his mid-forties, Nico insisted to his confidants that he was four hundred years old, rendered immortal by the astronomer Tycho Brahe in 1601 in an alchemical experiment gone awry. Sarah was never sure what to believe when Nico was around. What was indisputable was that Nico knew a lot about a great number of things, including chemistry. Sarah herself had been the beneficiary of a rather unusual drug he had replicated. She knew what he could do. But this was Pollina. And it wasn't a game.

"I have found something." Nico lowered his voice. He looked

around the restaurant, then slid an object across the table, wrapped in a napkin. Sarah unfolded it to reveal a book.

The cover featured a cartoon drawing of a white-bearded man dressed in what looked like a green jumpsuit, sporting an enormous Druidic headpiece topped with a crescent moon, and carrying a flaming torch. Behind the Druid, a few badly drawn goats wandered across a hilly background. The sky was lit by a rainbow, across which ran the title: *The Every Soul's Guide to Alchemy! 50 Fun Recipes for Living, Loving, and Levitating!*

"We're joking, right?" Sarah looked up.

"Nay."

"You want to use this on Pollina?" Sarah flipped the book open and read at random. "'We must shut off our rational, doubting, linear modal selves and listen to the harmonies contained in the Creator's majestic dance!'"

"I know," Nico sniffed. "The usual dreadful hippie twaddle. I was attracted to the cover, which I believe depicts William Price of Llantrisant, whom I knew. A darling man, and quite cheerful, for a Druid. Imagine my surprise when I'm leafing through it, merely to entertain myself with all the drivel, and I find . . ." Nico flipped the pages and pointed.

"'*The Will to Heal*, by Philippine Welser,'" Sarah read. Under the title was a list of ingredients involving a lot of symbols and drawings.

"Whoever put this silly book together," Nico explained, "decided to throw in an actual alchemical formula. In the author's acknowledgments I found a sentence thanking the von Hohenlohe family, so I suspect he got it from them. The von Hohenlohes' castle was conferred on them by Ferdinand of Tyrol, and they have what remains of Ferdinand's *Kunstkammer*, which includes

Philippine's book of medicines. The point is, it's real. It's an actual recipe of Philippine Welser."

"Okay, for those of us who lack your colossal scholarship . . . ?"

Nico sighed. "Philippine Welser. The wife of Ferdinand, uncle of Emperor Rudolf II."

"Oh, God. Not Rudy again." Tales of Rudolf's eccentricities were as ubiquitous in Prague as inexpensive beer and marionettes.

Nico, unperturbed, continued on. "An archduke, Ferdinand, married Philippine, a commoner, in secret. She was a talented healer and became famous in the Tyrol as something of a good witch. Most of her formulae were lost, and what has survived is, as I said, in the hands of a very close-lipped family. This is her tonic to incite the process of healing. A sort of spark to the engine. Pollina's immune system is sluggish. It needs to be awakened."

"Nico . . ." Sarah growled. Every skeptical fiber of her being was on guard.

"I'm not going to sit here and do nothing," Nico said sharply. "Alchemy is my talent, and I'm going to use it."

"Which talents are we using?"

Sarah turned to see Max Lobkowicz Anderson standing behind her chair. Sarah and Max had . . . there wasn't an easy explanation for it—slept together by mistake, fallen in love, almost gotten killed—during the summer she worked at the museum Max had opened in Prague, which housed his family's art and artifacts. They had kept up the affair for almost a year after she returned to Boston, until the pressure of maintaining a long-distance relationship while trying to establish a career had overwhelmed Sarah, and she had broken it off. Max, she knew, was now seeing a British historian who was researching a book in Prague. And Sarah? Lately there had been a brief but energetic fling with a tennis player. The tennis player wasn't Max—nobody was Max—but when it came to relationships, Sarah wondered if hers was more of a serve-and-volley game. She didn't really have time for long rallies.

Sarah stood to give Max a hug, and then collided with his chin as he went in for the double cheek kiss. Nico snorted. Sarah noted that the scent of the guy she had once fallen for now carried the unmistakable trace of another woman's perfume. Gardenias. A flashbulb went off, briefly blinding Sarah. Max turned to the paparazzo leaning precariously over another table.

"Please, Jerzy," said Max. "This is a private evening. If I pose for one, will you take the night off?" The photographer nodded, and Max offered his profile to the camera.

"Our little princeling has become quite the celebrity," said Nico dryly.

"Ticket sales at the museum are up." Max settled himself in the chair next to Sarah. "As are donations. The press is useful." Sarah knew that Max struggled to keep his family museum afloat so that he didn't have to sell off any of the treasures his ancestors had amassed. It wasn't a job he had asked for, but he had taken it on as a duty to his family and to future generations. During the summer she had spent authenticating Beethoven manuscripts at his museum, Sarah had watched him struggle with the responsibility of being thirteenth in a line of princes. Now she saw that the cuffs of his dress shirt were monogrammed. Apparently, he had adapted.

"We're talking about Pollina," said Sarah.

Max touched her shoulder in sympathy.

"You know she's been playing weekly concerts at the museum," he said. "I've tried to get her to cut back a little, but . . ."

"I know," said Sarah.

"I would do anything for Pols," said Max.

They all sat in silence for a moment. Plates of roast pork and dumplings arrived, along with another bottle of wine, which Nico again largely appropriated. He began telling them about the time when, after a week of heavy rains, the Vltava had overflowed its banks and submerged several areas of the city, including the Prague Zoo. More than a thousand animals had to be evacuated in extremely dangerous and dramatic conditions, including lions, tigers, rhinos, and hippos. Nico waxed rhapsodic over the aquatic feats of Gaston the sea lion, who escaped his enclosure as the water rose and swam all the way to Dresden. He described the anguish of the Czechs, weeping for the loss of their dear old elephant Sabi, who had been put down as the water rose to her ears. Of course, Nico being Nico, this led to the tale of a young male gorilla called Pong, who went rogue during the deluge and whose breakout had been hushed up by the authorities.

"I have seen him," Nico said. "I, and a few others for whom the tunnels below Prague hold no terrors. For that is where he lives to this day. He feeds on fruit. And, I believe, carp."

"You're drunk," said Max. Sarah realized this was true. The little man was listing sideways. He had certainly imbibed enough, but Nico's tolerance was legendary. He had once told Sarah that he had to drink solidly for nearly a month before he could become even slightly inebriated.

"I tell you I have seen his huddled form, slipping into the shadows!" Nico shouted. "And once . . ."

And that was when Sarah heard the splash, and a cry.

She looked over the railing into the inky darkness of the river, and she heard it again.

"Oh, shit." She pushed back her chair. "I think someone might be out there in the water."

"Very funny." Max joined her at the rail. "Nico has become quite the ventriloquist. It's one of his less amusing talents."

But through the light of the torches surrounding their table, they could both see someone struggling in the water just below them. Max called to one of the waiters, then pulled out his phone. Sarah looked down at the water, saw the white flash of a hand shoot up, then saw it disappear. The person wasn't that far away, and Sarah couldn't just stand there and watch someone drown right in front of her. There wouldn't be much time. She kicked off her shoes, climbed up on the railing, and dove in. The water was freezing. She surfaced, spluttering.

"There," called Nico, grabbing one of the torches and holding it out over the water.

Sarah paused for a fraction of a second to get her bearings, then kicked hard in the direction Nico was pointing to, trying to remember everything she could from high school lifesaving class.

It was nearly impossible to see anything in the water. Floating cans and plastic water bottles knocked into her head. The current was swift, carrying her close to the middle of the river. Sarah thought she could hear the sound of oarlocks on a rowboat, but when she yelled, no one answered.

Then she heard a gasp and a choked cry, close.

"Hey!" she shouted, stroking toward the splashing figure. A man.

Sarah ducked under the water and came up next to him, reaching to get an arm around his neck. The man panicked and, flailing, fought her at first, and she was pushed momentarily underneath the water. Sarah yelled versions of "It's okay" and "Stop kicking me" in as many languages as she could remember. When she got to *"Arrête!"* and then, more absurdly, *"Pax!"* the man finally went limp and let himself be towed along. Sarah wondered if he was dead. He was wearing something incredibly heavy that slowed her down and nearly exhausted her strength—a sleeping bag? Who jumped into the river wearing a sleeping bag?

Now she was having to swim against the current, burdened, and the distance suddenly seemed impossibly great. She could hear the voices on the shore, but she was growing tired very quickly. It occurred to her that many people who jumped into rivers to save others drowned themselves. Her legs felt heavy and it was getting hard to keep her chin above the water. She had a minute, maybe two, before she would have to drop the man and save herself. If she could. His long beard had wrapped itself around her arm like a manacle.

Again Sarah heard the creak of oars in an oarlock. Someone was definitely out here. Maybe Max had found a boat. She called out again. No answer.

And then, *ping*.

Something hit the water next to her head.

Sarah recognized the next sound. A gun being cocked.

Ping. Ping.

She dove under water, pulling the man with her. Fear mixed with outrage in her brain. *Bullets? Are you fucking kidding me?* Was this how she was going to die? Wearing out-of-season snowman underwear? There was so much she hadn't achieved yet, professionally. Who would remember her? She needed more time!

Who would help Pols?

Stop it. It was Pols's voice in her head. *Don't think. Swim.*

Sarah opened her eyes as her face emerged from the water, took a deep breath, and kicked hard toward the lights of the restaurant. She heard the creak of oarlocks again and ducked under the water, still kicking, still towing, until her lungs were depleted.

"Sarah!"

Max. Max was in the water.

"I'm here." She moved forward, towing her burden. "I'm here! Someone's shooting."

Max grabbed her hard around the ribs, almost polishing her off, but he had also brought a float ring. Together, dragging the man, they moved toward the wharf, where Nico and the entire staff and clientele of the restaurant were ready to help pull them out. One of the waiters worked to revive the man, breathing into his mouth, as Sarah lay on her side, gasping. Shock would set in soon, she knew, and she would begin to shiver. A waiter wrapped table linens around her, and Max, dripping wet, was rubbing her arms and telling her she was amazing through his own chattering teeth.

"Someone was shooting at me," she said. She had forgotten about the way Max's hands felt. How could she have forgotten?

"In the river?" asked Max. "Are you sure? I didn't hear shots."

"Yes," she choked out. "I heard the gun. Then bullets . . . hitting water."

Max frowned, staring out over the Vltava. Sarah listened to the crowd of Czechs and tourists buzzing around the man the way people did when something awful happened, like a flock of wild turkeys in the presence of a snake. She tried to say more but she was cold and exhausted. And Max being so close to her, touching her, was confusing. She heard sirens in the distance and looked over at the man, catching a glimpse of his long scraggly hair and beard. What she had taken for a sleeping bag was actually a heavy brown embroidered cloak over robes. Some kind of priest? Or was it a costume? The man wasn't moving. Nico caught Sarah's eye and shook his head.

So her efforts had been in vain. The last of the adrenaline left her body and she began to shake. Max put his arms around her.

"You were so fast," he said. "And I could see you . . . but then I couldn't . . . and I jumped in, and I thought . . . she can't . . . I have to tell her . . ."

"It was stupid of me," said Sarah. "I don't know what I was thinking. . . ."

Wait. What were they talking about? Max didn't smell like gardenias now. He smelled like foul river water, but underneath that, it was him. Max. His smell was still intoxicating. She was going to kiss him. He seemed instantly aware of her desire and, as always, met it with his own. His face, his lips, were close to hers. They had just jumped into one river, why not another? She had just chosen life over death. How much time did any of them have?

"*Ack*." The bearded man suddenly opened his eyes and coughed up a lungful of brackish water. "*Bluuuuck*." The crowd murmured, pressing forward. Max ordered them back. The man struggled to sit up, turning his head and looking straight at Sarah. His features were fine, his eyes a very pale blue. He said something Sarah couldn't understand in a thick, strangled voice, then closed his eyes.

The waiter felt for the man's neck, and began performing CPR, but after a few minutes Sarah could see that it was no use. The man was dead.

"Max? Max?"

A red-headed woman, wearing a long white coat and gloves, pushed her way through the crowd to where Max was crouched next to Sarah. He immediately let go of her and stood up.

"Max, what happened?" The woman grabbed his arm. "Are you all right? My God, look at you. You're soaking." The woman's accent was the kind of plummy, drawly English that Sarah associated with BBC news presenters and Agatha Christie mysteries. "Harriet," said Max.

Harriet began ordering people about, calling for a blanket for Max, and brandy.

An ambulance arrived. Sarah was given a thermal wrap and had her vitals tested. A technician complimented her on her blood pressure as Max explained the events to Harriet. "Sarah managed to pull the man from the river, but . . ."

"My God," the woman murmured, stroking his arm. Now that circulation had returned to her body, Sarah had time to take in Max's new girlfriend. Harriet's red hair cascaded down her back in a cluster of perfectly disorganized pre-Raphaelite curls. Her white coat buttoned tightly around her waist, then flared out. Her gloves, Sarah saw, had actual gauntlets. Where did she shop? The Edwardian Gap? Sarah took a guess that Harriet did not wear off-season snowman underwear. Probably silk stockings and garters. Sarah called Nico over to her.

"What did he say?" she asked. "The man. Before he died. Could you understand him?"

"He said that he was John of Nepomuk," Nico whispered in her ear, "and that he was pushed."

The ambulance took the dead man away. Sarah told the police about the shots, and they notified the water patrol. Sarah was formally introduced to Harriet, which was awkward, since Sarah was still wet and reeking of Vltava, and Harriet was wearing white gloves. The two women nodded at each other.

"Nico, get Sarah back to my place," Max said, tossing a set of keys at the little man. "I'll be along in a minute." They left him to the tender ministrations of Harriet, and Nico drove her to Max's "place"—the Lobkowicz family palace at Prague Castle that Max had converted to a museum, where Max kept a private apartment.

Sarah noted the feminine toiletries in Max's bathroom. Harriet seemed quite ensconced. When she finished showering, she saw that Nico had rather wickedly laid out a choice of robes for her: a man's dressing gown in heavy silk, monogrammed with Max's initials, and an ornate Japanese kimono reeking of gardenias. Sarah searched through Max's clothes until she found a T-shirt, sweatpants, and a cashmere sweater that had escaped the busy monogrammer.

She found both Max and Nico in the living room, waiting for her. Max's wolfhound, Moritz, rushed forward to lick her toes. Max handed her a glass of whiskey, not quite meeting her eye. Sarah was grateful for Nico's presence, which would keep them from discussing anything too intimate.

"Did anyone call the morgue?" Sarah asked. "Do we know who that guy was?"

"He said he was John of Nepomuk," Max reminded her. "Who was a fourteenth-century saint."

"Right." Sarah took a sip of whiskey. "So our guy was either high or delusional."

Nico shrugged. "Our guy was speaking Medieval Latin and Bohemian."

"Okay, so a language history student," suggested Sarah. "Driven mad by declensions and pursued by the Mob for unpaid backgammon debts. Someone was *shooting* at us."

"John of Nepomuk was pushed into the Vltava in 1393," said Nico. "Reportedly because he wouldn't reveal to the king what the queen's confession was all about. John of Nepomuk is the saint of the confessional. The saint of keeping secrets."

Max and the little man exchanged a look.

"You think it means something?" asked Max.

"Everything means something." Nicolas narrowed his eyes. "I have been feeling for months now . . . a sense that someone is looking over my shoulder. Following me. Or maybe I am following him."

"Maybe we're not the only ones looking . . ." Max glanced at Sarah.

"Looking for what?" Sarah asked, although she knew the answer to this. Max believed his family had long been members of a secret Order of the Golden Fleece. The Fleece—a book that reputedly contained the answers to the deepest mysteries of life and death—had been missing since the seventeenth century. Sarah had once tried to help Max on his quest, but she couldn't get involved in all that now. She was exhausted and more than a bit impatient. This was always the way things were in Prague: mysterious, watery, elusive. It was like the minute you got off the plane here, all firm ground dissolved. And you did crazy things. Like falling in love.

"I think it's a warning." Nico took a big gulp of whiskey. "A sign."

I don't want signs, Sarah thought. *I don't want warnings and strange portents. I want answers.*

"I'll be going to London tomorrow," Nico continued. "There are some things from Philippine's recipe that I would like to acquire for Pols. Max, I trust that this conversation will remain very much under your hat?"

"If you mean Harriet," Max answered stiffly, after a brief glance at Sarah, "then, yes. Yes, of course. I haven't told her anything about . . . anything. If you think Philippine's medicines might be helpful, I'll go through the library here and see if I can find anything related to her work. Worth a shot."

"And Sarah—"

"I'm leaving for Vienna after Pols's concert." She stood up. "I have my own quest."

"Do you have the key I gave you?" said Nico, moving forward and taking up her hand.

"Yes," she said, confused. Sarah fingered the key she wore on a chain around her neck. The little man had given her the key during the summer she worked in Prague. As far as she knew, it only opened one door, and that door was here, not in Vienna. "Why?"

"No reason. But watch your step. You must remain *en garde*, my dear."

"Don't worry," Sarah promised. "What could possibly happen to me in Vienna?"

TWO

$\mathcal{S}$arah woke early the next morning, surprisingly none the worse for having hauled a fourteenth-century saint out of the Vltava the night before. Of course she didn't really believe the man was actually John of Nepomuk, whose statue, with its crown of golden stars, she had passed many times on the Charles Bridge. She had also seen the saint's tomb—a mind-boggling tribute to what the Baroque could do when it got its hands on a shitload of silver—in St. Vitus's Cathedral. No, the most likely explanation was usually the correct one: the guy she had fished out of the river was a nut job in a costume. She was also not prepared to believe that the nut job was on some sort of rival crusade to find the Golden Fleece. Max imagined mythic quests around every corner. He was about a half step away from seeing Rudolf II on a piece of toast.

Max had been very generous, putting her up for the evening at the Four Seasons, where he said the manager was a friend. Sarah appreciated the high-thread-count sheets, but was horrified by the prices on the room service menu. No eggs should cost that much unless they came with the actual chickens and a handsome farmer who would rub your feet while you ate.

Sarah opened her computer and sent an e-mail to Alessandro, her former Boston roommate, advising him of her train times. It was Alessandro who had alerted her to the work of the nanobiologist Dr. Bettina Müller. He was teaching at the University of Vienna this year, and she would be staying with him.

The events of the previous evening almost seemed like a dream now. Nico. The restaurant. The dive into the river. The shots. Saint John's pale blue eyes staring at her. Max's hands. The feeling that she had made a mistake in letting him go. The desire to kiss him. Harriet.

Telling herself she was allowed to be curious, Sarah had done a little Internet search on Harriet Hunter before collapsing into bed the night before.

Max's new girlfriend was pretty famous in Britain. Her academic credentials were impeccable—her PhD was from Oxford and she had published in her field. But she was best known as the host of a popular television show, *Histories & Mysteries*. Naturally, Sarah found some episodes of it on YouTube. Dr. Hunter practiced what was called archaeological history. In her programs she re-created the banquets of seventeenth-century kings, spent the night in freezing castles, slept on a straw-tick mattress, and used a chamber pot. She squeezed her petite but well-endowed frame into corsets, donned bonnets, attempted an exit from a tiny horse-drawn carriage while wearing an enormous crinoline. She took a bath in goats' milk, plucked a goose, fought (unloaded) pistols at dawn. She punctuated her speech with Shakespearean exclamations: "Oh, pish!" "Heigh-ho, what have we here?" "What tilly-vally!" There was nothing she wouldn't explore, investigate, or ingest.

"It's 1598 and Oswald Croll is writing his *Basilica chymica* here in Prague," ran one documentary clip. Dr. Harriet was dressed in a floor-length magus robe and stood before a table of glass beakers and pewter dishes. "We can—if we dare—follow his instructions for the making of a magical amulet: two ounces of dried toads ground to a fine powder, one complete menstruum of a virgin, one dram of unpierced pearls, one dram of coral, two scruples of Eastern saffron . . ." Apparently Dr. Harriet had not dared to try—or, more likely, was prevented from quaffing on-air—the collected monthly of some suitably innocent schoolgirl, but she promised her viewers that Croll believed his amulet was a surefire preventative from diseases both astral and venereal.

All of this had earned the historian a raft of snarky comments from her colleagues, who accused her of pandering, of trivializing history, of sensationalism, and of—horror of horrors—bad taste. The kind of things that generally got said of any academic who achieved a modicum of fame, published something more than five people wanted to read, or wore lipstick.

But really, the woman was impressive.

And, Sarah had to admit, a good choice for Max, who was also sort of an odd duck. Perhaps the sudden rush of feelings for Max was just the result of having a near-death experience, Sarah thought, as she set herself firmly toward Josefov, where Pollina's parents kept an apartment for their daughter. Her brain had been flooded with chemicals and she hadn't been thinking clearly. Anyway, she would be leaving for Vienna in the afternoon. Better for everyone.

"They tell us her immune system no good, and it worse if she has stress. So we try not to worry her. We act normal."

Pollina's caretaker, Jose Nieto, was waiting for Sarah on a street of glassware shops, holding the leash of Pollina's elderly mastiff, Boris. Jose told her that the girl did not know how sick she was, and they needed to keep it that way.

"But she knows how she *feels*," Sarah argued. She was skeptical, anyway, about the ability of anyone to hide things from Pols.

The girl's blindness—and possibly her genius—had rendered her exceptionally observant. A bus pulled up and discharged a single-file line of young Chinese women in pink velour tracksuits. Prague was beginning to feel like a Hogarth painting entitled *The Triumph of Capitalism*.

"She say she feel fine, fine, fine. But when she think no one hear, she cough *bad*." Jose had looked after Pollina since birth. Now he had dark circles under his eyes. "Her parents, they just leave," he continued. "They go to Afghanistan for the archaeology. They nice people, but they don't worry! Always I see rich people worry about stupid thing like if bread has gluten, but they just say, 'Oh, darling, you must rest and not work so hard.' They no understand her."

The first-floor apartment was large and luxurious, though Sarah had to assume that while the art had been chosen by Pollina's parents, the decorative touches had been added by Jose, who had a flair for whimsy. A row of Egyptian statues sported tiny bandanas. Sunglasses and a pipe had been unceremoniously added to an African ceremony mask. The crucifixes, however, had been left in their original state.

Pollina was seated at a grand piano. She was playing a little tune of just five notes over and over again, as if in a trance: E. B. C. A. G.

Sarah, whose mind automatically sought to classify these things, didn't recognize the strangely compelling little passage, and wasn't even sure which key the girl was playing in. Pollina stopped abruptly.

"Why did you break Max's heart?" Pols demanded without preamble.

"I brought doughnuts from Boston." Sarah placed the carton of requested Dunkin' Donuts on the coffee table for the expats. Sarah was all too familiar with Pols's blunt opinions. The last time they had spoken, the target had been her career. Was Sarah *sure* that teaching was *really* what she wanted to do with her understanding of music? Pols had an unerring nose for weak spots.

"I thought," Pols continued now, coming forward and touching Sarah's hand in greeting, "that people strove their whole lives to find love."

Sarah sighed. Pollina was a genius, but she sometimes got very romantic notions into her head and she *was* only thirteen. How to explain that love and life didn't always go easily together? It wouldn't be obvious to Pollina why it was so important that Sarah make her own career and place in the world before she attached herself to someone else, that she and Max were leading very different lives.

Sarah kept her tone light. "Let's face it, I'm no princess."

Pols absorbed this as she munched on a doughnut. The changes in the girl were dramatic, but Sarah found them difficult to assess. Was her friend older looking because she was in fact heading into full teenager status, or had her illness aged her prematurely? She was not much taller, still slight, but her face had definitely lost its doll-like roundness. She was moving slowly, but then Pols always moved slowly, unless she was playing the piano or violin, when she was capable of Dervish-like agility and Titanic power.

"I see you as a conductor," Pols said at last, having demolished the doughnut. "When I'm done with my opera you should conduct it."

"Was that what you were playing when I came in?"

"Yes. That was the theme." Pols straightened her back. "The whole thing flows from those five notes, which are encrypted throughout the entire work. Or will be."

"What's your libretto?"

"I'm writing it myself. But I need to work fast. Mozart was twelve when he wrote *Bastien und Bastienne* and *La finta semplice*."

"Well, those weren't great operas." *But it's good that she's feeling competitive,* Sarah thought. *She's a fighter.*

"No, not truly great. They showed ambition but not compassion. The music was there, but emotionally he was still immature," said Pols. "Like you, kind of."

At noon, Sarah slipped into the back row of Lobkowicz Palace Museum's Music Room. The 7th Prince Lobkowicz had been a major supporter of Ludwig van Beethoven. Word had apparently gotten around that the current Lobkowicz was patron to another extraordinary genius. The place was packed.

I'll know how Pols really feels, Sarah thought, *when I hear her play.*

Harriet Hunter took the seat next to Sarah, togged out today in a green corduroy frock coat buttoned over a white silk blouse and green and black vest, with narrow black velvet pants. A sort of nineteenth-century cross-dressed look. You had to give the woman points for style.

"How are you feeling?" Harriet whispered, searching Sarah's face. "After your plunge last night? Max said you were into the river before anyone else had sorted out what was happening. And you think someone was shooting at you?"

"I might have been mistaken about that," Sarah said, hedging. "There was a lot going on." So Max had told Harriet about the gunshots, even though Nico had counseled discretion?

"Max said you're working on a book?" Sarah asked Harriet, hoping to steer the conversation away from drowning madmen and mysterious plots.

"A novel." Harriet smiled. "Although it requires a great deal of research. My heroine is Elizabeth Weston—the poet? They called her 'Westonia.' No relation of yours, Max says."

"Weston is a common name," Sarah said, though the name Westonia had given her a bit of a jolt.

"In her day Elizabeth Weston was more famous than Shakespeare," said Harriet. "I'm taking a bit of a risk, imagining her as a modern woman, looking back at her life and accomplishments here in Prague. But it's atrocious she's been so forgotten. I'm hoping to really make her come alive for a modern audience."

"Sounds great," said Sarah. *Although in my experience,* she thought, *it's not hard to make history come alive in Prague. The hard part is making history stay dead.*

According to Nico, Westonia had been the name Tycho Brahe had given to one of his little alchemical experiments, the result of which had been a perception-expanding drug that both Sarah and Max had taken. Westonia allowed you to see the past, see it so clearly that it was like time traveling. Nico had said that Brahe had named the drug after Elizabeth Weston, though Sarah had no idea why. She wondered if Max had said anything to Harriet about it. Probably not. The whole thing was pretty hard to believe and anyway the ingredients for making it were all gone.

Harriet squinted at her program. Sarah wondered if she would take an eyeglass on a velvet ribbon from her waistcoat pocket. "What does dear Pollina have in store for us today?" Harriet murmured. "Oh God. Strauss. Well, we must endure. That's for you, is it? I hear you're off to Vienna. I admit I find Vienna something of a sphinx. You'll meet quite a lot of them there. Sphinxes. And not just on buildings and lampposts."

Sarah smiled politely.

"Oh, you are prepared," Harriet laughed. "That was a very Viennese smile. Giving away nothing and concealing everything."

Max came and sat down on the other side of Harriet, who took his hand. *They make a nice couple,* Sarah told herself sternly, hoping she wouldn't be forced to make small talk, since at the sight of Max all her resolution dissolved and she had to admit there was just a tiny possibility that she might leap over Ms. *Masterpiece Theatre* and grab Max by his monogrammed wrists and tell him that—

Fortunately a hush fell over the room as a tall, silver-haired woman carrying a violin entered the Music Room, followed by Pols, walking slowly with one arm on a uniformed museum guard. The crowd instantly grew silent and attentive as the young girl seated herself at the piano and the violinist arranged her own music on a stand in front of her.

The first piece—"Vienna Blood" by Johann Strauss II—was perhaps better translated as "Vienna Spirit." It was Vienna as it liked to think of itself: sprightly, charming, and sensual. But Pols seemed to be finding something else in the music, as if the charm of Vienna concealed something broken. She was giving the merry waltz an almost sinister quality, revealing a darker truth. Pollina then launched into Schumann's "Träumerei," a piece usually played slowly and introspectively. The young girl broke that convention immediately, handling the ascensions with a nervous and almost threatening pace. Next was Mozart's Piano Sonata no. 14. The ease with which Pollina played this was breathtaking, but Sarah saw she was distracted. Her thin face occasionally broke into frowns or smiles, as if she were conducting a conversation with the composer, sometimes praising and sometimes scolding. The violinist and a teenage cellist wearing a yarmulke and a prayer shawl joined for the final offering: Luigi's Piano Trio, op. 97. (Sarah always thought of Ludwig van Beethoven by his favorite nick-name.) According to a contemporary account of Beethoven's performance at the premiere, "In *forte* passages the poor deaf man pounded on the keys until the strings jangled, and in *piano* he played so softly that whole groups of notes were omitted." It had marked Luigi's last public performance as a pianist.

Pols was in the middle of the second movement when she started coughing. She tried valiantly to keep playing, but finally stopped, chest heaving.

Sarah and Max both ran down the aisle to help the girl to her feet.

"I'm sorry," Pollina whispered.

"I'm going to find someone who can help you," Sarah promised. She looked at Max over the girl's head. His eyes said, *Hurry.*

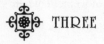 THREE

Nicolas Pertusato was not in the best of spirits. This was annoying, since he had been imbibing the best of spirits for a long time now and should have been feeling more cheerful. Of course, plane travel was no more a comfortable experience for him than it was for people with less abbreviated statures. On the one hand, he had more leg room than most adults. On the other hand, he could not make use of the overhead bins without engaging a flight attendant, and there were no attractive ones on this particular flight to London. You had to fly to Dubai to get a shapely stewardess these days. Although the ones on Japan Air were still fairly delectable.

Nico watched the giantess in the window seat next to him attempt to eat her dinner. Like the other behemoths on the aircraft, her arms were wedged so tightly in the seat she could use only wrist movements and a kind of lizardlike head bobbing to forage. That was diverting.

Well, and the appearance of Saint John of Nepomuk in Prague had been intriguing. The whole episode did have the ring of the kinds of practical jokes Nico and his friends used to play in the past. Except someone had shot at Sarah. That was simply not cricket.

"I only sell you one bottle and yet you have three empties." The depressingly mannish Czech airline . . . person . . . pointed to the row of vodka bottles on his seat tray. Nico sighed. Why would you *not* take something that rolled past you at hand height?

He was drinking a bit much these days, and he had seen Sarah notice it, but he had a lot on his mind. He really did want to find the ingredients for Philippine Welser's medicine. It would be nice to do something for Pollina. Sarah was skeptical about the old herbal remedies, but Nico had seen the miracles those healing women had worked. Certainly antibiotics and anesthesia were major improvements over biting a strap while someone sawed your leg off, but modern medicine had its blind spots.

What would modern medicine have to say about himself, for instance? Nico knew that somewhere the cure for his condition must exist. Tycho Brahe had made him immortal from a formula he had stolen from one of Emperor Rudolf's books. The book of the Golden Fleece. Sarah had seen the book—under the influence of Westonia—but then had lost the trail. Nico and Max had spent the better part of the past two years trying to pick up the trail on their own, with no luck. Sarah had reported seeing Tycho Brahe discussing the Fleece with the old mathematician and alchemist Dr. John Dee, and Nico had been all over Europe hunting through Dee's old diaries and artifacts. There was plenty to be found—the Bodleian Library at Oxford had a trove of Dee's diaries, but nothing even remotely Fleece-y.

The thought of blowing the one solid chance he had at shucking off the old immortal coil had thoroughly depressed him. *Carpe diem* was fun only as long as you had a *diem* to *carpe. Carpe eternum* was a drag. If he was hitting the bottle a little harder lately, who could blame him?

Nico took a train from Heathrow to Paddington, deciding to

detour for a pint at a favorite haunt from the old days. It might cheer him up a little.

The Windsor Castle pub in Kensington loomed up before him. Oh, the divertissements he'd enjoyed with his friends here! Like the time he had dispatched town criers to stand under the Duchess of Kent's window and announce her beheading. Nobody knew how to punk properly anymore. Or spy! Computer hacking had brought all kinds of boring people into the trade, and the market was flooded, which drove down prices. Barely enough to keep a man out of the circus. Not that he had to worry so much about money anymore. Nico ordered a tankard of pear cider and considered the Barbour-clad Sloane Rangers on their cell phones around him. These days he only picked pockets if he was in a good mood. He watched a couple of lawyers in Zegna suits bend themselves in half to try to squeeze through the door to the back room, which was only four feet, six inches high, then strode through himself, head held high.

"Looks like it was made for you, mate," remarked the ironically muttonchopped barkeep.

"It was," said Nico and headed for the loo, recalling—just in time—that it was no longer acceptable to urinate out the front window onto the street. Sometimes when he got drinking, his chronology became a trifle confused.

Several pints of cider and a shot of Irish whiskey sloshed gently in his stomach as he walked down Piccadilly, ignoring the curious—then deliberately uncurious—reactions of passersby to his unusual person. Only very small children were honest about staring, the little cretins. Gods, London had really lost its stink and become incredibly clean. So depressing.

The British Museum was famously enormous, a receptacle for

all the loot the Brits had managed to impolitely carry off while visiting any number of foreign countries (and sneering down their noses at the locals). What a mania for collection they had! The Elgin Marbles, endless amounts of statuary, pottery, jewelry, and other artifacts—all had been "rescued" from savage territories in order to be displayed here for all future generations of snotty British schoolchildren. At least the Rosetta Stone was now under glass—until just a few years ago, anyone could rub their filthy jam-stained hands over it. And why not? Full of foreign scratchings, it was.

How I long to be done with you all, he thought, making his way through the lofty hallways, squeezing through hordes of blank-eyed tourists wearing headsets.

He did look forward to seeing the galleon again. According to official records, the ship—which was also a clock and an ingenious automaton—was made by Hans Schlottheim, and it was believed to have once been in the *Kunstkammer* of Rudolf II. Nico happened to know that Philippine Welser was the one who had given it to Rudolf. It would not be an easy thing to steal, but that only made it more of a challenge. He would . . .

Nico stared at the empty glass display case. Inside where the automaton should have been, where it had been since 1866 when his old friend Octavius Morgan had donated it to the museum, there was instead a small white index card that read simply *Removed for curatorial purposes.*

This was not amusing. Whenever Nico needed to "borrow" something from a museum, he replaced it with one of his own *Removed for curatorial purposes* cards. He had them in the paper stock and fonts of about fifty different museums. It was extremely efficient, because it meant days or even months would pass before some nosy curator actually checked with the other curators and realized none of them had the object. He had "borrowed" this galleon himself, the last time he was in London.

What to do now? Nico looked around the museum. All these horrible children running around in perfect health, and Pollina . . .

No. There were other places he could find useful items for Philippine's recipe. Nico stopped at another pub to mull and had a couple pints of a really lovely amber ale and another whiskey to wash them down, which took the edge off his headache.

It was important that he not get too attached to the idea of saving Pollina. *You know what happens when you get attached.*

Nico's next stop was the British Library. It had the only copy outside Austria of Philippine Welser's *Book of Useful Medicines*, with marginalia by John Dee and his partner, Edward Kelley. This might be useful, though Nico had gotten very irritated with old John Dee. It was hard to know what the man had truly believed. And by the end, Edward Kelley had filled Dee's head with so much nonsense that the old necromancer didn't know his ass from his pointy beard. Poor Dee. And when you knew the details, poor Mrs. Dee.

Nico submitted his request at the library's desk and waited an unconscionably long time—with a few trips to the loo to fortify himself from his pocket flask—before the Jamaican librarian returned.

"I'm very sorry. The materials you requested are not here."

"Not here?" Nico pulled himself up to his full height. "And where might they be, then?"

"They have been removed," said the librarian with maddening indifference. "That's all the note says. Removed."

An hour later, and four more members of the staff interrogated, and Nico left the library still no further on his quest. No one seemed to know where Philippine's book had ended up, and even the records that should have informed them who had last looked at the materials had gone missing.

This required a bit more whiskey. But he wasn't done yet.

Nico arrived at the Science Museum an hour before closing and made his way to the fifth floor. He skirted a group of foul-mouthed schoolboys and made a brief inspection of camera locations and other security devices. Nothing a few magnets, a mirror, and a little patience couldn't get past. He made his way to the Giustiniani medicine chest. A nice little example of sixteenth-century pharmacopoeia. One hundred twenty-six bottles and pots within the case still contained their original elements. He only needed two of them for Philippine's recipe. Theriac and eagle bezoar.

No.

The medicine chest was gone. Not only gone, but in its place stood a small figurine of Khnumhotep, manager of ka-priests in ancient Egypt. Khnumhotep had no business being in this particular case of Renaissance medicine. His presence was an outrage, a deliberate insult.

Khnumhotep was a dwarf.

Nicolas Pertusato had an opponent. Game on.

Three hours later he was, Nico realized, not *quite* able to follow the lines of cobbles in the sidewalk. It might actually be that he was truly drunk now. He could not perfectly recall, for instance, what year it was.

Or what century.

Lincoln's Inn Fields. He had been here often enough. Oh, yes. He was right near Soane's house. Soane! Soane was excellent company. Soane would be helpful.

Nico made his way to number 13 and rang the bell.

"Soane!" he yelled up at the windows. "Soane! Open up! I want to raid your medicine chest."

"It's closed," said someone behind him, striding past. Some uncouth ruffian without a hat. Where was his own hat? He seemed to be filthy. Luckily, Soane would let you in if your feet were clean.

Nico tried the door again to no avail. Soane must be upstairs, having a wee nip himself. Since his wife had died, he'd hardly gone out at all, and Nico knew he'd be grateful for a visit. Soane wasn't comfortable at social gatherings, though his perceived deficiency wasn't height, but class. The son of a bricklayer, he had worked his way up to being a prominent architect for all the toffiest toffs in London's West End, but his real passion was teaching, and he had opened up his fascinating little house to visitors just a few years earlier, welcoming anyone with an interest in classical architecture and antiquities and offering them guided tours and cups of tea. Soane's Museum and Academy of Architecture, he called it, which Nico found rather pretentious. Soane's Future Jumble Sale, more like.

Fortunately, among his collectibles was a certain desk with a certain drawer (number 13) that contained a nice sampling of alchemical ingredients.

Nico made his way around back, where he knew a way up the drainpipe and into the second-floor window. It was on a rainy night like this that Nico had helped Soane build a funerary monument to Fanny, Soane's wife's dog. They had gone out in the middle of the night and found an unmarked headstone in the churchyard of St. Martin-in-the-Fields, brought it home, then Nico had inscribed it. *Alas, poor Fanny!* it had read.

Soane knew how to laugh.

The window was stickier than he remembered, but Nico eventually jimmied it open and made his way through the darkened house, keeping quiet so as not to wake the dogs. Soane could be a bit squiffy about lending things. He would get what he needed first, and then go wake up his friend. Nico tiptoed down the stairs to the basement, feeling his way in the dark, which wasn't easy since Soane was perhaps the biggest of all British pack rats. He never saw a Greek or Roman cornice or chunk of masonry he didn't want to bring home.

There it was. The desk. And there was the drawer and now . . .

No.

Removed for curatorial purposes. But this was Soane's home. The only curator here was *Soane*. This was beyond a joke. Furious, Nico charged toward the staircase, tripped, and fell face-first into something very hard.

Oh, for fuck's sake. He had fallen into Soane's marble sarcophagus. Soane had bought it from an Egyptian dealer and it was reputed to be more valuable than anything like it in the British Museum. To celebrate its arrival Soane had thrown a party for three hundred people and made them come in and view it in shifts, with the house all lit by candles.

Nico banged his head against the side of the sarcophagus in frustration. It would do him no good. He could bash his head for hours and there would be intense pain, blood, and probably a twenty-year headache, but he wouldn't die. And Oksana would give him hell about the bruises.

The alcohol was already wearing off. Of course Soane wasn't here. This really was a museum now. Soane had died in 1837. Nico had attended the funeral.

So many funerals. He would stand at the graves of them all, every last one of them.

FOUR

$\mathcal{S}$arah had brooded about Pols during the long train ride to Vienna, ignoring her Ohioan seatmate's breathless, excited narration of every landmark—"A church! Another church! A farm!"

The way Pols had played her first piece, "Vienna Blood," had felt like a warning. Schumann's "Träumerei" was also known as "Dreams of Childhood," but in Pollina's interpretation the dreams had been twisted and haunted. The girl's preternatural ability was very like the young Mozart's, and she wanted time to be able to develop it as he had. But she knew her body was turning against her, as Beethoven's had. Though she would never say it out loud, she had been sending Sarah a clear message in her choice of pieces: Pols was perfectly aware of how sick she was. And she was anxious, and frightened.

$\mathcal{A}$ crackly *"Wien Meidling"* had announced her train's arrival in Vienna. Sarah made her way outside the station to a queue of cabs, greeting the driver with the Austrian *"Grüss Gott."* For her ride through the city that was the adopted home of Beethoven and

Mozart, she had to listen to '80s pop blaring on the car radio. Duran Duran's "Hungry Like the Wolf," then Gloria Estefan demanding party and siesta.

Vienna. Outside the window, low industrial buildings were gradually replaced by lovely edifices of stone, and curving boulevards bisected with tram tracks. Sarah was relieved to see how orderly, how expansive, how cosmopolitan and polished Vienna appeared. After the warren of Prague's Easter egg–hued streets, Vienna looked refreshingly straightforward. Prague was a place where you could easily believe alchemists were lurking about. Vienna, although geographically farther east, had a decidedly Western European ambience. This was the kind of place where the frontiers of modern medicine were being pushed forward by scientists, not magicians. Sarah began to feel a surge of optimism. It was like Nico said. She wasn't going to sit and do nothing. She was going to use her talents. No moping, no hand-wringing.

Her friend Alessandro's apartment was located just outside the "Ring"—the wide boulevard that Emperor Franz Joseph had ordered built in 1857 to replace the old city walls and which now enclosed the historic center of Vienna.

"*Bellissima!*" exclaimed Alessandro, opening the door of his apartment to Sarah. The lanky and beautiful Italian was wearing an oddly cut dark green suit with leather piping and an Alpine hat, complete with feather. He planted a firm kiss on her lips and grabbed her ass.

"Ah, good," he said. "So often the acquisition of the PhD is ruinous to the *culo*. But yours has survived intact. Congratulations, Frau Doktor Weston."

"*Danke,*" Sarah said, giving Alessandro's own perfectly formed *culo* a good swat. Sarah had heard signorina after signorina testify in operatic terms as to the quality of Alessandro's lovemaking through the thin walls of their Boston apartment, but had never felt the urge to try it herself. Fortunately, Alessandro had not taken this as a challenge, and he treated Sarah as a sister—or, as he had once said, like a brother. Now he released her and ushered her into a tiny and immaculate living room.

"University arrange this nice place for me. I take down all the Klimt posters. At Harvard, you could tell if a girl would sleep with you by her poster. Modigliani—*sì*. Klimt—*no*. I want to set the right mood."

"Well done. But the outfit? Why are you dressed to go stag hunting with an archduke?"

"It is part of my very clever plan." Alessandro produced a garment bag from the hall closet and waved it with a flourish. "There is a ball tonight, and the scientist you wish to meet, Frau Doktor Müller, she will be there. You and me, we make friendly with her and then, boom, she say yes to enrolling Pols in the study."

It wasn't a bad idea. Alessandro's charms were legendary, and no woman seemed ever to say no to him. If anyone could sway Bettina Müller, it was Alessandro, especially at a ball.

"Do I dare ask what's in the bag?"

"This is a Tyrolean Ball. A special event being held at Rathaus. Traditional dress, this is mandatory. These Austrians are very serious about their balls."

Sarah's laughter was cut short when Alessandro whipped off the garment bag.

"Yeah, I'm not wearing that." The gown was an upscale version of the dirndl, or traditional Alpine peasant dress. There were three layers to the outfit—a white scoop-neck cropped blouse with puffy elbow-length sleeves, a midnight-blue velvet dress with an embroidered bodice, and a forest-green silk taffeta apron.

It came with white tights and black flat shoes. She would look, Sarah thought, like an extra from *Chitty Chitty Bang Bang*.

"You'll wear it for Pols," said Alessandro. "And I will promise not to post pictures on Facebook. Maybe."

Sarah took the dress from him.

FIVE

Alessandro had slightly underestimated Sarah's dress size and slightly overestimated her shoe size, so once she was dirndled up and shuffling along, Sarah felt like a well-trussed duck. Remarkably, their costumes caused nary a second glance as they strolled through streets where every third building was a landmark of historic or cultural significance. Alessandro pointed out the Secession Building, where artists like Gustav Klimt, Koloman Moser, and Carl Moll had made their stand against the *gemütlichkeit* culture of middle-class coziness and complacency that reigned at the end of the nineteenth century in Vienna. And then Café Museum, originally designed by Adolf "ornament is crime" Loos, where the artists had gone to drink coffee, argue, and seduce beautiful women into modeling and more. They reached the Opernring and the lit-up State Opera House came into view, decorated to within an inch of its life in Neo-Renaissance splendor and topped with equestrian statues.

"This has tragic story," said Alessandro. "When the building was completed, Emperor Franz Joseph said the building sat a little low. And so one of the poor *architetti* killed himself in shame, and the other died of a broken heart."

"Never read reviews," said Sarah, struggling to catch a deep breath in the dirndl.

"Or give them." Alessandro nodded. "Franz Joseph felt so bad that after, whenever anyone ask of him what he thought of some building, he just said, 'It is very nice. I like it very much.'"

They passed a blindingly pink coffee shop: Aida. Alessandro explained that Aida was a chain, but a good example of a *Konditorei*, a pastry shop favored by women who went to gossip and eat pastries, as opposed to the more macho *Kaffeehaus*, where men went to gossip and eat pastries.

"Mark Twain said that, outside of Vienna, all coffee was merely liquid poverty," Sarah commented.

"It is true." Alessandro sighed. "The coffee is heaven. But the food is awful. Knödel. A crime against pasta."

Alessandro steered her toward Maria-Theresien-Platz, so Sarah could take in the enormous white and pale gray edifices arranged around the edges of a vast green square. Beyond this lay the even more massive Hofburg complex, with its monuments to the power of the Hapsburgs and the time when Vienna had been the seat of the Holy Roman Empire, powerful and seemingly indestructible. Now all of these places were simply part of Vienna's perfectly preserved past. There was something, Sarah decided, a little smug about all this magnificence. Well, historically, Vienna had had the reputation of being a decadent, indolent city. Beethoven had once sneered in a letter that "so long as an Austrian can get his brown ale and his little sausages, he is not likely to revolt."

Moving along, they passed the Volksgarten, the enormous Greek Revival–style Parliament building, and then turned into the approach to the Rathaus, Vienna's imposing city hall, dressed to the nines in Gothic splendor, and boasting a statue of a knight in armor atop its lofty spire.

"Cheese and rice," muttered Sarah (a favorite expression of her father's) as they sailed into the majestic *Festsaal*. The ceremonial hall stretched the entire length of the building. She took in the barrel-vaulted ceiling, the parquet floors, the three-sided gallery, the statues and arcades, and the ornate flights of stairs. She counted sixteen chandeliers. Already there was a huge crush of people, all costumed, all wearing expressions of delight and anticipation in the frivolity to come. Members of an orchestra were settling themselves in one of the niches.

"I'm not going to have to waltz, am I?" Sarah asked, stumbling slightly in the overlarge shoes. "I don't exactly have the moves like Ginger."

"I will lead," Alessandro said with a mildly sadistic smile. "Marie!" An exceptionally tall woman surrounded by a group of young ballgoers turned and then strode toward them, smiling, her wide shoulders and the stiff flounces of her many petticoats cutting a swath through the crowd. "Sarah, this is my friend Frau Professor Marie-Franz Morgendal. Marie-Franz teaches history of science at the university. She is also big Beethoven lover."

"Frau Doktor Weston," said Marie-Franz in careful, accented English. Her voice was deep and warm. "I read your book on Beethoven and enjoyed it very much. It was wonderfully insightful!" Sarah's university had published her doctoral thesis on the correspondence between Beethoven and the 7th Prince Lobkowicz. Sarah had not mentioned in her book that some of her insights had come while she was on the drug Westonia, which had allowed her to actually *see* Beethoven and hear him play. It wasn't the kind of thing you could tuck into a footnote.

"Please call me Sarah." She had heard that Austrians were

very big on titles, but "Dr. Weston" still sounded very strange to her.

"Yes? Then you must call me Marie-Franz. Sarah, I see that you have also tied your apron strings to signify you are an unmarried lady?" Sarah looked down at her apron, bemused. She hadn't known she was sending a signal about her marital status.

"What is the tying that signals 'troublemaker'?" asked Alessandro. "Sarah should have this."

Marie let out a booming laugh as they were joined by a tiny, beautiful girl, whose pink hair and tattoos gave the whole dirndl thing a punk twist. Alessandro introduced the girl as Nina Fischer and explained that she was one of Bettina Müller's grad students. Nina seemed fully aware of Alessandro's plan and offered Sarah some advice.

"Play it cool, yes?" she said to Sarah. "Frau Doktor Müller is brilliant, but she can be a little . . . I don't know if you have this word in English." Nina switched to German, in which Sarah was fluent, and Sarah learned that Doktor Müller was "tricky." Nina then introduced her escort, who must have been at least twenty years older than Nina and had the half-avaricious, half-desperate look of someone who knew his dates with young women were numbered, and he needed to make the most of them. "This is Heinrich von Hohenlohe," said Nina, managing to look both proud and a little embarrassed as she pronounced the aristocratic "von." But the name caught Sarah's attention for a different reason. She remembered that Nico had said the von Hohenlohe family had the healer Philippine Welser's papers and was highly possessive of them. Given the too hungry look of this guy, Sarah was glad that Nico already had the recipe he needed.

"Is she here?" Sarah asked Nina. "Doktor Müller?" There were hundreds of people milling about. This was going to be difficult.

"She will be late," Nina said. "She always is. In the meantime, you should enjoy yourself."

Sarah was just hoping not to split a seam before Dr. Müller showed up.

Heinrich touched her shoulder. "Do not be offended," he shouted over the din, "if no one outside of our group asks you to dance. It would violate tradition. People come in couples or groups, and it would be considered ill-mannered to prey on a member of someone else's party, although ogling is allowed." Heinrich ogled Sarah, as if to demonstrate its acceptability.

When the orchestra leader announced, *"Meine Damen und Herren, alles Waltzer,"* and "Tales from the Vienna Woods" began, Sarah begged Alessandro to let her just watch the dancing for a moment. Each couple made their own swirling little circle while at the same time the entire crowd swirled counterclockwise, like an elaborate clockwork mechanism with hundreds of gauzy, glinting, moving parts. It was beautiful, it was romantic, it was slightly absurd, and it was fabulous.

When Alessandro led her into the next dance, Sarah had a moment of panic as she tried to recall where her feet were supposed to be, and then, to her great surprise, she was doing it, waltzing. Not perfectly, but definitely waltzing. She had to splay out her toes to keep the shoes on, and had an ongoing fear that the laces holding in her bosom would snap and release the hounds, and yet it was fun. Alessandro handed her over to another university colleague, who was more precise, and her technique improved. Then she danced with Heinrich, whose hands were predictably sweaty. But still no sign of Bettina Müller.

Marie-Franz suggested they go up to the gallery, where the view of the dancers would be particularly lovely. *"Vai.* I will wait for Bettina," said Alessandro. Sarah and Marie-Franz made their way to one of the grand staircases, a marble and wrought-iron affair with columns supporting pointed-arch vaults. Their progress up was slow, as Marie-Franz continually stopped to introduce Sarah to more people. On the mezzanine they looked down on the swirling couples in costume and Sarah tried to remind herself which century she was in. Taking out her cell phone to snap a few pictures helped.

"Adele!" Sarah turned and Marie-Franz introduced her to a man she named as Herr Kapellmeister Gerhard Schmitt, and then to his wife, Adele, a willowy blonde who clung briefly to Marie-Franz as the taller woman stooped to kiss her cheek. "Frau Doktor Weston joins us from Boston. She's only just arrived."

"Frau Doktor Weston, I kiss your hand. I hope our meager entertainment is not a bore," said the man, as his wife rolled her eyes theatrically. Sarah couldn't tell if the woman was unimpressed with the splendid scene or her husband. The Kapellmeister had a mane of very blond hair, and Sarah thought the name was familiar.

"Not at all," said Sarah. "It's—"

"In the regular season," the blonde interrupted, "it is not uncommon for women to get fat injected into the balls of the feet, so they can dance all night long." She spilled some of her drink on Sarah's dirndl and lurched sideways into the professor. "I wish I had your sense of humor, Marie-Franz. I wish I could laugh it all away."

Before the professor could respond to this, the man said, "Enjoy your evening," and led his wife away, his eyes lingering on Sarah's breasts.

"You recognized him perhaps?" asked Marie-Franz after the couple were out of earshot. "Gerhard Schmitt is a composer, and director of the Vienna Chamber Orchestra. He has taken the old title of Kapellmeister, though he is known in the press as 'the Lion of Vienna' on account of the hair. Ha! Adele is a harpist. I've known her since we were children. She's not always so . . . unstable."

"You seem to know everyone."

"Oh, we're terrible gossips here." Marie-Franz laughed her infectious, booming laugh. "And it is more that everyone knows me! Not that I am famous. But you see, I used to be *Herr* Professor *Franz* Morgendal. And now—" Marie-Franz gestured modestly to her dirndled bosom and flipped up the ends of her thick, wheat-colored hair.

Sarah put the deep voice, the height, the hands, and the slight hint of Adam's apple together.

"Some people think I should drop the Franz from my name, because it is confusing," the professor explained. "But I just like the way Marie-Franz *sounds*."

"It's very musical," Sarah agreed. "And why not please yourself?"

"*Yes!* I did not take the hormones or do the surgeries so that I could make people uncomfortable or comfortable. I did it so that I could live my life as it was intended in my soul. *Yes!* I use the word 'soul' even though I am a professor of the history of science and in the history of science they have never proved the soul. Only its expression."

Sarah raised her glass in salutation. She rarely used the word 'soul' herself, but she was definitely in kinship with living your life as you feel it was intended.

"*Geniesse das Leben ständig! Du bist länger tot als lebendig!*" said Marie-Franz, clinking glasses.

Constantly enjoy life! You're longer dead than alive!

They returned to the main floor. A tall man, resplendent in a Tyrolean uniform, had joined their group and stood chatting with Nina and Heinrich. The man's hair was dark, but his mustache and beard, groomed to a point, were red. His entire bearing and grandeur were very like the statue of the fifteenth-century Viennese notable he happened to be standing in front of.

"My brother, Gottfried," said Heinrich. Gottfried bowed stiffly.

"Gottfried is a rider at our famous Spanish Riding School," said Nina. "He's also a terrible snob, so don't expect him to ask you to dance."

Gottfried looked at Nina coolly, then offered his arm to Sarah. By this time, Sarah felt as though she had had enough of the waltzing already. Her toes were aching, her ribs felt oddly numb, and she was anxious about the continuing no-show of Bettina Müller, but she took his arm.

Gottfried, Sarah noted as they danced, smelled like an intriguing combination of oiled leather and fresh hay. Her sensitive nose also picked up an interesting crackling energy. And the beard was very sexy. Under different circumstances, this would all be worth exploring (and it would be one way to get her mind off Max), but Sarah was at the ball to find Dr. Müller, not pick up hot guys, no matter how Tyrolean. Still, she tried making conversation with Gottfried, asking him about the Spanish Riding School.

"I'm sorry," he said. "I do not speak your language."

"I'm speaking to you in *German*," Sarah pointed out.

"Yes. You are speaking German as the Germans do. The accent is unpleasant. You must learn to speak like an Austrian." Sarah had noticed a difference herself, with Nina and Marie-Franz, but it was mostly intonation and cadence. They had understood her perfectly. Nina had been right; Gottfried was a snob.

As they pirouetted past Alessandro, she saw that he was now talking to a small brown-haired woman with enormous glasses. Bettina Müller at last? She got rid of Gottfried by claiming waltz-induced dehydration and asking if he would mind getting her something to drink, which he seemed to be able to follow without her resorting to mime. She moved quickly over to Alessandro and the woman.

"Frau Doktor Müller, please allow me to introduce my dear friend Frau Doktor Sarah Weston," said Alessandro.

The woman's small hand was quite strong. Her glasses obscured most of her delicate features and magnified her eyes strangely. "So nice to meet you," said Sarah, flashing her most charming smile, the one she used for job interviews and talking her way out of speeding tickets.

"Yes." Bettina Müller looked intently at Sarah, who held the woman's gaze. She felt a surge of adrenaline course through her body. Sarah had met a few geniuses in her life. Pollina. Her first mentor in neuromusicology, Professor Sherbatsky. Beethoven, when she had been close to him on Westonia. This, she felt certain, was another. Here was a woman who could help her friend.

"Sarah just arrived today from Prague," Alessandro said. Bettina Müller was still holding Sarah's hand, and now the pressure increased, but the woman was no longer looking at Sarah. She seemed to be transfixed by something over Sarah's shoulder.

"Yes. Excuse me. I must go," she said abruptly.

"But I insist you allow me a dance! If you have another partner I will wait. Or challenge him to a duel." Alessandro said this with the full weight of his considerable charm, but the woman was backing away, still staring at something past Sarah. Sarah turned, but the ballroom was crowded. She was losing her chance.

"I'm so sorry, Dr. Müller," said Sarah, moving forward, "but I came all the way to Vienna to see you. I must speak with you; it's very important. Perhaps we can arrange a meeting—"

"I know who you are," the woman muttered. "I reviewed your friend's records and turned her down. She is too young."

"You don't know her," said Sarah. "She has an iron will. I think she can take the treatment. I know she can. Please. You may be our last hope."

The woman was pale, Sarah noticed, and her hands were shaking. Sarah could smell the fear on her.

And suddenly Sarah felt it, too. Danger. It was incredibly powerful. All the hairs on Sarah's neck went up.

But just then a group of ballgoers surged in between Sarah and the doctor as the orchestra struck up a new tune. Sarah tried to push past them, muttering *"Bitte. Bitte. Entschuldigung,"* but when she finally did, Bettina Müller had disappeared.

"Merda," Alessandro said, appearing beside Sarah.

"I'll go to her lab tomorrow." Sarah's brief sense of danger was gone, replaced with determination. Pols wasn't the only one with an iron will. "I'll find her home address and wait outside."

Nina joined them.

"What happened?"

"She left," Sarah said. "It seemed like something spooked her, actually. Not me. She wasn't really looking at me. Something was . . . wrong."

"I told you she was tricky," said Nina. "We'll think of something else. Now, come on. I'm trying to ditch Heinrich. Let's get something to eat. But not here. Only old rich people eat at balls. The rest of us go to a *Würstelstand*."

"Beer and hot dogs." Alessandro sighed. *"Schifoso."*

Nina rolled her eyes and laced her arm through Sarah's.

They moved through the crowd, passing Gerhard Schmitt—the Lion of Vienna—and his unstable harpist wife, apparently in the midst of a fierce argument. Sarah looked around for Gott-fried, but couldn't find him in the crush.

At the *Würstelstand*, Nina insisted Sarah sample her favorite, a cheese-filled hot dog known locally as "sausage-with-pus." Sarah decided at this point it was safe to risk dirndl failure and ate her hot dog and talked with Nina, trying to come up with an-other strategy for getting a meeting with the skittish doctor.

"I can mention the case again," Nina offered. "Not that she listens to me. Ah, shit—" She looked at her phone. "It's Heinrich. I suppose I better go back or he'll be pissed." She tossed down the rest of her beer and headed back to the Rathaus.

"You want to dance more?" Alessandro asked, but Sarah was way too frustrated to waltz. Also, she was ready to de-dirndl.

"I'll go with you to the university tomorrow," Sarah said to Alessandro in the cab back to his apartment. "Do you know where Bettina has her lab? Maybe if I can catch her on the way in or out—"

Sarah's phone beeped and a text appeared. The number was blocked, but the message was clear. Sarah leaned forward and ad-dressed the driver.

"I'm sorry, but we need to change our destination!" She handed her phone to Alessandro, who read the message out loud.

Sarah—can you come to my lab now? Must talk. Alone. —Bettina

SIX

Alessandro directed the cab to leave them at Borschkegasse, and he pointed out the building where Bettina Müller's lab was located, a newer, modern edifice tucked behind yet another row of Vienna's white Neo-Baroque giants. Alessandro wanted to come with her, but the doctor had specifically stated that Sarah should come alone, so he loitered near a fountain on the campus *Platz*, nervously smoking a cigarette. By the time she returned, Sarah figured, he would probably have picked up a sophomore. Or three.

There were still a couple of lights on in the laboratory building. Someone had put a piece of tape over the lock on the front door and left a card directing a pizza delivery to the third floor. Dry-erase boards and posters lined the walls of the entranceway, bearing testimony to the work being done in the building: schedules, reminders about safety precautions, a challenge from the Molecular Medicine team for a night of disco bowling.

Bettina's lab was on the second floor, at the end of a long hallway. Sarah had to use the flashlight app on her phone to navigate, as the overhead fluorescents were off. This made her a little uneasy. The previous night was bullets in a river, and Nico had said she should remain en garde. Difficult to do when dressed like a naughty beermaid. Sarah reached into her purse. Her choice of weapons was either a pen or the plastic sword from Nico's Barbatini, which had somehow ended up in her evening bag. She wondered what he had taken in exchange.

The door to Bettina's lab was standing open, but the lights were off.

"*Hallo?*" she called. "Frau Dr. Müller? *Es ist* Sarah Weston."

No answer. Sarah felt for the light switch inside the door and clicked it, but nothing happened. She shone her phone around the room, getting partial glimpses of long tables, stools, cabinets, sinks, lab equipment. The room smelled powerfully of bleach.

She jumped at the sound of scratching and a mechanical clink. She directed her light toward the noise and discovered a row of numbered cages. Sarah had seen plenty of white lab rats, but these were all gray, some drinking water, some sleeping, one little guy starting to exercise vigorously (or neurotically) on a wheel. Sarah stepped backward, slipping on a laminated poster depicting two soapy hands and the injunction *Waschen Sie Ihre Hände!* that had fallen to the floor. She heard a distinct tearing sound.

Then she heard the elevator door opening and the sound of heavy footsteps coming down the hall, several voices speaking at once.

"*Hallo? Hallo?*" Sarah stepped outside the lab and was momentarily blinded by the beam of a powerful flashlight hitting her directly in the face. For the second time in as many days, she heard the click of a gun being cocked.

At least, Sarah thought, she wasn't the only one at the police station in a dirndl, though hers was the only one with a side seam busted open. She counted a half dozen people in ball costumes, two of them in handcuffs, singing a spirited version of "Das Schönste auf der Welt" at the tops of their lungs. The officer who was transcribing Sarah's statement looked up at the sere-naders, frowned, then informed Sarah that the song was a fine one if sung properly, in tune.

Well, she had definitely arrived in Vienna.

There had been quite a scene with the police. After Sarah had explained to the officers what she was doing in the lab and they had holstered their guns, one officer had been dispatched to col-lect Alessandro from the *Platz*. By then, Nina Fischer had arrived.

It was Nina who sent the police to the lab. Bettina Müller, it seemed, had phoned Nina in a panic, saying she had gotten a text from a blocked number telling her that her laboratory had been broken into.

"But she couldn't come herself," Nina explained. "Because she was already on a train."

Sarah showed the police her own message from the doctor, though it, too, was from a blocked number. Nina was allowed to look in the lab, though she said the only thing she could find missing was Bettina's own laptop, which the doctor might very well have with her. Sarah, Nina, and Alessandro were all taken to the station to make statements. They filled out form after form, repeating all their information, and signing reports. Neither the *Polizei* nor Nina was able to reach Bettina Müller, who, by the end of the evening, was under suspicion of having stolen her own laptop from herself.

"Perhaps she is not getting phone reception on the train," Nina offered, outside the police station.

"Do you know where she lives?" Sarah asked. "I'm sorry. I'm really not a crazy stalker. It's just that I urgently need to speak with her. She did invite me to the lab tonight. . . ." *If she had even sent that message.*

"I don't." Nina raked her fingers through her pink hair. "Somewhere near the Naschmarkt, I think. She always breakfasts there. Shit. But, look, she should be back by Friday at the latest. That's when our team always meets. And there is a concert that night, at the Konzerthaus. She never misses when Kapellmeister Schmitt is conducting."

"I'll stay till then," Sarah said, frustrated. "Maybe she'll be back in touch."

In the morning, Alessandro left to teach his class on synaptic connections, and Sarah decided to breakfast at the Naschmarkt, an open-air market near the Secession Building.

A year ago, Sarah thought, as she made her way down the wide boulevard of the Museumstrasse, she would have been thrilled just to *be* in Vienna. The summer she'd been invited to Prague to catalog Beethoven's papers for Max, she had planned to visit Vienna until Prague had nearly consumed her, literally. Now she figured she could use the time waiting for the return of Bettina to explore the city, visit all the places where Beethoven had lived. (Though that might take more than two days. Beethoven was a notoriously bad tenant and had lived in nearly seventy different apartments.) She could go to the Lobkowicz Palace here, where the *Eroica* had premiered. She could visit Beethoven's grave in the Central Cemetery.

Sarah stopped in front of the Secession Building. Sporting clean classical lines, it thumbed its nose at the huge and heavy Baroque, Gothic, and Renaissance pastiche that surrounded it. The gold filigree ball atop the building was commonly thought to look like a cabbage, but Sarah thought it looked sort of like a golden brain. She paid her admission fee and made her way downstairs to see Klimt's famous *Beethoven Frieze*—inspired by Luigi's "Ode to Joy" and painted for a 1902 exhibition that was an homage to the composer. Painted on thin plaster, it had never been intended to outlast the 1902 show, but had ended up being sold, cut into seven pieces, and stored in a furniture depot for twelve years before being sold again, this time to an industrialist and patron of Klimt, August Lederer. Conveniently for the Nazi leaders who "collected" art, the Lederer family was Jewish, and so the Nazis dispossessed them in 1938 of their extensive Klimt holdings, including the frieze. After the war, ownership of the frieze returned to the current heir of the Lederer family, living now in Geneva; but conveniently for Viennese art lovers, an export ban was placed upon it. Eventually, in the 1970s, the heir sold the frieze to the Austrian government, probably because at that point it was desperately in need of repair and the sale was the only way to save it. A tragic history for a work that had been inspired by a symphony meant to celebrate the equality and brotherhood of man. But at least everyone could look at it now. For a fee.

The mural encircled the whole room and was observed from an elevated platform. A pair of stylish Brazilian women were taking pictures of the frieze with their phones when the guard's back was turned, apparently intending to reproduce it in a master bath. The frieze's narrative began on the left wall: female robed figures, eyes closed, floating with arms outstretched in front of them. Genii, Sarah read in the pamphlet. "Yearning for Happiness." The women looked like they were dreaming.

Sarah's own dreams the night before had been filled with the sound of Pols's horrible coughing. Coughing that had taken on a three-quarter-time melody, as if to rebuke Sarah for every step she had waltzed the night before.

She focused now on three supplicating naked figures in the panel before her, a kneeling man and woman, and a girl behind them. They were pleading in front of a knight in golden armor, turned away from them in profile. Behind the knight were two more female figures. The brochure identified them as "Ambition and Compassion." Sarah found it hard to look at the simple figure of the naked girl. She looked resigned, as if she didn't much expect the golden knight would help her.

The next panel was titled "Hostile Powers." Skeletal gorgons with snaking golden jewelry, a naked crone with pendulous breasts lurching behind them, and a lascivious siren with tendrils of long red hair, legs bent and pulled up to her chest, watched over by a richly garbed procuress. In the center, a giant, black, winged, gorilla-like beast with mother-of-pearl eyes and jagged, broken teeth.

Sarah thought about the hostile power threatening Pols. Not a huge hairy monster with wings, but something too small to be painted. A defective chromosome. It would be easier, Sarah thought, glancing back at the knight in armor, if the threat were something she could pick up a golden sword and take a satisfying swipe at.

In the final panels of the frieze, the Arts (more floating women, and one with a lyre) led to the higher plane, where Man and Woman embraced in a mystical union and a chorus of stylized women sang. Sarah contemplated this for a while. She had never really thought of the Ninth Symphony in terms of visual images. Did she agree? Was this what the "Ode to Joy" looked like? No. It was too artificial, too sensual, too . . . pretty. Beethoven, she thought, would not have cared for it.

Thinking this made her intensely lonely for Beethoven. It was absurd to "miss" Beethoven, but she did. The Westonia-drug-fueled visions where she had seen the great man, heard him speak, seen him play . . . they had changed her forever. She had felt connected to him so profoundly. And now here she was, in a place where there should be traces of him everywhere, looking at art that supposedly honored him. And he was invisible to her.

Sarah left the museum and headed to the Naschmarkt, feeling melancholy, which wasn't helped by a drizzle of cold rain. She ordered a mélange, the Austrian equivalent of a latte, and a *Topfengolatsche*, which was Austrian for "You have gone to pastry heaven. You're welcome." Sugar inspired, Sarah wondered if maybe Nina Fischer knew of any similar work to Bettina's being done somewhere else. Sarah thought she had run down every other avenue when she was in Boston, but maybe . . .

Her phone beeped.

I had to leave. My life is in danger.

What the hell?

Dr. Müller? Sarah texted back. *Where are you? And how do I know this is you?*

After a moment, her phone beeped again. There was a photo of her own cover letter on Pols's medical records. Then another message.

I can help your friend. Will you help me?

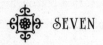 SEVEN

Nicolas Pertusato woke up in a very comfortable bed at the Ritz. The woman next to him was snoring. Nico studied her, curious. She lay on her back, but her large breasts pointed skyward in defiance of all gravitational law. Silicone. Nico lifted the sheet and inspected her pubic hair, or, rather, the lack of it. Just a narrow strip. It was definitely the twenty-first century, then.

Nico lay still for several minutes, running through an internal checklist in his brain. He reminded himself of the current day of the week, month, and—most important—year. For extra credit he named the phase of the moon: waxing gibbous. He cataloged the state of his physical health. Remarkably, he was not hungover. After leaving Soane's he had gone to another pub, perhaps two, and he remembered picking up a wallet and also—more vaguely— this creature.

Nico sat up.

Why had he been so despairing yesterday? Really, looked at in the proper light, the whole thing was actually . . . interesting.

Someone had been alchemy shopping all over London. That in itself wouldn't be so surprising—there were millions of crackpot theorists around, on scavenger hunts for the Holy Grail or Excalibur or Bigfoot. It was entirely possible that someone had conceived a quest for the Golden Fleece. But someone knew that *Nico* was looking for it, too. Someone had sent Saint John to Nico's restaurant of saints. Someone had left a dwarf figurine in place of a medicine chest. No wonder he hadn't been able to find anything of John Dee's that traced back to the Fleece.

Who was his antagonist? Anyone who could connect him to the Fleece had been dead for hundreds of years. And even then, the only people who knew that he had briefly held the book could be counted on one hand.

Sarah knew. But Sarah wanted nothing to do with alchemy, even though she had a PhD in it. What did she call herself? A neuromusicologist? Please. An alchemist by any other name would smell as sulfurous. Max? Max was desperate to find the Fleece, not to use it, but because he believed it was part of his family's duty to protect it. Secret Order of the Golden Fleece, sworn protector knights, and so forth.

Anyway, to work. Nico still had a few tricks up his sleeve. His opponent might have temporarily gained the upper hand, but now Nico was invigorated. Inspired. There was nothing like having a worthy adversary to liven things up.

Sherlock Holmes had needed a Moriarty to bring him out of his chronic ennui.

And so had he.

Nico hopped out of bed, took a bath, and decided a shave was really in order, as he needed to look respectable for today's plan. He had just lathered up when his evening companion stumbled through the door, collapsed in front of the toilet, and heaved. Nico soaked a towel in cold water and handed it to her.

"Oh, thank you," she said, in quite cultured tones, closing the lid and then sitting on it. She was a lovely woman, but Nico turned his attention to his chin. He hadn't shaved in about fifty years. He didn't get five o'clock shadow. He got half-century shadow.

"Last night was quite an experience. I'm beginning to remember it now. You are incredibly . . ."

"I know," said Nico.

"Oh." Nico could see in the mirror that she was staring at his naked back. She leaned forward and touched him. "I remember. Your scar. Got in a fight with gypsies, I believe you said?"

"I never fight with gypsies." Nico examined his teeth. "Nor should you, if you ever come across one. No, this was self-inflicted, I'm sorry to say."

"You stabbed *yourself* in the back?"

"It seemed funnier at the time," Nico conceded.

"Also . . . your wrists."

Nico glanced down at the very faint white lines that marked his wrists.

"What if I told you I couldn't kill myself even if I wanted to? What if I told you I was immortal because of a scientific experiment gone awry, that for four hundred years I've watched all my friends die, everyone I loved or cared for, while being unable to die myself?"

"I would assure you that this is a delusion. Not common, maybe, but one I've seen before, with varying specifics. I would tell you that such delusions can be treated."

Nico looked at her and she laughed shyly.

"I'm a social worker. My name is Lucinda, in case you've forgotten. Lucinda Smythe-Crabbet."

He had forgotten. There were just too many names. And this creature had three of them. And a title, he now recalled.

Really, Nico thought, after bidding Lady Lucinda a fare-thee-well outside the Ritz, he had always acted rashly when it came to women. You would think that after a couple of centuries he would have gotten this under better control, but no, humans were built to be irrational and could evolve only so far, no matter how long you lived. You might get past one or other of the big three—desire for love, fear of death, belief in God—but not all three at once. Buddhist monks came close, and Nico had met some severely autistic children who had surpassed the human condition, but Buddhism required intense meditation (which he was far too Epicurean to practice) and the other was denied to him by virtue of his genetic makeup, imperfect and frozen as it was.

At eleven a.m. Nico presented himself at gate A of the east wing of Blythe House, the massive Victorian building that had once been a National Savings Bank and was now used as storage for the spillover collections of a number of museums. The red and white brick edifice was topped with coils of barbed wire. From the outside it looked like an insane asylum. The inside was even worse: dirty glazed yellow tile, crumbling staircases, dimly shadowed corridors. But it had quite a lovely, cheerful staff, and all one needed to gain admittance to have a look at a certain object from the Wellcome Collection was an appointment. Once buzzed in, Nico made his way to the porter's office, presented his credentials, and received a yellow plastic visitor's pass. He was met by a Miss Ponds, who was delighted to show him the object he had requested.

"I expect you've been to see the permanent collection at the Euston Road museum?" she chirped. "It's wonderful. But of course, it's only a tiny portion of what Henry Wellcome gathered during his lifetime. He had agents all over the world hunting down artifacts, curiosities, medicines, tools, anything to do with the human body. Most of this would seem very primitive and wrongheaded to us now, of course. But it's a fascinating glimpse into the history of medicine. There were over a million objects in the collection, you know."

Nico did know. He had been an agent for Henry Wellcome in the early 1900s and had once spent a harrowing six months in Khartoum in his employ. Henry had been the first to market medicine in tablet form to the general public, and his pharmaceutical company had made him immensely rich. The man had been obsessed with immortality, was totally without a sense of humor, and had bizarre notions of temperance, insisting that none of his employees touch alcohol. Despite all that, Nico had rather liked him. Like most true eccentrics Wellcome had fewer prejudices about the differences of others, at least other *men*, and had treated Nico well, even making one of his custom medicine/tool chests in just his size. He still had it.

Miss Ponds was punching a security code into a door. Security here was very good, no need for cameras in any of the individual rooms, which was lucky for him. Miss Ponds gave him a pair of plastic gloves and they stepped inside a narrow cell lined with shelves.

"Now, let's see . . ." she said, bending down. Nico whipped a syringe out of his pocket and stuck it firmly into Miss Ponds's conveniently upturned ass.

"Oops-a-daisy," she said, before collapsing on the floor.

Nico ran his eyes over the shelves. He had requested to look at a particular specimen: a stuffed ram's head mounted on wheels. The top portion of the head opened up to reveal a compartment. In fact, Nico had no interest in this object, which he felt was obscene, and not in the way he usually found pleasant. No, he was after something a bit older, something he had given Henry from his own personal collection, as a joke, and to make up for all the things he had bought with Henry's money and never handed over.

"The box is late seventeenth century," he had told him, presenting it. "You can see that it contains some sort of powder within. The man who sold it to me swore it was *electuarium mithridatum.*"

Actually, the box contained the crushed bones of an elk that had belonged to Tycho Brahe. Albrecht had been his name. As much as an elk can be an asshole, Albrecht had been an asshole. Henry had been delighted with the box, and with what he thought was the acquisition of a sample of the seventeenth-century antidote against poison and infectious diseases. According to the Wellcome Collection database, the box was housed in this room, as item #7963.

Yes. Here it was, neatly tagged and with the false description of the contents lettered in tiny script. Holding his breath, Nico carefully opened the jar. The powdered remains of Albrecht had survived.

Score one for the dwarf, thought Nico. He could manage a fair bit of alchemy with genuine seventeenth-century elk bone. Particularly when the elk in question had died while under a massive dose of beer and Tycho's Westonia. God knows where Albrecht had thought he was when he fell down the stairs to his death. Cavorting with mastodons, perhaps.

Nico pocketed the box and replaced it with one of his cards: *Removed for curatorial purposes.*

"Mhmm," mumbled Miss Ponds. Nico bent to her side and helped her to her feet. "What happened? Did I faint?"

"It seemed as if you were going to." Nico dusted, perhaps a trifle too enthusiastically for Miss Ponds's taste, the knees of her skirt. "Perhaps you bent over too quickly."

"Oh. Oh, how strange. I'm so sorry."

It took a few minutes before Miss Ponds's composure was restored, and then a dull half hour while he pretended to admire the ram's head snuffbox and make a few notes.

Nico exited the building and hailed a cab.

"Heathrow," he told the driver.

EIGHT

$\mathcal{S}$arah strode through the Naschmarkt, searching the stalls for a glimpse of Bettina. Had she not left town after all? Was she following Sarah? What game was this woman playing? Another message arrived.

There is something in the refrigerator of my apartment that must be returned. Use maximum discretion. No police.

Whatever was in the refrigerator, Sarah was guessing it wasn't leftovers.

What is it? And who do I return it to?

But the return message read only: *Paniglgasse 18. The concierge will let you in. Tell no one or I will not help you.*

How do I know you will help me? Sarah texted furiously. This wasn't what she had imagined would happen in Vienna. This wasn't how scientists operated. . . . This was as bad as fucking Prague!

I can save your friend. Do this for me. I will contact you tomorrow.

$\mathcal{S}$arah got directions to Paniglgasse, which wasn't far. It was a lovely residential street, with nothing sinister about it. An efficient Viennese mom unloaded two strollers and a standard poodle from a smart car while her somber towheaded children in wool coats with velvet collars waited like tiny sentries. Sarah tried to be reassured by this as she walked through an arched entrance into the courtyard of Bettina Müller's Neo-Baroque building. A large golden retriever lay protectively across a doorway, and at her approach sat up and barked. This action was followed by the opening of a ground-floor-level apartment door and the appearance of an exceptionally tall and thin old man, bald, his trousers belted slightly below the region of his armpits. He stood glaring at her like an Austrian eagle. Sarah introduced herself in German.

"Yes!" he interrupted sternly. "I am Herr Dorfmeister. Frau Doktor Müller has told me to expect you and that you would be picking up a package."

"Yes."

"I will give you the key." He frowned. "I have been instructed to do so."

It occurred to Sarah that it was probably a good idea to make as many friends as she could with people who knew Bettina Müller. She needed allies. Or someone to run screaming to if Bettina's refrigerator contained a human head.

"Herr Dorfmeister, what is the name of your dog? She is very beautiful."

The transformation was magical. Herr Dorfmeister melted. He patted Sarah on the shoulder. He smiled. He introduced his dog, very formally. Her name was Candy, after Candice Bergen, whom Felix Dorfmeister admired as a great actress, particularly for her work in the television show *Murphy Brown*. Sarah was familiar, of course, with *Murphy Brown*?

Sarah, who had no idea who Candice ·Bergen was, smiled agreeably and, when Candy brought Sarah a mangled tennis ball, instituted a vigorous game of fetch in the courtyard. Apparently thoroughly charmed now, Herr Dorfmeister found the key and showed her to where the old cast-iron elevator was and how to work the doors.

"Apartment 6," he said. "And Frau Doktor Müller asks that you not let the cat in under any circumstances."

Sarah entered Bettina's apartment to the sound of gentle tickings, whirrings, buzzings, and clickings. She saw that the kitchen was directly to the right of the entranceway, but Sarah needed a sense of who this woman was, and decided to explore. She moved into a large, high-ceilinged room and revolved slowly in the middle of it, her eyes wide.

She was surrounded by clocks. Clocks of all sizes and shapes. Clocks in brass, silver, gold, pewter, porcelain. Long case clocks and smaller mantelpiece clocks mounted on shelves. Clocks surrounded by carved figures, clocks with swinging pendulums, clocks that showed the movements of the planets, pocket watches mounted in glass cases. The actual furniture of the room was IKEA utilitarian and very light on personal ornaments: no photographs; no figurines or mementos. More shocking to Sarah was the absence of books.

She looked over the rest of the apartment and found a small room that seemed to be used for random storage and laundry, a large bedroom, and a bathroom. The bedroom and bathroom showed signs of normal use: all the closets contained clothes and shoes and the bathroom cabinets were crammed with cosmetics and unguents. Bettina used a heavy perfume, something with a lot of musk in it. The bedroom had a giant flat-screen TV and huge Bose speakers. And about a hundred more clocks. Not all of them were functioning, but the ones that were seemed to be working harmoniously with one another. Their tickings gave the apartment a strange sort of pulsing vibrancy. Like being surrounded by heartbeats, Sarah thought. No. Like being *inside* a heartbeat. It wasn't unpleasant. It was actually kind of . . . soothing. The apartment was very stuffy, though. She was sweating.

The kitchen had all state-of-the-art appliances. A half-drunk glass of wine and plate of rice and vegetables in congealed sauce sat on the table next to take-out cartons. Sarah turned to the refrigerator. An Einstein magnet held a schedule of the Vienna Chamber Orchestra to the door. Several dates were circled, including one for the coming Friday.

Sarah opened the door. No food, not even shelves, which had apparently been moved to make way for a large white box.

A box large enough for, in fact, a human head. Maybe even two.

It wasn't terribly heavy. Sarah set it on the floor and loosened the lid. Inside, she found a rather beautiful golden model ship with a clock on its prow. It was elaborately constructed, with little figures on the deck and furled masts and everything. The whole contraption sat on wheels. It looked old. And valuable.

Stolen? Bettina was obviously an obsessive clock collector. It was hard to imagine a dangerous black market for clocks, but Sarah knew that art smuggling was big business, and this thing was definitely art. It would account for the secrecy. *No police.*

Why had Bettina put it in the refrigerator, which she couldn't even lock? Sarah's mother, who cleaned houses for a living, had once told her about a client who kept her diamonds in the freezer. Was it something like that? Or because it was really hot in Bettina's apartment and the heat would damage the clock? Sarah threw open the kitchen window to let in some fresh air. There was nothing on either the object or the box to indicate where it came from, or where Sarah should return it. This was going to be tricky.

Sarah sat down at the table, trying to re-create Bettina's evening in her mind. She had returned home from work, enjoyed a little pad Thai, and then she had gone to the ball. To meet her accomplice in trafficked goods? To get in a little waltzing? Sarah had thought the woman seemed thoroughly spooked and she had—according to Nina—jumped on a train before receiving a message that her lab had been broken into.

Was Sarah being set up? Or had Bettina gotten into something way over her head and was hiding out now?

Out of the corner of her eye Sarah noticed a thin gray cat sitting on the windowsill, staring at her. Crap! Herr Dorfmeister had said something about not letting a cat in. The animal gave her a triumphant glance and streaked straight across into the hallway, where it began furiously scratching at one of the closet doors. Sarah managed to get the cat by the back of its neck, holding it out at arm's length. The feline attempted a few wild scratches on Sarah's arm before she tossed it back out the window and shut it.

Okay. She needed to move smoothly, swiftly, and in a planned direction. First thing was to find out where this contraption belonged. Sarah pulled out her phone, took a few pictures, then began searching the Internet. It turned out that the item was pretty unique, and that the combination of "ship clock gold" was all it took.

It belonged in the British Museum.

The person with obvious museum connections was Max, but Sarah was reluctant to involve him. There were limits to what you wanted to do for your ex. And he might tell Harriet, and Bettina had told her to tell no one. Nico was another obvious choice, but Nico was better at stealing than returning.

It would be better to get it into the hands of a local museum curator somehow, someone who would be able to see it safely restored to London. Sarah thought about whom she could ask for help without implicating them.

By the time Sarah had repacked the ship and found a bag under Bettina's sink to put it in, it was all settled. She had texted Alessandro, asking only if he knew anyone in the museum world in Vienna, and he had suggested Renato, a second cousin of his whom he had never met but who was a Facebook friend and worked at the Kunsthistorisches, Vienna's gargantuan art museum. Within a couple of minutes, Sarah and Renato were also Facebook friends, and she sent him a message asking if he would advise her on an "art-related problem." Renato messaged back that he was working late at the museum this evening, but could meet her at nine, in Maria-Theresien-Platz, and they could go for a drink. Anything for a friend of a Facebook friend/cousin/ Italian.

Social media, plus nepotism, plus nationalism. Fifteen minutes, a couple of messages, and she was in.

And so Sarah set off across Vienna, carrying the ship in a bright yellow BILLA supermarket bag. She hoped she looked like a local on her way home from shopping, and not like a newly minted art thief.

NINE

Since Sarah had not wanted to leave the box unattended in Alessandro's apartment, she had spent the afternoon flipping through Vienna guidebooks and more or less babysitting the model ship. She had found out what she could about it: a sixteenth-century "galleon" possibly owned by good old Rudy II. This object was right up his alley. Fully automated, it had once been able to trundle down the length of a table, playing music from the organ on its hull, the toy sailors in the crow's nest striking hammers to announce the time, electors processing on the deck before the seated emperor, and cannons firing smoke.

She had found nothing on the Internet about the galleon having been stolen, which was reassuring. She tried to come up with legitimate reasons why a nanobiologist would have a treasure from the British Museum in her fridge, but quickly gave up. For Pols's sake, she would do as she was told without asking questions.

Sarah had spent some time studying Renato's Facebook profile. His picture was of a bust of Apollo, which Sarah hoped meant he had a sense of humor. Of course, that didn't mean he would be okay in helping her with trafficked goods. At least she didn't have to worry about Alessandro, who had neurology rotations at the hospital and wouldn't be home until late.

So Sarah read and looked at pictures of Vienna's tourist attractions. The guidebooks, she noticed, stayed clear of the city's most recent history (no Hitler tours) and instead focused on the glories of Imperial Vienna, the Secession and Jugendstil, the café culture, the music. Sarah had already noticed that nearly every shop window in the city contained images of either Klimt's *The Kiss* or a portrait of Empress "Sissi," the melancholic, anorexic, and ultimately assassinated wife of Emperor Franz Joseph.

It was dark when Sarah arrived at Maria-Theresien-Platz, another grand testament to those ultimate size queens, the Hapsburgs. Two massive structures with identical Neo-Renaissance façades, the Kunsthistorisches and the Natural History Museum, faced each other across an expanse of formal gardens, complete with fountains and statues. A gigantic monument to Maria Theresia presided in the middle of the *Platz*, with the plump and motherly looking empress holding out one hand as if to say, "Welcome, my dears. Don't muck up the shrubberies."

Comfortably settled on a throne atop Corinthian pillars, Maria held in her other hand the Pragmatic Sanction, the document her father, Charles VI, had worked for during his reign, which would secure her succession since there were no male heirs. Maria Theresia would hold on to the throne for forty years, pop out sixteen children (including the next emperor, Joseph II, and one Marie Antoinette), and fight a couple of nasty wars. She was one of the few Hapsburgs who wasn't inbred, though she had plenty of crazy ideas. Violently anti-Semitic and superstitious.

"Sarah?" Renato greeted her in English. He was a slight, dark-haired man with a long thick scarf wrapped around his neck.

Sarah held out her hand and Renato touched her fingers lightly with his gloved hand. Sarah saw that part of his face was covered with a blistering rash.

"My condition is called seborrheic dermatitis and it is not contagious," he said quickly, in a slightly mechanical tone that let her know he had said this very often. Before she could respond, he pointed with his chin at the statue of Maria Theresia. "One of my favorite monuments in Vienna. She always reminds me of my mother, who sits exactly so in the chair at the salon in Piazza Navona while she's having her hair done."

"Does that make you Joseph II?" Sarah smiled.

"No, Marie Antoinette." Renato laughed. "So, shall we go for a glass of wine and discuss your art-related problem? I have a very boring life so I was really grateful for your message."

"Actually . . ." said Sarah, who then ran through a creative version of "helping a friend who had been given something she thought had been stolen."

"I know this is a terrible imposition," Sarah said, hefting her bag. "And I don't even know if this thing is real. But if it can be done discreetly, it seems the best thing to do is get it back to the museum it belongs to. If it is the real thing, it's probably incredibly valuable. At the least, it's very old."

"How old?"

"Sixteenth century."

"Pfft." Renato made the Italian man's noise of dismissal. "That's not so old." He appeared to think things over for several minutes, then asked, "Do you know where it is supposed to be?"

"The British Museum."

Renato whistled.

"Show me?"

"I can't really whip it out in the *Platz*," said Sarah. "It's big." She hefted the BILLA bag. Renato pinched the bridge of his nose, thinking again.

"Okay, here's the plan." Renato's eyes were now twinkling with excitement. "We will go in through the security guard entrance, which actually has the fewest cameras. I will bring Thomas, my favorite guard, a nice espresso. I will introduce you as my friend. Then I will ask if we can use his service elevator, which I am not supposed to do, but he will let me and he won't search your bag because it will all be very friendly and so forth. You will use your feminine wiles on Thomas. Then we'll go straight to my tiny office, which is inside the antiquities wing. Everyone in that part of the building will be long gone, and the security guards only patrol outside the wing. They find the inside too spooky, apparently. Or maybe they are afraid of me."

"Okay, that sounds good. Then what?"

"Then you show me what you have and then we figure out a nice safe place to leave it and then we go get a drink and a nice pasta."

"Mille grazie," said Sarah. "If something goes wrong, act really surprised when they haul a priceless artifact out of my bag."

"This is so exciting," Renato said. "Nothing like this ever happens in Vienna. Or maybe just never to me."

"Sadly," said Sarah, "things like this happen to me all the time."

The first part of the plan went surprisingly well, though Sarah made no attempt to use feminine wiles on Thomas. It was clear that the man had eyes only for Renato, who made jokes and seemed relaxed, but whose hand shook when he handed the barrel-chested guard the espresso. Sarah thought that the audacity of smuggling "loose" art into a museum might have caught up with his nerves, but in the service elevator Renato admitted that seeing Thomas was pretty much the happiest part of his day, and that he had nursed an enormous crush for several years.

"I look at beauty all day long," he said. "But, you know, it's all long-dead beauty. Still, a guy can dream."

"He obviously likes you," Sarah said. "Maybe you should—"

"He's just a nice person," Renato interrupted. "He's way too perfect looking to be into someone like me." The elevator doors opened and Sarah stepped into a twilit ghostly hall. The floor was a beautifully laid out geometric pattern of black and white marble. The ceiling was vaulted and decorated with elaborate stucco designs and paintings. Her nose was flooded by the scent of lavender.

"Holy smokes," she said. "Is this place . . . perfumed?"

"Piped in the vents." Renato nodded. "Very subtly. You have a good nose." He led her across the hall to the antiquities wing, unlocking a door and waving a magnetic card over a sensor. She followed Renato through room after room of busts, cornices, jewelry, small figures, lamps, coins, and pottery. It was a huge collection. Although, Sarah thought, she had hardly visited a museum that didn't seem to have an enormous amount of Greek and Roman antiquities. Had anything those people touched *not* made it into a museum? Or was it just that if something was made four centuries before Christ, you couldn't just toss it, even if it was only a comb?

Renato unlocked a small door in the corner of a room filled with sarcophagi and she found herself in a small, book-lined office, just like hers back in Cambridge. Only better organized. And where she kept a silly papier-mâché bust of Beethoven that a friend had made for her, Renato had the bust of Apollo from his Facebook page. Renato saw her admiring it.

"Two thousand years old, and still working it, right?"

She set the BILLA bag on Renato's desk. "For an antiquities expert this might not seem so impressive, but have a look." Renato took off his thick gloves and replaced them with a thin fabric pair, textured at the fingertips. She saw that the skin on his bare hands was also peeled and patchy. It looked painful. She complimented him on the gloves.

"I made them myself," he said, handing her a pair. "Latex and I are not friends. The gods have a terrible sense of humor, bless their hearts."

Sarah glanced at the gleaming pale curves of Apollo's face in the corner. Greek and Roman statues, she knew, had originally been painted in bright and lifelike colors. Only time had worn them down to smooth whiteness, rendering them exquisite and remote. Did Renato choose antiquities because things of the past were easier to be around? Or was it like her feelings about music—to be near greatness, to try to understand it, to show it to others, was the thing that gave a point to existence?

"This is like Christmas!" Renato gently cut away the paper and bubble wrap to reveal the galleon. "What a lovely toy. Beautiful craftsmanship." He bent down to examine the figures on the deck of the ship. "What do you know about it?"

"It was made by a German clockmaker. Rudolf II had it at some point. It's an automaton, though apparently it doesn't actually move anymore and the clock, obviously, has run down."

"Well, it's fifteen centuries after my period, but it looks authentic. We have Rudolf II's *Kunstkammer* here, on the other side of the building. This would fit right in."

"Any ideas on how to get it back to the British Museum?"

"Actually I think it will be quite easy." Renato grinned. "We just got a crate from them yesterday. Two vases for our January show. I'll just tell them that this was in the crate, too. Someone obviously packed it by mistake."

"Will they believe that?"

"Oh, stuff like that happens all the time. Things go missing; they get broken or vandalized. Stolen. Mostly this doesn't get reported, since it's always very embarrassing. Once the Brits have it back, they won't ask a lot of questions. Everyone will just point the finger of blame at someone else." Sarah's relief was so intense that she spontaneously hugged Renato, who seemed surprised but pleased.

The galleon would go away, and now Bettina would *have* to help Pols.

"A really big dish of pasta," said Sarah. "And a really expensive bottle of wine. You've earned it."

They set about rewrapping the galleon. When Sarah tilted the automaton so Renato could position the plastic, the tip of her finger caught something on the underside of the ship. The hands of the clock face on the prow of the ship swung around, which caused a hidden compartment door to slide open.

"Oh, crap."

"Did you break it?"

"No. I found something, though."

Renato came around the desk and peered over her shoulder. "Secret chamber. How cute."

Sarah tilted the galleon so they could peer inside, and a tiny cannon emerged from the compartment, clicking into place.

"Very cool," said Sarah, as they both leaned forward.

Sssssssssss. The tiny cannon directly in front of their faces released a cloud of spray, exactly like an aerosol can. They both jerked back, only just not dropping the galleon. Sarah looked at Renato, whose eyes were streaming. Her own felt like they had just dilated to three times their normal size.

"Gesù Cristo!" Renato reached for a tissue, coughing. "What was that?"

Sarah wiped her face, which was lightly misted, and sniffed the back of her hand.

"Please tell me that we did not just get sprayed with anthrax."

Sarah shook her head. She examined the cannon carefully, but it appeared to have shot its entire wad. She brought her hands to her nose.

"It smells like . . . amber."

She laughed. Renato laughed, too. Soon they had to sit down they were laughing so hard.

"Wait," Sarah spluttered. "Why are we laughing?"

"I . . . don't know." Renato flapped his hands helplessly. "We should be screaming!"

This made them laugh even harder.

"Are we high?" Renato gasped. "Did we just do sixteenth-century crystal meth?"

"I'm so sorry!" Sarah felt like her face was going to crack from laughing. "How do you feel?"

She stood up and Renato stood up, too. Sarah looked around the room. Her vision seemed to be clear, her senses all firing. She just felt so . . . energized. Elated.

"I'm loving this!" said Renato. "Let's pack this golden bong up and leave it in my superior's office. I'll write a message saying it was delivered to me by mistake and we'll let her notify the British Museum."

It turned out to be absurdly fun to wheel the box on a little handcart across the museum's spotlit rooms. They deposited the galleon in another office, and then Renato gave Sarah a whirl-wind tour of all his favorite works of art. Sarah thought the Kunst-historisches had to be the most beautiful museum she'd ever been in. Marble floors, velvet couches and chairs for resting, huge doors. Spandrel frescoes by Klimt in the main hallway, along with a giant Canova of Theseus defeating a centaur. "Come see the Tintoretto!" Renato would whisper and they'd go racing into a room. "Come see the Salome!" They couldn't stop laughing. Sarah looked at a portrait of Archduke Ferdinand of Tyrol, Philippine Welser's husband, and thought she saw the little lamb on his Order of the Golden Fleece turn and wink at her.

"I feel like . . . skipping," said Renato. "Is that crazy?"

"No!" said Sarah. Skipping sounded incredible! Why didn't she skip anymore?

"Come on!" Renato clapped his hands. "I'll show you my favorite room in *my* wing."

They skipped through the beautiful rooms.

"Wheeeee!" said Renato, slapping the ass of a life-size Zeus.

They came to a room shrouded in darkness.

"Stand here." Renato positioned her in the middle of one wall and then flicked a switch. Beams of illumination shot out from the ceiling. The room was full of pillars of different heights, from waist to shoulder high. Atop each pillar, in its own individual spotlight, was a sculpted head. They were all pure white marble, and all incredibly lifelike. She was staring at fifty disembodied heads.

"Sarah Weston, I would like you to meet my friends," said Renato, walking among them. "This is Vespasian, and this is Marcus Aurelius, and this is a commodore I like to call Bob. And this is Julia and this is also a Julia, and this is little Knabe, dear Mädchen, and this is Gay Face. Tell me this *ragazzo* wasn't the toast of the taverna on a Saturday night!"

As Sarah laughed, the marble face of the young man with huge beautiful eyes seemed to frown for a second.

And then the fifty disembodied heads began to talk.

"Hey," said Marcus Aurelius angrily, "I feel funny."

"Did he just say that?" asked one of the Julias. "Or did I?"

"The heads are talking," said the other. "Wait. What's happening?"

"Be quiet!" cried Gay Face. "I need to think!"

"Renato?" whispered Sarah. "Are you hearing this?"

But Renato wasn't listening. He was staring at his hands. *"Guarda,"* he said. He held his hands up and then touched his face. He turned to Sarah. The blotchy patches of skin were fading, evaporating. His skin was luminous.

"Oh," gasped Vespasian. "You look wonderful."

Renato whipped off his sweater and T-shirt and Sarah saw the angry red skin all over his torso. But the weals were fading, replaced with healthy, olive-colored skin.

"Madonna santa," said Renato. "I've tried every drug—prednisone, cyclosporine, every immune suppressant out there—and nothing's ever worked. Sarah, this is a miracle."

The marble heads were all admiring his physique. Bob the commodore whistled.

Renato dropped to his knees and began to thank every holy figure Sarah had ever heard of.

"San Franceso, Maria, Gesù, Buddha, Giove, grazie, grazie, grazie," Renato was crying. *"Grazie Minerva, Diana, Zeus, Dio, Gaia! E tutti i dei africani e indiani, grazie!"*

Sarah looked at her own hands. They seemed the same, but of course she didn't . . .

"Grazie, Apollo!" Renato shouted. *"Grazie, Zeus!"*

The heads were now all talking at once, shouting, calling to each other, demanding to be heard. Renato leapt to his feet.

"How long will it last?" he shouted to Sarah over the din.

"I don't know!" she yelled back. "I don't understand what's happening!"

"Thomas." Renato grabbed his sweater. "If I have only five minutes like this, I want to be touched." He rushed for the door.

"Wait!" Sarah called.

"I'm sorry," he said over his shoulder. "I'll come back!"

As the door clicked behind him, several of the male voices burst into laughter and shouted encouragement after Renato. "Men!" said a Julia. "Always thinking with their cocks!"

"Did Bettina rig the clock with some kind of drug?" Marcus Aurelius wondered.

"Or was it something from Rudy II's time?" one of the child heads piped up.

"Rudolf had a lot of ailments," said Gay Face. "Why not seborrheic dermatitis?"

"This is crazy," said Bob. "It's like LSD or something!"

"Why would Bettina put a drug in a clock?" asked Vespasian. "That makes *no* sense."

"What if the drug cures more than skin disorders?" Mädchen wondered.

"They are speaking my thoughts," said Julia. She smiled at Sarah. "Yes, I just said that. And yes, we are."

"What if the drug acts on the whole immune system?" Septimius Severus shouted.

"Or is this all a hallucination?" Marcus Aurelius whispered.

"What if it is Bettina's drug?" interrupted the North African soldier. "What if it could help Pols?"

Sarah ran to the door.

"I hope I don't set off any alarms!" shouted Bob.

"I don't care!" Julia shouted back.

Sarah staggered through the rest of the antiquities display, but quickly became disoriented. Statues in various rooms called out to her, confusing her even more. "Did I come through this one?" they cried. "This doesn't look familiar!" The life-size Zeus muttered, "I remember that," as she ran by him.

Sarah was now at the main staircase of the museum. In front of her was the giant Canova. *The museum guards,* Sarah thought, *they must be patrolling around.* Would they be able to hear the statues, or was it just her? *Don't speak,* she thought furiously at the centaur-slaying soldier. *Do not say a word.*

The soldier raised his head, narrowed his eyes at her, and then thrust his pelvis forward. He had sprouted a ten-foot-long erection. Sarah ran down the stairs and then ducked behind a pillar. She could hear footsteps and saw the sweep of a flashlight across the marble floor. She looked back at the Canova, who was still watching her, and stroking his massive erection.

Sarah tried hard to think of nothing at all, in order to keep Canova quiet. She was trembling all over. Her body was burning up. She was . . . dear God. She was having an orgasm.

She needed to get back to Renato's office. She should take the clock with her.

She needed to . . .

Sarah clamped her hand over her mouth, trying to stifle the moan that was coming from deep inside her chest. She stumbled across the hall and groped for another door. Unfortunately, this one set off an alarm when she opened it, and Sarah crashed through two more doors and then suddenly she was outside, in the cold air. The statue of Maria Theresia loomed up before her. Sarah ran toward it, hoping she wouldn't be followed by a squadron of security guards.

Or that she would be. And they would lay her down here, right here on the ground in front of Maria Theresia's horsemen.

"Me, me, do me," said the four horsemen in chorus. Sarah started running again.

The second orgasm came as she reached the gates of the Volksgarten. "Ohhhhhhh," she groaned, passing a pair of older women. "Sorry, ate some bad chicken." They didn't quite believe her, she feared.

She wanted to tear her clothes off, touch herself all over, grab any other person . . .

Where was she going in such a rush anyway? This could be the best night of her life.

Another orgasm came as she pulled out her phone. She needed to get a message to Bettina. Did she know what was in the galleon? Sarah had another orgasm, right under a statue of Empress Sissi. Every cell in her body was filled with intense joy, vibrating in unison. Sarah sang out in ecstasy, all thoughts banished. She finally knew the truth. It had been revealed. Nothing else mattered but this feeling.

"Pull yourself together," Sissi snapped. "I am no prude, but . . ."

"Anyone who starts a sentence with 'I am no prude' is a total prude!" Sarah shouted. God, even her fingernails felt pleasurable. "You were a melancholic. You didn't even like food! There is nothing wrong with me!"

"Is the drug stimulating the vagus nerve?" asked Sissi. "That's how they treat epilepsy and depression, both of which Rudolf II may have suffered from."

Sarah stared at the empress.

"You read this online last month when you were researching a cure for Pols." Sissi sounded very smug. "The vagus nerve acts on several parts of the brain and nervous system in ways we don't yet understand. They're exploring the use of vagus nerve stimulation in other diseases, including Alzheimer's. It has anti-inflammatory properties that may make it useful in treating heart disease, colitis, and arthritis. And it's very long, connecting the brain to the—"

"*Okay!*" Sarah shouted. She fought down another orgasm and dialed a number on her phone.

"You should call Max and admit you're still in love with him," said the empress.

"Fuck off, Sissi," said Sarah. "It's not that simple."

The call went through at last. "I'm sorry to bother you but it's an emergency," she told Alessandro. "I need a drug test."

TEN

Max Lobkowicz Anderson, shifting uncomfortably under the stern gaze of a priest, was trying to pinpoint the exact moment when his life had gotten really weird. You could, he thought, go all the way back to the day five years before, when his father had called him to say that the Czech government had decided to restitute twenty-two castles and palaces that had been seized from the family in 1948. In a single gesture he had been transformed from a guy taking a few years off to find himself (drums, weed, Southern California) to landowning European aristocracy.

Max looked around him at the somber and magnificent interior of SS. Cyril and Methodius's Cathedral and tried to concentrate on the mass. He wasn't raised religious and, though he enjoyed the rituals, had never quite been able to decipher these things. He had come with Pols and Jose. After a few minutes of rest, Pols had been able to finish her concert, but Max was really worried about her. He was doing everything he could to keep her from getting overtired, which today meant bringing them to the mass in his car rather than have them take the tram. And that way he could get a good lunch into her afterward, too, at a restaurant she liked next door to the church. Nico, back from London, had used the offer of lunch to tag along, though Max was sure he, too, was keeping an eye on Pols.

Max was eager to get back to his grandfather's secret library in the basement of the palace, where he'd found some books about Philippine Welser. He was intrigued by Philippine's husband, too. Archduke Ferdinand (Order of the Golden Fleece, naturally) had been a courageous soldier, but seemed ambivalent about his princely duties and a lot more interested in alchemy.

There weren't many people in the cathedral today, though it was an impressive place. Like much of Prague, it was steeped in a complicated history and awash with emotions great and terrible. It was here that the Czech patriots who had assassinated the Nazi *Reichsprotektor* Reinhard Heydrich had made their last stand on June 17, 1942. Despite a misfiring pistol, they had managed to wound the bloodthirsty and cruel Heydrich on May 27, and the squad, which had parachuted in from London, had evaded capture while he languished. But when Heydrich finally kicked the bucket, the Gestapo had gone into high gear, and tortured people until they got answers, including showing one child his mother's head in a fish tank. Once the Nazis knew that this church was the hideout, they began to try to force out the squad with tear gas and bombs. You could still see the bullet holes in the walls and visit the crypt where the squad had committed suicide rather than be captured. All that had happened right here, where Max was sitting, not paying attention to the priest.

You could say his life had really gotten weird when he had first taken the drug Westonia. After the drug, Max had never been able to see anything quite the same again. Walking around the palace (his palace) in Prague or the castle (his castle) in Nelahozeves, he knew he was surrounded by the energy of great lives, great passions. Like it wasn't intimidating enough to be surrounded by portraits of your illustrious ancestors sporting the Order of the Golden Fleece on their fucking doublets.

And then there was the knowledge that his ancestors had been part of some *secret* Order of the Golden Fleece, a book containing the mystical theory of everything, or spells of ultimate power, or maybe just a load of crap. None of his ancestors had bothered to leave Max any clear instructions about what it was. Or where it was. Or how he was supposed to protect it. Or if there were any other members to the secret order other than him. Or what the secret handshake was, or if there were annual meetings. If they had left instructions, they had been destroyed or misplaced. Or hidden. Or used to line pie tins by an illiterate housemaid, like some of John Dee's papers had been.

Every other day he got an invitation to join a secret order. It was part of who he was now, the thirteenth in a line of princes. He had been courted by the Knights of the Triangle. The Brotherhood of the Rooster. Gentlemen of the Bronzed Codpiece. Maybe the secret Order of the Golden Fleece was just another version of those. An excuse to dress up in costumes and try to pretend you were as cool as the people who founded your dynasty.

Maybe one of those books in the basement would contain something helpful.

Max looked at the little man seated next to him. Nico believed that the knowledge contained in the book of the Fleece was science, but an advanced science that, four centuries later, modern science was only beginning to catch up to. Like Westonia, which activated glial cells in the brain and allowed you to experience nonlinear time. Which turned out to be the real nature of time. Now it was understood that particles could be in more than one place at one time and that there were probably multiple universes. What else was spelled out in the Fleece? Did the knowledge go all the way back to the Greeks or further? Was it some kind of basic manual for use of the planet, like the unified field theory that Einstein had dreamed of? Had the alchemists, unfettered by the strictly labeled confines of modern science, students of physics, medicine, biology, chemistry, and astronomy, as well as philosophy and religion, discovered the basic laws that dictated the universe and the way to manipulate them?

Nico had been helping him track down clues to the Fleece, but right now the only quest that mattered was finding something to help Pollina. Nico was now planning on going to Vienna to help Sarah.

Sarah. She was unlike anyone Max had ever met. She was tied to these deep mysteries of his life, she understood them better than anyone else, and yet she was constantly rejecting them, too. And rejecting him. She had made it clear she had no interest in joining their lives, which he knew she imagined would be some sort of prince consort tedium of fund-raisers and parties and inherited, unearned privilege. He had been too irritated with her uncompromising certainty to try to make her see it all differently. Also she wasn't totally wrong. Max had quickly learned that being the head of a museum meant you spent at least five nights a week either asking people for money at your own fund-raisers or trying to poach potential donors from other nonprofits.

Yes, he was still in love with her, but if he was honest, it *was* hard to picture Sarah in his world. He could picture her delving into a manuscript with a look of intense concentration or pulling him into the cloakroom of a restaurant, putting one hand over his mouth and the other hand down his pants. But helping him to arrange catering for a fund-raising event? Being diplomatic and charming to investors? It was like putting pearls around the neck of an eagle: the combination diminished both things.

And he wasn't going to turn his back on his life to follow her.

First off, he was pretty sure she didn't want anyone following her. And second, the museum would fall apart, and everything his grandfather had tried to save would be lost again. This time forever, sold at auction. He couldn't be responsible for losing a four-hundred-year-old fortune. If his future children wanted to walk away, he'd be fine with that, he wouldn't force it on anyone, but Max's parents were gone, and he had no siblings, and this was apparently his lot in life.

What were you supposed to do when the person you loved didn't fit into your world?

Max's thoughts were interrupted by a shout coming from the nave. People turned in their seats, scuffling and shushing.

"They're coming! They're coming!" a man was shouting in Czech. The priest stopped in midsentence. All around Max, heads were craning to see what was happening. He stood up.

A wild-eyed man in a tattered and dirty gray pinstripe suit and blue and white tie was being restrained by one of the church functionaries, a slender young man who was no match for him. Max strode forward to help, with Nico at his heels.

"Max Lobkowicz!" exclaimed the man, grabbing at Max's jacket. "Thank God! But you shouldn't be here—it's too dangerous. They'll kill you, too. It's terrible, sir; we've heard on the radio what they've done . . . the families, all dead . . ." He started to cry.

Max, taken aback, turned to look at the church functionary, who was calling for security.

"Sir," the man whispered, still clinging to Max and staring at him with panicked eyes, "I can't find my cyanide capsule! You must help me. Shoot me now before they get me! Shoot me!"

And then a security guard was grappling with the man and hauling him away. After a brief speech of apology from the priest and a blessing on the poor man's soul, the mass resumed. Max noted that Nico had disappeared.

"You knew that man?" whispered Jose.

"No . . ." said Max. "But he seemed to know me. He called me by name."

Pols said nothing, lost in prayer. Max wasn't sure if she had even been aware of the whole thing until she asked about it after the service was over.

"Someone off his meds, I guess," Max said.

"And Harriet was here?"

"Harriet?" Max was surprised. "No."

"Oh. I thought I smelled her."

Max decided to let that one go.

The incident was the talk of the family-style restaurant next door, which was where most of the congregation adjourned for Sunday lunch at long tables with pitchers of beer. No one had gotten a good look at the individual in question, and so the interruption was largely blamed on drugs. The Czech Republic had the most liberal laws concerning drug possession in the EU, but there was always grumbling about the African narcotics peddlers in Wenceslas Square. The popularity of violent American films and television was also mentioned and decried.

Max, happy to see Pols tucking into a bowl of soup between Jose and the priest, found himself in conversation with a young man from the church. It turned out he was part of the staff who worked at the museum run out of the crypt. "Oh, these reenactors," he said, shaking his head. "They make us crazy. I don't know how he got into the crypt. We usually keep it locked during mass. His costume and makeup were very accurate, I will say."

Max tried to remember what he had learned about Operation Anthropoid, the plot to assassinate Heydrich. He knew it had originated in England, where Czechs who had fled formed a government-in-exile to work with the allies to infiltrate the Nazis. He knew that because his grandfather had been a part of the government-in-exile. His grandfather Max Lobkowicz, whom he resembled closely.

Jan Kubiš, a paratrooper, had thrown the grenade that killed Heydrich. After the assassination, the Nazis suspected that the men had been sheltered in the town of Lidice before escaping to Prague and hiding in the church. Hitler had every man in the town of Lidice executed and the women sent to Ravensbrück concentration camp. The town was burned to the ground and then the ruins were leveled. Five thousand people died in the reprisals.

Max walked to the cashier to pay as Jose helped Pols get her coat on.

"Thoughts, my friend, on our little interruption?" It was Nico, pulling him into the hallway of the restaurant.

"The man was dressed in old clothes," Max said. "About seventy years out of date. And did you see the look in his eyes?"

"Remind you of anything?" The little man seemed uncharacteristically intent and serious.

"Yeah, the whole thing was exactly like when Sarah pulled Saint John of Nepomuk out of the river. What happened? I assumed you followed them?"

"The security guard took him out and told him never to come back. The man took off running through the streets. Seemed terrified out of his mind. I tried to keep up, but . . ." Nico shrugged.

"I don't think it was a historical reenactment," said Max.

"Nor do I. And I made some calls, to see if anyone was able to identify Saint John at the morgue."

"And?"

"The body has disappeared."

 ELEVEN

Alessandro, his normal Italian insouciance replaced with real concern for Sarah's well-being, had insisted on keeping her overnight and doing blood work, a urinalysis, hair and skin samples, a functional MRI, and a positron emission tomograph. He had examined her saliva and ultrasounded her abdomen. He had even looked in her ears, which was somehow more intimate than sharing a bathroom with him back in Boston.

Sarah sat on the table, in a paper gown. She had been unable to make eye contact with Alessandro when she described having the most powerful orgasms of her life, but fortunately he had retained his professional composure. At least for now. She had a feeling she would be in for some serious teasing later.

"Where you get this drug?" demanded Alessandro for the hundredth time. "And don't tell me again this story 'someone at club must have slipped something in my drink.' What club? Where is Renato?"

Sarah sighed. She trusted Alessandro, but she couldn't get him involved in the galleon and Bettina. There was too much at risk. She had been texting Renato during her examination, but so far he hadn't responded.

"I'm sorry," she told Alessandro. "One minute I was fine, having a great time, and the next minute I felt totally strange. Renato was with friends. I didn't want to worry him."

"First night I pick you up at police station and last night you are high as a kite. Sarah . . ."

"Please don't ask me any more," she said. "You know I have my reasons."

"It will take a while to analyze the data," Alessandro said, collecting a sheaf of papers. "What I see from the preliminary results is something *un pochino strano*."

"Strange as in . . ."

"I know you. You are like horse, never sick. Have you *ever* been sick? In your life?"

"Of course."

"I am asking because so far, everything in your body is . . . *perfect*. But too perfect. Everyone has something. Even healthy, spinning class, yogurt-eating, hot *ragazza* like yourself will have *something*. Bilirubin slightly higher, white cell count a little off, but your levels, *cara*, are optimal across the board. There is no inflammation anywhere in your body. You don't have a yeast infection or a toenail fungus or even a trace of gingivitis. Is very strange. Is like someone hit the reset button."

"I was thinking all the symptoms were just vagus nerve stimulation."

"Possibly you are right about that. Your striatum, she was lit up like a Christmas tree. Your nucleus accumbens was bombarded with dopamine."

"A lot of autoimmune disorders come from degeneration of that part of the brain, right?" said Sarah. "Parkinson's, Huntington's?"

"*Sì*. It also seems to be the center of addictions."

Sarah nodded and jumped off the table.

"You've been a rock star, Alessandro," she said. "How on earth are you going to explain running all these tests?"

"I make love to the lady in charge of billing." Alessandro smiled. "While her cats watch."

Sarah met Renato later that morning in his office at the Kunsthistorisches. The museum, which had been all hers last night, was now thronged with tourists. She averted her eyes as she passed the centaur and greeted Renato. The curator's skin still appeared smooth and clear. Renato told her that he had left his phone in his office last night and passed out cold a few hours after taking the drug. By the time he had gotten to the museum, his superior had already discovered the box with the galleon and a courier had come to remove it. He had told no one about the drug.

"But, Sarah," he said, "what did it do to me? What did it do to you?"

"I don't know." Sarah shook her head. "It might have been a sort of supersteroid, suppressing the immune system. It might have . . . repaired it. I don't want to get your hopes up. And I think you should get some tests done."

"By who?" yelped Renato.

"Alessandro. You wouldn't have to say what we took."

"Sarah." Renato locked his office door and then took off his sweater. His chest and arms were beautifully olive. But then Renato turned around.

The smooth expanse of skin was now delineated with darker patches.

Sarah picked up her phone and fired off another text to Bettina. *Galleon on way back to British Museum. I need answers.*

Renato had stripes like a tiger.

. . .

"You don't think," Renato said in the cab over to the hospital, "that I'm suddenly going to sprout claws or, like, fangs or anything, do you?"

"No." Sarah tried to sound calm and confident. "The skin isn't raised; there's no . . . hair or anything. It's just pigmentation. Some kind of side effect. And it's only your back."

"I don't want to sound ungrateful," said Renato in a high voice—he was clearly fighting down a certain degree of panic, "but I really don't want to become a tiger. All things considered, I'm a vegetarian."

"Alessandro will run some tests. He'll be discreet. I haven't told him about the galleon. Too complicated. We were at a club last night; someone slipped us some drugs in our drinks. You don't even have to say that you had a skin condition. Just have him look at the stripes."

"Okay."

"You're going to be fine. How do you feel?"

"I'm freaking out."

"But other than that?"

"Other than that, I feel great. I mean, look at me." Renato held out his arms, wonderingly. He ran one slim brown hand over the other, then touched his chest. Tears came to his eyes.

"Sarah, whatever this is, I don't want to change it. I don't want to go back. I don't even want to know what it was. You have no idea how good it is to feel my own skin. Touch me. Please. I don't mean . . . just touch me."

Sarah ran her hands down Renato's forearm. When they reached his hand, he gripped her fingers.

"How did the tiger get his stripes?" He laughed softly. "God works in mysterious ways. But you were right, you know. Thomas did like me. I thought, when I ran up and kissed him, he would ask me what happened to my skin. But you know what he said? He said, 'What took you so long?'"

S arah stayed with Renato and Alessandro long enough to ascertain that all of Renato's vitals were normal. The blood work would take longer.

"I cannot say if the marking on his skin will be permanent or no," Alessandro said when they were alone together in the hallway. "I think it is an allergic reaction to this drug. Every person has stripes on their skin, called Blaschko's lines, only on most people the pigment differentiation is so faint you cannot detect this, unless you look under strong UV light. Or sometimes with allergy, you see this."

"Is that related somehow to the vagus nerve?"

"Not that I know of." Alessandro shrugged, then added, "There is one other explanation. Genetic chimeras—people who have two sets of DNA instructions in their cells—often have visible Blaschko's lines. Maybe the drug is confusing Renato's DNA. I need to know what it was, Sarah. Stop with the nonsense about someone slipping you something. Renato is not as good a liar as you."

"It's hard to talk about." *To say the least,* thought Sarah.

"There is more?"

Sarah thought of the empty cannon with regret. If there had been any left, they could've tested it.

"No."

"You can find more?"

"I don't think so."

"Please, Sarah, *ti voglio bene.* You must not take whatever it is again. These different symptoms are strange. I am not convinced there won't be further repercussions. DNA is not GPS. It will not simply reroute if you take a wrong turn."

No response from Bettina. Sarah needed a long walk. She headed for the Donaukanal—the arm of the Danube that bordered the city center. The Danube, she found, was far from blue here— more an olive—but the walls along the pathway were a riot of colorful graffiti: cartoon characters, tags, messages, faces, figures. In some places the ground was littered with the discarded tips of spray cans. This was a different view of Vienna, younger, more energetic, struggling to define itself, literally. Yet even here Austrian sensibilities prevailed. The violence of a dripping black *Fuck cops!* was mitigated by something Nina had told her at the ball about city officials making it legal for graffiti artists to work on designated sections of the wall. The technical quality of the art probably benefited (no rushing to get through before Der Fuzz showed up), but it took a bit of the element of anarchy away.

Bikes zoomed around her as she dialed her phone. Jose answered. "Pollina at the palace. I go to pick her up soon."

"How is she today?"

"She taking new medicine, but she no like. She say it make her joints hurt. Oksana say she not understand why nothing working. She want to know if you meet the doctor in Vienna." Sarah felt something in her chest tighten and squeeze.

"I'm working on it."

"I go to mass every day," Jose said. "I pray to Jesus to keep her safe."

Prayer. That was what people did when there was nothing else left to do.

Sarah wandered over toward the Hofburg complex, pausing

outside Michaelerkirche as horses and carriages clomped past. The church contained, she knew, the largest Baroque organ in Vienna, a superb instrument by Johann David Sieber. She thought she might have a look since she was here.

It couldn't be that she wanted, like Jose, to pray for Pollina, could it? She hadn't prayed since . . . since her father died.

But if Sarah had been motivated by some latent desire for a compassionate Almighty, the sight of Michaelerkirche's high altar knocked it out. Meant to evoke a flight of angels escaping from Hell, it looked to Sarah like someone had assembled those little gold babies people hid in cakes and stuck them into lumps of putty. Putti putty. Gothic Play-Doh. There was nothing here for her but creepy art. She was about to make a hasty exit when a burst of music sounded above her.

Johann Sebastian Bach's "Fuga sopra il Magnificat."

Ah, hell, thought Sarah, leaning against a pillar and surrendering herself to the cascade of sublime sound. God in words and God in pictures left her unmoved. But God in music?

Her phone, which she had set to vibrate, buzzed in her pocket.

Thank you. Galleon an unwelcome gift, I assure you. I need answers, too. Someone stole my laptop. I need it back. You must help. It is not safe for me to return to Vienna yet. I will message you again.

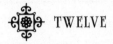 TWELVE

ollina Rutherford was tired. Her head was very
stuffy and she couldn't breathe through her nose. God was in-
creasing His tests of her every day. She took her hands off the keyboard and began massaging them. Oksana had taught her some
stretching exercises, and Pols was supposed to do them every few
hours. The girl stood up. Max had given her a private rehearsal
space at the palace and outfitted it with everything she might
need.

"Boris. Yoga mat," she said in a loud, firm voice.

She listened to the sound of her elderly mastiff rising, heard
the jingle of his collar make its way to a corner of the room, then
cross to her. Boris nudged her knee and deposited his favorite
chew toy, a mangled stuffed lion missing its tail, at her feet.

"Good boy," said Pols. Her dog was becoming nearly as deaf
as she was blind. He was also pretty blind. It was important to
consider his feelings, though, and be encouraging. Boris may not
be able to see her, or hear her, but he knew she wanted something,
and he had offered her the best thing he possessed.

Pollina shut her mind to the thought that Boris would not be around forever. It would be impious to feel sad about Boris dying, since his death would deliver him to the arms of God. Also, she still had music to learn today.

A blind musician could learn music in one of two ways. The first was to read Braille manuscripts, a laborious and time-consuming process, as she had to use one hand to read and the other to play, and then switch, and then combine both parts. Pollina had once described this process to Sarah as being like trying to understand a book by reading every other word, then going back and reading all the words you missed, and then combining them. Sarah had gotten in touch with several assistance programs for the visually impaired and found a network of people who volunteered to record themselves reading scores for the blind, note by note.

Pollina wondered how long it would take Sarah to realize that science was good, but art was better. Sarah was a natural conductor and she needed Sarah to conduct her opera. She had decided that it would be about the Golden Fleece. There would be a lot of conflicting musical motifs, and Sarah would be able to control the musicians. She could be quite impressive when she put her mind to it, and very perceptive for a sighted person. Pols reached down, scratched Boris's head, and, feeling that she had rested long enough, sat back down at the piano. She put the earbuds of her iPod back in.

Memorizing Mozart took a lot of concentration. She had to be quite disciplined and focus simply on the notes until she had it. Otherwise she had a tendency to drift while learning, feeling Wolfgang's thought process, his energy, his joy, his pain. These things were very distracting.

Pols flexed her fingers over the keyboard and repeated a passage. And again. And again. Her mind was drifting. She was tired. She was dreaming a lot. Bad dreams. About Sarah, and a round white room. She didn't feel very well, to be honest. There was pain. Sometimes it was in just her lungs, and sometimes it was everywhere.

And the pain was bad. She needed to think about something else. Someone else. That was the way out of pain.

Sarah is in danger.

The voice was clear in her head. Pols stopped playing and stood up.

She heard voices in her head. She always had. These voices came from God, and so there was no question of Pols being crazy. She was not crazy. Sarah was in danger.

Nico had said he would be going to see Sarah in Vienna. Nico was a good protector, but he didn't always take things seriously. She should speak with him. Pollina thought he was probably with Max in his study.

"We're going to go see Max," she shouted at Boris. "Good boy." Boris barked an assent, pleased to have a job. They moved into the hallway. Pols knew the palace well and she did not need her cane here. She moved down the hall, touching the walls lightly with her fingertips.

Oksana was in Max's office, too. Pollina could hear her voice in the hallway. Oksana wasn't happy with the way her body was responding to the drugs. Maybe she would make the doctors stop forcing her to take them. They really only seemed to make things worse.

It would not be right to eavesdrop on their conversation. It would, however, be polite to wait until they stopped talking. And if she accidentally overheard things from the hallway? Well, she couldn't help having good hearing. She was blind and her nose was stuffed up! She only had two operating senses!

"This man who accosted you in the church," Nico was saying,

"I can't find any trace of him. I checked homeless shelters and mental health clinics."

"Maybe faster to ask my friends to find him," Oksana said.

"Is there any place the Russian mafia isn't connected?" Max asked.

"No," said Nico and Oksana simultaneously.

"You want me also run check on Harriet?" Oksana asked. "Is routine in good families to do background check on girlfriends. The ones who don't, they are sorry."

That's when Pollina heard it. A very small noise coming from the door next to Max's office. But that was Max's bathroom. She moved quickly to the door and wrenched it open.

"Oh!" said a voice, and then the sound of the toilet seat squeaking and movement. Harriet, Max's stupid girlfriend. "Oh, hello!"

"Sorry."

"Oh, not to worry. I had quite finished and it's just us girls!" Toilet flushing, and then Harriet stepped past, clacking in her high heels. "Pollina, dear, may I help you with anything?"

Pols could hear a sudden silence from Max's office.

"Bathroom," she mumbled, stepping in and shutting the door. Well, Harriet wasn't going to make her a liar. She would go since she was here. She reached forward.

Funny. The lid was down. She hadn't heard Harriet put the lid down, just flush. And the top of the lid was warm. So Harriet had just been sitting there? No. Pollina had heard bare feet on the tiles of the bathroom and then Harriet had walked past her in heels. She had been standing on the toilet. Why?

The answer became clear when Pols stood on the toilet herself. She was smaller than Harriet, but reaching up she could feel that the sound was coming through a small grated vent. A taller person could put her ear against that vent. Pols didn't need the vent, though. Her ears were sharp enough to hear what Harriet must have been listening to.

"Oh, Harriet," said Max, in his office. "Come in. Nico and Oksana were just leaving."

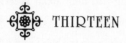 THIRTEEN

"How you find her missing computer?" asked Alessandro. "You are not a detective. Let the *polizia* find it. She is *pazza*."

It had crossed Sarah's mind that Bettina was possibly a little *pazza*, or at least in the throes of some kind of paranoid nervous breakdown. Since she was feeling not quite ten pins up herself, she had confided in Alessandro, but only to the extent of saying that she had gotten a text from the doctor, and that Bettina had asked her to find her stolen laptop.

Alessandro announced he was making a *risotto con funghi porcini*, opened a bottle of Brunello, and ordered her to begin chopping onions and parsley. "I am doubling the recipe. You need your strength," he said. "My mamma was from Milan and she make me risotto before every one of my exams. My father was pure Napolitano, so he make pizza. I was a very fat *bambino*."

Sarah sipped her Brunello and weighed her options. She felt trapped. It sounded as if Oksana and the team of doctors in Prague had basically thrown up their hands. Whether Bettina Müller was crazy or not, Sarah couldn't just walk away. Not yet.

Together she and Alessandro decided that Nina Fischer, Bettina's grad student, should be her first stop. She might seek out Marie-Franz, too, while Sarah was at the university. The professor had been there a long time. At the very least, she could fill her in on what Bettina's colleagues thought of her.

Why would someone steal a laptop? When Sarah's last machine had died, it had been annoying, but not devastating. Everything was backed up, so she guessed Bettina's concern wasn't so much about what she was *missing*, it was more about *who* had her stuff and was looking at it. Not surprising, since in addition to her research, Bettina was trafficking in stolen art and possibly in illegal hallucinogens. Sarah could be walking headfirst into several different kinds of criminal intrigue. She poured herself another glass of wine and, just for good measure, added another scoop of risotto to her plate.

She awakened from a tumultuous sleep on Alessandro's pullout sofa at eight, regretting both the extra helping and the final grappa he'd insisted on as a "*digestivo.*" She had dreamed that she was in a round white room, surrounded by doors. She was holding Pollina in her arms. There was something she had to do to save Pols, something urgent, behind one of those doors, but if she picked the wrong one . . . There had been a woman there, too, dressed in clothes constructed from strange discs of gold. Sarah had felt the weight of the garments as if she were wearing them herself.

"I cannot die," said the woman.

Time was running out. Sarah began to open a door, and as the certainty washed over her that she had made the wrong—*terribly, terribly wrong*—decision, she woke up shouting, "No!"

. . .

A lessandro took her to historic Café Landtmann for breakfast on their way to the university. Waiters with white jackets and black bow ties executed a complicated ballet around the restaurant, ducking in between tables, swooping and gliding between the chairs. The café sat next to the Burgtheater, another titanic white building, one of the biggest theaters in Europe, built to satisfy the desire of Empress Maria Theresia, who wished to have a playhouse near her palace. In 1943 "Die Burg" had hosted a notoriously anti-Semitic production of *Merchant of Venice*. At the time, almost all the Jews of Vienna had already either fled or been sent to camps, but perhaps the gods of Tragedy and Comedy that sat atop the building, at least, had been offended by the production. The building had been almost totally destroyed in World War II. And then restored, as Vienna had been restored. Up from the ashes.

At a nearby table an Englishman ranted about the poor curation of the Freud Museum, while his wife did a crossword and complained of "*Platz* fatigue."

"This café was the favorite place of Dr. Freud," Alessandro said to Sarah.

"How do you think Freud would have interpreted a dream of a round white room?"

"You want a penis," guessed Alessandro, a little too loudly. The couple sitting near them looked over, and the man laughed a little.

"I thought you were a neuroscientist." Sarah took a sip of her mélange. "What about short-term memory consolidating events into a hierarchy according to emotions and a lot of random synapses firing during the process?"

"*Sì*," said Alessandro. "And then there is my *nonna*'s idea that the dreams are the reality, not this. I like best Freud's idea that it is always about sex." He licked his spoon lasciviously.

Sex, but also violence, Sarah thought, were the undercurrents of Viennese history carefully papered over with postcards of Sissi and dancing white horses. A hundred and forty years had passed since Johann Strauss wrote his waltz "Vienna Blood," and there had been quite a lot of real blood spilled in the city since then. The final decimation of the Hapsburg Empire, two world wars, the attempt to wipe out an entire race. And yet, the famous cafés of Vienna with the famous waiters still served the famous coffee and cakes. No wonder the city had been the cradle of psychoanalysis.

Sarah went to the bathroom, leaving Alessandro perusing one of the many newspapers hung on wooden poles for the customers' use. As she passed the glass case of sweets, she heard a gruff "Grüss Gott," and turned to see the bearded horse rider she'd met at the ball entering from the street and saluting the maître d'. She remembered he smelled good but had been exceptionally rude, so she pretended not to see him and kept going, but when she emerged from the ladies' room he was waiting for her.

"Frau Doktor Weston? I am Gottfried von Hohenlohe. We met at the ball."

"Yes, I remember. Are you coming from another one?" Sarah indicated the loden cape he wore over a three-piece suit.

"No." He looked down at his cape, puzzled. "It is cold today. This is Austrian."

Sarah smiled, trying to imagine an America where it was considered natural to tog out like Betsy Ross.

"Ah, you tease," he said with a smile. "Because I was so rude at the ball. You must forgive me. I am ill at ease around beautiful women."

"I doubt that. I'm glad you are able to understand my German today."

"You are picking up the accent, I notice."

He touched her arm and Sarah felt all her senses kick into gear. Rude or not, Gottfried definitely had a certain magnetism.

"Gottfried," called a voice from a near table. Sarah saw it was the schlumpy older guy from the ball who'd made such an incongruous pair with Nina. He was carrying a leather briefcase and wearing what she guessed was an expensive raincoat, but somehow on him it looked messy and rumpled. Nina had definitely picked the wrong von Hohenlohe.

"You remember my brother, Heinrich," said Gottfried. "Are you in Vienna long?"

"A few days." Sarah nodded. "I should get back to my friend," she said. "Nice to see you again."

"Perhaps you will allow me to give you a tour of the Spanish Riding School some day after morning exercise." Gottfried handed her his card, which had nothing but his name in raised letters. He took a gold fountain pen out from under his cape and wrote his number underneath. "The stallions are quite remarkable up close."

I bet they are, she thought with a sigh. She pocketed the card, thanked him, and rejoined Alessandro.

"Not interested?" he asked, since of course he had been observing the whole thing. "I thought you and Max were over."

"Maybe interested, but I've got other things to do here," said Sarah. She didn't want to talk about Max with Alessandro—or anyone, for that matter. The feelings for him that had resurfaced when she was in Prague were confusing, and there was enough confusion without going into all that. So she switched the conversation over to Nina as they left the café.

"How well do you know her?"

"We only sleep together once," he said, making Sarah laugh. Of course he had. "I know when she was sixteen she ran away from little village outside of Salzburg. I remember this because

Salzburg is town of strange movie *The Sound of Music* which you force me to see."

Sarah had taken him to an outdoor showing on the Boston Common, where people had dressed up and sung along, which the Italian had found alarming, though not alarming enough to prevent him slipping off with a girl dressed as a warm woolen mitten.

"Is she really dating that older guy?" Sarah asked. "Heinrich? Seems like an odd match."

"She is odd girl." Alessandro shrugged. "This thing with the raccoon eyes and the hair and the tattoos, the Italian girls they do not do that. They like to be beautiful, as beautiful as possible. I know Nina only start working for Bettina this past semester, helping in the lab. What else can I tell you? Ah. Her labia, she is pierced."

"Not helpful," said Sarah. "But thanks."

"Who *doesn't* have a grudge against Bettina?" said Nina, whom Alessandro and Sarah had arranged to meet on one of the benches outside the immunology building. It was cold, and Nina had suggested they move up to the lab, where she needed to check in on the rats. Alessandro had gone to work, which Sarah was glad about. She didn't want him distracting Nina.

"She dismisses all of her grad students at the end of every semester," the girl was saying now. "And yet she's so brilliant that we all line up again, like lambs to the slaughter."

Nina threw a white lab coat over her ripped plaid jeans, Doc Martens, and Debbie Harry T-shirt safety-pinned together, and started making notes on the rats. She said that Bettina had sent her a message to keep things running, but hadn't left any more instructions than that. They moved back and forth between

German and English, which Nina spoke very idiomatically, though with a thick accent.

"She basically told me she was hiring me because I grew up taking care of goats," said Nina, surveying her rodent charges in their cages. "I guess I should thank my asshole father who made me work on the farm since I was three years old, since because of him I have no problem with blood and shit. I clean up after the rats. And then I cut them open."

"So you have talked to her since the break-in?"

"She sent me a couple texts, but she's being really cagey about where she is. Not that I blame her. Weirdos send her hate mail all the time. Religious zealots or just regular people who hear about what she's doing and think she's going too far. But that's what gets me off about nanobiology. It's a crazy *inventive* branch of science, like mad scientists, you know, and Bettina is one of the maddest scientists in the field."

That Sarah didn't doubt.

"People just don't get it, but then, most people are idiots. Yeah, and a lot of sick people write to her, too, begging her to help. So she has to deal with that. Oh"—Nina blushed—"sorry. I forgot about your friend."

"It's okay," Sarah said. "But can you tell me anything about the work? I know that at least part of it is on cytokines, and I know people think cytokines are now believed to be the 'software' of the immune system."

Nina seemed relieved Sarah wasn't offended. Despite the punk exterior, she was as friendly as a puppy, and hugely enthusiastic about her work. It wasn't difficult to picture the country girl who had run away from goats and ended up with rats.

"Cytokines are hot right now," Nina explained. "We know they send messages, but not why they sometimes screw up and send bad ones. Where the bad input is coming from. It might be in the DNA itself. Maybe from what we call the noncoding part."

"Bad messages." Sarah nodded. "So you need to tell the DNA to send a different message."

"Exactly. That's what Bettina has figured out, how to do it. But I can't tell you much more than that. I don't even know myself. I do the grunt work. Not that I'm complaining. It's totally a privilege."

"How do you send a message to DNA? I mean, how does a drug do it? And is it a pill or a . . . a mist?" Sarah wondered if the drug in the galleon was part of Bettina's experiments. It had certainly had an effect on the immune system. But Nina showed no glimmer of recognition.

"A mist? That is funny. Okay, first you take carbon, right, like just plain old ashes from the fireplace?"

Ashes to ashes, thought Sarah. How appropriate.

"You give the carbon atoms an electric charge so they form into a lattice on their own, like nano-size chicken wire. Then you roll that into a tube, and that's the vehicle for whatever you need to attach to it and send into the cell."

"And because it's made of carbon just like everything else, the body doesn't recognize it as an enemy substance and doesn't fight it off?"

"You got it. It can zoom right into the nucleus of the cell and even attach to the DNA itself."

"That's really . . . nano-Frankenstein."

"It's fucking rad. And guess what the best molecule for attaching to the nanotube is? Gold. Molecules of gold."

"Gold? So basically, the most cutting edge of science involves ashes and gold?"

"Fucking poetic, right?" Nina nodded. "But it works. In theory. Uh-oh." She stared into a cage where a rat was curled up in his nest. "Number 47 has gone kaput." She snapped on a glove and pulled out the dead rat.

"Did he . . ." Sarah thought this would be a good time to ask just how far Bettina's research had been tested. If rats were still dying from it, then she would call off the search right now.

"No, this guy is part of the control group." Nina laughed. "He just died like we all die if nobody fixes our shit. I should probably get going on him." She laid the rat on the table and unwrapped a bag of medical instruments.

"Oh, of course." Sarah watched her pull out a scalpel. "Thanks for talking with me."

"Sorry I can't help you more. You should talk to Bettina. She's really okay. She's kind of looked out for me, in a funny way. I seem to attract protectors." She laughed again.

"I saw Heinrich von Hohenlohe at Café Landtmann." Sarah smiled. "He's your . . . boyfriend?"

"Oh, he's just useful." Nina shrugged. "We met at a club and he bought me and my friends all drinks one night. He's okay. He says he'll get me a job at the pharmaceutical company where he works when I graduate. You need connections in Vienna."

Pharmaceutical company? thought Sarah. Maybe Heinrich's interest in Nina wasn't purely sexual after all. A pharmaceutical company would be very interested in what Bettina was up to. Nina was clearly whip smart, but that didn't mean she wasn't still a naive goat girl when it came to the ways of men.

"Has Heinrich ever visited you at the lab?"

"God, no. I'm supposed to work alone here. So many rules. If she knew I was even talking to you she'd be paranoid. Everything with Bettina is *eine sehr grosse Sache.*"

Maybe even a bigger deal than you know, thought Sarah.

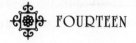 FOURTEEN

Well, she was making a little bit of progress. Heinrich could certainly be considered a suspect for the missing laptop. Sarah thought it might be worthwhile to take his brother, Gottfried, up on the offer of a tour of the Spanish Riding School; she could ask a few discreet questions.

It was hard to get a sense of Bettina from Nina, though, who seemed pretty in thrall to the doctor. Would she help Pollina or not? What kind of person was she? Sarah hoped Marie-Franz might be able to give her the skinny. The professor had seemed pretty up on everyone at the ball.

Frau Professor Marie-Franz Morgendal worked at the main building of the University of Vienna, a short walk from Bettina's lab. The pleasant inner courtyard's arcade was lined with niches containing busts of the college's illustrious dead. Since the university had been established in 1365, these were numerous. Sarah studied the profile of Schrödinger. Bettina was like Schrödinger's famous cat, Sarah thought. Here and not here.

Sarah looked around at the young people chatting, smoking, and enjoying the sunny October day. She tried to determine if Austrian students looked any different from their American counterparts, and decided they did not, except that possibly, here, berets were worn without irony.

Sarah inquired at the front desk and learned that Frau Professor Morgendal was giving a lecture. She followed the instructions to an auditorium paneled in wood and furnished with steeply banked rows of ornately carved wooden pews, which gave it a churchlike feel. The lecture had started, and Sarah slipped into a back pew. It was nice to see a few black, brown, and Asian faces among the students. Walking around Vienna's Innere Stadt, she had noticed that it wasn't only the buildings that looked incredibly white.

"We don't just hear music," Professor Morgendal was saying to about two hundred students, all pecking away on laptops and tablets. "We *feel* it." The professor was an imposing presence, with her height and elegant wingspan, her deep voice, and her well-cut suit. Sarah wondered how the Viennese establishment had taken her Hansel-to-Gretel gender switch. The students certainly didn't seem to care.

"I want you to keep this concept of feeling music in mind as we talk about an eighteenth-century doctor here in Vienna. You will recognize his name. Franz Anton Mesmer. From him we get the word 'mesmerized' and also the phrase 'animal magnetism.'"

Sarah had heard of Mesmer, and knew he was considered the father of hypnotism, but in a vaguely discreditable way. She was interested to hear where Marie-Franz was taking this lecture.

"Mesmer was born in 1734." The professor flashed portraits of Mesmer on the large screen behind her. "He studied divinity, philosophy, and law before turning to medicine. His dissertation, *De planetarum influxu*, was completed here at the university and outlined what would be Mesmer's idée fixe for his entire life: that the planets influenced the human body by means of a universal fluid, an impalpable and invisible gas that permeated everything. What do you think people called him? Crazy! Ha!"

Sarah thought of the recent discoveries of dark matter and dark energy, which were in fact impalpable and invisible and permeated everything. Not so crazy, Mesmer.

"Like many physicians of his time," Professor Morgendal went on, "Mesmer was interested in the healing properties of magnets. In the Middle Ages, Paracelsus had written about magnets, which were thought to be able to attract illness to themselves, be it a menstrual cramp or a demon in the liver. This notion made something of a comeback in the latter part of the eighteenth century, and Mesmer began to wonder if the universal fluid in the body might be conducted—controlled—by use of magnets."

More images flashed on the big screen, scenes of Vienna from Mesmer's day. Drawing rooms, horse-drawn carriages, servants in livery, and men in powdered wigs. This was the Vienna of Empress Maria Theresia. Pleasure seeking, arrogant, decadent, and frivolous.

"Mesmer experimented. He went, it must be said, magnet crazy. *Ha!* He magnetized everything: plates and cups, clothes, furniture, mirrors, musical instruments. Pets. Flowers. He would magnetize water and then instruct his patients to soak their feet in it while holding on to cables he attached to trees in his garden that he had magnetized. He wore a magnet in a pouch around his neck."

Professor Morgendal flashed a seemingly incongruous photo of a bar called Viper Room.

"By the 1770s Mesmer had married a wealthy woman and set up very nicely for himself in Vienna. His house and clinic were at Landstrasse number 261, which I cannot show you because it is no longer there, so instead I show you this bar, which is possibly on the site though we are not sure, but in any case serves a fine schnapps. Ha! Mesmer's house was called a 'miniature Versailles.' He served excellent food and wine and, above all else, excellent music. Haydn, Gluck, Piccinni, Righini. Mozart's first opera, *Bastien und Bastienne*, premiered in Mesmer's garden."

Pols had mentioned this opera, Sarah remembered. She liked that Mesmer had stuck his neck out for the young Mozart, who had not been easily accepted into musical circles in Vienna. There had been trouble over productions of his juvenile operas, jealousy, and sabotage. He had needed patrons and supporters.

"Word of Dr. Mesmer's magnetic cures spread throughout Vienna," the professor continued. "It was Mesmermania. And what is a party without a hot tub? Mesmer constructed a *baquet*: an oaken tub of magnetized water with jointed steel rods poking through the covered lid."

The next slide showed an engraving depicting well-dressed ladies standing around a big tub in groups, holding strange rods. *Right,* Sarah thought. *It is always about sex.*

"The patients would apply the rods to whatever part of their body was ailing. You can imagine the spectacle: women mostly, a few men, touching themselves with rods, moaning and shrieking, Mesmer striding around them, stroking all the bodies with his own magnetized wand." The students, clearly loving the lecture, laughed. "During all of this—and this is crucial," continued Professor Morgendal, "there was always music playing. He used a glass *armonica*, which is different from a harmonica, please note. 'Gentle music,' we are told, though I have not yet found exactly what was played."

Sarah hoped it wasn't the eighteenth-century version of bad porno music, although it was funny to think of boom-chicka-wah-wah being played on an armonica—a graceful instrument composed of glass bowls mounted horizontally on an iron rod, connected to a treadle. You pumped the treadle, the bowls spun, and you used the friction of your fingers to produce tones by touching the glass.

"There was a rumor," the professor said with a smile, "that the sound of the armonica caused one to go insane." She threw up her hands. "It is impossible to describe any of this without it sounding like the most obvious form of medical chicanery and exploitation, not to mention a night at the Berlusconi mansion, but Mesmer was a serious scientist, a man of steady and calm temperament. He approached his work methodically and deliberately, always seeking approbation and acknowledgment from the established medical community. And he had good reason to believe he had stumbled upon a significant cure for nervous ailments. And his patients, who look so mad to us, also had good reason." The professor paused for a moment, making sure her audience was rapt.

"Because Mesmer's cures actually *worked*. He never claimed that his magnetic cure would heal something like a broken leg or a bullet wound. But if the disease had its origin in the nervous system, Mesmer was your person. He cured hundreds, treating many patients gratis. Hysteria, anxiety, convulsions, rashes, headaches. We have letters, accounts from his time, of these cures. His fame grew and grew, until the nasty gossip of his detractors forced him to leave the city."

Professor Morgendal showed a slide of the human brain.

"We began with the idea that we don't just hear music, we *feel* it. That's because sound is a construct of our brains—what we think of as 'sound' is just how our brain classifies waves of energy that make our ear bones vibrate. The brain 'reads' those vibrations according to patterns established in the limbic, or emotional, system. Then the vagus nerve acts as the conduit from the brain's limbic system to the nervous system in the body."

Sarah thought about the galleon drug and its effect on the vagus nerve and on the immune system. She had been thinking about music and the brain in an entirely different way. Sound therapy was still considered a bit on the fringe end of science. She leaned forward, making a mental note to learn more about Mesmer.

"So sound stimulates the brain and nervous system. Indian drummers and African shamans use music to send their listeners into a trance that leads to a vision in which patients are healed. Energy expressed as music. Music leading to trance. Trance leading to healing. Mesmer did the same—music, baths, rhythmic stroking all contributing to a trance state, or hypnosis, that led to healing. But Mesmer believed that he himself was the cure. He was correct and incorrect. What he had stumbled upon was what we now call the placebo effect, the 'will to heal' within the brain, and how that will to heal might be unblocked or encouraged."

The placebo effect. There had been many interesting studies on this—including one where the placebo was prayer. A congregation had been enlisted, and the members dutifully prayed for specific patients. Some of the prayer recipients were told about this; some not. The ones who were told did heal slightly faster than the ones ignorant of the prayers headed their way. And the "will to heal"? Nico had said something about that, Sarah remembered. Yes, that was what he had called Philippine Welser's recipe in that book. A will to heal. A spark to the engine.

"We know that much illness is a question of our bodies malfunctioning on a cellular level. Cancer, the immune disorders, depression. Our software malfunctions. If the placebo effect can be harnessed to repair it—think of such a thing." The professor smiled. "Drug companies do not want us to dream this dream. But many people who are ill reject it as well. The responsibility of being your own cure is too much. Historically, people have been willing to subject themselves to the most poisonous of treatments rather than change themselves. In other words, meditation is hard, but pills are easy, and they feel reassuringly more like science. But what if Mesmer and the shamans, who are the history of science, are also its future: what if music is an energy that can provoke the brain into healing the body?"

A pretty big what-if, Sarah thought. She had grave reservations about the body's ability to heal itself of genetic defects through good vibes, meditation, and nice tunes. All that could help, sure. But Pols was a devout Catholic who prayed every day and played music in what often looked like a shamanic trance. And she was dying from a defect on chromosome 20.

She caught the professor as she left the lecture hall. "Frau Professor Morgendal?"

"Marie-Franz, please! Sarah, what a pleasure."

"Your lecture was fascinating," Sarah said. "I hope you don't mind that I listened in?"

"I am honored and delighted."

"I was so interested in what you were saying about the vagus nerve and the immune system. And some of Mesmer's work seems very prescient. You made me want to read more about him."

Marie-Franz stopped at the door of her office. "You could say that Mesmer was chased out of the city in disgrace not for failing, but for succeeding in a way no one could explain. You have read *Wittgenstein's Vienna*? It says, 'Few cities have been as unkind as Vienna, during their lifetimes, to those men whom it proclaimed cultural heroes after their deaths.' I am thinking of writing a book about Mesmer. To bring him back to his rightful place. Do you know that the Neue Burg has *lost* his armonica? The very instrument he used to make the healing music. *Lost it!*" With that she disappeared into her office, calling over her shoulder, "Come in, come in. Forgive the chaos."

Sarah followed her into the small space, which was lined with bookshelves and contained a number of esoteric instruments, many of them musical. "Chaos" to an Austrian evidently meant a few papers on the desk and three unshelved books on the floor.

"That's no longer true today, though?" Sarah pressed, seeing an opportunity to twist the conversation in the direction she desired. "About Vienna being unkind to its great thinkers? So much innovative, cutting-edge work is being done here. Like the scientist I met at the ball the other night, Bettina Müller. Do you know her?"

Marie-Franz pursed her lips and appeared to be considering her words carefully. "Slightly. Frau Doktor Müller is brilliant. And like many brilliant people, I think she is not always understood." The professor held up a small package. "I have to return this now to Narrenturm. Would you like to accompany me? It is an interesting place."

"I'd love to," Sarah said, hoping to swing the conversation back to Bettina. The normally chatty and open Marie-Franz was holding something back about the doctor, she could tell. "What's Narrenturm?"

"A place where you can get an old medical model of the human ear, among other things." Marie-Franz waved her package.

Before leaving the building she showed Sarah the university's library—the largest in Austria—and an enormous ceremonial chamber with copies of murals by Gustav Klimt.

"The original paintings horrified the faculty of the time, who found them pornographic and perverted. Klimt returned the money and demanded the paintings back—with a shotgun. Later, they were all burned by retreating SS officers," Marie-Franz said.

"We can add Klimt to our list of misunderstood Viennese geniuses."

"Maybe the two things go hand in hand," Sarah suggested. "To be a radical, you must have conventions to rebel against. My impression of Dr. Müller is that she is a genius. And everything in Vienna is so huge, it's not surprising that there'd be a rogue nanobiologist here, studying the very small."

"Yes, perhaps," Marie-Franz agreed as they left the main building. "And I believe she is a genius. Her work is extremely well respected here. Revered. They say she will win the Nobel Prize someday."

"I wanted to talk to her more," Sarah pressed on. "But she left quickly. She seemed upset or . . . frightened of something. I'm sorry to be such a gossip."

"One thing you must know right away about Vienna is that we love two things above all else," said Marie-Franz. "Music and gossip. So when the gossip is about music we are thrilled. The rumor is that Dr. Müller is having an affair with Kapellmeister Gerhard Schmitt."

Of course she is, thought Sarah. *When does this woman get any work done?*

"The Lion of Vienna?" Sarah tried to keep her tone casual. "Oh. I'm sorry . . . you are friends with his wife, I remember."

"I would never bring it up with her, of course. One doesn't. And they have children, so you see . . . Also the other rumor is that Dr. Müller started the rumor of the affair herself, and that Gerhard denies the whole thing and says she is crazy."

Ahhh, Sarah thought. And if there were incriminating photos or letters on Bettina's laptop that showed she *wasn't* crazy? Gerhard might want those back. Very badly. Or maybe the unstable harpist wife was after Bettina. Was that why she got out of town? Seemed a little extreme, though of course no one wanted a harp launched at their head.

"Narrenturm," Marie-Franz said, waving her arm as they rounded a corner. Sarah looked up at a squat, mustard-colored, perfectly round tower that looked more like it belonged on the set of a King Arthur movie than a twenty-first-century college campus.

"I want to see if you can guess what it was built to be," said Marie-Franz. "Some people can. And dogs. They won't come near."

As they approached the flaking paint of the building's entrance, Sarah felt a strange sensation—a wariness. She didn't just smell something off, she felt it in her bones. The feeling intensified as they walked through a whitewashed arch that led into a narrow, semicircular interior courtyard. Pigeons fluttered and the sound only amplified the sensation. *Dread,* Sarah thought, categorizing. But it wasn't the kind she usually experienced when forced to endure strip malls or romantic comedies. This was old-school dread.

"An insane asylum?"

"Well done!" Marie-Franz applauded. "Ha! The Tower of Fools. Dates back to 1784. Now it is a medical museum. Mesmer's own writings on the treatment of the mentally ill helped influence its construction, although he was already in exile by the time it was completed."

Marie-Franz left her package with the porter, and Sarah followed her into a narrow hallway that curved around the inside of the building. It had been a long time since the crumbling brick walls had been painted; scuff marks and handprints and scratches were everywhere. It was easy to imagine the inmates clawing these walls. Every few feet along the stone-floored hallway was a heavy wooden door with a small iron-grated hatch.

"Emperor Joseph II had the tower built according to numerological principles of healing," the professor explained. "The circumference of sixty-six fathoms represents God, and it has twenty-eight rooms on each floor for both the lunar month and the Kabbalah number for 'God heals the sick.' I'm sorry. This is not good subject? I forgot Americans do not like to talk about religion."

Sarah realized she was staring at the circular hallway with its row of doors.

"No. It's just . . . this just reminds me of something."

"You've seen photographs? Or perhaps—ha!—you were once interred here and are remembering the past life experience?"

"A dream," said Sarah, mentally shaking herself. "And I don't believe in reincarnation."

"What about the idea of genetic memory?" Marie-Franz suggested. "An unconscious connection between others?"

"Communing with memories in my DNA? All the way back to the Mitochondrial Eve? The Y-Chromosome Adam?"

"Why not?"

"Maybe. Or maybe Alessandro is right," said Sarah. "And really everything is all about sex."

"Ha!"

Each former cell housed a different, slightly dusty exhibit. Yellowed information cards seemed to have been typed on a manual 1940s Remington. Nothing was left to the imagination: a display about tuberculosis featured not just brightly colored wax models of lungs and eyes, but also *actual* tubercular organs suspended in cloudy liquid inside large glass jars.

Another room contained a brash array of large-scale models

of human sexual organs—giant vulvae and three-foot-long penises, artistically infected with syphilis and gonorrhea, painted with grisly pockmarks and oozing chancres.

"I make all of my students come here so they will never forget to use a condom," said Marie-Franz.

They passed twisted skeletons bent almost in two, drawings of flesh-eating bacteria, jars of hundred-year-old deformed fetuses. A glass vessel marked *Lack of folic acid* contained a baby whose two eyes, two arms, and two legs were in all the wrong places. Sarah made a mental note to buy condoms *and* vitamins and followed Marie-Franz out of the chamber of horrors into the fresh air.

Crazy, Sarah thought, is subjective. Psychotics and schizophrenics would have been locked up in Narrenturm, along with, possibly, epileptics or homosexuals. The building to house insane people had been designed after numerological principles. Mesmer had thought that he had special powers to cure people, and people who agreed with him had actually been cured. Music had the power to change your brain.

"Scientific curiosity is a wonderful and terrible thing, is it not?" asked Marie-Franz. "What a time we live in, when we begin not only to understand how our clockwork mechanism functions, but also to develop the ability to reengineer it. Some call this arrogance."

"I don't accept that," Sarah answered. "Are we just supposed to throw up our hands and say, 'Oh, whatever God, or Mom and Dad, or Mitochondrial Eve gave me is what I am and shouldn't be changed?" She had been thinking of Pols as she said it, but when she caught Marie-Franz's amused eye, she realized she was preaching to the reengineered choir.

"But even I will say that the lines between what we *can* do and what we *should* do are not always clear," said the professor.

"I agree, the lines are not always clear." Sarah nodded.

And they weren't, ever. Science marches on, with its discoveries about folic acid and venereal disease, but the one thing we can't ever seem to understand, that still consistently makes us *pazzo*, Sarah thought, are all the emotions attributed to the human heart.

Gerhard had called Bettina crazy.

It was time to do a little Lion hunting.

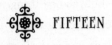

 It had taken Oksana less than twenty-four hours to get back to Max. She and Nico met him at a café in Old Town Square. Nico ordered drinks for Max and Oksana with a wave of his hand as rain beat against the windows, driving even the most stoic tourists indoors. Nico, Max noticed, was having a sedate cup of tea.

"Strange thing," Oksana said, which made Max lean forward over his *pivo*. Oksana was never surprised. It was a prerequisite for being married to the little man. "This crazy man, he *gone*."

"Gone, like there's no trace of him?"

"One trace. Fingerprints on crypt door."

You *are* impressive, thought Max. "And? Who is he?"

Nico smiled and squeezed a square of lemon into his tea. "His name is Jan Kubiš."

"Jan Kubiš died in 1942, shot by the Nazis."

Nico smiled. "And John of Nepomuk died in 1393. And yet they're baaaack."

Max frowned. Within a stone's throw of where they were sitting, Tycho Brahe was buried, a burgomaster had been defenestrated, twenty-seven rebel leaders from the Battle of White

Mountain had lost their heads . . . If the dead were coming back to life in Prague, things could get really weird, really fast. "What the hell is going on?" he said.

Nico smiled delightedly. "I have no idea. What I want to know is, who's next?"

Oksana was less happy. "Dead should stay dead. Who is doing this?"

"Moriarty," said Nico. "I can feel it."

Max thought of what Sarah had said, that someone was shooting at her that night on the river. "Whoever they are, they're possibly very dangerous."

"I can find no connection between Saint John and Jan Kubiš," said Nico. "Other than the names, of course." The little man seemed positively gleeful. "Do you think we will see a raft of historical Johns coming back? John the Baptist. Jan Hus. I am hoping for John Dee. Also for John Denver."

"Both Saint John and Jan Kubiš died in Prague," said Max.

"Yes. There is that. Time is getting very thin here in Prague."

Max hated to ask, but he had to. "And Harriet? What did you find on her?"

"Good as gold," said Oksana, before her Russian pessimism kicked in. "So far."

❧

Harriet Hunter made her way through the twisting streets of the Malá Strana toward Letenská Street. Despite the driving rain, she could see her destination. The Gothic spire of St. Thomas was a familiar landmark in Prague; its height made it easy to orient by. Harriet appreciated that. Things had gotten a bit muddled.

Women love or hate; there is nothing in between.

Elizabeth Weston had written that.

Her hands were shaking. It was a weakness, to need something this badly. People could exploit such a weakness.

She hadn't always been this way.

There had been a point, hadn't there, when she had stood at a crossroads? Only she hadn't known it then. Did one ever know that kind of thing? She had always been passionate. That was her trouble. "Susceptible" was her father's word for her. "Impressionable," was her mother's rebuke. Well, Father had been susceptible, too, to women other than Mother. And the biggest impression Mother left was the ruby red imprint of her lips on the edge of an ever-present highball glass.

Harriet could not remember a time when she had been terrifically fond of what was going on in the present.

It had never been enough for Harriet to merely study history. She had wanted to live it, to feel it. It had been a kind of crusade. It still was. Because she was passionate. This wasn't weakness, it was strength.

She hurried, a little, down the cobbled streets.

It had all started with Elizabeth Jane Weston. Harriet had "discovered" her at university and her first book (unpublished) had been a straightforward biography of the now largely forgotten poet. It had been a labor of love, in all senses of the phrase, and she had felt herself in such kinship with her subject that she, too, had taken to writing verses in Latin and spending long hours at prayer. She had even plucked her eyebrows in imitation of her favorite portrait of Elizabeth.

"Reads like historical fiction" had been the reaction of potential publishers.

"The author intrudes herself . . ."

"Far too many sentences begin with 'We can imagine' and 'It's easy to imagine.'"

And, most horribly: "Preposterously overwrought and managing to be both overwritten and undercooked, simultaneously."

But one had to use one's imagination a little! Elizabeth's poetry and letters were enough to fill a volume, but that had been done, and nobody outside of a few dusty scholars gave a damn. She had to be made to come alive, to breathe, to laugh and cry and think and act. And for that, Harriet had precious few "facts" to work with. It wasn't even enough to fill an episode of *Histories & Mysteries*. She could've wrapped up everything known about Elizabeth Weston's life in one five-minute clip. Four minutes if she did it while walking and they cut away to maps and portraits and things.

Harriet wanted more than that for Elizabeth. Elizabeth needed to be restored to her rightful place! Harriet had scarcely been aware, as she was writing the book, that she was going beyond traditional scholarly speculation into the realm of imagination.

She had to admit that her love and admiration of Elizabeth Weston had also contained a measure of impatience. Liz's stepfather was one of history's most notorious charlatans. Edward Kelley! A man who was apprenticed to an apothecary, left Oxford under a cloud, was pilloried in Lancaster for forging illegal deeds and coin, was arrested for digging up a corpse and trying to communicate with it in Lancashire, and claimed to have stumbled upon mysterious alchemical manuscripts and magic powders while wandering in Wales. A man who claimed to speak directly to angels, a man who claimed to have transmuted base metal to gold, a man who had killed another man! A man who claimed that angelic communication had demanded that he and John Dee share the favors of their wives! This was Elizabeth's stepfather!

And Elizabeth says nothing about him, only that she was "content," and that he treated her as his own.

In this, Elizabeth was like Harriet's mother and the rest of her mother's circle, tight-lipped women who behaved as if you were screaming the bloody house down if you so much as sniffled, who thought questions were "impertinent," and who never, ever, ever told you anything you wanted to know. Or like the dons at school, who were always trying to crush her enthusiasms. But Harriet felt—she *knew*—that there was much more. And a historian—a real historian—was very much like a detective. One had to be very dogged and persistent and leave no stone unturned. One of those stones was empathy and another was imagination.

And all of these people—Elizabeth Weston, Edward Kelley, John Dee, Rudolf II—were long dead, and even contemporary accounts of what they had said, what they had done, were just that: *accounts*. Stories. Impressions. Harriet had kept a diary since she was ten years old. There wasn't much in it that was actually true. She could write an account of what people had said or done in her presence today, five minutes ago. Would it be *accurate*? Would it be *factual*?

So, anyway, she had gone into television.

And then, two years before, after a perhaps ill-considered attempt to interview Moravian puppeteers in Brno, Harriet had gotten an e-mail from a woman living in the Czech Republic, in the town of Třeboň. The woman worked in some sort of publicity capacity for local tourism, and wouldn't Třeboň Château make for a "rather colorful" segment? She would be more than happy to act as a translator and/or guide, if Harriet ever wanted to visit.

Harriet had visited Třeboň before, when she was preparing her book on Elizabeth, and relished an opportunity to return.

Třeboň Château was where John Dee, Edward Kelley, and their families had retreated when they had temporarily worn out their welcome in Prague. Třeboň Château was where Kelley had received the angelic injunction regarding wife swapping. Harriet decided to do an unofficial scouting trip, and since her Czech was far from perfect, take the woman up on her offer. The woman— Harriet couldn't remember now what she had called herself—had been fantastically helpful and made a wonderful tour guide of the château. She pointed out details that even Harriet's sharp eyes missed.

She had just followed her into a small room, and was pulling out her camera to take a few photos, when the woman had taken a small atomizer out of her pocket and sprayed it directly in Harriet's face.

Harriet's first thought had been anthrax, and she had opened her mouth to scream. The woman lurched forward and covered her mouth. For a moment they struggled, and then Harriet had begun to feel *most* peculiar, and something—other than the thought that she had just been blasted with anthrax by a tiny, blond, blue-eyed terrorist—began to distract her and she stopped struggling. What was it? What was happening?

The woman said, "Look. Look around you. Tell me what you see."

Harriet looked. The walls surrounding her were the same walls but the light was different, and the colors were different; everything was shimmering and fading. Now it was dark and the room was crowded with furniture, and in the center of this stood a small child in a long white nightdress.

Harriet's fear had vanished. It wasn't exactly like a dream. It was more like what had happened to her sometimes, as a small child, when she had pretended *very* hard. She had spent her life trying to re-create that feeling, and give it to others. And now here it was, being given to her.

She focused on the little girl in the nightdress. The child was filled with powerful emotion; Harriet could feel it coming off her skin in waves. Fear? Yes, fear, but something else as well. The child's white face was beaded with perspiration. Harriet moved slowly toward the girl and reached out a hand, which passed straight through the child's shoulder, as she had thought it might. What she had not been expecting was the jolt of electricity that almost brought her to her knees. The girl remained as she was, her eyes fixed on the doorway, where, presently, a man appeared. A man with a cap slipping sideways on his head, revealing mangled ears.

"Come, girl," the man said, holding out his hand. "It is time."

The girl took the man's hand. Their bodies were ringed with some kind of phosphorescence. Harriet started to cry, without knowing why. Perhaps because the little girl wanted to cry, but would not allow herself to? Perhaps because she, Harriet, was so happy to be seeing this?

"Can we follow them?"

Harriet felt a hand on her back then, and the low voice of the woman spoke again.

"Yes. Do not run. Do not speak of what you are seeing. Do not attract attention. All shall be well."

Harriet had breathed deeply, inhaling a curious scent that seemed to her dazed brain to be a mixture of amber and olives. She felt the muscles of her face relax and her shoulders fall. The hand on her back remained, pleasant and reassuring. She had followed the man and the child into the hall.

It was very dark. The man held a candle, which threw shadows on the walls around them but did not illuminate much. Harriet could just make out the outlines of a tapestry, a low bench, a chest. The man led the child down a flight of steps, and Harriet reached a hand out to the banister, relieved to feel solid wood under her fingertips. From her earlier tour, Harriet knew they were heading in the direction of Dee and Kelley's laboratory. When they reached the laboratory door, the man unlocked it, and the little girl looked down the hallway. For a moment her eyes seemed to meet Harriet's own. *She's wondering if she can run,* Harriet thought. *She's wondering how far she will get before he catches her.*

Pity and morbid curiosity mingled in her brain, but the hand was firmly guiding her on, and when the man had at last managed to open the heavy door, Harriet slipped in behind them.

This room, too, was nearly pitch-black, though the man lit another candle, illuminating a kiln made of round tiles, patterned with symbols in red and black. The smell coming from the oven was noxious, and Harriet covered her face with her hands, her eyes and nose burning.

"Watch," the woman's voice said again. "Watch what happens."

The man took a long pair of pincers and removed something from the kiln, something that glowed darkly blue. He moved with this over to a long table.

"Bring the candle," he ordered the girl.

Harriet watched as the man plunged the blue stone into a dish of dark liquid that immediately began to turn milky white. The man held the dish to his lips and blew over it softly.

"*Omnia quia sunt, lumina sunt,*" he whispered, speaking the Latin words awkwardly.

All that is, is light.

Harriet felt the little girl beside her shiver. The hand at her back, too, was shaking.

The man handed the girl the dish. She held it in her small hands, her eyes shut tight, her face streaked with tears.

"Drink," said the man.

The next thing Harriet knew, she was sitting on a park bench. The woman was sitting next to her, with a book in her lap. They were in the château's park, in the present day. People wearing jeans and trainers passed by on bicycles. Harriet's stomach rumbled.

"What . . ." Harriet pressed a hand to her rib cage.

"I read your book," the woman said, in a low voice. "And I have followed your career with great interest. I was waiting for the right time for us to meet."

"My book?"

"*Elizabeth Weston: Venus in Exile*."

"How? Did you work in publishing?" Harriet took a deep breath.

"You got many things right," the woman continued. "I was surprised. And intrigued. Frankly, I was a little alarmed at how you might have come by that knowledge."

For a moment, all of Harriet's questions vanished in a thrill of triumph. She knew she had been right! "Preposterously over-wrought," indeed!

"But, of course, you got many things wrong," the woman continued. "You made me too emotional."

"I remember," Harriet said, her voice beginning to rise. "You sprayed something in my *face*. We were standing in a room and then you . . . and then I . . ."

"And then you saw." She put her book down and faced Harriet. "You saw my stepfather give me something to drink."

Harriet let this sink in for a moment. The questions were forming fast now, but the one that came to her lips was the simplest

and most obvious one. Harriet could never bear having a story interrupted.

"Did you drink it?"

"I did."

"And what happened?"

"For a while," the woman said, "nothing. Or so I thought. But
I was wrong."

And then the woman, whom Harriet now knew to call by her
real name, Elizabeth, began to talk in earnest. She talked for a
long time. She talked about the book they would write together.
About the things Harriet could see with this drug that she had
learned to make. A drug that would allow Harriet to see the past.
A drug Elizabeth would be happy to provide in return for Harriet's cooperation in a few small matters. They talked until the
shadows fell and then Elizabeth asked Harriet to walk with her.
And Harriet, who had not known she was at a crossroads, had
followed.

Harriet was at St. Thomas's Church now. She had gotten the
e-mail the previous night with the second chapter and the instructions on where to claim her reward. Harriet had already sent
the first chapter, which covered the events at Třeboň, off to her
agent, who was surprised but pleased Harriet was going in such a
commercial direction. It was raining harder than ever as she entered the church and made her way to the inner courtyard, stepping briskly down the covered loggia until she reached a familiar
slab of stone set in the wall.

The tomb of Elizabeth Weston. She reached up high and
found the niche in the bricks. Her hands stopped shaking as they
found the tiny box that had been left there for her. One pill inside.
Just one. Where should she take it? Charles Bridge? Wenceslas

Square? Why not here? She swallowed the pill, sighed. It would begin soon.

She reached out a hand and traced the Latin with her fingertips.

The tomb of Elizabeth Weston.

The empty tomb.

The Tenth Muse

· THE TRUE STORY OF ·

Elizabeth Jane Weston, Poet

---

by

Harriet Hunter, PhD

CHAPTER TWO

In which I am wronged, again.

By the time I was fourteen my stepfather, Edward Kelley, had forced a number of potions down my throat. So I wasn't terrifically distraught when he was arrested and thrown into prison. Not for anything he did to me, of course. I was a girl and his stepdaughter and the phrase "child abuse" would have caused a good laugh in the 16th century. No, my stepfather had enraged the emperor—possibly the one man in Prague even dippier than Kelley. All of our family's property was seized. We were left destitute. My saintly mother took to her bed, which was understandable, but not very useful. My brother was at school. I was painfully aware of just how bad our situation was due to my excellent education—I was fluent in English, Czech, Italian, German, and Latin, and well versed in mathematics, botany, philosophy, poetry, astrology, and astronomy. Shocking for a girl of this era to know so much, say you? Well, how many people—let alone adolescents—do you know in *your* era who can speak five languages?

Don't get me wrong, I love the current era. I consider the microwave oven to be the apotheosis of human civilization, right after Scotch tape and RevitaLash. But I digress.

So, there we were, friendless and penniless. I began to write. I sought assistance from all quarters of the world, sending out letters and poems and odes and prayers. I described in the most delicate terms the condition of my family and our plight. Since you, dear twenty-first-century reader, are unlikely to have much of a grounding in the linguistic arts (r u mad @ me? ☺), I will put it in terms your electronically numbed brain can grasp: I was the original blues singer, and, man, could I let rip.

> *My daddy's in jail.*
> *My momma's a mess.*
> *The larder is empty.*
> *And I ain't got not one single dress.*
> *I got the sixteenth-century blues, let me tell you,*
> > *the one-six-oh-oh blues.*
> *Things are so bad that gettin' a case of the clap*
> > *would be damn fine news . . .*
> *I got the sixteenth-century bluuuuues.*

Imagine that in Latin. It killed! Every fortnight I received a letter of praise about my mellifluous verses from one exalted person or other, but none of them actually lifted a snot-caked finger to help me except dear Georg von Baldhoven, and his concern was getting my work published so he could make a fast pound of flesh off it (literally, as he ran a brothel to support his printing press, things being then about as they are now in the book trade). My stepfather was never released from prison. My brother died. My mother died. It was just me, hovering around the edges of the court at Prague, relying on the kindness of strangers. Not a good place for an apple-cheeked young lassie to be.

And I was a wee lassie indeed. My mother had blamed our diet of thin porridge, thinner porridge, and porridge-flavored water for my stunted growth. I was in my twenties, yet appeared to be still on the cusp of my teens. And unfortunately, there were men even before Nabokov coined the term "nymphet" who had a real yen for that sort of thing. And were willing to pay top florin for it.

Women back then were considered property, you see, like chairs and donkeys and cloth of Flanders (my list is in ascending order of value), and if you no longer had a father to own you, and you weren't married, well, anyone could claim you at the nearest lost and found. And do with you as he pleased. Which usually involved you getting a good sniff of his boils. Pun intended.

Fortunately, I had become one of the most celebrated women of my age. My verses brought delight across Europe. I received letters from kings, naming me the English Virgo, the Tenth Muse. Like Cher or Madonna, I ascended to the heights of single-namedom—I was "Westonia." But writing turned out to be no road to riches. No movie deal was "inked." I was a woman alone with no cash. Being a rock star wasn't going to protect me from the wolves forever. Literally the wolves—there was a pack living in what is now Prague 4. So, like many women of a certain age, I got out of the entertainment industry.

I married one Johannes Leo. I did not plight my troth for love. Johannes had a position at the imperial court and had promised to help with my petition to the emperor to get my stepfather's property back. It wasn't as selfless on his part as it sounds, since Johannes now under the law owned me, and anything I earned or was restituted would all go to him. So we were pretty well matched.

I promised God to be a good wife to Johannes, a promise that I kept despite God's disinclination to show Johannes the path to fresh breath or flatulence control. (To my list of mod cons I heart, let's add toothbrushes and Beano.) And I desperately wanted children. I gave birth to six, one after another. All three of my sons died. My youngest daughter was born simple, and another had fits of such violence that she had to be tied to her bed and a nurse set to watch her at all times, lest she swallow her tongue. Portia, my beloved firstborn, so brilliant and clever and beautiful, had poor lungs and suffered fits of coughing and weakness that broke my heart. I did not think Portia would survive.

There is no greater grief than this. To bring children into the world and then see them die, or endure a living death of illness. I came to believe that it was my womb that was corrupting them. That my blood was fouled. As I've mentioned, my stepfather tested his potions and spagyric tinctures upon me when I was a child. And as a young woman I became his assistant. I helped him to the best of my ability, which soon became greater than his. I saw many things. Many things neither of us understood at the time.

But now my children were suffering for having had to live inside my damaged body. I created a small laboratory in my home and began testing things secretly, trying to find a solution, but to no avail. I was bequeathing my children nothing but death or pain.

I prayed very hard.

And at last I was shown a way. In the midst of my prayers

one evening I heard a voice. I knew it instantly to be the voice of God.

I admit that it surprised me to find that God was a woman, and that Her voice sounded so much like my own! She had quite the vocabulary. God sang to me, soothed me, and promised me help. I thanked Her and vowed to do Her work. *I will be with you always*, God promised. *You are precious to me. You are my true daughter, as He was once my true Son. You will have many trials. Hang in there.* [I translate for you from the ancient Greek.] *But I will save you and you will do my work. There is a way.*

Where? I asked the voice. *How?*

When your stepfather was in prison, the voice answered, *what was the one thing he asked for more than anything else? More than food, more than blankets, more than his own freedom?*

He asked for the Book, I said. *The Curious historie and awfull magick of the ancient and wonderfull golden fleece.*

Yes. That is the Way.

I thought hard about the message I had received. Emperor Rudolf had confiscated all of my stepfather's property, including his books (the arresting guards seemed keen on the illustrated ones, hoping for anatomical representations of impossible acts involving twins, I suspect). How do you take something back from an emperor? None of my letters or poems or Johannes's entreaties had ever convinced him to part with even a chamber pot. But perhaps I had erred in seeking the help of men. God was woman. Would not a woman help me?

That was not a rhetorical question. I really had no idea. I did not have many women friends. But I had always admired Polyxena Pernstein, a noblewoman, a good Catholic, and a lady of exceptional learning (not as exceptional as my own, but she knew her diphthongs from her troches). Polyxena and her husband, Zdeněk, a dullard with a penchant for *Blutwurst*, were intimate with the emperor.

Later that evening, when Johannes was lying on top of me, shoving himself inside me, I did not have to resort to my usual mental trick of repainting the frescoes on the ceiling. My mind was racing. A poem in praise of Polyxena was not difficult to pen. I could tweet Latin in my sleep. The result of my efforts—slightly more than 140 characters—was an invitation to dine at Lobkowicz Palace.

All I wanted was for Pretty Polly to use her influence to ask the emperor to let me borrow one damn book. *Prithee, God has told me that I need to recover a book my stepfather practiced from so that I might find a way to reverse whatever curse I am suffering under and my next child can be born healthy.* How hard is that?

And yet Polyxena didn't get it, that pampered bitch. She sipped wine and fed her lapdog a better dinner than her servants got and told me that the death and illness of my children was, after all, God's will. Which was ridiculous because I had spoken to God at length and knew for a fact it wasn't Her will.

I cursed the Lobkowicz family and all their descendants.

I cast the net a little wider, writing next to a man my stepfather had known, the powerful and influential Tycho Brahe. I told him that I knew there was a book in the emperor's keeping that had belonged to my stepfather, an important book, "leant" to my stepfather by Archduke Ferdinand (copied in secret without his knowledge). I said I knew the book well (a lie) and could help him interpret its meanings and formulas if we studied it together (a truth). I followed this with an epigram of praise for his genius, which took me less time than the rest of the letter, since it was a repurposing of some lines I had intended to send to Johannes Kepler. (To my mind, a far superior astronomer, but Kepler was no friend to alchemy.)

While I waited for an answer from Tycho, my need became ever more urgent. I discovered I was pregnant again. And try as I might to find the right combination of herbs and tonics to soothe the violence that was tearing my darling Portia's body in two, Portia could not stop coughing. She grew weaker and weaker. I will not attempt to describe the terror and sorrow of that time. Not in any language. Let us leave that alone.

Finally I received a letter from Tycho. Would I perhaps pay him a call at Baron Kurz's summer palace, where he was currently in residence? There was something he wanted to discuss with me.

Brahe greeted me cordially, though his foul abortion of a dwarf had the effrontery to address me as well. I hid my face in my wimple and ordered him from the room, holding my hands protectively over my swollen belly. He skittered away.

Tycho Brahe claimed that he did not have the book and had never seen it. But he began to question me about certain alchemical phrases. As if he were testing my knowledge, though I could immediately tell that my knowledge was greater. We thumbed through various alchemical texts.

"That is the image for *Solve et coagula*. Dissolve the fixed and fix the volatile."

"This tells you that any plant matter will do, but the bark of an oak tree is best."

"When you notice the particles falling like a gentle snow inside the retort, you must remove the oil."

"Elk bone, ground very fine."

He pressed me further. Did I know what was meant by . . . ? How would I translate . . . ? And so on.

It seemed from the specificity of his questions that he had seen the book, perhaps only briefly and on the sly, since the emperor was so protective of it. He made casual mention of a drug he had heard tell of that allowed one to see many things that had happened in the past. Did I know of such a drug? Since I needed to let Brahe see he could trust me, I suggested an exchange. I told him I did know of such a drug—I had helped my stepfather make it often. If I told him the formula, then would he help me find the antidote to what was poisoning my womb? He quickly agreed, and I sketched out the formula for him as I remembered it.

"I will call it 'Westonia' in your honor," he said. He was excited, humming.

"Now you will help *me*," I said sharply, less interested in branding and more in saving my children's lives.

I suggested that he test things on his dwarf. If Brahe gave the dwarf the substance my stepfather had poisoned me with, and the preliminary versions of the antidote didn't work, the only harm that would befall the dwarf was that he would not be able to father healthy children. And what loss was that to the world? He could just keep testing the antidotes on the dwarf until he found the one that worked.

Brahe laughed. "Oh, yes, Jepp is very useful."

$\mathscr{I}$ returned to my home and my children and my flatulent husband. I wrote to Brahe repeatedly, but he did not answer me. I suspected that he had never planned on helping me at all, but I had no recourse, and soon, no strength to deal with him. Portia was gravely ill. And my pregnancy was advancing. Another baby.

We are dying, I thought. We are all dying.

Finally the answer from Brahe came. *I cannot help you.*

That is all he said. *I cannot help you.*

I cursed Tycho and that malicious dwarf. And my stepfather. And the emperor. And my husband. And the fleas on his head.

The baby was born dead. I held this last baby, this last child borne of my curse, and I decided that I could go on no longer. In that moment I took the powder I kept under my pillow. A simple powder. Obtainable in any apothecary's shop. And I asked God's forgiveness. When God did not answer, I took the powder anyway. I thought about taking Portia with me, to spare her the last ravages of her illness, but some part of me hoped that perhaps God would spare her in the end, if I offered myself in her place.

*T*hey said I died in childbirth.

I remember thinking: *This is what it means to be dead. This kind of sleep. Perhaps this is Purgatorio, where I must atone for the sin of taking my own life until I may be admitted to Heaven.*

They buried me with my child at my breast. I could hear Portia weeping outside the casket. Her thin sobs. *Portia, Portia. I will wait for you, my darling. We will be together.*

They buried my body in the cemetery of the Church of St. Thomas.

And I lay in that coffin for some time before I realized something very important.

I was not dead.

And that made me very, very angry.

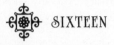 SIXTEEN

G*eschichtsbewältigung*, shouted the sign in large black letters on a white background. It was the only object in the otherwise empty room. The word meant "coming to terms with the past."

Sarah had just missed him again.

Finding Gerhard Schmitt had turned out to be about as easy as stalking a real lion in the wild. After leaving Marie-Franz and the university, Sarah went first to the Konzerthaus on Lothringerstrasse, the home of the Vienna Chamber Orchestra. It turned out to be—no surprise—a massive white building trimmed in gold. She was knocking on the stage door when a helpful bassoonist came along and told her that Herr Kapellmeister Schmitt was speaking right now to a group of schoolchildren at the Haus der Musik, Vienna's museum of sound and music, which wasn't far. If she hurried, she would catch him.

Sarah dashed up Schwarzenbergstrasse, raced into the Haus der Musik, jumped from foot to foot as a group of British tourists counted out their euros, finally bought a ticket, and sprinted up the stairs, bisecting groups of schoolchildren as she wound her way through the labyrinth of the museum to the room where a guide had said the Kapellmeister was speaking. *I'm on a roll,* Sarah thought, *getting information out of people. This will be easy.*

She was not on a roll. Gerhard had gone.

Thinking through her next move, Sarah wandered back through the Haus der Musik's highly interactive and well-curated exhibits. She would have loved this place as a kid, Sarah thought as she passed children wearing headphones, listening to different frequencies. She lingered just a minute at a display of Beethoven's household expenses in one of his sixty-eight different apartments in Vienna ("marrow, 8 kreuzers"). When no one was looking, she pressed her hand against the pale green door from Beethoven's last residence. *Luigi, come out and play with me.*

Yep, I'm just as crazy as everyone else.

The final exhibit of the museum consisted of a virtual Zubin Mehta inviting participants to take a turn at "conducting" the Vienna Philharmonic on a video monitor. Sarah watched a boy of about ten attempt to set a tempo for the "Radetzky March." His parents laughed and applauded as the boy struggled to wave his arms in a regular beat and the recorded performance alternately lurched or dragged.

It was silly, but Sarah felt a stab of pain in her chest. She had studied conducting as an undergraduate, a requirement for all conservatory students. She remembered raising a baton for the first time in front of a roomful of players. She had felt no fear, which wasn't saying much, for Sarah. But the experience had been better than sex, which was saying a lot, for Sarah. One of the best moments in her life, really.

There weren't many world-class women conductors. There were plenty of world-class women scientists and historians, though. Had she somehow taken an easier path, without realizing it? She, who had always been so fearless? Pols had told her she should be a conductor. Why wasn't she on the path to becoming the Lioness of Boston?

Jesus, what *was* it with Vienna? she thought, heading down the stairs and out onto the street. It made you all introspective and melancholy. No wonder half the intellectuals and artists who had lived here ended up committing suicide. Maybe it was just hard to stand up to all the architecture, all the greatness of the past. *Geschichtsbewältigung* indeed.

Sarah called the Konzerthaus to see if Schmitt had returned, but was told he had not. "I am a reporter for the *Boston Globe*," Sarah said. "I was hoping for a few minutes of the Kapellmeister's time this afternoon." Gerhard, she then learned, was attending an auction at the Kinsky Palace. She set off to cross the Innere Stadt of Vienna.

Her plan could use a little finessing, anyway. What would she do if, when confronted, the Lion just said, "She is crazy/I don't know what you're talking about/Yes, I took her laptop and you can't have it." Threaten to cut off his hair? Threaten him with her plastic sword?

She would tell him about Pollina. The man was, after all, a musician. Whatever was going on between him and Bettina was none of her business.

Sarah turned right on Krugerstrasse, which became a lovely pedestrian-only street, and crossed swanky Kärntnerstrasse, passing Café Mozart and traversing the triangular *Platz* toward red and white banners denoting the majestic white stone (shocker!) façade of the Lobkowicz palace, completed in 1687. Beethoven had walked on this street. For a moment she thought she could see the back of his head just in front of her. *Hey, Luigi, turn around!* Wishful thinking. To see the past you needed really good drugs.

Vienna was a difficult city to hurry through. It was so

distracting. Sarah crossed Michaelerplatz and looked up at Looshaus. The Modernist work of architect Adolf Loos had so shocked Emperor Franz Joseph in 1911 that he ordered all the curtains on the windows of his palace that faced the "horror" to be permanently closed. The big scandal had been merely the house's simplicity, and its windows' lack of ornamental detail. It was now considered a masterpiece.

It was easy to imagine how startling the building would have been, though, especially to people used to something like the Palais Kinsky. Sarah drew up in front of the white (you don't say!) and yellow building, which fronted on a lovely little *Platz*. A dynamic pair of scantily clad sculpted gents held up a Baroque doorway to the palace. She moved into a white rotunda crammed with more statues and massive cast-iron lanterns, before she was politely blocked by a uniformed concierge. The auction, she was told, was a private one. Sarah flashed her Boston Public Library card.

"I am a journalist," she said. "I am here to meet Kapellmeister Gerhard Schmitt."

But the impassive concierge didn't laugh and kick her to the palatial curb. Kapellmeister Schmitt, she was told, had already left the building.

Sarah made another call. The Kapellmeister would not be able to speak with her. He was in rehearsals for the rest of the day at Theater an der Wien. Sarah looked at her map. The theater was about four blocks away from where she had just come from.

Sarah decided that she could schlep no more *Platz*es and jumped on a tram.

Theater an der Wien was quite cheerful looking: yellow and green. The Papageno Gate at the entrance featured the feathered sidekick from *The Magic Flute* playing his pipes, and the front door was open, which was refreshing. Apparently the management didn't mind tourists taking a peek at the famously ornate interior. She wouldn't have to try to brazen her way in as some sort of Lois Lane.

The inside of the theater was overwhelming. Sarah stood completely alone in a jewel box of red and gold. She turned around and around, gazing up at the massive height of the stage, the frescoes adorning the round ceiling, the tiers of boxes. So many performances, so much history.

Entranced, she walked up the stairs onto the stage and stood where Beethoven had stood, conducting the premiere of his only opera, *Fidelio*. The composer had lived onsite for several months beforehand, finishing the work. It had been a difficult time in a life filled with difficult times. Beethoven had struggled with the work. The occupation of Vienna by the French had depressed him and hurt his finances. And his hearing was going.

So he had done what he had always done in difficult times. Written music that didn't quite sound like anything else and challenged his listeners to follow him or not.

She closed her eyes and breathed. Then she raised her hands, feeling the heroic measures of the *Fidelio* Overture in the tips of her fingers. The opera told the story of a woman, Leonore, who must rescue her husband, Florestan, from the prison where he has been unjustly incarcerated.

It was electric. *Luigi, I can feel you.*

And she could see the orchestra, all eyes on her. The music had to come out of silence, had to emerge from emptiness inexorably, inevitably. She coaxed the violins gently as they began their faint melody, then signaled the percussion. E minor. Every member of the orchestra needed to be engaged in this battle. No one gets left behind!

The sound of a door shutting somewhere broke her concentration. What on earth was she doing?

"Hallo?" she called. "Anyone here?" She crossed into the wings and found herself backstage. She tilted her head back, peering through the darkness up into the soaring flies, making out lights and ropes and metal catwalks.

"Hallo?" she called again. Really, she thought, anyone can just walk in here? Surely the management didn't want people tromping around on the stage or poking through the sets and scrims. At any rate, the Kapellmeister was probably in the rehearsal rooms of the building somewhere, and not here on the actual stage. Sarah stepped back into the theater and was halfway up the aisle when she heard a collection of voices. Her sharp ears caught Gerhard's name being used. She hesitated.

"Okay, Fritz? Bring down the platform, please," someone shouted backstage. "Kapellmeister will want to see it. *When* he shows up."

A hydraulic motor sounded and two men in work clothes came onto the stage.

"Hey!" one of them shouted, spotting her in the aisle. "What are you doing here? This is a private rehearsal!"

"I'm so sorry," Sarah apologized. "The door was open. I am meeting Kapellmeister Schmitt." A large platform, draped with billowing fabric, was slowly descending toward the stage.

"I'm glad to know he's still coming," the man said dryly, before turning away and shouting more orders. "Karl! Get the door! Put out that damned sign!"

"Do you know"—he turned back to Sarah—"where the Kapellmeister is?"

Sarah did know, but for the moment all she could do was point to the platform now hovering just above the stage.

The Lion of Vienna lay sprawled across the platform's edge. The angle of his head told her that he was very, very dead. And next to him, clasped in his arms . . . a woman. Surely there was another girl in Vienna, Sarah thought desperately, who had hair that particular shade of pink?

Someone other than Nina Fischer?

 SEVENTEEN

"There you are!"

Max looked up from his desk and smiled. Harriet was glowing and looked happy, which was nice because lately she had seemed kind of off . . . tense and nervous. So it was good to see her looking like her usual self, which was sort of a funny thought since Harriet was dressed as Polyxena Pernstein, 1st Princess Lobkowicz: long dress in some stiff white fabric with red sleeves and gold florets and a high white ruff. She had been filming in the palace this morning, before the museum opened. A program on the Lobkowicz family for the BBC, which Max hoped would spark some more tourist interest.

"That suits you," Max said, nodding at the costume and sliding the little book on Philippine Welser he was reading into his pocket.

"Thank you, darling! My figure fits into period dresses quite well. Most women these days are too tall. I hardly ever have to have things specially made. And I actually don't mind wearing a corset. I rather like it, actually."

Max rather liked it, too, though he wasn't crazy about the ruff, which looked like one of those cones you put on dogs to keep them from licking wounds.

He had been glad that Oksana's digging around in Harriet's closet had not produced any skeletons.

"Everything go well?" he asked.

"Very. Come and look at the footage? I think you'll be pleased."

"Can I look tonight? I've got to go to Kutná Hora today."

"Kutná Hora?"

"You know it?"

"Of course." Harriet leaned against his desk. "I considered doing an episode of *Histories & Mysteries* at Sedlec Ossuary, several years ago. But they wanted heaven and earth for filming rights. The Beeb isn't Hollywood, and I'm afraid Hollywood has spoiled the Czech Republic. Thankfully, you are not so greedy. What takes you to Kutná Hora?"

"Oh . . . potential board member lives there. So . . . just boring museum stuff. Sorry."

Harriet smiled. "Not to worry. I have plenty of work to do."

"How's your book on Elizabeth Weston coming?"

"Writes itself," trilled Harriet. She came over to give Max a kiss. Then a deeper one. Then she pulled him up and began stroking the front of his pants. Harriet really did get turned on by history. She liked reenacting scenes. They'd done Cleopatra and Mark Antony, and Napoléon and Josephine, but they hadn't done any from this particular era and Max wasn't sure how he was supposed to deal with the ruff.

"I guess women in the sixteenth century couldn't have a lot of spontaneous sex," he mumbled as he tried to undo the heavy buttons of her bodice. "Too much clothing to take off."

"Women," Harriet said, turning around, hoisting her heavy

skirts up, and presenting her creamy naked pale ass in all its glory, "have always known how to manage these things."

An hour later, Max was zooming past orderly rows of pine trees and plowed-under fields in his red Alfa Romeo convertible. The Czech Republic boasted the highest highway mortality rate in Europe. People here hadn't been driving that long and the cars were mostly old. But you had to drive fast, because everyone else did. Unfortunately, it was too cold to have the top down, though the sun was unexpectedly bright today. Max reached forward to the glove compartment to get his sunglasses.

"Looking for these?" asked Nico from the passenger seat. The little man—who was wearing Max's Dolce and Gabbana shades—handed Max a pair of oversize pink ladies' sunglasses.

"Cool, thanks." Max put them on, pretending to look undisturbed. It was a game they played, and like all the games one played with Nico it had no real beginning or end, just an endless circle of parries and thrusts, moves and countermoves.

Max could not remember his mother's funeral, but he knew that was when Nicolas had first shown up in his life, telling Max's father that he had been a friend of the departed woman, and thereafter making occasional appearances. For many years their relationship (as well as Nico's lack of visible aging) had largely gone, by Max at least, unexamined. Nico was a fact, not necessarily good or bad, though some kind of loyalty bond did exist between them. When Max's father had died, Nico had been the first person Max had called. Nico had come. And when, later, Max had taken Westonia and had seen the little man, four hundred years earlier, on a street in Prague, it had not seemed so very surprising. Suddenly everything about Nico and his presence in his life, and his lack of visible aging, had made complete sense.

Harriet, Max knew, did not like Nico very much. It was a problem. Sometimes Max wanted to strangle the little man, but he couldn't stand anyone saying a word against him. The only time Max had ever punched someone was when his roommate at Yale had referred to Nicolas as "your crazy midget buddy." Admittedly, during his visits, Nico had overly enjoyed college life and eventually been banned from New Haven after an incident involving a stolen ibis. Anyway, Max hadn't told Harriet the truth about the real reason for coming to Kutná Hora, or about going with Nico, and this was a problem, too. If Harriet was going to be a part of his life, he would eventually have to tell her about . . . everything.

Of course, the main problem with Harriet was that she wasn't Sarah. Not cool to make comparisons, but he couldn't help it. You couldn't help who you loved.

"Kutná Hora was a ringleader in the Bohemian Uprising against Philippine's father-in-law," said Max. "I want to check if there's anything about her or Ferdinand that's been overlooked in the archives there at the Gothic Stone House. And the Alchemy Museum has what exactly?"

"A drinking horn made with the talons of a griffin. The story is that the beast gave his talons to Saint Cornelius and that the drinking horn will neutralize any poison."

"And it . . . does?"

"No." Nicolas fiddled with the radio station. "I just want to impress all my buddies at the next Dungeons and Dragons convention."

"Okay."

"It belonged to Edward Kelley," Nico said, relenting. "I don't need it myself; I just wanted to see if it's still there. I'm testing a theory."

"You really think Kelley is your Moriarty? You've always said what an ass he was. You said Tycho Brahe thought he was an idiot."

"Do you know what Tycho recommended for the cure of epilepsy?" Nico switched off the radio. "The head of a person who has been hanged. Decapitated by other means is okay, but only if it was execution and not accident. Crush the head with peony seeds until you get a nice powder. Don't take it at the full moon."

"So, they were all idiots in some ways. Kelley, John Dee, Brahe, all the alchemists."

"They were relentless. They always had to know more. It made them cruel. Ah, we're almost there. Kutná Hora. It hasn't changed much."

"When was the last time you were here?"

"Not in this century," Nico said, briefly; and then, after a pause, "Nor the last."

Nico stared at the road unspooling in front of them. The thought that he might have a real opponent out there had invigorated him, but, he realized, it had also brought back memories he had long pushed aside. Things he had never talked to Max or anyone else about. Tycho Brahe had changed his life—Tycho was Nico's Dr. Frankenstein—but it wasn't Tycho that he was thinking of now.

After Brahe died, Nico's life in Prague had become very difficult. He had tried to make his way back to Denmark, to Sophie, the Master's sister. Sophie Brahe had been Nico's first and greatest love. The most gifted alchemist he had ever known, and the first person who had ever treated him with kindness. But he had been robbed on the journey, and beaten, and thrown into prison. The notebooks in his traveling bag had been enough for a conviction of heresy. It was worth wondering what would have happened if he had not escaped before his execution date. Would the fires have raged about his person and then blown out? Would he have had to spend the last four hundred years with third-degree burn marks covering his body? When he had at last arrived in Elsinore, Sophie was nearly insane. He had cared for her, he and Livia, Sophie's maid. And when Sophie died in 1643 he had tried to slit his wrists. No matter how deep he made the cuts, the blood had refused to gush, though they had remained open wounds for about a hundred years. Livia was a fair alchemist herself, and she had done her part to help him, even experimenting on herself with various combinations of drugs. They hadn't really come close. Livia had only managed to extend her life to age 143.

Nico was still here.

He had almost given up on dying, and it had nearly driven him mad. And now there was a glimmer of hope. If the Fleece had been found, or if there was a serious alchemist in the game, then the end might actually, finally, be nigh. It gave him such purpose, to think he might die soon. He would like to make a lovely death. Oksana would miss him, but Oksana was tough. He would like to help Pollina if he could, before he went. He would like to help Sarah, if she would let him. And he would like to know that Max was okay. You couldn't help who you loved.

"'Removed for curatorial purposes,'" said Max, reading the card. They had found nothing about Philippine or Ferdinand in the archives at the Stone House, either. "Okay, let's talk to the curator. This isn't the British Museum; it's three rooms. There will be records, something."

"There will be no records." Nicolas smiled. "There aren't many records of where I've been, either, my dear, or what I've done. One learns how to cover one's tracks. I've spent a couple centuries walking backward in my own footprints, dragging sleds behind me, erasing, deleting, obscuring. Don't worry about it. I have an idea."

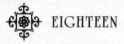 EIGHTEEN

If there was one thing that Vienna loved more than pastries and balls, it was funerals. The Lion of Vienna was being given what was known locally as a *schöne Leiche*, or "beautiful corpse." City fathers, members of the music world, religious leaders, nobles from the houses of Esterházy and Von Thurn und Taxis in full regalia, and thousands of distraught fans lined the streets as the black carriage (its glass sides revealing a stylish black Secession-style casket) pulled by four black horses with black plumes and driven by a coachman in a black top hat made its mournful way from St. Stephen's Cathedral across the center of the city and out Simmeringer Hauptstrasse to the city's massive Central Cemetery. And the flowers!

"Gerhard gets the Rose Parade and Nina gets a discount urn with a smiley face on it?" asked Sarah as they abandoned the famous #71 tram ("Took the 71," Sarah had learned, was a Viennese euphemism along the lines of "kicked the bucket"). She and Alessandro made their way on foot the remaining half mile to the cemetery, all traffic hopelessly snarled.

Nina's father had refused to leave the farm and come to Vienna to claim his errant daughter's remains, and since Nina had expressed a wish to one of her friends that she be cremated, Alessandro and a few of her friends at the university had passed the hat to pay for the arrangements. Sarah had tracked down a number for Heinrich von Hohenlohe and left him several messages, asking if he would like to contribute to the funeral for Nina, or at least attend it. He had finally returned her calls, saying he was sorry that Nina was dead but had no intention of mourning the loss of someone who was, as he put it, "two-timing" him.

"I can't say I really blame him," Alessandro had said. Having met Nina on the first day of classes, Alessandro found himself in the odd position of being her oldest acquaintance in Vienna, and as an "adult" the task of choosing the urn had somehow fallen to him, a responsibility he had quickly off-loaded to Sarah. She had been a little taken aback by the selection of urns offered at the funeral home. She had been shown one shaped like a Sacher torte, one that was a replica of a soccer ball, and a clear jar where the remains could be admired like potpourri. Sarah had chosen a basic black cube, but apparently there was some mix-up, because when she got home and removed the urn containing the ashes from the cardboard box, it was the smiley face. It was highly possible, she thought, that it wasn't Nina at all inside the box, but someone's beloved dachshund.

At least, she thought, the urn wasn't emblazoned with the image of Empress Sissi. Bad enough that poor Nina's greatest fame was being linked to the insipid empress by a strange historical parallel.

For *Mayerling Redux!* screamed the headlines of one of Vienna's sensationalist papers. In 1889 the beloved son of Empress Sissi and Emperor Franz Joseph had died in an apparent murder-suicide at the family's hunting lodge in Mayerling. Crown Prince Rudolf was thirty, a married man with a child, and his lover a pretty baroness of only seventeen. Beyond the scandal, the incident was considered to be one of the factors precipitating World War I. At the time the Hapsburgs were able to cover up many details and even convince the church to allow their son to be buried in the Imperial Crypt.

In contrast, the double death/suicide of Nina Fischer and Gerhard Schmitt at Theater an der Wien was being treated with absolutely no discretion by anyone, it seemed, and had been picked up by some foreign papers. Nina's life story, from goat girl to tattooed and pierced grad student in nanobiology, was combed over and her powers of seduction assessed. Apparently one of her roommates was part of a local coven of witches and had brought Nina to at least one "moot," or gathering, which made great press, including a British photo-essay headlined *The Lion, the Witch and Their Wardrobes*. Gerhard's romantic liaisons and musical career were chronicled, his colleagues interviewed.

Two people remained silent. Frau Schmitt remained barricaded in the couple's Innere Stadt apartment, refusing all interviews. And Frau Doktor Bettina Müller, given merely passing reference in the press as Nina's mentor at the university, was described as "out of town" and "unreachable for comment."

Sarah herself had narrowly managed to avoid fame as the first to discover the bodies. After interviewing her and the stagehands and releasing them, the *Polizei* had apparently locked down all official details of the case, and fortunately no photos or grisly details had been leaked to any tabloids.

But Sarah could not get the gruesome picture out of her head: the two bodies entwined on the platform, the gun still in Gerhard's hand. There had been a lot of blood and . . . bits of brain, too.

She had seen Nina that very morning . . . so alive. Sarah remembered the way Nina had said, "I seem to attract protectors," and laughed. Sarah parsed their conversation in the lab over and over in her head, but could not fathom how, only hours later, Nina could be lying dead in front of her.

Nina and Gerhard. It was hard to wrap her head around. Some of Nina's friends offered theories: Nina was always on the hunt for a father figure (see Heinrich), was attracted to difficult geniuses (see Bettina), and was known to be sexually adventurous ("Not so much, really," said Alessandro).

But why had Gerhard killed her and then killed himself? Surprisingly, this seemed to be the least mysterious part of the case for everyone else. Perhaps because Vienna had long held the odd title of Europe's suicide capital, and there was no shame in taking this method out of complicated problems, love triangles, or even just apathy. Indeed, she was told that the police never released information on the means and method of the deaths by suicide . . . too many people would copycat.

At the police station, answering questions about why she'd happened to be backstage in Theater an der Wien, Sarah had debated mentioning that Bettina Müller was the obvious connection between Gerhard and Nina. If the police forced Bettina to return to Vienna for questioning, Sarah might be able to corner her. But if Bettina was tied up in a police investigation, would she be willing or able to help Pols? In the end she did give them Bettina's name—she felt she owed that to Nina. But the policewoman interviewing Sarah had merely nodded and said Frau Doktor Müller was being "very cooperative."

That was particularly galling, since she was being anything but with Sarah.

Frankly, Sarah was ready to go home. Renato had called to say his tiger stripes had faded, and his seborrheic dermatitis had returned. He had made discreet inquiries of a curator in the British

Museum, but the galleon had been thoroughly cleaned before being put back on display. Alessandro had not been able to determine the drug's ingredients from its effects on Renato and Sarah, which was disappointing, and seemed to mark the end of that lead. The only good news was that Renato and Thomas were happily dating.

Bettina wasn't answering any texts. Sarah had not found her laptop, and half the people she could ask about it were dead. The computer could be anywhere. She felt like the woman was yanking her chain. If Sarah had to start over in the search for someone who could help Pols, then the sooner she began the better. As soon as Nina was taken care of, she would leave.

Sarah had gone with Alessandro to a kind of memorial for Nina with her offbeat assortment of friends at her Leopoldstadt apartment. Girls and boys alike wore raccoon eyeliner that ran in rivulets down their faces. Alessandro had made black squid ink pasta. Today all Nina's friends were meeting up to scatter her ashes. Lili, the Wiccan roommate, said they wanted to do it in the Central Cemetery on the day of Gerhard's funeral, as a sort of romantic gesture to unite the lovers. Without any official permission, of course. Fortunately, the place was so enormous—nearly six hundred acres—it would be easy to find a quiet corner. Alessandro wanted to attend the ceremony, and afterward they were joining Marie-Franz for a farewell drink. Then Sarah was getting on a train back to Prague.

So here she and Alessandro were, at the funeral of Gerhard Schmitt, following friends, family, and hordes of black-clad chamber orchestra subscribers who, to what Sarah imagined would be the maintenance man's horror, had brought an enormous pride of stuffed lions to pile on the Kapellmeister's grave.

They made their way along the cemetery's leafy alleys past

elaborately carved and inscribed grave after grave. It was beautiful but oppressive. The man at the funeral home had told them that being buried alive was such a common fear among the Viennese that for a long time people had asked to be interred with a string around their finger that ran all the way to the cemetery guard's HQ, so if they woke up they could ring for assistance.

"Did it ever happen?" she had asked.

"Oh, all the time. Because of decomposition, you see. The hand would move and the bells would ring. So eventually the night watchmen just ignored it."

Sarah had spent the previous evening with heart-stopping dream after dream of waking up in her own coffin. It wasn't much of a break from round white rooms.

Her heart stopped again for a moment at the sight of Beethoven's name emblazoned in Gothic letters across an obelisk. *I'm here, Luigi.* She was reminded for a moment of visiting her father's grave at the cemetery. A slab of stone—no matter how pretty—was not the right tribute for greatness. Sarah lifted her head and looked at the sky, as she had done at her father's infinitely more modest burial site. We look to the heavens, she thought. Even when we don't believe there's anything up there but space. But at least space is infinite.

There was a whole musical neighborhood in the cemetery, and Gerhard was fortunate enough to have earned a spot not too, too far from the cool kids' lunch table. It was amusing, at least, to imagine Beethoven, Schubert, and Brahms shooting spitballs at each other for all eternity. Sarah spotted Gluck, Czerny, Schoenberg, three Strausses, and the more recently interred Austrian superstar Falco, famous for "Rock Me Amadeus" and "Der Kommissar."

For the actual burial rites, Gerhard's inner circle was protected from the crowds by velvet ropes. A long motorcade awaited the luminaries for when the service was over. Sarah, Alessandro, and Nina's half dozen tattooed and pierced friends paid their respects to the Lion and then moved away from the crowds to a private glade behind some large family crypts.

"Maybe each of us say something about Nina?" Alessandro suggested as they formed an awkward circle around the urn. Some of the girls were still in their teens, Sarah guessed, and this was probably the first time someone close to them had died.

Sarah hadn't spent a lot of time thinking about what she would like her own funeral to be, but she imagined good music, brief, spontaneous tributes, not too morbid, preferably funny. It would be nice to be the impetus for some we're-still-alive sex in the parking lot of the funeral home.

"We could chant her spirit to the afterlife," said a short girl with a spiky green haircut whom Sarah knew only by her nickname of Rabbit.

The Wiccan Lili, swathed in black velvet, who had been weeping nearly continuously, brightened. "I think she would like that."

"I brought a drum," said a lean whippet of a boy, pulling a small bongo from his backpack.

"Is pagan thing?" Alessandro whispered nervously to Sarah, surreptitiously crossing himself as they all lay down on the grass on their backs, heads surrounding the urn, hands joined to form a circle. The boy began to drum.

Sarah, looking up at the cloudless, crisp blue sky above them, was expecting something silly about the Goddess welcoming Nina to her secret circle, but instead Rabbit simply began repeating Nina's name slowly over and over, in rhythm with the drum.

"Nina Nina Nina..." They all closed their eyes and picked up the chant. At first Sarah's musically trained mind focused abstractly on the sounds alone and the cadence. The chanting forced you to breathe in rhythm, like during yoga, or sprinting. The drummer increased his tempo, and the chanting kept pace. Sarah felt a strange sensation—as if she were floating, like the woman in Klimt's *Beethoven Frieze* at the Secession, floating above the world, but still connected to it. It was impossible to distinguish her own voice from the others', her own self from the grass, the earth, the trees, the sky. She told herself the euphoria was merely oxygen deprivation from the chanting, but there was something quite lovely and final in the moment when the drumming ceased, the voices, too, and she opened her eyes in silence to see a lone bird silhouetted against the sky, flying away.

Maybe Nina had gotten a better send-off than Gerhard after all.

"Changes in cerebral blood flow during chanting are *fascinating*," said Marie-Franz in the kitchen of her sleek and modern apartment later. Alessandro had told Sarah that it wasn't very common for the Viennese to invite someone to their home, so it was quite an honor. The place was decorated with an incredible assortment of African artifacts gathered during her travels, many of which she said were gifts from shamans she had observed as part of her studies. "It's been well researched using tomography scans. When you deactivate the left posterior parietal lobe, you have the sensation of floating, the transcendence of the physical self. During group chanting, people's heart rates sync up, but even more so if the people know and love each other. It's *astounding*."

Astounding had been discovering Gerhard Schmitt's wife draped across Marie-Franz's couch, still wearing a fur coat.

"I threw myself on Marie-Franz's mercy," Frau Schmitt had called out when they came in. "I couldn't bear to be with any of those horrible sycophants. God! Or all those dreadful public officials. What a ridiculous charade! Marie-Franz, can you make me another one of those lovely drinks?"

So Sarah had left Alessandro to comfort the widow and accompanied Marie-Franz to the kitchen, where the professor was mixing a Viennese specialty of Aperol and Prosecco.

"We shouldn't mention that we knew Nina, right?" Sarah whispered. "Or Bettina?"

"I don't know. Most importantly, we should get some food in her, I think."

But when they returned to the living room, Sarah had only gotten out a "Frau Schmitt, I'm so—" before the widow interrupted.

"Please God, don't say you're sorry. And call me Adele. I saw you with her at the ball. The little Nina. She was a friend of yours?"

"An acquaintance, yes. We were friendly."

"Then it's me who should be saying I am sorry." Adele downed her drink. "And I am. In fact, every tear I've shed has been for her."

"You are very compassionate," murmured Marie-Franz.

"Oh, *you* know," said Adele. "I don't have to pretend in front of you. My husband was a *monster*. That poor girl . . ." She began to weep.

Marie-Franz moved to the sofa and put an arm around her. The widow leaned into the much taller woman gratefully for a moment, and then stood up abruptly, pulling a cigarette out of her bag. Alessandro lit it and she patted him on the arm, still crying.

"It could have been anyone," she said. "My husband had many women. I will be honest with you, I had thought of killing him myself. Now I only feel pity. Even for Bettina Müller, I feel only sorry for her. You are shocked by this?"

"Surprised," admitted Sarah. So the rumors of an affair were true.

"When my brother's little boy was so ill, cancer, Bettina worked with his doctors. That's how Gerhard and I got to know her. She worked around the clock to use the boy's own cells to create an antibody against the cancer. She warned us it was dangerous, and for a while we thought we would lose him, but last spring he turned thirteen. I truly believe she's a miracle worker. How could I hate such a woman?"

As Adele sang the praises of her late husband's mistress, Sarah wondered if she was giving up too soon.

"She said she would help a friend of mine, but she's being incredibly strange about it."

"That's Bettina all over," said Adele. "Suffers from terrible paranoias and persecution complexes. It's that thing, you know, like the man in—what's that film, *A Beautiful Mind*? The geniuses, they always have some mental hiccups. And she is probably saying she will not help you?"

Sarah nodded.

"She always says that, but it is to fill the time while she is thinking about the cure. She does not want to disappoint. There is a saying that 'Vienna is a city of people who have missed their vocation,' but I can assure you Bettina is not one of them."

Sarah absorbed this. "Someone stole Bettina's laptop a few days ago," said Sarah. "She says she needs what's on it to help my friend. Did you or your husband find it? Or—?"

The widow looked at Sarah and began to cry again, large tears that rolled down her cheeks. "No," she said. "I know nothing of this. But I will search the apartment when I get home." She took Sarah's hands in hers. "I do not want your little friend to die. We have had enough death. Enough pain. It is time to find room in our hearts for love. Let us drink to love."

As Sarah raised her glass, Alessandro leaned in. "We should leave now to grab your bag and make the train," he whispered. "You ready to go?"

She was still pondering this question when they got back to Alessandro's apartment and found someone waiting for them.

"Darling," said Nico. "What on earth have you been up to?"

 NINETEEN

Café Bräunerhof was doing a lively business. The whole city was buzzing with talk of the recent death of the Kapellmeister and Nina. Not that Nina was being talked about so much. She was just *"das süsse Mädel"*—"the sweet girl"—of an important, wealthy man. Who really cared about her? The girl had no family, and what little she had didn't want to claim her.

Heinrich nodded to a few members of the city's industrial elite, who were poring over the *Financial Times, Il Sole 24 Ore*, and the *Wall Street Journal*. He bit into a *Punschkrapfen*. His brother would be meeting him soon. They would talk, and they would talk about family, as they always did.

Heinrich and Gottfried's mother had made the brothers promise on her deathbed that they would do whatever it took to hold on to their inheritance. She had also made them promise that they would employ a surgeon to surgically stab her corpse in the heart before she was put into the ground. (She had the common Viennese fear of waking up in her own coffin.) It had cost three hundred euros. They had done the same thing for their father, too, although the bullet Father had put through his own brain had taken most of his head off.

Their estate had been in their family since Archduke Ferdinand had conferred it on the von Hohenlohes in 1570. Land and an estate that, sending his mother spinning in her grave, would be sold to an American entrepreneur in a matter of months if Heinrich wasn't able to turn things around. The American entrepreneur had made his fortune in infomercials. According to *Fortune* magazine, the American was "the *Emperor* of Infomercials," a phrase that had made Gottfried apoplectic.

"They call this man an emperor because he has sold collapsible colanders and nose hair clippers?" his brother had fumed.

"They call him an emperor because he has sold a *billion* collapsible colanders and nose hair clippers," Heinrich had explained. "Also zirconium jewelry, plus-size swimwear, robotic vacuum cleaners, a device that allows you to hang wallpaper very smoothly, a brassiere that can be inflated or deflated—"

"We are descended from not one but two Grand Masters of the Teutonic Knights," Gottfried interrupted, lifting his chin. "They fought in the Crusades."

"And they fought valiantly and well." Heinrich knew the story went faster when you played along.

"You've seen their armor in the Neue Burg, the dents, the scratches. And this is what you propose as *our* course of action?"

The thought that his own brother looked down on him twisted Heinrich's stomach, which was already doing battle with a combination of goose liver, Zimtstangerle, and rum-soaked cake frosting.

Gottfried was not only the heir, the scion of their house, but he was the gifted one, the one with brains and talent and charm. Even his epilepsy was considered a sign of his nobility, having been inherited through the Hapsburg line. A line that also carried notable examples of insanity.

Gottfried planned on having children as soon as he found a woman who met his breeding standards, which involved dental records, genealogy, a lengthy questionnaire on Austrian history, and a 5K timed run. And Gottfried intended his eventual sons to inherit the von Hohenlohe estate, as they had, and their father before them. But the estate needed to be saved, first.

Gottfried had become a rider at the Spanish Riding School and Heinrich had taken a job—his forebears would have shuddered at the word—as a consultant with a pharmaceutical company, telling people that his family had a long connection to medical innovation through Philippine Welser. But the truth was neither of the brothers was as interested in Philippine as they had been in their lineage of Teutonic Knights. Heinrich's contract was to provide "public relations assistance," but in reality they had hired him for his connections in Austrian society. As a descendant of the old aristocracy who had attended the best schools (where his mediocre marks were interpreted as a sign of patrician restraint, not dimwittedness), he could weasel his way into conversations with high-level Austrians anywhere and sniff out any developments that might be interesting to his employer. They called it "research," but it was really gossip, which came naturally to Heinrich.

Then the company had come to him, and after praising his discretion and effectiveness, had asked for a very delicate service to be rendered. When they mentioned the sum that they were prepared to remunerate, he had felt his prayers had been answered.

He had agreed to provide such services. There was an EU official to be gently bribed to pass some legislation beneficial to the company, then a little off-the-books banking business in Switzerland. A sensitive negotiation made over a cotoletta at Bice in

Milan. Always just gentlemen doing business, of course. As the need for tact and discretion had increased, the rewards had kept pace. But so had the risks.

This latest assignment was not just gentlemen doing business. Since Gottfried was the one so rabid about holding on to their inheritance, Heinrich had damn well asked him to help. Which may have been a mistake. Was certainly a mistake. Yes, things had certainly gotten out of hand. Gottfried's fantasies had a way of taking over things. Heinrich had some difficult choices to make now.

Heinrich swallowed a second *Punschkrapfen*, then nervously checked his upper lip for traces of pink frosting, as he saw the slim (damn him!) silhouette of Gottfried making his way into the restaurant. Gottfried got all the women: beautiful, intelligent, sophisticated women who slept (Heinrich imagined) in between silk sheets and whose well-tended bodies were lithe and dexterous and who whispered naughty things in educated voices. Nina had refused to sleep with Heinrich, so the last act of sexual congress he had enjoyed had taken place with a middle-aged Laotian prostitute in a 15th district brothel boasting a selection of "internationally themed" boudoirs. The "America" room had been decorated with chuck wagon wallpaper and gingham upholstery. It had been necessary to keep his eyes tightly shut while he screwed, which defeated the purpose. You kept your eyes closed when you fucked your wife, not your mistress. Not that the prostitute counted as a mistress, but still.

Heinrich's feelings for his brother were as layered as a Viennese pastry. Love, fear, jealousy, hatred, admiration, and resentment. Heinrich suddenly remembered how Gottfried, as a child, would order a Dobostorte in a café and proceed to dismantle it, casting aside chocolate and buttercream and cake to eat the only part he liked: the slivers of caramel.

Yes. That was what Heinrich had to do now. Turn his mind from all those layers of feelings and focus on the one that was most useful. The one that would get them closer to their goal.

There was work to be done. They would do it together.

The Tenth Muse

· THE TRUE STORY OF ·

Elizabeth Jane Weston, Poet

by

Harriet Hunter, PhD

CHAPTER THREE

———∞∞∞———

*In which I reveal exactly what
I did after I died.*

Yes, dear readers, there I was, in my coffin, having officially died in childbirth and unofficially by my own hand.

I have thought, from time to time, that I should write a short book on how easy—relatively—it turns out to be to escape from one's own coffin. It would be a bestseller in Vienna. Of course, some modern coffins are made out of metals like aluminum or steel, and in that case one's goose would be quite cooked, or asphyxiated as it were. A very painful route.

It is possible that I ran out of oxygen before I freed myself, and another person doing what I did would not have succeeded. My chest hurt at one point quite dreadfully. But I believe my methodology was quite sound and is another example of how well I think under pressure. Six feet of dirt pressure in this case.

My coffin was made of wood, and the pressure of the earth above it crushed an egress around my midsection. They had buried me with my child. The child was dead, truly so. I moved the small body off my chest and removed my heavy dress until I was wearing only my linen shift. I took the crucifix from around my neck and used it to enlarge the hole, packing as much earth as I could within the coffin. I ripped a piece of skirt from my dress and made a loose bag of it around my head in order to keep the dirt from falling in my mouth and nose. When it was possible, I stood up, my arms above me, thrusting myself out of the hole. I leveraged my foot on the coffin and rose to a height where my hands were able to break free of the ground. I could feel cold air on my fingertips.

What a sight it would have been, if anyone had been there to see it.

I had not been buried long. The earth was still fresh, and crumbly. I pulled myself free. It was night. I stood there, covered in dirt and some blood where the wood of the coffin had scratched against my skin. Shivering in the night air.

I did not know what to do next, so I walked home, across the graveyard and then through the narrow streets, slipping into the shadows and hugging the walls whenever I heard footsteps approaching.

At my home, all was still. I thought about waking Johannes. He would scream. They would all scream. And run from the house. What could I do? What had I become? This was well before zombies had entered popular culture, please remember. I thought I might be dreaming.

No. I knew.

I knew I had been wrong. My stepfather had not poisoned my body against childbirth. He had poisoned me against death. He had found the tonic for immortality. The Elixir of Life! If you think masses of people have tried to crack the formula for

Coca-Cola—think again. The Elixir of Life was sought for a thousand years by crazy alchemist and king alike—though not by a single woman, I'd like to point out. Had Kelley even known what he had done? How could he? I had never died—or tried to die—until now.

Also, if my stepfather had known, he would never have shut up about it. The man didn't talk to just angels—he talked to anyone who'd listen. I mean anyone. One-legged beggars ran from the man in the street.

I crept into the house. I could hear Portia coughing her wracking cough from her room. Portia. Portia had wept over my grave. Portia should know that I was still alive. That I would never leave her.

And then the coughing stopped, and the house was still and most terribly silent. I went to my daughter's room.

Portia was dead.

I cannot say exactly what happened next. I know one part of my brain continued to behave as perfectly and wonderfully as it had ever done, for later I found myself with clothes, a cloak, a pair of shoes, a knife. Some money. But I was grieving for my daughter, and my grief was perfect and wonderful, too.

I left Prague. I wandered a very long time. I hid, and I learned, and I waited and I planned. And I lived. On and on and on, I have lived.

*Y*ou would think that my grief and longing for my daughter would have lessened over these many years—these centuries. You would be wrong to think so. She is my light in the darkness. Portia. Waking or sleeping, she is my dream.

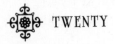

TWENTY

"Vienna as dull as ever?" asked Nico in the taxi. He had insisted on taking Sarah to his favorite place for dinner. She had agreed, since it had become immediately obvious that she needed to separate Alessandro and Nico, who disliked each other as much as they adored Sarah, and perhaps for that reason.

"Why does the little person think he can break into my apartment and make fun of my sofa?" demanded Alessandro after Nico made a crack about pink being the new black. "Is not pink, is rosé. And why he wipe his hands on my towel? No one touch my towel but me. That is why I put out the guest towellinos."

Having achieved enough détente to get Nico into a taxi before Alessandro threw him into a boiling pot of gnocchi, Sarah gave the little man the short version of her adventures: Bettina's disappearance, the theft of the laptop, the stolen galleon, the murder/suicide of Gerhard and Nina, and Adele's testimonial to the scientist's skill.

"A moment, please," Nico said. "That galleon. Did it have a secret compartment?"

"How did you know?"

"You forget, I watched it trundle down Rudolf's table.

Sometimes he challenged people to find the secret hiding place. You found it?"

Sarah told Nico about the drug.

"I don't think Bettina knew it was there. She's an avid clock collector, so maybe this was some sort of bribe. She called it an 'unwelcome gift.'"

"Tell me more about this Bettina person."

"She's brilliant; she's frightened; Adele said she's paranoid, but Bettina does get hate mail"—Sarah shrugged—"so maybe her paranoia is justified. I don't know much more than that."

Nico pondered this, brows furrowed, fingers tapping on the cab's armrest.

"What happened in London?" Sarah asked. "Did you get what you needed for Pols?"

"No," he said. "I'm sorry, Sarah. The whole trip, it was like someone was one step ahead of me. There's hardly a decent powder to be found in London. And we have a leaky time problem in Prague. Another dead man." Nico told her about Jan Kubiš, adding, "Either hell portals are busting out all over or the Fleece has been found. I rather think the latter, because of all the missing alchemical ingredients. I believe someone is using the Fleece's secrets to bring people back from the dead. My question is: why?"

"Um, my question is: *how?*" Sarah said. "Because that's impossible. I don't mean that's 'weird,' I mean that it's *impossible.* I'm willing to believe that alchemy was an early form of science, and that perhaps the early alchemists unwittingly stumbled upon things of incredible significance, but that's going too far. Saint John? Jan Kubiš? Those people are dust now. Bones and dust."

"Yes. Don't misunderstand me, I am not talking about resurrection. Both of the men appeared in the place they are said to have died. Nepomuk in the river, and Kubiš in the church crypt.

As if they were wrenched from the past at the moment of their, well, passing. As if time were being bent. And that is not impossible. Einstein did not think so. String theorists do not think so."

"But to move an actual person from one time to another . . ."

"For that you need a portal." Nico nodded. "Or maybe a really, really big magnet."

"You sound like Mesmer." Sarah shook her head.

"Franz Mesmer?" Nico smiled. "Knew him in Paris. He cured my mistress's chronic yeast infections."

Nico's favorite place turned out to be a *Heurigen*, or wine bar, in Heiligenstadt. Sarah had always longed to visit Heiligenstadt. It was the place where Beethoven had spent many summers, escaping the heat of the city and communing with nature. Just as in his day, rows of neat vineyards still looked down on narrow cobblestone alleys of ancient houses surrounded by green fields. Sarah had seen engravings of Heiligenstadt from Beethoven's era and though of course there were changes, it was still quite recognizable, especially the leafy little square in front of the village church. A couple of wizened old men in fedoras were smoking pipes on a bench under the trees, eyeballing a pair of shapely young ladies passing by with miniature pinschers on brightly colored leashes.

Beethoven's most seminal visit to Heiligenstadt had been in his darkest moment, in 1802, when his deafness was becoming apparent.

I would have ended my life—it was only my art that held me back. Ah, it seemed to me impossible to leave the world until I had brought forth all that I felt was within me.

It was here that Beethoven had chosen life over death, Sarah thought.

"I like this one," said Nico, leading her under an awning into a long, narrow cobbled courtyard of a *Heurigen*. Rough wooden tables and chairs balanced precariously on the stones, and waitresses in dirndls brought pitchers of wine to customers.

Sarah had condemned Gottfried as pretentious for dressing in Austrian *Tracht*. But is it pretentious, or even kitsch, she wondered, if it's not done for effect, but just because that's the way it's always been done? Perhaps she would find out. What with Adele's perspective on Bettina and Nico's appearance, she had decided to postpone her departure, and in the taxi had made a date with Gottfried to tour the Spanish Riding School tomorrow. She would try to discern what he thought about his brother's possible larcenous tendencies.

Sarah and Nico sat at a small table in the corner, under the grape vines trellised over the courtyard. Tables of locals laughed and gossiped over carafes of icy, lemony Grüner Veltliner. Some of the windows of the *Heurigen* were still the old bubbly hand-blown leaded glass. She ran her fingers over one of them, wondering if Beethoven's fingers had also traced its surface, having a drink with friends. It would be nice to see Beethoven happy. It would be nice to have a drink with him, take a walk in the countryside afterward. *Picnic, Luigi?*

"That the galleon was here surprises me," Nico said. "It suggests a link. Either Bettina Müller *is* Moriarty—"

"She'd have to be pretty busy," said Sarah. "Nanobiologist by day, thief of all things alchemical by night?"

"Yes, it suggests nimbleness to an unlikely degree. Perhaps Moriarty sent the galleon to her in order to harness her skill. If she could analyze the drug inside she could reproduce it. I'd really like to talk to her."

"Get in line. The drug seems to stimulate the vagus nerve, which seems to temporarily reset the immune system. The effects fade, or did in my friend Renato's case. Do you have *any* idea of what might be in it?"

"No, but I know who gave the galleon to Emperor Rudolf," said Nico. "Philippine Welser. She might very well have had Schlottheim build a little compartment inside it to hold medicine for Rudy's many ailments. So it wasn't just a clock or an automaton. It was a giant pillbox."

"But the effect on me was crazy. I was hearing voices. I mean, my voice projected upon other things." Sarah decided against describing the multiple orgasms.

"You do not have an autoimmune disease, so it merely stimulated an already healthy vagus nerve, causing hallucinations, a feeling of warmth, and usually a significant arousal of the . . ."

"Yes," said Sarah. "So maybe Philippine came up with an early form of steroids, which work only if you keep taking them and can have consequences for the rest of your body. Like Renato and his stripes. But it's still serious medicine. It wasn't placebo effect stuff, you know. It was a *drug*."

"I understand, but you should know that this modern idea that one drug should work the same on different people—that's not medicine, it's commerce. There's no knowing how it would affect Pols. Still, I'm glad you finally appreciate Philippine's genius."

"I met the family, the von Hohenlohes, who have her book. Heinrich is the one I was telling you about, who works for the drug company. He's not very friendly, but I'm meeting his brother tomorrow."

"Good," said Nico, putting his hand over hers to calm her. "But tonight we relax."

"I can't, really," said Sarah. "The connections . . . things are starting to coalesce, but . . . I just keep thinking that the answers are out there, just out of my reach, and if I just figure out a way to put everything together . . . I keep thinking about Bettina's research, how progressive it is and yet how simple. Ashes and gold. The galleon. Philippine's book. Mesmer and his armonica. We've got to try everything, no matter how crazy it sounds. I wasn't there before, but I am now. I'm ready for the fucking witchcraft, you know. Bring on the witchcraft."

"This is how it goes," Nico said softly. "This is the worst part. When you love someone."

"Don't say it," said Sarah. "I don't want you to say it."

"The price of love is loss."

Sarah choked back the despair rising in her throat. She would not give in. There was still time to fight, and she would fight. *Until I have brought forth all that I feel is within me.*

The waitress came, took their orders, and walked away.

"I have a little surprise for you." Nico held one palm aloft and passed the other over it. Like magic, a pill appeared in the center of his tiny hand.

Sarah looked at the pill, then glanced at Nico, then stared at the not-perfectly-circular pill again. It couldn't be. The ingredients were gone. No longer obtainable. Weren't they?

"It can't cure Pols, but it's going to take you where you want to go," whispered Nico. "All you have to do is open your eyes."

"Westonia," said Sarah.

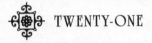 TWENTY-ONE

Harriet was dying for a hit, but of course she had to wait until Max was asleep. She was surprised at how *relieved* she had been the other day to see Max's Alfa roll back into its parking space underneath the castle. Not everyone came back from Kutná Hora, and she had become rather fond of Max. It was possible they could have a future together when this was all over. It might be rather fun to be chatelaine of the Lobkowicz households. She would do it so well. And Mother might actually be pleased, for once, even if Max was American. He was so nice, and so dishy, and so svelte and slim hipped. Harriet pulled him up out of his chair and over to the bed. He looked gorgeous in costume, even if he wasn't very clever with accents or sticking to character in their private moments. She began undressing him.

Of all the assignments Elizabeth had given her, Max was by far the pleasantest. Elizabeth had rather a bee in her bonnet about the Lobkowicz family, ever since Polyxena had let her down, but so far all Harriet had had to do was watch and see if Max turned up anything valuable, and make sure he didn't get too close to the truth. It was terrible bad luck that he had been present for both John of Nepomuk and Jan Kubiš—she'd had to endure a real tongue-lashing from Elizabeth and a threat that if she wasn't more careful, there would be no more Westonia. Harriet shuddered to think how Elizabeth had fired shots to try to dissuade do-gooders from saving Saint John before she could retrieve him herself. What if Max had been harmed? And she had a bit of a fright when Max had mentioned Kutná Hora . . . but here he was, safe as houses, sitting on his sofa and accepting the very stiff martini she had just poured for him. She fingered the pill inside the silk pouch in her pocket. Soon Max would be off to Elysian dreamland, and she could get back to where she belonged. . . .

"You haven't told me much about your childhood," said Max, as Harriet settled herself astride his hips.

Oh, God no, thought Harriet. He doesn't want to *talk*. What an eccentric man. She unbuttoned her modest, high-necked nightie and let her breasts spill out. Talking could take hours. And the past was beckoning to her . . . she could feel history's siren call. Every time some new detail emerged, some conversation, some previously misunderstood corner of the past was illuminated. But it was more than scholarly interest. It was like the most gorgeous dream and the most engrossing book and the most fascinating movie all combined at once. She needed to divert Max, and divert posthaste.

"I've brought a special treat for us." She reached behind her pillow. Zounds, if this didn't keep him from a chat then nothing would.

Max's eyes widened briefly. "Is that what I think it is?"

"A fourteenth-century English *phallus*." Harriet did not care for the unpleasant American word for such devices. "Ivory. A very special auction at Sotheby's. The inscriptions are particularly amusing."

She held the elaborately carved ivory tower between her

breasts and pointed to the first of the curving lines that circled it. "'At this mark the virgins tarry, going no farther if they wish to marry.'"

"Aha," said Max. "Okay."

"I'm the Wife of Bath, and you—" Harriet leaned over the side of the bed and brought out a rough hemp robe from her bag. "You are the Friar." Max looked wonderful in a cowl.

"*Canterbury Tales*?" said Max, allowing her to dress him in the robe. "I'm not sure we covered this chapter in high school English class."

"No, I expect you wouldn't have." Harriet settled herself on the bed and pulled the hem of her dress up to her hips. She parted her legs and keeping her eyes locked on Max, slowly slid the ivory tusk inside herself up to the first line.

"Whoa," said Max. Harriet smiled at the look in his eyes. Heigh-*ho*.

"Mhmm. You read the next bit."

Max rotated the lingam in order to read the line of script. "'At this line the good wives stay, when their husbands are away.'"

I do adore my work, thought Harriet. This was much more fun than *Histories & Mysteries*, where they sometimes censored her impulses. She caressed her breasts and spread her legs wider. "Oh, dear Friar," she said, "'Tell me also, to what purpose or end the genitals were made, that I defend / And for what benefit was man first wrought?'" Chaucer really was divine. She wriggled her hips.

"Something, something, something, 'they were not made for naught,'" answered Max, who tended to paraphrase quotations in these moments, poor darling.

"Do read the next line, Friar."

Max obeyed and slid the merry Maypole up to the next line.

"'Touch the naughty wench's spot, where the door to Heaven is sought.'" Max began to kiss the insides of her thighs.

"One more," Harriet pleaded, writhing. "The last line, Friar. Read it. Oh, I beg you. Read it to me."

"'Pass this point and go straight to Hell, after giving a good loud yell.'"

Harriet, always receptive, complied.

It was three a.m. when Max awakened from a bad dream he didn't remember and found that Harriet was no longer sleeping beside him. He wasn't sure if she had left the palace or not. Her clothes, shoes, and coat were gone, but her purse still lay on the chair where she had flung it before unpacking her . . . things.

He pulled on the friar robe to go searching for her. He hoped she wasn't sleepwalking. If she wandered into any of the museum rooms, she'd set off the alarms. But she was nowhere to be found. Possibly she had left and simply forgotten her purse. Definitely not the girl next door, Harriet. For all her professional accomplishments and confidence, he sensed there was a vulnerability there she was hiding. It made him feel protective, which was nice.

Well, he was awake now, might as well do some reading. Pols had asked him for books on the Golden Fleece for the libretto of her opera. It was nice to talk to someone about Fleece lore. So far his search through the secret library hadn't turned up anything useful about Philippine's cures, but he had found some interesting things about Ferdinand, his collections, his interest in architecture, and his happy marriage. Pols loved hearing about Ferdinand and Philippine, too, and he enjoyed reading to her. Ferdinand and Philippine had really come alive for him—they no longer seemed like distant historical figures but flesh and blood people. Ferdinand's struggles to please his demanding father, his inconvenient ardor for Philippine, whom he had spotted on a trip to Augsburg and fallen madly in love with—Max felt like he and Ferdy would have a lot to talk about. He was beginning to wonder if the Archduke hadn't been the original member of the secret Order of the Golden Fleece.

Max made his way down the stairs to the subterranean basement, followed a narrow hallway into a small, windowless room, and rolled up the rug that concealed the trapdoor. He descended into a tunnel, walked in a crouch for thirty meters, pulled open a second trapdoor, and then ascended into the secret library of his palace.

His grandfather Max had sealed this room before fleeing the Nazis in 1939. He had left all his most prized possessions here. Not the priceless art or artifacts or jewels, but letters, books, and the strange alchemical arsenal. Though many of the books mentioned the Fleece, none so far seemed to contain a clue about its whereabouts, but it was going to take a while to get through everything. Max grabbed a couple of things he had set aside earlier about Philippine and Ferdinand to take upstairs. Two books and a folio of heavily annotated architectural drawings. He reversed his path, moving through trapdoor-tunnel-trapdoor. He could renovate this lower part of the palace, and make it all easier, but it was . . . let's face it . . . totally badass to have trapdoors and secret passages.

He came up in the little windowless room. This had been Sarah's room, when she had been at the palace two summers ago. Sarah. Talk about inconvenient ardor.

Max sighed and flicked the flashlight app on his phone to make his way up the stairs. He heard a scuttling in the narrow hallway. Damn. The rats were back.

· · ·

Harriet tried to stand, but couldn't quite manage it. The robed figure had walked past her in the darkness, with ancient tomes under his arms. Who was it? Martin Luther? Richard of Wallingford? The Venerable Bede?

No. No, she was in Prague. The drug let you see into time, but it didn't let you see across space. She could see only things that had happened here. Thank God she had realized at the last second it wasn't a figure from the past, and stayed where she was, out of sight. It was Max. That was close. Harriet wondered what time it was. Max was probably looking for *her*. She'd need to reappear with a story about needing some air. A tiny little lie. And while she was at it, she would have to dissemble just a wee bit to Elizabeth, too, and tell her she'd seen a monk. With a wand of light! Elizabeth seemed to be doubting Harriet's skills to see the past. But really all she needed was a little more practice. And a bigger dose of Westonia. One pill was not nearly enough. Elizabeth was so mean with the stuff. Harriet kept begging her for a *big* bag, big enough to see all of the Napoleonic Wars. All in good time, Elizabeth said. Pish! But she needs must do as she was told.

Harriet screwed her eyes shut and breathed deeply. The drug worked so erratically! Sometimes it took hours before anything happened, and sometimes it happened right away. Harriet wanted to do what Elizabeth asked, but Elizabeth didn't realize how blasted difficult the whole thing was.

Or how much she was demanding.

After they'd met at Třeboň, Elizabeth had shown Harriet her lab in the abandoned mines beneath the village of Kutná Hora. Elizabeth had explained to Harriet that she occasionally needed subjects to test her drugs on. Drugs that every once in a while proved fatal, which was why Elizabeth only experimented on very bad people. "Rapists," she had said. "Child pornographers." Harriet tried very hard not to think about that part. She was aware that occasionally some new bones were added to the piles at Sedlec Ossuary, after being chemically treated to look like old bones. She was aware because Elizabeth sometimes had her do the treatment. It wasn't all whortleberries and roses, being handmaiden to a genius. Or being a drug addict. A *history* addict, she told herself. After all, what's wrong with being addicted to history?

She had to trust Elizabeth. Elizabeth was the only one who could give her what she needed, feed the need she had created that day at Třeboň, the need to see the past. And it was insanely impressive what Elizabeth had accomplished! Things that the rest of science was only beginning to admit were possible. Especially considering what she had had to endure and how she had been forced to keep moving, never letting anyone realize how slowly she was aging. It was being a poet, Harriet thought, that had allowed Elizabeth to become such a gifted scientist. That and her initial training in alchemy. She actually *knew* how to decipher those complicated metaphorical manuscripts! No more guessing.

And of course Elizabeth's cause was full of poetry, too. It was four-handkerchief-weeper stuff, really, about trying to die because of grief and then finding out you had to live with grief. And then all the feminist bits. Her insights about current culture. Harriet was pretty sure the Man Booker Prize would be hers for those. If there wasn't some immigrant narrative that year. Of course, Elizabeth's sense of humor needed to be cleaned up here and there. People now didn't find beheadings all that funny.

It was all going to make an extraordinary novel. The question was, how did the story end?

Harriet stood up. She felt ghastly, and her mouth was dry. There wasn't much doing down here in the hallway. Maybe nothing interesting had ever happened down here.

On his way back upstairs, Max passed the practice room and heard noise. He flipped on the lights to reveal Pollina, who was unaware he was there. The daily walk from her apartment to the palace had been proving to be too much for her, and Max had given her and Jose rooms here to sleep in, so that she could play whenever she felt up to it. She was determined to finish her opera.

He would wait for a pause and then tell her about the books.

Max leaned against the door frame of the practice room, stroking the grizzled head of Boris, and watching the girl play. The dog leaned heavily against his leg. Boris might be mostly blind, and nearly deaf, but he was a hero. Boris, Max thought, was far braver and more loyal than he was.

Pollina was experimenting with equipment Max had just bought for her: an electronic piano (full eighty-eight keys), plugged into a specially designed laptop (Braille keyboard and voice activation), which automatically recorded everything she played. Pollina had asked for this, and Max, desperate for ways to feel useful to her, had immediately complied. He couldn't hear what she was working on—she had plugged in and was wearing the enormous headphones—but the slight plonk-plonking sound of her fingers hitting the keys was oddly soothing.

As the girl played, Max used the sleeve of his monk's robe to gently rub the cover of the folio he'd retrieved from the secret library. A gleaming six-pointed golden star began to emerge. At first Max thought it represented the Jewish star, but when he opened the cover, he found that the loose collection of pages were in Latin.

Veteres ritus et ritualia stellae aestate palatium Ferdinandus. Max flipped through the handwritten pages, recognizing the floor plan and some of the drawings. It looked like the Star Summer Palace, here in Prague. Someone had made a series of handwritten notes on it, probably the builder.

Max knew a little about the star-shaped palace. Ferdinand had built it for Philippine as a sort of vacation home. Except, looking at the alchemical notations on the drawings, Max wondered if it was more than that. . . .

Pols turned, startling him. Of course she had known he was there. Her senses were incredible.

"What's that thing you're reading?" she asked. "Is it for my opera?"

"It's very late," he said. "Let me help you back to your room. We'll read together tomorrow."

Harriet staggered up the stairs. The drug had *finally* kicked in on her way up, but she hadn't seen anything historically interesting at *all*. It had just been Sarah Weston and the dwarf Nico that Elizabeth had warned her about, marching up and down, up and down, dragging some third person and *giggling*. It had been odd, but not at all useful, and she hadn't been able to push past the energy of either of them. Sarah, in particular, had been crackling, sending sparks right and left. It wasn't the first time Harriet had encountered Sarah while on Westonia. The girl had mucked up half of Prague with her energy.

Another figure appeared at the far end of the hallway. Max again. Damn it, she had lost the thread. Harriet hid herself and watched Max help the little girl down the hallway. Pollina didn't like Harriet, she'd made that bloody clear. Moritz snarled at her, too, the unholy cur.

She needed to get back to bed and tell Max she'd gone out to look at the stars.

Harriet tried the door of Max's office. Locked, damn it. She needed something to give to Elizabeth. Elizabeth might stop telling her the story if Harriet didn't deliver. And the novel wasn't finished.

 TWENTY-TWO

"You like horses?"

Sarah nodded, though she had pretty much no experience with the animals—she wasn't exactly from a horsey set—and had thought the whole Lipizzaner thing was just something for the tourists.

But Gottfried was a thorough and passionate guide, and she found herself growing interested. He explained how the original horses were brought to Austria from the Spanish court by Maximilian II in the 1500s, how they were trained for war, and how all of these snowy white stallions in neat rows of stalls were descended from six foundation sires: Pluto, Conversano, Maestoso, Favory, Neapolitano, and Siglavy. They were ridden in the mornings, with performances for tourists in the Winter Riding School in the evenings. This time of day was rest time for horses and riders. Sarah smiled and nodded, not taking much of it in, waiting for an opportunity to bring up Heinrich.

She had declined Nico's offer of Westonia the night before. As much as she longed to see Beethoven in Heiligenstadt, there was only the one pill and there were other places in Vienna where it might be more useful to see the past. She and Nico had made a plan, which he was setting in motion while she got a little closer to half of the uptight von Hohenlohe brothers.

"You seem a little . . . distracted?" Gottfried finally asked as they watched one of the horses work on a single piece of straw, looking for all the world like an ex-smoker.

"I'm sorry," she said. She'd been having more nightmares about Pols and the round white room. Always with the sense of having picked the wrong door. Sometimes there was the woman in gold, other times a dragon or a giant appeared. She shook off the memory and said, "A friend of mine, a little girl, is very sick. I'm worried about her." Why not tell him some of the truth, she thought.

"I am sorry to hear of this." Gottfried put his hand on her arm. It was funny, he had a very comforting touch. Probably it was from working with these horses, who all did seem to be kind of high-strung. His hand continued up and down her arm. "Tell me about your friend."

Sarah began to describe Pollina, and her illness, and how she had come to Vienna to research a cure, and how doing so had led her down some peculiar alleys.

"I've even been looking into homeopathy," Sarah said, her fingers absentmindedly rubbing the brass stall decorations. "And older healing methods. I actually came across a famous Tyrolean healer. Philippine Welser."

"Ah, yes, of course." Gottfried nodded. "My family possesses a book of her recipes. It is one of our treasures. Our family home belonged to Archduke Ferdinand and Philippine. Do you know Innsbruck?"

"No. I haven't been able to travel that much in Austria," said Sarah. She tried to sound merely curious. "I'd love to see the book."

"I would be delighted to show it to you."

Sarah took a deep breath. Good. She was finally catching a break.

"Yes." Gottfried nodded. "Your friend will need you to be strong and calm. You can help her that way. Take another deep breath."

Sarah inhaled the scent of Gottfried, the scent of horses, the scent of hay, and felt her shoulders relax a little.

"Good. Shall we continue?"

"Yes." Sarah nodded. "This is exactly what I needed, actually." As soon as she said it, she knew it was true. She had been racing from one baffling, sad, and frustrating event to another ever since setting foot in Vienna. But tonight she would take Westonia and she would get some answers. And if Gottfried took her to Innsbruck, maybe there would be something in the family archives there that might help Pols. Now, how to introduce Heinrich into the conversation?

"Please, show me more." She smiled.

Gottfried rolled back a brass and lacquered wood door to open a stall. "So. The stallions are always named for the sire and dam. This is Conversano Bonadea 2002, meaning he is directly descended from those two founding horses, and born in 2002. All of his sons will also be named Conversano."

"And his daughters?"

"All fillies take the name of their mother. The breeding is kept one hundred percent pure."

"So no stealth visits from a randy Shetland pony?"

Gottfried smiled and ran his hand along the stallion's thick arched neck. "*Na Du—mein wunderbares Pferd,*" he whispered affectionately. "He's a powerhouse under saddle." Gottfried rubbed the horse's withers and the animal stretched his neck around in gratitude, rubbing Sarah's arm with his velvety nose.

"It must be very prestigious, to be a rider here," she said.

"It is a great honor to be selected. But lately I have become unsatisfied. The horses are too fat, too bored. They should have more time in the country. They should be allowed to be *horses*."

Conversano blinked. His eyelashes were white and long.

"This is a prison," Gottfried continued, gesturing to the marble stalls and rose granite mangers. "The horses are kept here nearly twenty-four hours a day. They are descended from warhorses. The best of the best. And look at them now." He slapped the belly of the stallion, who farted. "Fat. Nervous. Like my brother, Heinrich."

Perfect, Sarah thought. "He must be very sad about Nina."

Gottfried shrugged. "He is unlucky with women."

"He seems kind of unhappy in general. Does he enjoy his work? He works for a pharmaceutical company, right?"

Gottfried sniffed. "Heinrich enjoys nothing. He is neurotic. Like Pluto over there."

He pointed to the stallion in the stall across the walkway. It was biting the stall divider and sucking in air. "It's called cribbing," said Gottfried. "It's like people who bite their nails, or border collies who lick their feet or chase their tails. Animals who should be doing real work, but instead are kept as *pets*. These horses have become lapdogs who dance for the tourists and line the pockets of the government. I am always telling the *Oberreiter* that I do not want to see these beautiful horses go the way of the rest of Austrians," said Gottfried angrily. "Forgetting their real power."

Sarah looked at Gottfried's lean, muscled body.

Gottfried caught her eye and smiled. "Strength is merely the ability to overcome fear. Most people are ruled by fear. You have noticed this?"

"I have."

"I don't believe fear drives you, Fräulein Weston."

"No, it doesn't," she said simply. "It doesn't stop me, either."

"We are alike, then."

They looked at each other for a moment. And then Gottfried stepped forward and kissed her. Long, hard, and with a significant amount of talent.

"I've been wanting to do that since the ball," he said.

Sarah felt an electric current running up and down her spine. The muscles of her legs were taut. She seemed to be lucking out in the stables in more ways than one. Conversano nudged her shoulder again. It was as if the horse was pushing her toward Gottfried. *Hold on a second, buddy,* Sarah thought. *Let me just think this through for a minute.*

But when Gottfried put his hands on her shoulders and moved her back against the wall of the stall, Sarah found thinking to be an extremely difficult activity, except for the part of her conscious mind that recognized—*Ooh, limes*—as she tasted him. Gottfried's mouth was urgent and confident. The red beard was very soft. Sarah arched her neck like a Lipizzaner and let Gottfried plunge his hands into the V of her dress. Sarah caught Conversano's eye. The horse was built to be free, to be powerful, to do what he wanted. And he had been tamed, and trained, and denatured. She would never let that happen to her. She had a sudden desire to be absolutely, primally naked. And for Gottfried to be naked. For basically everyone in the world to be naked. God, she was burning up.

Soon Gottfried was whispering, "Let me have you, let me have you," in her ear, her throat, her breasts.

They were both drenched in sweat. Gottfried slid her sweater over her head and then undid his shirt. He had a black cross tattooed on his chest, right above his heart. Underneath this were three words: *Helfen, Wehren, Heilen.* Help, Defend, Heal. Gottfried picked her up and sat her on the lip of the stall. Sarah grasped the frame. His hand moved in between her legs, his fingers deep inside her.

Gottfried unzipped his pants. Even Conversano seemed impressed. Sarah threw back her head and laughed in delight, which caused Gottfried to laugh, too, deep in his throat. She wrapped her hand around Gottfried's cock, which was hot to the touch.

Purse, she thought. *Condom. Oh, God.*

Sarah pressed her lips against the cross on Gottfried's chest and for a moment she thought she heard the ringing of armor, the stamping of horses on the battlefield, tasted blood and sweat. And fear. And faith.

She wrapped her legs around his waist.

Everything was on fire. Gottfried's cock inside her was on fire, and her skin was on fire. And Conversano's cries were blending with hers, and all the horses were crying and stamping, urging them on, and her nose was filled with the scent of fire. She released herself into the fire, raining down upon it, as Gottfried let out a wild yell of satisfaction. And still there was fire.

No, there really was fire.

The stable was filling with smoke.

They realized the truth of it at the same time, pulling apart and then hastily reassembling pieces of their clothing as they stumbled into the walkway.

"*Mein Gott.* Where is it coming from?" Gottfried cried, racing from one stall to another. The stallions were panicking.

Sarah was dialing her phone. "No signal!" she shouted.

"The walls here are five feet thick! Go get help while I get the horses out."

Sarah ran for the heavy wooden door to the courtyard, which loomed huge and dark in front of her. Hadn't they left it open? Now she pushed as hard as she could, but found it immovable. She banged on it with her fists, barely making a sound.

"Gottfried!" she called. "Is there another way out?"

All of the horses' stalls had doors that opened onto the courtyard, but these were bolted on the outside. They were locked in.

Sarah could now see the source of the fire, and she ran through the thickening smoke to the huge pile of wood shavings at the end of the aisle, piled up for use as the horses' bedding. It was blazing with flames, throwing sparks toward the stalls. The heat from the fire was so intense that she couldn't even get to the fire extinguisher on the wall, and the fire was growing in height, nearly ten feet. She made her way back toward Gottfried, calling his name. The smoke was becoming so thick that she could hardly see, and the horses were neighing in terror and thrashing around in their stalls.

"We're trapped!" she shouted.

She found him in the smoke, two haltered horses plunging on either side of him, his eyes wide as he held their lead ropes, realizing there was no safety to lead them to.

She looked around for anything they could use to bust through the wooden door. She grabbed a shovel and tried battering, feeling instantly the futility of it. Why was no one coming? She looked around her. Even if she could find a corner of the stable that wasn't bedded in flammable materials, the smoke would get them within another minute or two. She could barely draw breath, her lungs burning with effort.

Crack! Crack! Crack! She heard what sounded like a battering ram coming from the next stall.

She crawled through the smoke and could make out Gottfried and Conversano. He was holding the horse by the halter and pleading with him.

"Capriole, *schnell!*" commanded Gottfried, standing upright alongside the horse despite the smoke.

The magnificent white stallion, huge black eyes ringed white with fear, nevertheless obeyed the command of his master. He lifted his front legs and jumped up, kicking out with his hind legs with huge force. His hooves crashed into the wooden door, beginning to splinter it. Sarah had seen pictures of the horses doing this move, but kicking out into the air, never against something. The horse, in pain from the impact, fell to his knees, sweaty and trembling with fatigue and fear.

"Again, Conversano, again," pleaded Gottfried. Sarah did not think the horse had it in him, but he groaned with effort, got to his feet.

"Again," said Gottfried, laying a hand against the horse's cheek. "Courage, my boy. Think of what you come from, not what you have become." The horse gathered himself and kicked out again. Sarah thought of fourteenth-century knights' horses, equine battering rams knocking down the gates of castles, and anyone standing behind them.

Crash! The wood was splintering.

She could feel the heat of the fire and hear its crackling. The horses were screaming. The smell of singed flesh and hair filled her nostrils. The bedding in the stalls was igniting from the flying sparks. They did not have much time before the entire place exploded in flames.

Sarah was struggling to breathe. Gottfried's face was streaked with black. He stamped out a spark that landed in the straw at their feet.

"Again, Conversano. Capriole," he commanded the animal. She saw Conversano's hind legs were bloody from kicking the wood. He looked finished. She met Gottfried's eye. He shook his head. Done.

No. She was not done fighting. Pollina wasn't done fighting. They were getting out of here.

She threw her arms around the horse's face. "Fight," she whispered into his ear.

With a huge effort, the horse leapt into the air and—*BAM!*— hit the door again with the full force of his entire fifteen-hundred-pound body, channeled through the springs of his hind legs into his massive hooves. The door splintered to pieces, and Sarah could feel the rush of fresh air. She stumbled out, gasping, as firemen came streaming under the arched entrance across the courtyard.

"Take him!" shouted Gottfried, tossing her Conversano's lead rope. Before she could cough out a word, Gottfried disappeared back into the flames.

Sarah led the bloodied and trembling horse away from the fire as the firemen hauled in hoses and shouted orders. She whispered to Conversano to keep walking, trying not to hear the screams of the other horses. Traffic was stopped in the street outside and tourists were being herded back, wide-eyed. The air was filled with smoke, and sirens sounded on all sides. Through these she heard a clattering, and when she looked back toward the Spanish Riding School, out of the smoke came galloping ghostly forms, giant white horses streaked with ash. Six, seven, eight, ten, she counted them as they churned around Conversano, majestic, panicked, terrifying, like the horses from a marble fountain come to life. People in the square screamed and ran from the frenzied horses, and cart horses on the far side of the square reared in their traces, hearing the primal call of the stallions.

A final horse galloped out of the smoke, and Sarah saw there was a rider atop him, no saddle or bridle, his bearing erect like a charging knight.

Gottfried had a bullwhip in one hand, and he cracked it to bring the stallions in line, circling his own mount with pressure from his legs, keeping the stallions in a smaller and smaller space until they came to a halt in a writhing mass of horseflesh.

In his other hand Gottfried held her purse. Her white bra, which she had not redonned in all the commotion, dangled jauntily, half out of the opening.

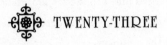 TWENTY-THREE

"The newspapers say it was faulty electrical wiring."

The morning after the fire, Sarah and Nico had made their way past Schmetterling, the vast steampunk greenhouse that housed, of all things, butterflies, and through the Hofburg complex to check out the damage to the stables.

"So much for German engineering," said Nico.

Sarah felt a moment of relief. In the confused hours after the fire, when she had found herself once more giving statements to the police, she had dazedly wondered if somehow the source of the blaze hadn't come from the heat off of her quite smoking encounter with Gottfried. She had left that part out of her statement, though. She had been taken to the hospital, and then gone back to Alessandro's apartment. At some point, she had lost track of Gottfried.

"Do not worry. I will find who did this," Gottfried had said in the square in front of Michaelerkirche. "They will be punished."

Standing now, surveying the damage, Sarah wondered if a team of engineers were currently being horsewhipped.

The stables were taped off, and police and firemen were still positioned outside the building. There was quite a crowd, taking pictures. Some people had brought flowers, though, miraculously, all the horses had been saved. Sarah read how they had been safely removed in trucks, taken to the stud farm at Piber.

"I don't like it," said Nico. "The game is no longer a game. This is twice that your life has been threatened." While Sarah was at the stables, Nico had conducted his own investigation. The little man had visited Bettina's apartment on Paniglgasse and thoroughly ingratiated himself with the concierge, Herr Dorfmeister. "I stayed away from the dog," Nico had said. "Dogs are uneasy around me. But we began a game of chess. I did not learn anything about your elusive doctor, but I have procured the key to her apartment. Should you care to make a visit."

"I want to take Westonia at Bettina's lab," Sarah said. "That seems more like the scene of the action. But first I want to see if there's anything at the Austrian National Library about the galleon and Philippine Welser. Now you've got me curious about her."

"Worth a try," Nico said as they turned back to the massive Hofburg complex and made their way to the library.

Sarah paused for a moment at the entrance to the *Prunksaal*, which was truly breathtaking, with its marble floor, wood paneling, frescoed ceiling, carved balconies, rolling ladders, huge gilded columns, and dizzying heights of books.

"There are three million printed manuscripts here," said Nico. "Not to mention one hundred and eighty thousand Egyptian papyri covering three thousand years of history. Let us hope they have a better smoke detection system than the stable. And that even Moriarty couldn't sift through that much data."

Disappointingly, there wasn't much at all about Philippine Welser. Sarah chalked it up to the fact that women, even remarkable women, perhaps especially remarkable women, hadn't rated much mention in the archives of history as chronicled by men. Nico had more sinister theories regarding Philippine's absence from the public record. Sarah did find some brief asides. Birth and death dates for the sons of her morganatic marriage to Ferdinand, one of whom became a cardinal. Descriptions of her extended family's vast holdings.

"Did you know Philippine's uncle went to South America?" Sarah called over to Nico, who seemed deep in his own search.

"Yes, her family were wealthy merchants. Her uncle lent a large sum to the emperor and in return was given Venezuela."

"Venezuela? Like, all of it?"

"Yes. In fact, the Welsers were the ones who named it, for 'little Venice.' They had many encounters with native tribesmen."

Sarah pondered this as she looked around the hushed roomful of people lost in ancient books, librarians hovering like priests. Philippine was wealthy, educated, interested in medicine, highly empowered for a woman of her era, and possibly in possession of medicinal plants from South America. No wonder she had hallucinogens up her sleeves. Very interesting.

"'*De re coquinaria*,'" Sarah said, reading the catalog entry. "'Handwriting. Over two hundred recipes and medical cures of the wife of the Archduke of Tyrol. 1545.'"

"That's the book the von Hohenlohes have," said Nico. "Anything about the galleon?"

"Nothing," said Sarah. "You don't think—no, never mind."

"Out with it."

"That Philippine Welser is involved in this? Personally, I mean. That you're not the only immortal. That *she* is your . . . Moriarty?" The moment it was out of her mouth, Sarah regretted it. Her skepticism was the only thing keeping her together right now. There was no time to go off the deep end into Fleeceville.

"My suspicions have been centered around Edward Kelley. I don't think it's Philippine. By all accounts, her interest was in healing the sick. She wasn't interested in manipulating alchemy for purposes of power. That's rather a guy thing, I suppose."

"Not always. Anyway, what *are* you looking at?"

"Rudolf's papers," said Nico, "which are numerous, despite the Swedish hordes scattering them on the four winds. One always likes to take a look, in case something's been overlooked. Why, just last year in the Bodleian some first-year chappie found a forgotten diary of Serafina, underparlormaid to the 4th Duke of Devonshire. I must say, I had some very toasty evenings with that wee lassie...." Sarah looked over his shoulder as he scrolled through the list. There were certainly plenty of interesting things: a book of herbals in French from 1573 with Rudolf's margin notes; an English volume in Latin inscribed to Rudy, which she would guess was a gift from John Dee; and a Styrian alchemical manuscript from 1584 by Johannes Erici.

"Who the bloody hell is that?" Nico mumbled.

Sarah frowned. "The notation in the catalog says he was an assistant to Tycho Brahe."

"Never heard of him. Tycho had a cousin named Eric, bit of a boozehound that one, and then there was Eric Lange, most amusing, loved answering the door in his wife's gowns, but neither of them ever wrote a book."

Sarah went to the call desk and filled out a form to request the volume. She had to leave her passport and sign a piece of paper in triplicate agreeing to the archive rules, which included a promise not to "kindle any fire within the Library," which Sarah tried not to take personally. She signed, and the librarian eventually returned with a cardboard archival box.

"When you are finished you will kindly return this to the desk and at that point your documents will be returned to you. No pens." He gave a curious glance at Nico.

"My assistant," said Sarah.

"Your slave," whispered Nico as the librarian retreated. "Although apparently you don't need me anymore, now that you have Alessandro Muscle-lini and the Gottfried von Heimlich Maneuver. They're like the new Axis powers."

Sarah ignored this and opened the box, whose spine was marked with an old inked number and the words *Die Alchemie. Johann. EW Erici. 1584. Rudolph ii-Sammlung.*

Inside was not a book, but another box. Sarah leaned forward to read the tiny black handwriting on the older archival box. *The Curious historie and awfull magick of the ancient and wonderfull golden fleece.*

"I suppose it would be too much to ask," Nico said, sighing, "that this would be the actual Golden Fleece? We could call it a day and go get some Sacher torte."

"I'm not after the Fleece." Sarah felt like slinging the box across the library.

"You don't think secrets of life and death could be helpful to Pols?"

They stared at the box for a moment.

"Well, no shimmering powerful aura of the ultimate keys to the universe and whatnot. So I'm thinking it's not the Fleece." Sarah tugged her turtleneck sweater up until the fabric was covering her mouth and nose. "But I'm not taking any chances," she explained. "In case some kind of mystical powder poofs out at me."

"You've gotten so conservative," Nicolas complained.

Sarah opened the lid, and together they peered inside.

A simple card. "'Removed for curatorial purposes,'" Sarah read.

"Bugger *me*," said Nico.

"What does it mean?"

"It means it's time to take the drug. You said you were ready for the witchcraft."

"Bring it *on*," said Sarah.

⚜

Gottfried stood in Frau Müller's apartment. It was the day of the concierge's weekly tennis game. The old man was very vigorous. A good Austrian.

Heinrich had come to him this morning and said that the most crucial information from the doctor's research was still missing. Everything on the laptop had been sorted through by the drug company's scientists, men whom Gottfried pictured as having spectacles and doughy girl hands. Heinrich's "superiors" were excited but not satisfied. There had to be more information. A flash drive, a disc, an iPad. Handwritten notes. They couldn't say what, wouldn't give details. Something.

Gottfried took a deep breath. It was unclear when he would have unfettered access to this apartment again. He needed to move quickly. He had not told Heinrich that Sarah had been asking questions about him, but he was uneasy.

Sarah. Sarah was . . .

Even during the fire she had not been too afraid to act. Gottfried wasn't used to other people being that way, just himself.

Help, Defend, Heal.

Sarah had a sick friend, that was why she wanted Bettina's research. Her motives were pure.

He had not eaten today. He had maybe not eaten yesterday. The horses were safe, but his head was hurting. He did not feel well. He did not have much time.

Gottfried faulted himself later for not having heard the

apartment door open, not heard the footsteps behind him. How could he have missed that? He had been so caught up in searching without leaving a trace that the old man was standing right behind him before he realized it.

"Excuse me, do I know you?"

Gottfried stood and gave a polite bow.

"Yes. I am a friend of Frau Doktor Müller."

"Frau Doktor Müller is away."

"Yes, she asked me to stop by. To check on things."

"Why are you searching through Doktor Müller's possessions? Excuse me. I will have to call Doktor Müller now."

The old man began backing out of the apartment. He was afraid.

Gottfried would have to act. There was not much time. He must not think. He must act.

The Tenth Muse

· THE TRUE STORY OF ·

Elizabeth Jane Weston, Poet

———✦———

by

Harriet Hunter, PhD

CHAPTER FOUR

~~~

In which I discuss what I have been up to for the past four hundred years.

Si meruit mortem, quid vita in corpore languet?
Si non, morte gravi cur graviora fero?
AEqua sunt poenae and crimen pendenda bilance?
Haec non, vulneribus fortius illud erit.

Hey, if I was meant to die, wouldn't I have kicked it by now?
Wouldn't death be easier than some of the crap I've put up
  with?
Who came up with the idea that 'you get what you deserve'?
I've gotten seriously shafted, and no mistake.

I, Elizabeth Weston, wrote those lines. Without spell-check or a compubrain that does your taxes and watches your weight and reminds you when to wipe your arse. I wrote those lines using nothing but a quill pen, a pot of ink, and a piece of vellum that I hersed, scraped, pumiced, and limed myself from a calf named Mitzi. (You think you know suffering? What about life before dishwashers? Washing machines? Tampons? Vacuum cleaners? You have no idea. No idea!)

I wrote those lines before I knew what had been done to me.

But maybe I had always known.

As I've said, I had received the best education possible and I could speak the languages of many countries, and the language of math, of the spheres, of biology and chemistry as it was understood then. Of course, my understanding has changed over the years, the decades, the centuries. The language of alchemy has been dismissed and discredited, then picked up in egregious form and perverted beyond recognition. Geneticists, nanobiologists—nothing new under the sun! Philippine Welser lacked the proper equipment to develop her talent, but the ideas were all there. The desires behind alchemy are still with us. In us. The union of two into one. To change one thing into another. To understand the stars, and the stars in ourselves.

I have never stopped loving God. Each year God has become more perfect in my memory, more cherished. My old quarrels with God, the pain and anger I once felt, those have long vanished. God and I are One now. I might as well hate myself as hate God.

What had been done to me was the work of man—of one man—but I did come to understand that I was chosen for special work. I'll get to that—be patient, it's quite delicious. Let me stress that in the meantime I have felt God's presence even in the worst of times.

When were the worst of times?

Well, the Reign of Terror was no picnic.

What would have happened if they had taken my head in Paris, as they did Charlotte Corday's? Would my body have simply risen from the guillotine and stood upright, decapitated, and walked through the screaming mass of people? Would I have then become a kind of monster, a headless horsewoman? Or would my head have plunked into the waiting sack, and when tossed in some hole set about quietly regenerating a body, like a starfish with a severed limb? Both extremely fascinating possibilities.

In 1794—one of the greatest years of terror in the Great Terror—I had been alive for two hundred years and had become adept at managing things. As well as a woman could in those days, which involved trickery on a scale that was exhausting.

Through much of the late seventeenth century I had stayed hidden, in convents, where a surprising amount of thinking and experimenting could be done. Indeed, a convent was a kind of early think tank for women, since it was the preferred choice of intellectuals wanting to escape marriage. The food and the accommodations were less than five star—oh, the gruel that I have known—but the clothing was convenient. And although I had some very tempting opportunities, I did not indulge in any same-sex relationships during those years. I was not banging Hildegard in Bingen. I was a very private person, for obvious reasons. I couldn't hide my age—or rather my lack of aging—for very long. Women are particularly observant of such things—you have no idea how many times I've been asked what my beauty secret is. Before Botox, I had to keep moving.

I did not seek love, or even affection, beyond the sustaining memory of my Portia, and I tried to keep marriage as a last resort, for the most desperate times only. But in 1747 I seized at what seemed like a golden opportunity. Charles was a homosexual, so he had no interest in forcing himself upon me. And he was an amateur botanist, so he had lab space in his castle in northern Ireland. He assured me that I would be able to continue my work, and in return my presence would provide certain protection for him and get his mother off his back. It was ideal. I could continue my work, and I would not be touched, nor forced to bear a child that would be born damaged.

Twenty years, that time. Twenty years of being able to work without interruption. I had long given up poetry in favor of pure scientific research.

And I had abandoned the quest for my stepfather's book. What was my stepfather capable of that I was not? Had I not been the greatest poet of my age? Had I not been chosen to actually not have an age, but for *all* ages to be mine? Why should I not be as great an alchemist as any of them? There had to be more than one way to Fleece a sheep.

Why could I not raise the dead?

Yes, that was my plan. To raise the dead.

A good one, yes?

I had to prepare for complications. How to make the undead stay undead, for one. Suffice it to say, I had things to learn. And experiments to carry out. And I had to be ruthless in my pursuit.

I made great strides that last year before Charles died and the accusations of murder and witchcraft ran me out of Ireland.

Earlier in the century I had trusted the wrong person in England with my money (despite the lessons of Tulip Mania the cretin *still* fell for the South Sea Bubble) and my finances were rocky. To complicate my situation I then . . . miscalculated during a brief stay in Scotland (Loch Ness gained one additional monster) and another hasty departure was necessary. I went to Austria, and that was where I met Franz Anton Mesmer.

Mesmer. I knew him for what he was, instantly. He was like my stepfather, Edward Kelley. Not in looks, for Mesmer had both his ears, and Kelley neither, thanks to a razor-sharp brush with the law. But like my stepfather, Mesmer was a man who had discovered something and knew that he had, but had not been able to understand the very thing he had uncovered. It was making him insane, like it had my stepfather, because their madness was so close to truth. It was the other side of the coin.

Mesmer believed that the body, like the heavens, was bound by an invisible, electric substance. And that this substance could be balanced using music. He believed in a harmonic spectrum of the body, the music of the spheres. Human beings could be tuned, but it took a Master Tuner. People thought he was a charlatan, but I immediately grasped the potential power of what he had stumbled upon. Right before the long-sought answer to a problem emerges from the tangle of my waking dreams, I often feel an intense physical vibration. I felt this in Mesmer's presence. I felt it when I saw him cure a young girl of an infectious lung disease. Mesmer always insisted that his cures would only work on conditions of the nervous system, but I began to see the ways in which the nervous system could be brought to bear upon all injury, all disease. Even, perhaps, upon the dead.

I got Mesmer to take me on as a patient.

"Tell me of your family," Mesmer asked, in our first interview. "You have a husband? Children?"

"I have loneliness," I told him.

"Ah." He nodded. "And how does this loneliness manifest itself? Headaches? Nausea? Nervousness? Fainting spells? Dizziness? Pain in your joints? Fever?"

"Regret," I said. "It is an acid in my veins."

Eventually I became his assistant, though he was quite paranoid and proprietorial of his methods. I learned to play his glass armonica, a series of glass plates on a spindle with a foot pedal to set them spinning. I even suggested some improvements for its design. Mesmer didn't like that I played it so well. He accused me of sabotage, of stealing his secrets. This was a lie, though I did eventually steal his armonica. But he was long dead by that point, and it was just sitting in a museum in Vienna. Sometimes I think of him and play a little tune from "Annie Get Your Gun" on it in his honor: "Anything you can do—I can do better." There, my dirty secret is out. I love show tunes.

Mesmer understood electricity and its role in the human body, and as I had come to see it, electricity must be the key to reanimation. (I mentioned this idea to Mary Shelley and she ran with it.) I learned a great deal from Mesmer before he was driven out of Vienna.

I went to France, too, but I felt I had milked the Mesmer cow dry and turned my mind in other directions. I had been in correspondence with Marie-Anne-Pierrette Paulze, wife and laboratory assistant of Antoine Lavoisier, the celebrated chemist. A smashing good *paille-maille* player, Marie was—the game that took the world by storm as "croquet." The Serena Williams of her age. We passed many a happy hour. I helped her translate English documents to French, and vice versa, and worked with Lavoisier on the element nitrogen, even suggesting to him the name for it—"azote" or "lifeless" in Greek. Then came the Terror, and Lavoisier's death. I went to Denmark.

The days, years, decades marched on. I moved from place to place, creating identities and then burning them as people began asking too many questions. I set up laboratories or worked in the laboratories of others. Mostly, of course, I had to work on animals. But opportunities did arise.

I made some important breakthroughs during World War II.

More decades passed. Science made huge leaps forward, and so did I. It became easier to work as a woman alone, to order the necessary equipment. I reached out to other women scientists from all nations and fields of knowledge—history, philosophy, astronomy, genetics, physics. I began to see possibilities beyond what I had imagined before. I do believe I have come full circle.

*F*or this last stage it became necessary to employ an assistant for a specific task that I could not do myself. I went through a couple of interns before I got to Harriet, who has many qualities that make her particularly fit for the task and who has ~~more or less kept it together throughout our association. I do not consider her addiction to be entirely my fault. Her mother is evidently quite the souse. These things are hereditary.~~ been a great help to me and is a brilliant mind in her own right.

I do hope her novel is successful. It will be lovely to see my early work in the literary arts restored to fame. Perhaps some heartsick teen will sing one of my poems on YouTube and I will go viral.

But, darlings, trust me. You ain't seen nothing yet.

 TWENTY-FOUR

"The lab will be locked," Sarah said to Nico on the way over. Their taxi passed operagoers massing in front of the Staatsoper for a production of *Die Fledermaus*.

"Please do not insult me," Nico sniffed.

Sarah didn't bother to hide her excitement from Nico. There was always a risk in taking Westonia, but she had gone as far as she could using other means and things had only gotten more confusing. On Westonia she would see who took Bettina's laptop and—with luck—where it had ended up. Then it was just a matter of getting her hands on it and delivering it to Bettina. The last obstacle would be removed. Bettina would not be able to put off helping Pols anymore. No more excuses.

But beyond all that was the anticipatory thrill of taking Westonia. The drug was the ultimate rush. Who knows what she might encounter if . . .

No. She would stay very focused. No looking out the window and trying to find Beethoven. It was time to get high and then get out of town.

At the lab, Sarah stood lookout while Nico removed a toolkit from a very beautiful brown leather satchel. "Bespoke," said the little man, patting the bag fondly, "and still in good condition despite its age and the fact that I once had to wrestle it away from a lunatic camel in Morocco. My relations with the animal kingdom in general, it must be said, have not been easy."

He had the door open in about three seconds.

Someone else must be taking care of the rats, Sarah thought. The brown specimens were all still in their cages (minus the one that had gone kaput during her last visit) and the place was clean and orderly.

"Okay." Sarah rolled up her sleeves literally and metaphorically. "I don't want to go back hundreds of years. Specifically, I'd really like to avoid a plague."

Nico produced the pill from his pocket and placed it on the table between them.

"You displayed remarkable control the last time," he said. "Just remember that this is not time traveling. You are expanding your awareness. So think of what you want to be conscious of—think of Bettina and the laptop—and move slowly. Please remember that if you start running I will not be able to keep up with you, and that without me the likelihood that you will run into traffic or into a wall or hurt yourself is very high. Remember Sherbatsky."

As if she could forget. She had seen her beloved mentor Absalom Sherbatsky on Westonia walk out a window to his death.

"And I know your Latin is horrible," Nicolas continued, "but you are familiar with the phrase 'quid pro quo'?"

"We want the same thing," Sarah said. "We want a cure for Pols."

"Perhaps we need a leash," Nico fretted, turning away to lock the door.

Sarah picked up the pill and bit it in half. She put the remainder in her pocket.

Hold on, Pols. I'm going to figure this out.

She was plunged—almost instantly—from the relatively calm sounds and sights of Bettina's rats hanging out in their cages to the sight of the siege of Vienna by Turkish invaders, which had apparently involved a lot of rape along with the usual screaming and blood and hacking of limbs. The vertigo was intense and she appeared to be floating. Sarah tried to get out of the lab, found the door locked, and managed to rip the doorknob off the door, a feat of strength that pleased her immensely, before Nicolas tackled her to the ground. He actually sat on her chest. She could see him, through a thick veil of smoke. Vienna was burning.

Max. Where was Max? He had kept her sane on Westonia, he had helped her. Nico was just muttering, "Don't scream, don't scream," over and over and pestering her to describe what she saw and she didn't want to. Max had told her once to find the music, hadn't he? Music. That was what kept you sane. Sarah shut her eyes and listened and then she found it. A series of single notes, played over and over. They sounded so familiar, and so peaceful, a ringing on glass, a frequency that made her feel calm.

When she opened her eyes, there was Mesmer, in a violet frock coat, sitting at an armonica. Bettina's lab was now a room filled with wooden pews like she had seen Marie-Franz teach in. Mesmer was surrounded by a group of men in powdered wigs.

"This is what I played," said Mesmer. "To bring her through the crisis. And then I removed the last wrapping from around her eyes. I stood before her and bade her look upon me. Her first remark was, 'That is horrid. Can that be a figure of a man?'"

The remark was met with general laughter, and Sarah laughed, too, shoving Nico off her and standing up. "It's okay!" Sarah shouted. "It's Mesmer. I think he's describing how he cured Maria Theresia von Paradies of her blindness."

Nico started to speak, but Sarah shushed him.

"My dog Anselmo was brought before her at her request," continued Mesmer to the circle of gentlemen. "And she said, 'The dog pleases me better than the man. His looks are far more agreeable!'"

This, too, was met with laughter, but Sarah saw that Mesmer hadn't really intended this as a funny tale. He was intent, elated. He was offering proof of his cures. Sarah had read about Mesmer's cure of Maria Theresia a few days earlier, after she had heard Marie-Franz's lecture.

Maria Theresia had been blind since she was four years old. Every doctor had been consulted, and no expense had been spared. The girl's father was a courtier at the court of Empress Maria Theresia, and the empress had taken a special interest in her namesake, who despite her blindness was a remarkably gifted pianist. After trying everything—which included bleeding and thousands of applications of the eighteenth-century version of electric shock therapy (Leyden jars and wires)—the girl's parents had brought her to Mesmer. He had taken one look at the spastic eye rolling (and probably another long look at the equally spastic, quarreling, and melodramatic parents) and insisted that the girl live in his home while he supervised her care.

Nico was just not getting how completely fascinating and extremely relevant all this was. He kept going on about laptops! Which, sure, a part of her understood was vaguely interesting, but she wasn't sure why. The people around Mesmer were leaving now, although one younger man remained. Mesmer was packing up his armonica.

"Maria finds noses very amusing," Mesmer was saying to his colleague. "She has a beautiful laugh."

"Herr Doktor, I must warn you," the younger man was whispering, "there are rumors circulating . . . the girl's father . . ."

"He is worried that the empress will no longer favor Maria," Mesmer cut in. "And he will lose the stipend she has been giving him for his daughter. And the mother is a hysteric. Those two are the source of her blindness. They and the doctors that have been torturing her."

"But the girl has been examined by the committee," the younger man said. "And they did not find the results conclusive."

"They were asking the wrong questions!" Mesmer exploded. "Asking her to name objects. Of course she was confused! Names are difficult for her still. She cannot reconcile what she is seeing with what she was feeling before. The names of colors—she has to relearn this. Even perspective. Yesterday we walked in the garden and she thought the rose trees were walking along with us, and the house was moving forward to greet us, rather than us approaching it."

"But she cannot play," the companion insisted. "It is this that worries the father."

"It worries her, too." Mesmer stopped and fingered the small pouch that hung from a cord at his throat. "This is the crisis that we must push past. She is melancholy from the new sensations. The sight of her hands on the keyboard confuses her. She told me she was more peaceful in her mind when she was sightless, but I have told her over and over again that the music will return. It is simply too much knowledge all at once. We are limiting her exposure now. All shall be well."

"Vienna is talking—"

"Vienna is always talking. You cannot hear the birds for all the gossip."

"They say you have personal reasons for keeping the girl. That you . . . that you and she—"

"Personal!" Mesmer exploded. "What I do, I do for science!"

"*Sarah!*" Nico was shouting. "*Pollina!*"

Pollina. What she was doing, she was doing for Pollina. That was why Mesmer was important. Why didn't Nico understand that? Oh. *Laptop.* Yes. There was something else.

"Bettina Müller!" Nico shouted.

Sarah turned her back on Mesmer and took a deep breath. Bettina Müller. Laptop. Twenty-first century. Lab. She could do this.

"And how are you, Hermes? You're looking very fit!"

Sarah turned to see Bettina Müller tap on the cage of Specimen #134. She was here. She had found her.

But it was hard to know *when* exactly the action she was watching had taken place. She had only seen Doktor Müller for a few seconds at the ball. Her hair was the same—heavy bangs and a severe pageboy—though now she wasn't wearing her thick glasses or the bright lipstick and rouge. She looked younger. Had she come too far back?

And then Bettina took her hair . . . off.

"Didn't see that coming," Sarah muttered as Bettina tossed the pageboy on her desk. The doctor's own hair was sparse and very blond, almost white. It didn't look like a buzz cut—more like premature hair loss, or perhaps the result of chemotherapy? Bettina opened the cage of Specimen #134. The rat slunk to the back of the cage and made squeaking noises, vibrating its tail.

"Don't be like that," Bettina cooed. "After all I've done for you? You have more gold in you than your average rapper. Show a little gratitude. And don't even think of biting me or I will remove your teeth."

The rat rolled over on its back, its paws curling and jaws open.

Bettina laughed. "Oh, so we're playing dead now? I know that trick. Come on." She held up a tiny harness. "Suit up, Hermes. It's showtime."

"Sarah, what are you seeing?" Nico pulled on her hand.

"Bettina is bald and she's trained her rats to submit to blood samples."

Hermes rolled over and reluctantly climbed into his harness and Bettina inserted him into a kind of trap on one of the lab tables that kept him immobile while she stuck a tiny needle into him. After this, the rat hung limply, but his eyes, Sarah could see, followed Bettina's every movement.

The doctor put the sample onto a glass slide under a microscope and began humming and then singing softly to herself.

"She's also a terrible singer," Sarah said. Hermes seemed to agree. He was twitching miserably in his harness. Bettina flipped open her laptop (*there* it was!) and began typing something rapidly. Sarah looked over her shoulder, but could make no sense of the data. Numbers, percentages.

Hermes squeaked loudly.

"Oh, shut up!" Bettina snapped at him. "You would have been dead of a nasty little autoimmune disease years ago if it hadn't been for me. And now you'll live forever. I could literally cut your head off and you'd probably just crawl around headless for eternity. Actually . . ." She smiled at the rat, who went very still.

"Nico," Sarah said softly, "this isn't . . . this isn't good." Bettina was singing again. Sarah recognized the tune now. It was from Leoš Janáček's opera *The Makropulos Affair*. An opera about, among other things, a singer who was granted immortality because of an alchemical experiment during the time of Rudolf II. Sarah had never seen the opera, but she remembered Sherbatsky playing it in class, and telling her about a famous production at the Met in 1996, when the tenor had suffered a heart attack while climbing a ladder onstage and had fallen to his death after singing the line, "Too bad you can only live so long."

Sarah was very close to either passing out or puking. Bettina didn't have a cure for Pols; she had a cure for death. And Bettina—she could see it in her face—was as twisted as a strand of DNA, as full of dark matter as the universe. Sarah had been played, and played well. If Bettina wasn't Moriarty—and she very well might be—she was definitely a modern-day alchemist, binding telomeres with gold. The alchemists had always been looking for a way to turn base metal into gold, and had sought the Elixir of Life. It had taken a couple hundred years for the techniques of science to catch up with intuition and speculation, Sarah thought, looking at the rat in his harness, but it had been done.

No more death.

Even if she could get her hands on this research, she wouldn't be bringing Pollina a cure, she'd be bringing her a curse.

She had failed.

"Sarah, talk to me."

But Bettina was putting the rat into a pet carrier now and rinsing out her slides. She flicked the computer off and, grabbing the bag with Hermes in it, left the lab.

"Bettina. We have to follow her," Sarah said dully. "Come on."

But once on the street, things got confusing again rapidly. Sarah was witness to a horrifying scene of a man being bludgeoned to death. At first she thought she had stumbled into the twentieth century, as the man was being taunted for being a Jew and she saw a yellow emblem on his frayed coat, but then she realized that it was a yellow circle, not a star, and from the clothing she guessed she was somewhere in the sixteenth century.

"Help me, Nico," Sarah whispered. "Touch me. Sing something. Anything." Sarah turned and realized that she was looking at two versions of the little man. They were not entirely identical. Nico I looked a little older—more weathered maybe—and was wearing a camel hair coat. Nico II was wearing a thick cloak.

"Sarah, what are you seeing?" She could feel his hand in hers.

"Two of you. Nicos. Nicii. What are you doing? Why are you so anxious?"

"Probably because I was depressed. The Age of Enlightenment was very groovy, darling, but mostly I just wanted to die. Where is Bettina now?"

Sarah's mind shifted. There was that. Both of the little men standing in front of her wanted the same thing, wanted it passionately, desperately. She was almost knocked off her feet by their collective yearning. They wanted to die. They wanted to die so very badly.

Nico had not been honest with her. He wanted to help Pollina, yes. But he wanted something more than that. Quid pro quo. Life for Pollina. Death for Nico.

She could see Bettina now, walking ahead of her with the pet carrier, and Sarah followed but she could feel Westonia loosening its fingers on her brain. It was like she was wearing bifocals. Look one way and she was passing a Starbucks. Look another and she jerked to avoid being stepped on by Franz Joseph's processional. She caught sight of a wan Sissi in a carriage, then streets filled with smoke and fire and the heavy sounds of bombing and explosions. Vienna was smoldering, dying, paying the price for its splendor and its poison. In one moment she was walking on the Ringstrasse, then seeing the Ring being built, then seeing it bombed, then seeing it built again. "It shouldn't look the same, but it does," she muttered. Nico II pulled the hood of his cloak up around his face and retreated into a crowd.

"History repeats," Nico said, pulling her by the hand. "Vienna may burn again. Mozart may live again. I can't go through it all, over and over. Sarah, please. You have to keep going."

Pollina. Pollina could be Mozart if she was given the time. Ashes to ashes, gold to gold.

Bettina was getting on a tram. Sarah felt her triumph, her purpose, and her intensity. She was glowing with it.

"A tram." She pointed.

"Yes. There's a tram coming."

The ride was a nightmare, since the two trams were not in sync. Bettina's tram was about ten seconds' worth of distance ahead of the one Sarah and Nico were on, and Sarah kept lurching forward and being dragged back by Nico. She watched a little girl sitting next to Bettina peer inside the carrier and say loudly, *"Oh! Es ist eine Ratte!"*

Bettina smiled beautifully at the little girl.

"Isn't he handsome?" she said. She stood up. They were at the Karlsplatz station.

"I'm exhausted," Sarah said to Nico. "I want to sit down. I don't want to do this anymore."

"Magnify that times four hundred years," Nico said, "and you'll get a glimpse of what I feel. Keep moving."

Sarah trudged alongside Nico, bumping into people. The Westonia was definitely fading now, possibly because she was just too tired to see anymore. When they turned onto Paniglgasse, Bettina vanished entirely.

"She must have taken it home," Sarah said.

"Taken what home?"

Sarah looked down at the little man.

"An immortal rat."

TWENTY-FIVE

Pollina woke up coughing.

She could hear Boris by the side of the bed. At her own apartment in Paris Street, she had instructed Jose to move her mattress to the floor, because her bed was too high for Boris to get on and off easily. And Boris was too heavy for her to lift. She would have joined him on the floor here in one of the palace's guest bedrooms, but in strange places Boris liked to sleep separately from her, in order to guard the door.

Her coughing worried him. He whined and paced if it went on too long.

Sometimes the coughing went on for a very long time. This bout was not bad, although her chest hurt. Her chest hurt all the time now, even when she wasn't coughing, and she was tired all the time. She was not sleeping well, because of her dreams, and so she was always tired. Her dreams were very bad.

Moving to the palace was a relief. Here, she could just walk thirty-five paces down the hall and then down a flight of ten stairs, step-step-step, half-turn, twelve stairs, step-step, right turn, then forty-four paces to the music room. She could do all that and still have energy to play. To compose. Max was helping her with the libretto for her opera about the Golden Fleece, reading her things he'd found about Ferdinand and Philippine. It made a perfect story for the opera. Ferdinand was curious and intelligent and in love, and Pols thought he sounded a lot like Max.

Pollina felt for her Braille clock, although she knew that it was evening. Time to get up for a little while, play a bit before going back to bed. Her brain registered the difference between day and night nonvisually; her body operated on the same circadian entrainment as sighted people. Her retinohypothalamic tract functioned. The same was true, Sarah had told her, for mole rats, who were also blind, and whose bodies also followed circadian entrainment. Blind rats had body clocks, too.

Sarah knew interesting things like that.

There had been a rat again, in her dream. And clocks. She had been dreaming of the rat for several days. She had read once that Helen Keller had described the dreams she'd had before acquiring language as being pure sensation, and the sensation was only fear. Later on, the dreams had shifted into narratives. Helen had described a recurring dream of a wolf biting her, an image Helen believed she had learned and adapted from the story of Little Red Riding Hood.

"When you dream," Jose had asked Pollina once, "how does it . . . what do you . . ."

"Are you asking if I see in my dreams?" she had snapped. "I don't see when I'm awake. How could I see in my dreams?"

"So what you dream?" Jose had asked. "Answer with not so much of the bitchiness, please."

"Sound," Pollina had explained. "It's sound and sensation, but mostly sound."

But this dream had been totally silent. And Sarah was in it.

Yes, she would get up and practice a little. She had not been able to practice very much earlier, because she had been so tired, and her chest hurt so much, and also she had had to go with Oksana to the hospital for more tests.

There was something wrong with chromosome 20 in her DNA. It should have been coding for a certain kind of protein that would cause bacteria to adhere to it and therefore be flushed out of her bloodstream. It was not doing this. And so the bacteria were proliferating, and that was why she kept getting infections, like pneumonia. They were going to start her on a new drug the next day. Oksana seemed hopeful about it.

But what if the defect in chromosome 20 had something to do with her blindness? There was a certain rare form of blindness that was being cured through gene therapy. Pols did not have this form, but more than 160 genes were linked to blindness. So really anything could happen with these drugs. And if the two symptoms *were* linked, then along with taking away the infections and the pain, they would take away the blindness.

And she knew she would lose the music if that happened. It was a greater fear than death.

If she was dying, she would accept it.

"If she doesn't improve, then we could be heading toward organ failure," she had heard. "We will have to watch how she reacts to this new treatment very closely. It is a risk, but we're really running out of options. If we don't try, then realistically she has maybe two months. Maybe."

They had not told her. But she had heard.

Different types of listening employed different parts of your brain. Sarah had explained this. The most complicated process was one neuroscientists called a "top-down" response. This was when you were actively listening to something. When you really concentrated on sound, signals were sent a special way in the brain. They moved through the dorsal pathway in the cortex, and the brain suppressed other sounds, like a set of headphones, so that you could concentrate.

She had heard Oksana. She had heard her doctors.

She was going to die very soon.

The treatment was not going to work.

She hoped that she didn't die before Boris did. She wouldn't want him to think it was his fault.

She should work. She was composing an aria for Philippine, in which she warns Ferdinand about the power of the Fleece. It would be horrible, though, to try to play and not be able to, because she could not lift her arms and because her chest hurt too much. She should not be afraid. If God wanted her to play, He would give her the strength. She would ask for His help.

Slippers. Robe. Cane.

Boris got stiffly to his feet. He did not really want to walk anywhere, but he would walk with her wherever she went. He would drag himself, if he had to.

When she turned right, outside her door, she could feel Boris understanding where they were going. His pace picked up a little, in the hallway leading to the music room. Pols could hear Moritz, Max's dog. Max must be near, then. She heard a series of notes on the piano. C2. E3. D4. The lid was down. Max was playing her piano.

Pollina entered the room and greeted Moritz. She had been told that Moritz "looked" like a wolf. It was funny how some people forgot and told her how things looked. Moritz had triangle ears that stood up, and forefeet that turned out slightly. He had a flat chest, and his back was a little sloped, so his hind legs were very slightly crouching. He had a long tail, and his coat was thick.

He felt very different from Boris. He was much less beautiful.

Pollina was sure that Boris was very beautiful because he had a smooth coat, and in her world beautiful things were smooth things.

"I'm thinking about why Ferdinand wants the Fleece," said Pols.

"What are you up to?" Max asked. "Are you hungry? I can heat something up." She heard him set down a glass upon her piano.

"That is not a table," said Pollina, moving toward the instrument.

"Hold up," Max said. "There is a bottle on the floor, right in front of your left foot. Okay, got it." He slid over and made room for her on the bench.

"What is in the bottle?" Pols asked. "I would like a small glass, please."

"You won't like the taste," Max laughed. "It's brandy."

Max was worried. He was worried about her.

"When someone is ill in old books," Pols said, "they give them brandy. They say, 'Get a little of this brandy down,' or 'Someone get him a brandy.'"

"I'm not sure you're sick enough for me to justify giving you brandy," Max said.

Pollina let that sit in the air for several seconds. Long enough for Max to replay it in his head two or three times. Max knew how sick she was.

"I think Ferdinand wants to protect the Fleece from falling into the hands of people who will misuse it," said Max. "But I also think he's curious about its power."

"But will he use it for good?"

It would not be right to pray to God to spare her life. She could ask for strength, for forgiveness, for courage. She could not ask for His will to be altered. It did seem that He intended her to die very soon. She wondered if in Heaven, she would be blind. But

God would not take her music away—surely? No. She would be able to play. And finally see the stars.

She held up her hand and Max put a glass in it, moving her fingers and palm so that she cupped the bowl of the glass.

"Some people say it's better at room temperature, and some say you should warm the glass first. Like this." Max moved her hand in small circles. "This is how they do it in old movies. There's a scene in *Rear Window* where everyone stands around just waving their brandy glasses. I don't think anyone ever takes a sip, but it looks cool. Don't do it too much, or it'll slop over the sides. Yes, Ferdinand wants to use the Fleece for good. Very much."

Pollina moved her glass in small circles, and then brought it to her nose.

"It smells nice," she said. "I like it." She took a small sip. It burned a little. She tried to imagine the liquid burning through the bacteria that had invaded her lungs. She hoped it was not also burning the tissue around her heart. The bacteria were eating that. They were nibbling at it, like rats.

"If Ferdinand had to choose between the Fleece and Philippine, which would he choose?"

"He would choose Philippine, in a heartbeat," Max said. "Back to bed for you, Luigi. I'll bring you a snack."

She heard Boris and Moritz get to their feet.

She did not want to die. She did not want to die. Please God, don't let me die. *Almighty Father, grant me mercy. Almighty Father, can I not serve you better on this Earth?*

She must finish the opera.

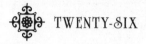 TWENTY-SIX

$\mathcal{S}$arah pulled Nico over to the side of a building, so she could rest, and described to him everything she had seen. By the time she finished, some of her energy had returned. Her mind was moving rapidly. This couldn't be the end. There had to be something they could do.

"The cat!" Sarah straightened up.

Nico, looking a little dazed, raised an eyebrow in query.

"When I took the galleon from Bettina's apartment," Sarah said in a rush, "I opened a window and a cat got in. I wasn't supposed to do that, Bettina specifically said so. But I forgot and the cat got in and went straight for a closet." They both began walking fast to Bettina's building. "The rat might still be there. You'll have to distract Herr Dorfmeister or something while I look for it."

But when Sarah and Nico got to Paniglgasse 18, instead of Herr Dorfmeister they were greeted by a teary-eyed, freckle-faced, red-haired crowd—men in *Tracht*, mothers with babies in arms, young children running about, and older people stooped with age, all bearing the same clear genetic imprint. Candy the golden retriever lay on the floor in the middle of the group, despondent. Apparently Herr Dorfmeister had passed away in his bed that afternoon, and his entire clan had gathered to discuss his arrangements.

"It is quite sad," said a young woman who introduced herself as Eva, his granddaughter. "But I suppose we should be grateful. He was an old man and he played tennis this very morning, then came home, lay down, and died peacefully in his own bed, with no illness. We should all be so lucky. Come in and have a glass with us. We are toasting Opa's memory."

"He was a lovely man and a very good chess player," said Nico, looking over the chessboard as Eva handed them both large dripping steins of dark beer. "I'm sorry we didn't get to finish our game. Dr. Müller"—he indicated Sarah—"and I will miss him very much." Sarah felt something being slid into her pocket.

"Please excuse me for a moment," Sarah murmured, and, handing her glass to Nico, she raced toward the elevator, pulling Bettina's key out of her pocket.

Bettina's heavy perfume had covered the scent before, but now that Sarah was focusing on it, she knew she could smell a rat. It had taken some doing to get to him, since Bettina had sealed up the wall of the closet very well, but after some vigorous demolition work, Sarah was able to find Hermes, looking a little drawn, inside a small cage with an automated feed and watering system.

She hauled this out and set the cage in the living room. They were both still sitting there, contemplating each other, when Nico entered. He joined them on the floor. Hermes perked up a little and moved to the edge of his cage, his tail wagging. He squeaked. Nico put a finger through the bars of the cage and Hermes put both his front paws on it.

"Hello, Hermes," Nico said gravely. "I am Nicolas Pertusato." With his other hand he pulled something out of his jacket pocket and handed it to Sarah. It was a chess piece.

"I am not so sure," said the little man, "that the old man went so peacefully as his *Sippe* think."

"What do you mean?"

"The game we started yesterday. It should have been my move. But someone made it for me. We should let him out."

"What are you talking about?"

"He wants to stretch his legs. He won't run away."

"No, about the chess game."

"Herr Dorfmeister made a move. We agreed to pause the game there."

"So he made a move for you."

"The man was nothing if not correct. Someone moved my queen. A very particular type of move, actually, most boldly done in Levitsky versus Marshall, 1912. It's called the 'shower of gold,' in which you appear to sacrifice your queen but instead trap your opponent."

Nico lifted up the door of the cage and they watched Hermes run joyfully around the apartment, up and down all the furniture, up the curtains, and over the clocks before he returned to drink some water, after which he took up a position on Nico's shoulder.

"He's not afraid of me." Nico smiled. "I haven't met an animal in over four hundred years that wasn't. But it makes sense. We are two of a kind."

"Okay, let me get this straight. You think someone murdered Bettina's concierge."

Nico shrugged.

"Bettina may be brilliant," said Sarah after a pause, "but I don't want her coming anywhere near Pols."

"Agreed," said Nico. "But I'm not leaving Hermes here." The rat sniffed around the edges of Nico's ears.

"When she realizes he's gone, she'll come looking for him," said Sarah, standing up.

"And I'll be waiting." Nico stood up also. "We leave for Prague immediately, I think."

"You're leaving for Prague immediately," said Sarah. "I've got one last piece of business."

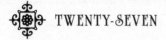

TWENTY-SEVEN

Gottfried von Hohenlohe leveled a disdainful glance at his brother, Heinrich, as he strode into Zum Schwarzen Kameel. Heinrich was wearing a boxy American suit with broad lapels and what looked to be Italian shoes. Disgraceful. Gottfried, who favored traditional Austrian *Tracht*, as their father had, wore a loden cape over a jacket with standing collar and staghorn buttons. He placed his Tyrolean hat neatly on the shelf, where members of his family had been placing their variously shaped hats since 1618 while they patronized what was first an exotic spice shop, then a wine tavern, and now a tony-yet-traditional coffeehouse. Gottfried stroked his red beard.

"Servus," said Heinrich, to which Gottfried gave a curt *"Grüss Gott."* The two men exchanged a quick and formal kiss. Though Gottfried usually preferred to stand, he settled into Heinrich's corner booth away from the prying eyes and ears of their fellow Viennese.

Gottfried wiped an imaginary crumb off his loden as Heinrich ordered, to Gottfried's horror, a Diet Coke.

"I'm watching my weight," said Heinrich defensively. He shifted uncomfortably inside his brown tweed suit. "That was a most unfortunate event," he said quietly. "We were lucky not to be seen."

Gottfried leaned forward and stared hard at Heinrich. "The important thing is that we were *not* seen. You must not lose your nerve. You must remain in control of yourself at all times."

"I could say the same of you, brother. Remember Thumbkin."

Gottfried refused to dignify this with a response. They both knew what had happened. When they were children, Gottfried had shot their mother's cat Thumbkin with a crossbow from the family armory, which was part of a historic collection, and which they had been forbidden to touch. Their mother had asked their father to punish Gottfried appropriately and Gottfried's father had taken him to the stables, produced a flask from a secret compartment, and given Gottfried his first taste of schnapps.

"You have killed today," his father had said. "And sometimes a man must take the blood of another creature. But make sure you have a worthy adversary. Always adhere to this rule and you won't go wrong: never shoot an animal whose head you wouldn't be proud to display in your trophy room."

"People are animals," young Gottfried had said, after a long silence and a few passes of the flask.

"We take no pleasure in killing people. We do it to defend our family, and to defend Austria. For this, honor is the only trophy."

Gottfried had never told Heinrich what had happened in the stables. His younger brother was not capable of understanding such nuance.

And now he, Gottfried, had done what was necessary to save their inheritance.

Heinrich lit a cigarette. "There is still the matter of the missing research."

"I tell you I could find nothing in the apartment."

"It must be somewhere."

"Very well," said Gottfried at last. "I will look into the matter further, and you will inform them of my new price." He slid a piece of paper across the table. Heinrich unfolded it and considered the number.

It would be enough to save their family lands and home for the next generation, his sons. He would do it for no less.

"I am sorry about the old man," said Gottfried, a shadow crossing his brow. "He was a good Austrian."

Heinrich nodded. "I know you are sorry. But how many good Austrians does my company employ? Forty-five thousand. Do these people not matter? And the fifteen billion euros that it earns for Austria each year?" Gottfried could always be won over with this line of attack.

"You are right. Many wars have been fought over less. We do this for Austria, as well as for the family."

"I have to get back to the office," said Heinrich. He passed his brother a bottle of antipsychotics. One of the company's most important developments, it had made normal life possible for hundreds of thousands if not millions around the globe. "One a day, remember? Please! It's better for everyone."

Gottfried nodded with great dignity and put the bottle in his pocket, knowing he would pass it off to a homeless man who sat outside the Café Hawelka with his dog. Yes, he might have some psychological qualities that people found unacceptable in this ridiculously sedentary era, but those same qualities had been highly valued in other times and would be again. People called the Hapsburgs insane, and look at the glorious Austrian empire they built, which once covered all or part of what was now Italy, Spain, France, Germany, Poland, Slovenia, the Czech Republic, Slovakia, Hungary, the Ukraine, Bosnia, Croatia, and

Romania. An empire that would still be intact if it weren't for the democratic movements of the twentieth century, which had reduced their homeland to a second-tier stop on the European tour, a tiny country known for sickly sweet pastries, singing families, and dancing horses.

You couldn't honorably assume only part of your birthright. You had to assume it all.

"And the American girl?" Heinrich stubbed out his cigarette.

"She knows very little." Gottfried kept his features impassive. "She is not important."

"My superiors do not think so. They think she knows quite a bit."

"You and I also know a thing or two," Gottfried pointed out. "But surely they will not ask that I eradicate my own brother?"

Heinrich smiled.

"They trust you," he said. "They trust us."

Gottfried burst into laughter. The sound startled Heinrich. He seldom heard his brother laugh.

"For myself, I have no fear." Gottfried narrowed his eyes. "And I would never let any harm come to you, my own flesh and blood. I would cut off the hand that touched you."

"I am not a scientist, I do not understand what it is they think she has found. But I have never seen them so eager," Heinrich said. "But this amount . . . it is a great deal of money."

"We are not asking for much." Gottfried flared his nostrils. "We are not asking to be as rich as a man who sells colanders on television. We are only asking that our name not be disgraced."

"Gottfried."

"We are only asking to preserve what is rightfully ours and pass it on to the next generation of von Hohenlohes, to keep Austrian treasures in the hands of Austrians."

"That is true."

"Very well," Gottfried said grandly. "It will be easy. Sarah has already suggested the means. I offered to show her Philippine Welser's book, and she was most interested and anxious to take me up on this. We drive to Innsbruck tomorrow. She will not be a problem."

"Good," said Heinrich, showing his small teeth. "Very good. My superiors, too, have a request"—here Heinrich leaned forward—"about the research."

Gottfried sighed.

"Yes? Let's have it. I have things to do. I cannot linger here all night."

"The scientist said she conducted her experiment on an animal. Rat number 134, she called it."

"Yes?"

"Well . . ."

"Please, brother. You have come this far. Do not hold back now."

Heinrich smiled weakly.

"They want the rat."

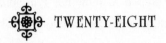

TWENTY-EIGHT

"Y ou can only grasp me with one arm," said Harriet. "Because you lost the other one in the Battle of Santa Cruz de Tenerife in 1797."

"Right." Max folded one arm behind his back. The linen shirt Harriet had given him to wear was itchy, the white wool vest smelled of mothballs, the dark blue wool jacket with epaulets had a disturbing bullet hole in the breast, and the flap-front trousers were just plain silly. And that was before you got to the two-cornered hat that looked like a giant black banana.

Harriet was doing a kind of interpretive dance around Max's living room. She was a good dancer and looked very pretty in her linen shift.

"I've just done my performance of Medea for you, the King and Queen of Naples, and a select few other guests"—Harriet was slightly out of breath—"and of course my husband, the British ambassador. You're lounging on the sofa, exhausted after your long journey from Aboukir Bay and defeating Napoléon in the Battle of the Nile."

Max lounged and tried to look exhausted.

"You're suffering from malaria, and since we last saw each

254

other five years ago, you've lost all your teeth, an arm, and one eye."

"Jesus. How old am I?" said Max.

"You're only forty, but you've fought a lot of battles. You've earned a reputation as being exceptionally brave, but also headstrong. You once chased a polar bear."

Max nodded approvingly and, using his left hand, sipped rum out of a tiny antique glass.

"That rum comes from Jamaica, where you were nursed back to health after a life-threatening bout of dysentery."

"Dysentery is *not* sexy," said Max, hoping Harriet wasn't going to want him to enact that part.

"Not to worry. I suffer from amoebic dysentery and so does my husband, Lord Hamilton, probably contracted right here in Naples."

"Okay, so we all have dysentery," said Max.

"I've been secretly in love with you for five years and awaiting your return."

"How does your husband feel about you putting me to bed?"

"In later years, we will all live openly in England in a ménage a trois. It will be an enormous scandal."

"Let's skip that part."

"Oh, Lord Nelson." Harriet fanned herself. "I haven't laughed this hard since playing charades with Goethe."

"Please, call me Horatio," said Max, doing his best imitation of an eighteenth-century British naval hero, downing the rest of his drink.

"Don't forget to keep one eye closed and one arm behind your back," Harriet whispered.

Max suddenly felt very tired. Very, very tired. Harriet swam before him. She kissed him. "I'm sorry," she whispered.

Max was dreaming. He was taking a bath with Sarah, but they were not alone. There were several other people there, including Harriet, which was awkward, and Beethoven and Mozart, which was just weird. He started to slip under the water and found he couldn't use his arms or legs to hold himself up. *I'm drowning.* No one else in the tub noticed him slip under or moved to help him. *I'm dying,* he thought, unable to fight his way to the surface. Gasping, Max struggled to open his eyes and finally pulled himself awake. He felt groggy and hung over. He was still wearing his Lord Nelson costume. Had he passed out after sex? But he hadn't drunk that much. Harriet had insisted on a period glass, quite small, for the draft Lord Nelson needed to take for his malaria. Wait. Had she actually given him eighteenth-century medicine? He struggled to sit up.

Moritz was pacing the floor. Max hauled himself out of bed, pulled on a robe against the chill, and padded over to let the dog out. He stepped into the hallway, then paused. Someone else was up. He could hear someone moving about. Pols? Harriet? The music room was empty. His office door was closed, but he heard the creak of his desk chair. Pols wouldn't be in his office, nor would Harriet. A thief? He gave Moritz the hand signal for silence, then went to his room and retrieved the small pistol he kept in his dresser. Just in case. Max returned to his office and opened the door silently, just a crack, and was at first relieved to see that the person *was* Harriet. He could just make her out in the light from the small penlight she was holding. But before he could say, "You scared the crap out of me," he thought to himself, *Why is Harriet in my office at night?*

Her back was to him. She was being very cautious, he could see that. Looking at everything on his desk, but putting it back exactly the way it was. Looking *for* something. She opened the drawers one by one, then pulled something out. From the size he guessed it was the Star Summer Palace folio. Harriet took the folio and tucked it under her coat. She turned toward the door.

Max flicked on the lights and strode into the room, grabbing Harriet by the arms. The folio fell to the floor. Moritz ran into the room, growling and showing teeth.

"What are you doing?"

"My God! My God, Max, What? I . . ."

"What are you doing?"

"Max, you're hurting me. Please."

Max let go of her arms and bent to scoop up the papers. Harriet stooped, as if to help him, and Moritz's growl went up a notch. The dog began backing her into a corner.

"Max, really, call him off. I couldn't sleep and I was looking for something to read. I didn't think you'd mind. I'm sorry . . . I didn't think." She reached out a hand.

Moritz bit Harriet. Right on her outstretched hand. Quickly, and without hanging on, but a nice solid puncture.

"Bloody hell!"

"Get out," Max said to her.

Harriet held out her hand, incredulous, as two red spots began to swell.

"He *bit* me."

"You drugged me. Get out."

"Max, don't be ridiculous. You're overreacting. Think."

"No. You're done here."

"I haven't done anything!" Harriet cried. "Just . . . looked. I am a curious person, darling. You know that. I'm a historian. It's what I do. Darling, this hurts like hell. There could be nerve damage. Put some clothes on and we'll talk in the car."

Max wished he had bitten her himself. It must have felt really good, he thought.

"Get out," he repeated quietly. "Right now, or he'll bite you again."

Moritz growled again and took a step toward her.

Harriet backed toward the door that led to the rest of the palace. "You're not thinking straight," she said. "We'll talk in the morning. You'll see this was all a silly bit of nonsense. And you owe me an apology."

Max marched her out of the office and down the stairs to his private entrance, Harriet protesting the whole time. He shut the door in her face.

Back in his office, Max put the folio down on his desk and slumped onto the sofa, his head in his hands. He had a pounding headache from whatever drug Harriet had given him to knock him out, and now that the adrenaline was abating, he felt groggy and exhausted. And angry and disappointed and embarrassed. What had Harriet been up to?

Whatever she wanted, she wouldn't get it now.

Moritz whined and licked his hand.

"Thank you," said Max. "God, I'm an ass."

"You were lonely," said a voice.

Max froze and looked up at the dog. Moritz was standing in front of him, wagging his tail, staring at him.

No. It was the drug. Max sighed, rolled onto his side, and closed his eyes.

"Sleep it off," said Moritz. "You must rest the spine you recently grew."

Max sat up again. "What the—?"

Moritz sat down in front of Max.

Max stood and slapped his own cheek.

"All right. Let's get back to bed."

"You could ask nicely." Max wheeled around.

Nico.

The little man emerged from behind the curtains at the window.

"How long have you been there?" Max demanded.

"Long enough. I was just about to surprise dear Harriet myself when you did such an admirable job."

"She drugged me," Max said defensively.

"So I gathered," said Nico. "Luckily she didn't drug your dog."

"He didn't do a very good job of telling me you were here."

"Maybe you should feed me more biscuits," said Moritz. And weirdly, the voice really did seem to come from Moritz and not from Nico.

"You little bastard," said Max. "I should have known."

"I'll teach you the art of ventriloquism if you like. It's quite useful. And now let us examine what Harriet was so interested in."

"It's drawings of Ferdinand's Star Summer Palace. And lots of notes and the usual alchemical hoo-ha. Maybe you can make sense of it."

"I will look. You should go back to bed and sleep off whatever Harriet gave you. From the smell I am guessing laudanum."

Max struggled to focus his sleepy brain. "Okay," he said, then turned back to Nico. "Did you see Sarah in Vienna?"

"Of course."

"How is she?"

"Same as you," said Nico. "Tall and stupid."

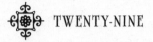

TWENTY-NINE

"Because I have been the worst houseguest since the Pilgrims showed up at Plymouth Rock," said Sarah, handing Alessandro a boxed edition of the complete run of the television show *The Golden Girls*, which for reasons imperfectly clear to her, Alessandro had often stayed up late to watch in syndication when they had been roommates together, and insisted was the greatest comedy ever made.

"My ladies!" he cried, embracing both it and her. "For this I forgive you. I even forgive you bringing a rat into my apartment."

Before Nico had left for Prague, he had handed Sarah another cage. "In case Bettina shows up asking for her rat, you'll have a decoy." The rat inside had arched its back, stamped his feet, and gnashed its teeth at her. Sarah had thought of Saddam Hussein, who had used doubles to throw off his enemies.

"Great," she said. "I'm calling this one Ares, god of war. I can't believe you found an open pet store."

"I found an open dumpster. You probably should not touch him."

"Got it," said Sarah, as Nico picked up Hermes. "Don't worry. I'll be okay. I'll meet you in Prague."

*S*ometimes *life gives you gifts,* thought Gottfried when Sarah appeared outside his flat carrying a cage with a rat in it. *Signs that you are on the right path.*

Getting into the room with Bettina's laboratory animals had been easier than he'd thought it would be, since someone had apparently torn off the doorknob. But rat #134 was not there.

"I'm petsitting for a friend," Sarah said, putting the rat in the backseat. "Long story. But I can't leave him alone overnight. Do you mind?"

Gottfried stared at the little brown rodent. Sarah had known Nina. Knew Bettina. This must be rat #134. Kept under constant watch by the scientist's cronies. Yes, of course.

It was all falling into place. He was driving Sarah and the rat to the countryside, where it would be easy to get the rat away from her and hand it off to Heinrich. Heinrich would be so pleased, and they would collect all of the money. The *Schloss* would be saved.

And as for Sarah . . . what? Well, he would see what signs life sent.

"I do not mind," he said.

*S*arah got into the front seat. If Bettina came after her, let her come. As always, Sarah carried with her in her shoulder bag a small kit containing a Swiss Army knife, waterproof matches, Band-Aids, potable water tablets, lip balm, and a condom. With such fortifications, a woman could survive or enjoy just about anything. She was not prepared to leave Austria without anything to help Pollina, and there were answers for her in the place where Philippine had lived. The woman clearly had mad skills. Maybe there was another recipe in her book that would be useful.

Maybe she could find out more about what had been put in the galleon.

Gottfried was wearing a jaunty green Tyrolean hat with a feather in its black and white braided hatband, and he produced a small box of chocolates and a bottle of water. "To sustain you on the journey," he said with a shy smile. He kissed her. Sarah had a brief flashback of fire, and then she inhaled Gottfried's particular scent of limes and leather and hay. For a moment she thought she could hear Conversano nickering.

Though Sarah offered to share the driving, Gottfried insisted on doing all of it so that Sarah could immerse herself in the scenery. Sarah would have immersed a little more successfully at a lower rate of speed, but Gottfried, like many European drivers, enjoyed traveling at well over a hundred miles an hour, weaving among trucks, cursing the idiocy of everyone else on the road, and treating the journey as if he were bringing serum to diphtheria victims, with the Mini Countryman in the role of Balto the husky. As they zoomed over mountain passes, through tunnels, and around hairpin turns, leaving the plain of Vienna behind and climbing up into the Alps, Sarah got a brief, tantalizing glimpse of storybook spires.

"Linz," said Gottfried.

"The pajama makers?"

"That is Lanz, who make ladies' flannel nightgowns so ugly and impenetrable that we call them Austria's most effective form of birth control. In Linz, Kepler taught astronomy, and you will be familiar with another famous son, the composer Bruckner. And of course you Americans always want to bring up Adolf Hitler, who spent his youth here before leaving for Vienna."

"Ah," Sarah said diplomatically.

"Even though Hitler was Austrian by birth, Nazism was a

very German idea. Germans should not rule over other peoples. You want happy times? Let Austria rule over Germany, not vice versa."

"Being so pro-Austrian I'm surprised you drive a British car," Sarah teased.

"Ah, but my *Schatzi* is made in Graz, here in Austria." Gottfried patted the dashboard with pride. "I make this drive often, but it is nicer with you here." He put his hand on her thigh. Sarah hoped the villa beds weren't too ancestral. Well, if need be they could improvise. Look what they had accomplished in a stable.

They passed through Salzburg.

"You will recognize from *Sound of Music*," said Gottfried with a sigh. "Seventy percent of the foreign tourists who come to Salzburg visit not because it is the birthplace of Mozart, but to see where the nun Maria captured the heart of Captain von Trapp."

"I've heard that Maria wasn't actually that popular with the children."

"Also, they did not walk over hills. Obviously, it is geographically impossible to cross to Switzerland from Salzburg by means of hills. The Von Trapps took the train. To Italy."

The highway ducked briefly into Germany, then shot up into twisty Austrian mountain roads that made her ears pop.

At last they exited in Innsbruck, which was nestled beneath some truly spectacular peaks, already snowcapped in October. The blue of the sky seemed brighter here, and the pastel buildings cleaner. It was not surreal, Sarah thought. It was hyperreal. It was high-definition reality.

The little car began climbing up one side of the valley in which the town nestled, and they made their way along a densely forested lane over which a huge gray stone wall loomed. Finally Gottfried pulled up in front of a massive iron gate.

"Wait here." Gottfried hopped out of the car, pulled an enormous ring of keys out of his pocket, and shoved a huge skeleton key into the rusted lock. He swung the gates open and got back in the car.

"The place is in deplorable condition," he said. "I apologize. We cannot afford a full-time staff." They continued up a long, winding lane. Sarah could see only another steep stone wall above them. "My father insisted the *Kunstkammer* be preserved in the right conditions, and the remainder of our fortune went to this. But there is only Heinrich and I to look after it."

"You can't open up part of it to tourists, as a museum?"

"We do not have the European Union–required facilities. There is no wheelchair ramp and very few bathrooms. There are no sprinklers for fire safety. No parking lot."

They passed under the stone wall through a tunneled arch and into a courtyard. Gottfried's family home was a gigantic hulking Renaissance castle and outbuildings, surrounded by a huge and densely overgrown park. The buildings were red and white, though the white had gone very gray, and the red was black in patches. There had been a fire here, probably more than one. Sarah got out of the car, carrying her overnight bag and Ares in his cage. She stepped over a fallen roof tile.

"It's quite beautiful, isn't it, in a wild sort of way?" said Gottfried. He escorted her past the tangled garden and up the hill toward the largest building, which was several stories tall and loomed over them.

"In 1563 when Ferdinand was named Margrave of Burgau and Archduke of Further Austria, which included Alsace and Tyrol, he bought this place, which was then a ruined medieval castle. Ferdinand was an odd person. As the second son of the Holy Roman Emperor he was not in line for the title, so he had great wealth but limited responsibility. He had been a brave warrior. But he was also very whimsical in his tastes."

"A fun Hapsburg." Sarah smiled.

"Yes, he loved learning, and collecting art and scientific specimens. He even welcomed unfortunate people with deformities—dwarfs, giants, hunchbacks, a family covered with hair—whom others at the time considered touched by the devil. He also fell deeply in love with Philippine, as you know, who was a commoner from Augsburg. I will show you their portraits. It was a politically disastrous marriage, and Ferdinand and Philippine's children would never be recognized. Hence Ferdinand's desire to hide his wife away from the court in Vienna."

"So you're not the first owner to bring an inappropriate commoner here?"

Gottfried frowned and nodded as he used one of his vast number of keys to open another creaking gate. Sarah followed him under yet another arch and into the most spectacular interior courtyard she had ever seen. All four walls surrounding her were sgraffitoed with hundreds of elaborate trompe l'oeil figures in an endless two-dimensional parade.

"Many of these figures have not been identified," said Gottfried. "But there are the nine Muses. There are the Worthies. The story of Odysseus is here. And here, my favorite: the Virtues. Faith, Hope, Charity, Justice, Prudence, Fortitude, Temperance, and . . ."

Sarah didn't mind being tested. She was good at tests.

"Divine Wisdom. I like that the artist gave her a dog."

"Ferdinand was also deeply interested in alchemy," said Gottfried. "So it's possible that these drawings have some alchemical significance. When he died, Rudolf took most of his uncle's *Kunstkammer* and absorbed it into his own. Some of the things were later recovered, or bought back, by members of my family."

Sarah studied the etchings. One figure especially caught her eye. A woman, standing on top of a star. In one hand she held a book, in the other a stylus of some kind.

"That is possibly a portrait of Philippine," said Gottfried.

Sarah traced the figure of Philippine, surprised at how much the image moved her.

"She looks very powerful," she said. "Usually sixteenth-century women are just shown praying, or reading a Bible and looking sort of defeated."

"Indeed. Her medicinal garden is back up in there." Gottfried pointed toward another wing of the castle. "Some of her plants survive to this day. Her book is in the family's private library. I will have to find the key."

Sarah saw that to the left of the Philippine portrait, the wall was studded with holes.

"Bullet holes." Gottfried nodded. "For a while, the *Schloss* was used as an army barracks. There are a number of bullet holes, all over the estate."

Gottfried took her hand and she followed him through a doorway into a small and simply fitted-out kitchen, which she guessed belonged to the caretaker. He set out a loaf of bread, a salami, and a hunk of cheese. From a stenciled cabinet he produced a bottle of wine, which he decorked by hitting the bottle with a knife.

"The salami is wild boar," said Gottfried. "I shot it myself."

Sarah decided Gottfried's online dating handle would be "Teutonic Throwback." She set down Ares' cage and he hopped around inside it, sniffing. Gottfried cut Sarah a slice of the salami. His knife went through the dense meat as if it were warm butter.

"Now you would like to see the book?" Gottfried asked after

they had eaten. "Or should we make love first? Love first, I think." He stuck his knife in the wall and reached for her. Ares shrieked.

"I suggest we leave your little rodent friend here with some cheese and water," said Gottfried, a little later. He stood and opened the door. Sarah walked through, feeling a trifle dizzy.

"I am distressed that none of these keys work," said Gottfried in frustration outside a locked storeroom on the third floor of the castle. Sarah had caught glimpses of cavernous rooms, furniture shrouded with dust cloths, as they climbed what had been a beautiful stone staircase, now chipped and a bit crumbly. "I'm sorry, Sarah," Gottfried said at last. "The caretaker is visiting his daughter today. I'm afraid I will have to run down to her house to get his set of keys. I hope you do not mind the delay. We will find the book. In the meantime I will let you into Ferdinand's *Wunderkammer*. I think you will be much surprised and it will give me pleasure to have you see it."

Sarah followed Gottfried back down and across the courtyard to another whitewashed building, this one with a beautiful wooden balcony, now sagging and in need of repairs, and not-quite-symmetrical gabled windows in peculiar shapes. He told her it had been built by Ferdinand specifically to house his collections.

Here, one or two modern improvements had been added. There was an alarm system, the lights in the barnlike second-floor gallery were on timers, and the rug running down the central hallway of the first floor looked new. The rooms were lined with rows of glass cases as well as freestanding exhibits. It was utterly silent.

"It is all displayed exactly as Ferdinand left it," said Gottfried.

"Except for this terrible rug my brother purchased. And we have updated the alarm system. The original was very . . . grisly."

Don't ask, thought Sarah.

There seemed to be a great number of objects. The space was filled, top to ceiling. "Not to pry, but you can't sell a few pieces and keep the castle?" she wondered.

"We are prohibited by law from breaking up the collection. Nothing can legally leave Austria," Gottfried said. "But there is not enough money. If we sell, we have failed. We will have lost everything. I would not survive this shame. No. It cannot . . . It is a thing I cannot . . ."

Gottfried's jaw was white with tension. He grabbed her hand and held it for a moment, hard. When he spoke again his tone was courteous and correct, but he did not meet her eye. He was, she thought, deeply embarrassed.

"Sarah, I will be back in a little while. Please feel free to examine anything you like. I do not have to tell you to be careful with my family's treasures. I trust you."

He left.

The wood floor creaked under her feet, and it was very cold. Though when she reached out to touch the thick, stuccoed wall, she found it warm to the touch. Interesting. It was fun to try to decipher what was in the cases without the benefit of a museum brochure, though here and there items were identified by small yellowed cards. The collection seemed to be sorted according to materials, such as coral, stone, gold, or wood, rather than type of object.

Sarah passed delicate corals carved into realistic models of mountains, a strange undersea coral crucifixion scene, and a coral chess set. Ferdinand was apparently a big fan of coral.

She'd be back in Prague the following day. Back with Pollina. She would see Max, too.

Would it be easier to see him with Harriet, now that she had enjoyed a dalliance with Gottfried?

Sarah passed a case that contained a miscellany of objects made from varying materials: a coconut goblet, a snake bracelet, a rhino horn mug, an ostrich egg, and a skeleton made of pear wood. Chosen for their oddness? For their beauty? For some legend attached to them?

Ferdinand had also collected musical instruments. Sarah paused in front of an eight-foot-long wooden alpenhorn, the local equivalent of the didgeridoo, and stared at a dragon-shaped *Tartolte*, another ancient wind instrument. This one was seemingly played by blowing into the dragon's tail. She became consumed by a desire to try it out. Well, why not? Gottfried said she could examine things. And wasn't that the advantage of a private collection? You could play with the stuff.

The tone was louder than she imagined, and pure. It reverberated through her. She remembered Marie-Franz saying "We don't just hear music, we feel it." That wasn't poetry, it was science. She ran her fingers over the strings of a lute with nine inlaid alternating stripes of ebony and ivory and listened to the dusty twang. She looked at a bagpipe and an olifant, a wind instrument made from an elephant's tusk that was (fortunately for elephants) quite rare. Sarah had only seen one in books, and she'd read of it in *Song of Roland*, in which Roland, a warrior in Charlemagne's army, blows an olifant and dies. When Sarah blew into it now, she thought she caught a brief image of the African plains the horn's original owner had once roamed, then felt a millisecond of intense pain, all over her body. It came and went so quickly she almost didn't consciously register it, but the instrument had left her with a terrible taste in her mouth. Like something rotten.

She came next to an inlaid wooden case, like a piano, but much smaller. She touched the keys, but no sound came out. This object had a small card taped to its side: *When you the hit keys, clappers will play glass bells (now missing). One of its kind.*

A precursor to Mesmer's missing armonica? She wished the glass bells were still inside. She headed deeper into the hall, where the light barely penetrated.

Her phone beeped as she stopped in front of the next case. A text from Gottfried. *I am delayed in Innsbruck. Many apologies. Will return as soon as I can.*

Don't worry, she sent back. *I'm perfectly happy.*

Sarah looked around. She felt deep in her pocket, for the thing that was still there. It was a risk, but it was time to take risks.

Now? Yes. Now.

She smiled and took the object from her pocket. Yes, it was a risk. But Philippine had created her cures here at the *Schloss*. Sarah could read about them in the book, or she could watch them happen herself. And so she ingested the rest of the Westonia, and waited for the magic to begin.

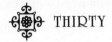

$\mathcal{S}$arah was looking at the Golden Fleece. She had gotten used to seeing the emblem on every third painting or façade in Vienna. And here it was, bouncing off a man's chest right in front of her. Sarah peered at the limp golden lamb emblem hanging from a chain against the black doublet, then peered into the man's face. This was undoubtedly Ferdinand.

She recognized the close-cropped reddish hair and beard. And the Hapsburg chin. Holy shit, they weren't kidding about the chin. The man's whole visage was exaggeratedly carved, almost cartoonlike with its large eyes, dented forehead, and hooked nose. And yet, there was something appealing about him, too, something powerful. He was playing a small flute: the *Doppel-unuchenflöten*, basically an early form of the kazoo. Now she could see that Ferdinand was surrounded by a group of courtiers, who were all playing similar instruments. They were giggling and laughing as they did, deliberately making their instruments honk and squeak and . . . yeah, they were making fart noises.

Sarah felt a flush of rage. She had saved this last bit of the drug, hoarded it, when it really belonged to Nico. She had not taken it when she was in Heiligenstadt, where she could have seen

Beethoven at one of the most critical moments in his career. Not taken it back to Boston, where she could have seen her own father, lost to her for so many years. She had saved it for when she thought it would help Pols, but all she was getting was asinine men making flatulence jokes?

Her heartbeat was accelerating. The outlines of other people, other times, were beginning to form all around her in the hallway. A girl, hugely pregnant, buckled to her knees in front of Sarah. The girl's hair was covered in a scarf, and her long, heavy dress was blue and rust colored. No, not rust colored. That was blood, soaking through the girl's skirt as she began to gasp and scream in hoarse, high-pitched shrieks. She saw a man and a woman, dressed in rich brocade and silks, though the man's breeches were open, and the woman's sumptuous gown was shoved up around her hips, a stockinged leg waving in the air, a silk shoe dangling half off as she squirmed underneath him. The man had one hand firmly clamped over her mouth. To stifle her cries of ecstasy? Cries of panic? It was so vivid, too vivid. Sarah could smell their sex. The rhythmic thumping and sliding and gnashing of their bodies and choked groans and cries were thunderous. Sarah clung to the wall, forcing herself to stand. Men in military uniforms now surrounded her on all sides. She remembered Gottfried telling her that the *Schloss* had been used at one point as a military barracks. These men were struggling to hold someone down, urging him to be calm, to be brave. They were shouting, half laughing, very drunk. Bloody. "I will have to take the leg," someone said. "Or he will die." Sarah saw a man, jacket off, sleeves rolled up, shirt stained in bile and blood, lifting a saw. The patient began to shriek. And the sounds coming from his mouth were remarkably similar to those of the bleeding pregnant woman and the copulating woman in brocade and silk. And the sound of the saw cutting through bone was like the sound of Ferdinand's flute, which was also like the sound of the copulating man. They had formed a chorus, through time.

This was history. Fear, pain, pleasure, music. Sex and death. The big death. The little death. This was what it looked like. What it sounded like.

There had to be music here, real music. She needed to be calm. Sarah shut her eyes and covered her nose in order to listen better.

At first all she could hear were the same macabre layers of shrieking and groaning, but eventually she found it. A light, twanging sound. A lute. A lute being plucked, not quite tunefully. Sarah began to grope toward it, feeling her way against the actual walls with her eyes tightly screwed shut so as not to be distracted by the bodies hurling themselves in her path. She was stumbling, blindly, into fields of energy, which seared her nerves and made her dizzy with confusion. She ran straight into a suit of armor that felt very much like it existed in the present day and Sarah found herself doing an absurd polka with the armor, crashing down the hall, trying to disentangle herself. At last she reached a set of stairs and she stumbled up them as her knightly dance partner clattered to the floor, chivalry thwarted, if not absolutely dead.

The sound of the lute was louder now, as she wove around passing phantoms crackling with emotion: lust, fear, lust, fear. And then, quite suddenly, a burst of pure joy. Sarah stared down at a thin adolescent boy, who was in turn staring at a single beam of sunlight coming from a narrow casement window above them. He held his hand out in front of him, caressing the light with his slight fingers as if he were stroking a cat. He was dressed in the formal court dress of the mid-eighteenth century, his fine hair caught back with a ribbon, his thin cheeks marked lightly with what looked like smallpox scars. His hand paused in the air, he smiled with deep satisfaction, then turned and ran down the stairs, out of Sarah's sight. Her heart was racing.

Mozart.

She was pretty sure she had just seen Mozart. Age thirteen or so, probably on the way to or from one of the family trips to Italy. He was about the same age as Pollina was now. Pollina would never see her own hand held in front of her face, but Sarah had seen the girl, in a Boston apartment crowded with dusty antique furniture, step into a shaft of sunlight from one of the deep bay windows. And Pols had felt the sun on her face and she smiled with the same kind of secret joy. Held her own thin hand up in front of her face, conducting the music in her head. This, too, was history. Not just lust and fear, but exaltation. Creation. Genius. Pols had the flame of genius within her. A flame as deep and dazzling and mysterious as the one that burned in the young man who had just walked past Sarah on the stair, two hundred and fifty years or one second earlier. There was something here that would help Pollina. There had to be. She had to find it. What was her own life, her own contrail of energy? Was this not her gift? She was being given now, in this moment, a chance to use those perceptions within her that had been strengthened. She could call forth from the melee the individual voices she needed to hear. Like a conductor, as Pols had said.

Sarah let the last of her resistance to the drug fall away from her. She closed her eyes, breathed deeply, and stretched out her mind, feeling it unravel from the center of her forehead like spools of unfurling ribbons.

The galleon. What was the powder that Philippine had put in the galleon?

"Gently," said a voice, just above her. Sarah opened her eyes. A man stood on the stair, dressed in black with sleeves slashed with red satin. Not Ferdinand, though bearing a slight resemblance to him. One of his sons? The outlines of his figure were hazy, fading into the air. A second man, dressed somewhat more simply though still elegantly, shifted something large and gleaming in his hands.

The Spanish galleon. Sharp and solid and gold.

Good, she thought. I can focus.

Sarah followed the two men up the stairs and into a large, high-ceilinged room lined with books and cabinets containing corals and other minerals. Globes and astrolabes stood on small tables. Maps covered a long refectory table. A fire burned at one end of the room, which was otherwise lit by candles. Sarah watched as the man carrying the galleon set it gently upon the long table, then, with a deferential murmur, withdrew.

"I am sorry but I cannot help you." The man in black and red turned to a figure by the window Sarah hadn't noticed before. A slim young woman, wearing a heavy black coat with a furred hood. There was something about her, something familiar. The young woman moved gracefully, swaying slightly, toward the table.

"I was told that the emperor gave it to you." The woman's voice, too, was soft, though Sarah could feel an undertone of acidity.

"I am sorry, Lady Elizabeth."

"Do you mock me?" the woman replied with a small smile, softening her voice. "By calling me this?"

"Surely you are used to hearing your name coupled with

titles? You are the tenth Muse, Westonia, the Virgo Angla. Perhaps I do you a dishonor to call you less."

Sarah watched Elizabeth Jane Weston receive these tributes with a melancholy flutter of her hand. What was Elizabeth Weston's connection to the galleon?

"I am a daughter, above all else," she said. "A daughter who must beg for the things that were stolen from her father's house in the dead of night by your emperor's men."

"Your emperor, too."

"Oh, we all bow before Caesar." Elizabeth curled her lip. "Please. May I look at it?" Sarah moved forward to see better and stumbled over something hard, at her knees. Something that hadn't existed in whatever time she had been following, but most definitely did in the twenty-first century. Sarah pitched face forward onto the floor. Something had cut into her knee and the smell of her own blood momentarily overwhelmed her. When she looked up, Elizabeth Weston and the man had vanished.

A crowd of figures appeared, jostling her, running past her, through her. Smothering her with their emotions, their desires, their fears and dreams. Everything twisted, twisted. Like chains.

She needed to move back further in time. Elizabeth Weston and Edward Kelley came after Philippine's era. She needed to focus. Music. Where was the music? Sarah fought through the layers until she found the gentle sounds of the lute again. She tried to tie her mind to the sound of the music. Water. Splashing water. Laughter. She groped up another flight of stairs, down a short hallway, and into a wood-paneled room decorated with a frieze of bathing scenes. In the middle of the floor sat a child, idly plucking at a lute.

Not a child. A dwarf. Not Nico. This was a woman, red faced and sleepy eyed. At one end of the room, Sarah could hear voices coming from behind a small door. The little woman plucked a string and then the instrument fell lax in her hands. Her head fell forward. She snored. Sarah opened the door.

She was in a bathroom. A literal bath room, with a large, rectangular tub lined with tin-plated copper sheeting taking up most of the floor. The entire room was painted with murals of sea creatures: fish of all kinds, crabs, frogs, toads, and snakes. Incense burned from two large copper pots.

A middle-aged man and woman sat across from each other, on painted benches in the water. The man was naked except for a pair of brief swimming trunks. The woman wore a backless, apronlike garment. They both wore caps on their heads. The man reached over and fiddled with a tap decorated with a lion's head. Water gushed out. Ferdinand. And . . . was this Philippine? Their faces were serene, blissful.

Sarah realized that these people were definitely on some kind of drug themselves. She could feel it wafting off their bodies. It was different from Westonia, gentler. Kinder.

Sarah decided to join them in the tub, curious if she would actually be able to feel the water. Yes, and it was hot and scented. Every part of her body felt soothed.

"You must hide the book," said the woman.

Hide it? Sarah thought. Why hide a book of cures? Particularly if they contained a recipe for what had to be the best bath salts ever.

"I will hide it," agreed Ferdinand.

"Bury it. Not here."

"I am designing a mausoleum for it," Ferdinand said softly. "A mausoleum disguised as a star. A star disguised as a palace."

"Good. No one knows?"

"Secrets are hard to keep in this world."

"And in the next, perhaps."

"Philippine." Ferdinand smiled and stretched himself sensuously. "This is wonderful. What a feeling. Tell me you are not tempted to experiment further with the secrets of this book?"

"I am content to cure the sicknesses that come to all of us. The headache, the sore, the wound, the pains of childbirth, the fever, the spirit that is perturbed. The secrets in your book are powerful and wild. I cannot be responsible for what they unleash," Philippine replied. "We must not go deeper than this. That is why you must bury the book deep enough that others will not be tempted. These things are not for us to know."

They weren't talking about Philippine's recipe book. They were talking about the Fleece.

They had the Fleece. Philippine was rising from the bath.

"Where are you going?" asked Ferdinand.

"There's a stable boy with Saint Anthony's fire. The poor lad is in agony."

"He can wait. Come back."

Philippine was wrapping herself in a robe, donning her slippers. Sarah had to follow her. Sarah must see, she must learn. Philippine was leaving the room. Sarah ran after her, and then straight into Gottfried von Hohenlohe.

Straight into him, and with a lurch that sent a thousand jolts through her skin, straight through him.

 THIRTY-ONE

$\mathcal{S}$arah gasped as she plunged through Gottfried's energy field, zapped by a sharp electrical current. She staggered for a moment, and when she regained her footing she turned back. Gottfried had been replaced by two young boys. One of them, the leaner one, carried a crossbow that was nearly as big as he was. The leaner boy's energy was . . . strange. It was pulsing and clicking, almost like a clock, or a bomb. The two ran down the steps and Sarah, pulled by some magnetic force she couldn't name, followed them into the garden.

"Gottfried," the plumper boy said. This must be Heinrich. She could see his sullen expression in this child. He pointed. "Look. Mama's cat."

But the boy Gottfried had fallen to the ground; the pulsing energy of his body had exploded and he was convulsing, his young body twisting and turning in unnatural ways, his eyes rolling back until they were all whites. Sarah looked at Heinrich to see what he would do.

He picked up the crossbow, took aim, and shot the cat.

The two boys vanished, only to be replaced by versions of themselves, seated at a chessboard in the garden. Their bodies flickered. They were little boys, wiry teens, young boys again, then in their twenties. Always playing chess, always facing each other across the board. Always the same hot rivalry, the same crackling tension.

"Heinrich," said Gottfried. "Your move."

The boys were intense, and the men more so. Gottfried was confident, but unhappy. Heinrich was angry. Angry and jealous.

"This may be our last game here," said Gottfried. He looked exactly like himself now. This had to be recent.

"Not necessarily," said Heinrich.

Gottfried made a move on the chessboard. Heinrich smiled and moved his own piece.

"I have beaten you at last, brother," he said.

"Your skills have improved." Gottfried leaned back in his chair. "I did not expect such a bold move from you."

"It's called the 'shower of gold.'"

Sarah's mind raced—where had she just heard about this chess move? From Nico. The move he claimed someone made on Herr Dorfmeister's chessboard.

"There is a woman named Bettina Müller," Heinrich was saying now, "a scientist. She works at the university. I've made friends with her assistant. This woman—Frau Doktor Müller—is involved in very important medical research. My company does not say what this is, but they are willing to pay a great deal to make sure she does not sell this research to foreign investors. This research will help our company, help Austria. This woman must be stopped. I need your help."

So it was Gottfried, Sarah thought with a chill. Gottfried, loden-wearing Austrian patriot horseman, not to mention sexual maestro, who had stolen Bettina's laptop?

Shower of gold. Shower of gold? Surely it wasn't Gottfried who had—

She needed to get out of here. Before Gottfried returned.

Sarah shut her eyes. Philippine. She had to find Philippine.

"Come to the grotto. Come see what Philippine has made."

Sarah opened her eyes. It was Ferdinand and Philippine again, surrounded by guests. A party. Musicians. They were drunk, laughing. It was nighttime and the guests held candles. They waved them around, making circles of light, and hooting. Sarah followed the crowd to the grotto, where a young man, elegantly dressed, sat manacled in a chair. The straps were made of leather and attached to metal locks. The man was laughing and struggling and the guests circled him, some taunting, some encouraging.

"It is a riddle!" Ferdinand cried. "Solve it and the chair will set you free!"

"You have to break the glass," Philippine said. "But the glass is inside the locks."

"I cannot . . ." the man gasped, and he rocked the chair.

"What is the riddle?" asked one of the guests.

"What can the blind man not do?" Philippine smiled. Sarah took a step back. Philippine seemed to be looking straight at her.

"The blind man can't see!" the young man in the chair cried. But nothing happened. The guests began calling out suggestions. Sarah took a step toward Philippine.

Help me, she whispered. *I don't have much time.*

"Philippine?"

It was Ferdinand. Standing next to her, looking straight at her. Her body felt . . . strange. Filled with energy but somehow unfamiliar, as if she . . .

Ferdinand took her hand. She could see him take it; she could see her arm rising; but she could only feel a slight electrical charge, a faint warmth.

She was holding the hand of Archduke Ferdinand, sovereign of Further Austria, who died in 1595.

Ferdinand led her toward the building that housed his collection of curiosities. Sarah could see her own jeans-clad legs and short leather boots, but she could also see, overlapping her present-day self, another self, someone wearing a fine dress of embroidered silk.

She hadn't just found Philippine. She *was* Philippine.

"I have something to show you, my princess," said Ferdinand.

It was the strangest sensation. They had overlapped, somehow. Like magnets.

"I'm no princess," said Philippine. Sarah had said these words, too, almost five hundred years in the future. She had said them to Pols.

"You gave up much when you married me," Sarah found herself saying now, as Philippine. "You endured your father's wrath and the scorn of your friends, and you missed the chance for an alliance which would have brought you even more power."

"I do not seek power."

"I am glad to hear it."

Ferdinand held Sarah's gaze for a moment, and Sarah could feel how strong the bond was between him and Philippine. The things they had both given up for love and the differences between them—where they came from, what they wanted—only served to intensify their connection.

Ferdinand led her up the stairs and into the long hallway of the *Kunstkammer*. Gottfried had been right, it was nearly the same in his time as it had been in Ferdinand's. No rug, no lights, fewer things on display. It seemed the oliphant hadn't been acquired yet;

perhaps the elephant was still alive. Ferdinand led Philippine (and Sarah with her) over to a small table. On it was an alabaster and marble toy castle, checkered and cantilevered like an Escher painting.

"It is a safe place, my darling. Watch."

His hands moved over the castle, pressing first one thing and then another. At last, the drawbridge of the castle opened, revealing an empty compartment.

"An amusing contraption, to hold such a serious thing," said Philippine gravely. "This is not a cure for the rash. This is different. This is . . ."

"Immortality," said Ferdinand.

Philippine reached into her pocket and removed a small vial.

"This is why the Fleece must be hidden," she said sharply to Ferdinand. "Do you understand what immortality means? Do you? Eternal life. Do you understand the temptation and the curse?"

"I do."

"You think you can withstand it? You think immortality can be hidden in a box? I tell you it cannot. I would rather these stones be immortal."

Philippine raised the vial and smashed it against the floor.

Ferdinand's face was white. But he took Philippine's hand and kissed it.

"You are right," he said. "Thank you."

Philippine withdrew a second vial.

"This is the antidote," she said. "I will put this in your castle within a castle. But I will not practice from that book anymore. You must take the Fleece away from here. You must bury it deep. It must be hidden until the end of time."

Time, thought Sarah. She didn't have much time. Gottfried would be coming back. Sarah could feel herself inside Philippine, feel the woman's blood all around her. And then, Philippine's voice inside her head.

"What do you seek here?"

Philippine's voice was infinitely gentle.

"I seek a cure for someone I love," Sarah answered.

"The need is great?"

"Yes."

"The need is always great."

"This is different."

"It always is."

"Please help me."

"We will help each other. You must go now. He is coming."

Sarah was standing in the same place, the same room, but she was completely alone. All the phantoms had disappeared, and she could feel that she was firmly back in the present, and the present alone. The drug had worn off, abruptly this time. The lights of the gallery had gone out. The clicking had stopped. The objects in the room were barely visible in the fading light coming in from a high row of small windows. She looked down.

She was holding a small vial.

She was holding the antidote to eternal life.

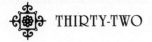

THIRTY-TWO

"Max. Max, wake up."

"Is it morning?"

"It is almost evening," said the little man. "You slept all day. We have work to do. Wake up."

"The folio?" Max muttered.

"Fascinating. In Ferdinand's own hand, with later notations by Edward Kelley."

"Kelley?"

"Kelley had access to all of Rudolf's manuscripts. How it came to end up in your family library is another story."

"So what's it all about?"

"The notations are instructions. And in some cases, spells. To be used in one location only, the Star Summer Palace."

"To do what?"

"Precisely. It has always been a mysterious building. No one was ever clear precisely what went on there. Or why Ferdinand designed it the way he did. They thought he was building a folly, or a love nest. But now I think the entire structure was designed for a specific purpose."

"Well?"

Before Nico could answer, Jose came barreling through the door, hair wild.

"It's Pollina," he said. "She send me text not to disturb her so I don't but finally I worried and—" A strangled cry came from his throat. "She's gone."

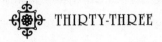

THIRTY-THREE

"*S*arah?" Gottfried. It was Gottfried walking down the hallway. Present-day Gottfried. The Gottfried who had stolen Bettina's laptop. The Gottfried who . . .

Sarah shoved the vial deep into her pocket. She needed to think about why Philippine had given this to her, instead of something that would help Pols, but right now she needed to get out of being in a secluded sixteenth-century castle with a potentially homicidal maniac. Where was her purse? Not that a Swiss Army knife would be much help if Gottfried was intent on killing her. She looked out the window, and judged the distance to the ground.

"I'm so sorry I was delayed," said Gottfried. "And I have bad news for you, I'm afraid. I was finally able to find the key to the library, but when I went in to get the book from its case, I found this." He showed her a card.

Removed for curatorial purposes.

"Heinrich must have lent it to some museum," he said. "I am surprised. Usually we let nothing out of our sight. Ah, well, but we will have a nice dinner anyway."

"Thank you for looking." Sarah's mind was racing. "I really do appreciate it. But while you were gone, I had a phone call. A work crisis. I need to get back to . . . to Boston. As soon as possible. I'm afraid I can't stay the night."

"Very well." Gottfried took her arm. "I will drive you to the airport and you can explain to me what a crisis in musicology consists of." He reached into his pocket.

A harsh blast of hot, white light hit Sarah's face like a bomb going off. It strobed as she closed her eyes and threw her arm across her face. She heard a thud, and a grunt, and then she was grabbed around the neck and forced into something—onto it—and she was shouting but she was *blind*, and someone was binding her, gripping her, and she could hear more grunting and thrashing and her wrists were locked into place and she felt metal across her waist and legs. She was manacled to a chair.

She could see spots. She could see black spots, and then colored whorls, and then she could dimly make out Gottfried on the ground in front of her. He was having a seizure, shuddering and convulsing. And standing over him was another man.

Heinrich.

She was strapped to a chair. Bound. She tried to kick her legs as hard as she could, but the straps held. Straps that fitted into metal locks.

"It's very effective, isn't it?" said Heinrich. "Ferdinand's little party game. He would make his guests sit in it, then lock them down and not let them loose until they had answered a riddle."

"What the fuck?" Sarah said. "Look at your brother! Help him!"

"I am well aware that my brother is having an epileptic fit. There are many causes of epilepsy, but they say in his case it is a defect on chromosome 20. The telomeres bind to themselves and form a ring. So his number 20 is an O, not an I. An old Hapsburg gene that has resurfaced. The price of all that inbreeding to keep the family close."

"Fascinating," snapped Sarah. "To repeat my earlier question: what the fuck?"

"Oh." Heinrich pursed his lips as Gottfried's convulsions ceased and he lay still, apparently unconscious. "I am afraid that you know too much for me to let you go. But thank you for the rat."

Thank God, Sarah thought. *Thank God we switched the rats.* "Bettina Müller is working on a cure for defects in chromosome 20," Sarah said. "Is that why you want the rat, to cure your brother? Because maybe I can help."

Heinrich laughed a small, tight laugh. "My brother's epilepsy has been useful. I see no need to cure it, especially since only an hour ago he threatened me. Told me to leave you alone. Gottfried's seizures are very easy to trigger these days, you know. All it takes is a burst of light. Sets off an electrical storm in the brain. Isn't it interesting, how it really does all come down to energy imbalances? Soon all scientists will sound like New Age hippies."

Sarah began carefully testing the strength of the metal and wood that held her fast. It was five hundred years old, this chair—it must have a weak point.

"He does not remember what happens during the attacks. So I have to tell him. Sadly, he is often violent. He will awaken to discover that he has hurt you, I'm afraid."

Heinrich slipped a noose over Sarah's head. A noose made of piano wire.

"Like the cat?" she asked quickly. "Did you make him think that he had shot the cat with the crossbow?"

Heinrich paused, staring at her, frowning. "How do you know that?" he asked. "Gottfried would not have told you."

"I know you killed Herr Dorfmeister, too," said Sarah, trying to twist around. She had to keep him talking until she found a weakness in the chair. "How did you pull that one off?"

"Gottfried went to see if he had missed anything in the apartment. He had a seizure. The old man called me. Gottfried wears a bracelet with my number on it. I took care of Herr Dorfmeister. But don't worry. For him, a nice old Austrian gentleman, I used a drug that causes a painless death. But I'm afraid you have no one but yourself to blame for Nina."

Sarah froze. "You killed Nina? And Gerhard Schmitt?"

"How pleasant it is to speak of such things openly. I could not share this even with my brother, you see, because he thinks I am weak, and it is better that way. It was only supposed to be her. I saw you together, going into the lab. I followed her, only to ask what you had talked about. She grew suspicious of my questions, began to accuse me of things, and that was when that blond fop showed up."

"Gerhard?"

"The little witch would sleep with him, but not with *me*? They accused me of spying, threatened to go to the police. I had no choice, you see."

It was no use. The chair was solid.

"My brother suspected, I think," Heinrich continued. "That's why he warned me to stay away from you. He is loyal, but I fear that eventually he would have cracked. His strange ideas about honor have become inconvenient. Perhaps it was fate that saved you both in the stables. If you had died then, I would never have gotten the rat."

"You set the fire in the stable," said Sarah. "You tried to kill us both."

Heinrich shrugged. "Among other things, I hate horses."

He began to tighten the garrote, then leaned over and whispered, "The tourists come to Vienna, and they enjoy the opera, and the Sacher torte, and they buy a souvenir hat and they think what a lovely civilized place Austria is. A little fussy, perhaps, but safe as houses. They forget the past. They forget what is in our stars." Sarah could feel the wire cutting into her throat. The room began to go black. The wire was cutting off the flow of blood to her brain.

"I will kill him, too. I will be the heir. My sons will be the sons to inherit. Gottfried cannot be trusted. If he told some American bitch he barely knows about Herr Dorfmeister . . ."

"No. I saw," Sarah whispered. "You won the chess game. In the garden. You beat Gottfried. It was the shower of gold. It was your move."

Heinrich stopped tightening the noose. "How did you know that?" The garrote loosened slightly.

"I saw you."

"That is a lie."

She had seen them. She had seen. The garden. The game. The chair. She had seen the chair she was sitting in before. In the garden. Philippine. Ferdinand. A riddle. What can't the blind man do? *The blind man can't see.*

You have to break the glass, Philippine said. *But the glass is inside the locks. What can the blind man not do?*

"You must be a witch," said Heinrich, tightening the noose again. "We burn witches here at the *Schloss*. You wouldn't be the first."

The blind man can't see. C. A note. A musical note.

As Heinrich's noose started to cut off her air again, Sarah began to scream. She wasn't normally the screaming type. But this was a very particular scream.

A scream in C. Every piece of glass has a natural resonance. Every material on earth has it. A frequency. Match the pitch and the molecules will vibrate. Do it loud enough . . . Sarah did not attempt a high C, but her pitch was perfect, and she could sing very loud.

As she did, she felt something vibrate and then shatter inside the metal locks as they released. Sarah's now free hands shot up and she lurched forward, grabbing Heinrich's throat and kneeing him in the balls as hard as she could.

Heinrich's scream came pretty close to a high C. Sarah shoved him roughly and he stumbled backward into a glass case, which shattered. A solid alabaster skull with ruby eyes rolled off one of the shelves and hit Heinrich on the head. He fell to the floor.

Sarah removed the piano wire from her throat, choking still. She could feel blood, but the cut wasn't deep enough, thank God.

Thank the past.

Gottfried was coming to. She sank to the floor next to him.

"Gottfried," she croaked through the burning in her throat.

"Heinrich," he whispered. "Heinrich, what have I done now?"

"Gottfried, it's not you. It's your brother. It's Heinrich who does these terrible things. It's not you. Heinrich is the murderer."

DAY 644,868

The road has been long. Very long. I have made mistakes. Harriet has not been the finest of necromancers. Her mind is marred by the drug.

St. Vitus is not the best portal. It has been corrupted.

The Charles Bridge portal isn't perfect, either. Too weak. Or maybe it was Harriet who was too weak. She overshot wildly. John of Nepomuk came out in the Vltava. He didn't last long, fortunately.

Then the incident at SS. Cyril and Methodius Cathedral. Too much pain there. And again, Harriet failed.

Harriet is quiet now. She was very upset that the little Lobkowicz princeling caught her spying. One would almost believe she had feelings for him. But she got just enough information to be helpful. First, when under the influence of the drug she saw Sarah Weston (no relation, since, as you know, dear reader, I have no descendants) open the portal in St. Vitus with a key.

293

Apparently this happened a while back. That was very interesting to me, though Harriet could provide very few details. And second, she reported that there is a map of the Star Summer Palace in the Lobkowicz library. This confirmed my suspicions.

And so I have decided to give young Harriet the ultimate gift. She has graciously agreed, although possibly she does not quite understand as to what. I have given her a full dose, and I believe she is currently watching the Swedes loot Prague in 1648. Perhaps she will see me being raped. If she does, she may stop wondering why I became so cruel, how I could hurt so many people along the way in order to learn what I needed to know. Why my ambition is not tempered with compassion.

*B*ut no more mistakes.

If you want to make sure something is done correctly, you must do it yourself.

If at first you don't succeed, try, try, again.

A stitch in time saves nine.

Twinkle, twinkle little star.

Life is but a dream!

*T*ruly, this is the Golden Age.

I am the Redeemer of the Alchemists. I am the Alchemist's Revenge.

I do not need Harriet.

I have found another.

I have sent the message to Max, and soon all the players will assemble to play my tune.

This is the greatest age of them all. I do not even need to hide so often. I am no longer the only woman who appears to be frozen at thirty years old! I can look thirty for decades. *O brave new world*, indeed.

And now I know where it is to be done.

I should have known.

I should have remembered.

But four hundred years is a long time.

I have known so many over the centuries—the wise, the illustrious, the terrible. The unkind. The merciless. The diseased. Much harm could be done, you know.

But what I do next, I do for love.

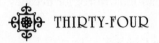

THIRTY-FOUR

Boris was dead.

Pollina was aware that she had been dreaming. Boris had been dead in her dream, or was he actually dead? Dead in life?

Dead in life. That could be the title of an aria, for Nico, for her opera. He was a character in it, too. A character who wanted to die.

Then it occurred to her that she herself might actually be dead.

She was awake.

She had died in her dream.

No, the first part of her dream had really been a memory. She had remembered walking to the Lobkowicz Palace with Nico. Right before Sarah had come back to Prague.

She had never walked up the Old Castle Stairs. She was surprised when Nico suggested they try this together one morning. Nico did not particularly enjoy steps any more than she did, and there were one hundred and twenty-one of them on the route. Nor did he like crowds, and the route drew crowds, because the views from it were said to be spectacular. But the stairs were lined with walls, and many of them were too high for Nicholas to see

296

over. Between counting the steps, and managing her cane, and being around so many people, and hearing them talk, and trying to ignore the pain in her chest, and the fear, it had not been pleasant.

But Nico had said that there were too many unpleasant things in the world to escape them. He had said that she needed to find a way to manage stress, not avoid it. He had said that the world was cruel, and that nothing could change the world from being cruel. He had been angry, and she could feel his anger through his arm, which was laced through hers.

"You would feel differently if you believed in God," Pols told him.

"Who says I don't believe in God?" he answered. "Once I believed that God was the great power of our universe and that God had created our world and everything in it and that God watched over all of us. Later it occurred to me that I had made a very naive assumption: that God had done any of that in a spirit of benevolence. So then when I prayed to God, I prayed that He would be less cruel, less vicious."

"So you hate God."

"I hate God with the same amount of passion that I love God," Nicolas answered. "Which is to say a very small amount. I cannot . . . care . . . anymore."

"You still have God's love," she said.

"And God's hate."

"You don't think God hates you because He made you smaller than other people, do you?" she asked indignantly.

"Whether He hates me or loves me He has left me here all alone," Nico said. "For eternity. Alone. Like our lonely planet. As above, so below."

She had pulled on his arm until they were against the wall.

And she had felt his face with her hands. She wasn't sure why she had done that. She had never wanted to before. She had never deliberately touched a man's face before. She had felt Nico's jaw, and his lips and his cheeks and his nose and his forehead up to where his hair began. His skin was very smooth, so she knew he was very beautiful.

And they had not said anything more.

But that hadn't been in her dream. Or had it? Her mind was confused. Was she dead? Was this what being dead was like? But where was Heaven? Pollina was starting to panic.

She must not panic.

Her dream. Yes, she had been thinking about Nico as she was getting ready for bed, and remembering that conversation and thinking about how it could be translated, musically, and then something had happened and she had fallen asleep. In her dream she had been walking down a smooth gravel path. The sun had been shining; she could feel it on her skin. But her chest was hurting and she was afraid. And sad. Because in her dream she had realized that Boris was dead, and would never run beside her again, and he would have liked this path, which was so straight and smooth, and therefore beautiful.

And then she had known that a creature was in her path, a creature that was not her dog, though it had four legs. It was a lamb. A golden lamb. But it was not beautiful. It was terrible, and it had jumped at her, and wrapped itself across her shoulders, and she had fallen to the ground and then she had rolled over on her back and she had felt as if she were broken and then she had thought, *It has killed me.*

Then she had woken up. Yes. She was awake now.

She was lying on her side, but not on gravel. It was hard,

whatever it was, and it was moving, vibrating and jolting. Pollina decided she would try moving her fingers and toes. They responded. Her tongue felt very thick in her mouth. She moved a little more. Her back was not broken. Her legs and arms could move, but not very far before they hit things that were hard. Metal. Rubber. She was in a moving box made of metal and rubber. She listened.

Her head hurt. Her chest hurt.

She began to cry. This surprised her. She had not cried in a very long time. When she was younger she had cried a lot, in frustration, because her hands were too small to play what she wanted to. She had met Sarah then. Sarah had played for her, until she had grown.

Nico would not grow.

Nico was lonely.

Boris was dead. She had gone to the bathroom the night before and brushed her teeth and she had been thinking of the opera she was writing, of Ferdinand and Philippine overcoming the obstacles to their love, but also of Nico's theme, of the bassoons. She would need to hear the woodwinds, to make sure they were all right. She thought they would be, but she would need to hear them played, with the strings, to make sure she had gotten it right. Max would have to arrange for the musicians to come and play it. Then she had drunk the glass of water by her bedside and gotten into bed. She had called Boris's name, to say good night to him, and he had not come. And she had kept calling for a while but in her heart she had known that he was gone. He was gone forever. She had gotten out of bed and she had found him, as she had known she would, stretched out in front of her door. Until the end, he had been her guard. He had kept her safe.

And then . . .

And then she had realized that something was wrong, inside her. Different from the other thing that was wrong. This was new. Because she always felt tired now, but this was not tired. This was . . .

And then she had a thought: *the water*. The water had not tasted right. She had noticed, and not noticed, because she had been thinking of the bassoons.

Cars. She could hear cars.

She was in a box in a car. She was probably in the trunk of a car.

Pollina began to pray.

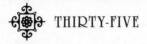
THIRTY-FIVE

A woman loves or hates; there is nothing in between.
So now, the dilemma is a binary question for you. Yes:
you will come at midnight to the Star Summer Palace
with the folio and Sarah Weston. Or, no: you will not
do these things and I will kill the girl.

Max read through the message for the hundredth time, and for the hundredth time looked at the clock in his office. Nico was standing on the window seat, staring out. Sarah would be getting to Prague soon. She had actually been on her way, when he had called her.

Of course Sarah would be bound up in this latest edition of *Hell Portals for Dummies*. Sarah had the key that Nico had given her. Once before when their lives were threatened, it had opened a door and they had watched evil fall into its fathomless depths. He hadn't told Harriet about the key or what it had done, but had she found out somehow?

He had hurt more than just himself when he had fallen for Harriet. Now Pols was in danger. They were all in danger.

"Max?"

It was Jose, standing at the doorway. Max turned to him.

"Pollina's parents. They are coming. They will be at the airport tomorrow morning." Jose held up his phone. He was trembling. "I tell them nothing. I say she is in hospital and situation is serious. I no tell them you let her be stolen when she is dying."

"We will have her back," said Nico. "Before her parents return." Max watched as the little man jumped down and crossed to Jose.

"Is it money?" Jose's voice was hoarse. "They want money? Because parents pay money. They want these things?" He waved a hand around at the library vaguely. "You give them every fucking thing in this palace." His nostrils flared. "Every stupid butter knife and old painting of ugly lady in bad dress. They want blood?" He thumped his chest. "I cut out my heart. I . . . I . . ." His eyes filled with tears.

"You must have faith." Nico spoke with great firmness and solemnity. "I would not say this of everyone, but in your case faith is a good thing. Because you are a good man. Your actions are good. Whatever your sins are, they are not against love. So I believe your life will be a happy one." To Max's surprise, Jose knelt down next to Nico, who gave him a kiss on the forehead and whispered something in Spanish. Jose embraced him for a long moment and then rose. He looked at Max expectantly.

"Jose is a knight. He wants you to give him a task," said Nico, as if he were translating. "Be a prince, Max. Delegate."

Max kept himself from ordering Jose to bop Nico in the nose.

"There are some airtight containers in the supply room," Max said. "Find one big enough for Boris and put him in the wine cellar. Pollina will want to give him a proper burial. Then call Oksana. If for any reason we are delayed, Oksana can help you stall the parents until we get Pollina back here. Keep your phone charged." Jose bowed and left.

Nicolas returned to the library table, where he had spread out the pages of the folio and where he had installed a rat in a cage that for some reason he had brought with him from Vienna.

"Okey-doke," Nicolas sang out, cheerfully. "I could really use an astronomical sextant for some of these instructions, but I think I have the basic idea of what's what. And now I would like to shower and shave and pick out something snazzy to wear. Be a dear and open up a bottle of Château d'Yquem."

Max crossed the room in three quick strides. His anger had found a new focal point. He would not threaten the little man physically (not because of political correctness but because Nico had once demonstrated to Max with an uncooked potato a move Nico called "the testicle puree"), but he wasn't going to let Nico treat this as another entertaining rotation in the great Wheel of Life, or whatever.

"They stole Pollina," he thundered. "She's sick and she's blind and they took her. And now they want Sarah in exchange. Stop acting like it's prom night."

"He doesn't want Sarah." Nico waved a hand. "He wants Sarah to open up a hell portal. And he found a very efficient means of getting her to do it. He won't harm the child, whom I will remind you is very close to dying anyway. But nobody wants her to be murdered. This will be prevented. You and Sarah will get her back. She is not important to him."

"Who? Edward Kelley?"

"Edward Kelley." Nico's eyes were shining. "Edward Kelley. Or possibly Dee. It has to be one of them, and from all the little tricks I'm thinking it's Kelley. Dee was rather a sweetie. I can't see him snatching little girls."

"Your 'Moriarty.'"

"Yes. Kelley must have taken the same drug Tycho forced on me."

"But why does Edward Kelley want to open a hell portal in the Star Summer Palace?"

"I don't know. Perhaps because that is where the Fleece is. Perhaps it is the presence of the Fleece that creates a hell portal. But if it's Kelley, he'll know what the antidote is. He'll know how to help me die."

"But how can you be so sure that Kelley will be able to kill you?"

"You cannot have the code for life without the code for death." Nico smacked the table with his hand. "Death is everything. Death, therefore, art. Therefore, religion. Therefore, sex. Therefore, drugs, wall-to-wall carpeting, salad forks, the Westminster dog show, Barbie, Twitter, soap on a rope, and ShamWow."

"ShamWow?"

"It's a towel. Very absorbent. Oksana ordered one off the Internet. I am trying to say good-bye to you."

"I know. Your requiem sucks. And you might be wrong. Even if it is Kelley, he might not be able to reverse the curse. If he had it, wouldn't he have used it on himself?"

"Edward Kelley has had a *choice*!" Nicolas thundered. "That is the difference. I have had no choice. I am Time's pawn. I am History's *bitch*."

"Okay, that's a little dramatic, even for you."

"Pandora opened a jar out of curiosity and all the evils flew into the world. She shut the jar and caught Hope in the lid. It's all I have. You've always been supportive of my suicide. Don't get soft on me now. This is my moment of exaltation. Kill not my buzz."

Nico leaned over and flipped open the door to the cage that held the rat. The animal immediately ran up Nico's outstretched arm, nuzzled the little man's ear, and then settled himself on Nico's shoulder.

"Don't worry, Hermes," said Nico, with more tenderness than Max had ever heard in the man's voice. "I would never leave you here alone. We'll go together."

"I can look after the rat," Max said.

"Not this rat."

A silence fell between them.

Max found that his anger had dissipated, replaced with a profound sadness. *You are the only family I have,* Max wanted to say. *Don't leave me.*

"You will have a family of your own," Nico said, as if reading his thoughts. "And you don't need me as much as you think you do. Also, I've stolen a number of things from you."

"I know you have."

"And if Sarah had let me sleep with her, I would have."

"Okay. The moment you're dead I'm shagging Oksana." Max turned away, trying to control the spasm in his throat.

"It all comes down to sex, apparently," said a familiar voice. Max turned. Sarah was standing in the door of the library. She looked like hell. She looked wonderful. "All right, I'm here and I'm ready to open a hell portal to get Pols back. The question is . . . what happens after that?"

"Precisely," said Nico. "It's very exciting."

THIRTY-SIX

During the drive from Innsbruck to Prague Sarah had tried to work through the possibilities of what she was about to face, and to make sense of what she had seen and experienced at the *Schloss*. She had told Gottfried about what Heinrich had confessed. He had called an ambulance for his brother—and the police. But she couldn't think about them now.

She had tried to keep the image of Pollina clear in her head, to let the girl know she was coming, that it would be all right.

Bettina Müller was not the answer. There was another answer. She would find it. She was not afraid.

Now, Sarah looked over her shoulder at Nico, in the backseat of the Mini Countryman Gottfried had not objected to her commandeering. Nico was dressed to the nines in a custom cream silk Armani suit with Bettina's rat in his lap. A rat that had been made immortal by twenty-first-century alchemy sitting in the lap of a man made immortal by the careless machinations of an astronomer in the first year of the seventeenth century.

Anything was possible, it seemed.

"Did you find anything out about the galleon at the castle?" asked Nico.

"I found something," Sarah said. "But not that."

She had the cure for immortality in her pocket. It was what Nico wanted, more than anything else. Had it been for Nico that Philippine had given it to her? Sarah loved Nico, but she hadn't been thinking of him when she asked Philippine for help. And Philippine would have known that, because for that moment they had been one. The ultimate desire of alchemy. Two into one.

Sarah looked at Max, driving with his usual breakneck speed westward across Prague.

"I love you," she said.

The car swerved, then straightened.

"I love you, too," he said.

The Star Summer Palace was not visible from the entrance of the park, which had been a hunting preserve in Ferdinand's time. Max parked the car on Libocká. It was freezing cold. They all pulled out flashlights, though the moon was full and luminous. Sarah knew that Max was carrying a gun. Nico slipped into the darkness and she began to run, Max keeping pace beside her, but stopped when they turned into the long avenue that led to the palace.

The building shone white and stark in the darkness. Max had told her in the car that the roof had been rebuilt several times over the years, but the original structure as Ferdinand had designed and built it was intact. A star disguised as a palace. A secret disguised as a star. She told him what she had seen at the von Hohenlohe *Schloss* in Innsbruck.

The gravel crunched under their feet.

She knew that in the past this place had been the scene of much violence. The Battle of White Mountain had been fought near here in 1620 and—Sarah paused as a horse, screaming and wild-eyed, and dragging a bloody rider behind it, his stomach pierced by a broken stave, thundered past her.

"What?" Max whispered, grabbing her arm. His touch restored her vision. The avenue was once again silent and peaceful. Sarah shook her head. The Westonia should have worn off hours before.

"I think the past here might be stronger than the present," she said.

She stared at the building before her. The foundation, Nico had told them, was a circle with a radius of sixty feet. From that rose six peaks of the star formation, each set precisely sixty feet from one another. The original height had been sixty feet from bottom to top. The interior was a series of circles and hexagons.

"We'll have to break in," Max said. "There's probably an alarm system, too. Although maybe . . ." He stopped talking.

A figure stood at the entrance to the building. A small figure, in a heavy long black cloak. A figure who now raised an arm in a bizarrely cheerful wave. Nico appeared beside Sarah, squinting.

"Who is that?" he asked sharply.

They drew closer. It was now clear that the figure was a woman, slim, with large eyes set in a pale oval face. Her features were very delicate. Her short hair was almost white.

"*You?*" said Nico.

The woman narrowed her eyes at Nicolas. "You were a foul abortion in 1601," she said. "And I see that time has not improved you."

"Elizabeth Weston," said Nico. "No."

"No," said Sarah. "That's Bettina Müller."

They looked at each other, then back at the woman.

"I am Westonia," she said with a smile. "The Tenth Muse. The greatest poet of her age. *And* I am Bettina Müller, the greatest scientist of this one. And a great many other names along the way."

"Okay, fine," said Sarah. "But right now I don't care what you call yourself. Because unless you hand over Pollina in about five seconds"—she gripped the bars—"you're just another cunt I'm sending to Hell."

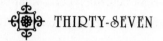 THIRTY-SEVEN

"Where is she?" Sarah rattled the wrought-iron gate. "Pollina. Now."

Bettina pulled a phone out of her heavy cloak and passed it through the bars. Sarah held it to her ear.

"Pols? *Pols?*"

"I'm fine," said the voice, Pollina's voice. "But, Sarah, don't do it. Don't do what she asks. It's profoundly wrong."

What is she asking?

"Where are you?" Sarah pressed the phone hard into her ear.

"I don't know."

"Can you get outside? Can you hear anything? Smell anything that would tell us where you are?"

Sarah glanced over and saw Bettina standing there calmly, arms crossed, watching her. Max and Nico, too, were waiting for a signal.

"Nothing. I'm locked in. But listen to me, Sarah. I need you to really listen."

"Okay," said Sarah, crouching down. Her heart was pounding, her breath making frosty clouds in the air. Only a mile or so away, it was just another late fall night in Prague. She could hear faint blasts of Donna Summer from a nearby club. And yet here she was, dealing with—what?—a crazed scientist? A four-hundred-year-old psychopathic poetess? She was going to stick with the former for now. She focused on what Pols was saying.

"I'm okay with dying," Pols said. "If this is the end, here, it's all right. Do you understand? I know I'm only thirteen, but I've done everything I hoped to do. I've loved and been loved. I've made music. I have had the best of life. And I'm going to die anyway."

"Don't say that." It couldn't end like this, over the phone.

"I've always known I wouldn't live a long life. I think if you look into your heart you'll realize you've always known it, too. So you must let me go. Let me go, Sarah. I will always be with you. Don't put such stock in this physical body. It's not what lasts. Love is what matters. You know that. That's what the visions have shown you, isn't it? Passion, in all its forms, that's what endures."

Sarah couldn't speak.

Pols continued. Her voice was clear and calm. "God has always had a special plan for me, and I don't want anyone messing with that. Okay?"

Sarah refused to accept what Pols was saying. If she did, she had the sense she would fall into an abyss there was no climbing out of.

"I'm coming to get you," she said. The phone went dead. Sarah examined it. A burner phone, no other calls on it.

"I love modern technology," said Bettina as she unlocked the gate. "You have no idea how annoying this all would have been in another century. Letters, carriage rides, messengers to bribe . . ."

"Spare me," said Sarah. Her adrenaline was heightening all of her senses. She could smell things on Bettina—metallic scents, herbs, something harsh and chemical as well. No fear. That was bad.

Bettina gave a tight smile as Sarah, Max, and Nico came through the gate. "I've given the security guard a little tranquilizer so we'll have the place to ourselves. And I've shut off the electricity—we don't want anything interfering with the natural energy of the site."

Max had his gun out in an instant and pointing at Bettina.

"I'm *immortal*," she said impatiently. "I'm surprised I need to spell it out for you all. If you don't do exactly as I ask, Pollina will die." She looked at Max. "Harriet will see to that."

Harriet stepped out of the shadows, eyes downcast. She was dressed in court costume of the seventeenth century and seemed barely able to stand. Her eyes were rolling. Drugged. She lurched toward Max, who held her by the shoulders, looking horrified.

"You did this to her?"

"She did it to herself," Bettina said calmly. "She was a very willing participant. But not a very good spy. Still, she is being rewarded. You will see."

"You've known about me?" This was Nico now, coming forward. "All this time?"

Bettina pursed her lips. "Only recently did you come to my attention. We've been looking for the same things, though I suspect for different reasons. I hope you enjoyed all my little cards. You know, several times I almost called you and suggested we go have a nice chai latte at Starbucks and talk over the old days. We should be friends. And yet—"

Nico's lip twisted in a sneer. "You cannot stoop so low. Nor can I. But . . . you found it?" The little man was trembling.

"Found what? I've found many things."

Nico looked toward the palace, hopeful.

She opened the front door for them, a heavy wooden Renaissance-era door crisscrossed with iron. It slammed shut behind them with a heavy clunk.

They were standing now in a foyer between two of the points of the six-pointed star. The room was empty, except for a pile of boxes in one angle of the star, and lit with torches that cast shadows on the whitewashed walls and stone fireplace. In the flickering light, Sarah could see empty-eyed plaster masks staring down at them. Laughing, crying, staring, grimacing. The hair on the back of her neck went up, and the key between her breasts began to vibrate.

"Charming, isn't it?" said Bettina. "Ferdinand did love his symbolism. Max, the folio?"

Max looked at Sarah. She nodded and looked away. She couldn't look at Max.

She needed to hold on to her anger, stoke its fire, keep it at the boiling point. Anger was good. Anger fed action.

"I've read it," said Nico as Bettina flipped through the papers. "The building is supposed to represent the cosmos and all that is contained within. All of the stucco work has alchemical parallels. Heroism, transmutation, incest, the chemical wedding. If the Fleece is here, it must be buried. Unless you already have it—?"

Bettina laughed. "Is that what you're after?"

"Fuck the Fleece," Sarah shouted. "I want Pollina back."

"Don't fight her." Harriet in all her finery slunk against a wall. "She *is* Elizabeth Weston. You should do as she says."

"Fuck the Fleece indeed," said Elizabeth. "I stopped looking for that a long time ago."

"Then what do you want?" Nico came forward and stared up at Elizabeth.

"To be reunited with my daughter," said Elizabeth.

"Oh, I remember," said Nico. "Which one do you want? The dribbler? Or the spitter? Or the cougher?"

With one hand Elizabeth grabbed Nico by the hair and threw him across the room. Before Sarah could even react, Max had Elizabeth by the throat.

"You may be immortal," snarled Max, holding the butt of his gun to her head, "but I will club you like a carp if you touch my friends."

"A Lobkowicz with something in his codpiece," said Elizabeth. "Polyxena would be proud. Let me go. Remember your little Pols." Max released her. Nico started to stand, and then sat down, heavily, his head in his hands.

"You want to die?" asked Sarah. She very much needed *not* to look at Nico right now. "And be with your daughter? Because I can send you to her. We don't need a portal. I have the antidote. I'll give it to you after you give me Pols."

She produced the vial from her pocket. Elizabeth stared at it.

"I have no idea what that is," she laughed. "But I don't care. Even if it is the antidote, I don't need it. I don't want to die."

"You can't want to live," Nico whispered. "Not anymore. This is a curse."

"You idiot," Elizabeth spat. "A curse? You have done nothing with your time if you can't think of anything better than dying. Ah, but your perspective is so small, isn't it? Four hundred years and a dwarf is still small. But woman? Woman has risen! Woman will continue to rise! *I want my DAUGHTER.* She will live forever by my side. Together we will live to see the end of man. And now I have a way to bring Portia to me. That's what I have been working for, all these years. I will bring her back. I will cure her sickness. And then, when her body is healthy and strong and pure, I will bind her telomeres with gold. And we will never be parted again."

"It is impossible." Sarah's mind was spinning.

"You understand, Sarah," said Elizabeth softly. "I know you do. The anguish at not being able to save the one you love? In that we are the same, we Weston women, aren't we?"

"Don't," said Sarah. "Don't try to girl bond with me. And how do you think Portia is going to be returned to you?"

Elizabeth spread her arms wide.

"You are going to take a dose of a time-perception drug, which a little bird tells me Tycho named after me. You will find Portia, and you will bring her with you through the portal. This can be done. I've been practicing." Elizabeth turned to Max. "You can vouch for that."

"Saint John," Max said. "Jan Kubiš. You brought them through. How?"

"Time," Elizabeth laughed. "Time brought me the answer. Time *is* the answer. The last century taught me that. Einstein taught us all that space-time can be bent by the presence of an enormously huge mass. Which is what a hell portal is, of course. A pocket of dark matter. But I needed the precise measurements of this power and how to manage it, which has taken practice. Another century. And I needed a portal here in Prague, near where Portia was. Not having a convenient key like mademoiselle here, I had to use a fair bit of alchemy to open the portals. I thought I had found all of them, until Harriet described the markings on the folio. Philippine bound this place very thoroughly with her spells so we must do things the old-fashioned way to find where the portal is hidden. And then I need you, Sarah, to open the door and be Portia's guide. According to Harriet, you're quite the little time-walker."

They were all, Sarah realized, looking at her now.

"I don't have any Westonia," she said. "I took the last of it in Innsbruck."

"Oh, Harriet will share. She's not much good on it herself."

Sarah looked at the wasted figure of Harriet.

"You really did find the antidote?" Nico was at her side now. "That's the 'something' that you found at the castle?"

"I broke the Westonia in half," Sarah confessed. "I took one half in the lab and the other at the castle. And I saw Philippine. I . . . I was her, I think. For a few minutes. She had made the elixir for immortality. And the antidote. She gave it to me. I can't really explain how it happened."

"Interesting," said Nico. "Especially since I have the other half of Westonia right here."

He produced a half pill from his pocket.

"But," she insisted, "I hid the Westonia in my pocket."

"And I stole it, and replaced it with half an Altoid."

"Then who . . . what? I saw everything. Ferdinand. And Philippine. I saw *Mozart*, and . . ."

Elizabeth and Nico exchanged a look.

"Placebo effect," said Elizabeth. "She doesn't need the drug."

Nico nodded. "She has the gift. I did wonder."

"Me, too, at the ball," said Elizabeth. "Scared the hell out of me. She has it."

"I have what?" demanded Sarah. "What happened to me?"

"My dearest one," said Nico, "It seems you never really needed the drug, after that first time. You only needed to *think* you had taken the drug. You're highly sensitive to energy fluctuations, to put it mildly. Sherbatsky suspected this, I think."

"So *unfair*," said Harriet. "She doesn't even care about history."

"You're saying I... But all the physical sensations... the sickness."

"I didn't say it was an easy thing. Perhaps you will get better at it."

Sarah thought of how she'd been catching glimpses of Beethoven all over Vienna. Did she really have the power to see him? Did she only need to give herself permission?

"Lovely," said Elizabeth. "No sense wasting good drugs. Ingredients are so hard to come by these days. I had to order powdered lion heart from some redneck animal dealer in Texas, for God's sake. Now. Sarah. Pols is waiting. Time, my dear. Time. We need to make a deal."

"Fine!" Sarah snapped. "What do we need to do to speed this show along?"

Elizabeth kneeled and bent her head in prayer for a moment.

"So you're not kidding?" Nico said. "You could bring back Aristotle, or Jesus, or Seabiscuit. And you're bringing back—"

Elizabeth was eye to eye with him. "Tell me, Jepp, wasn't there a girl... why, I believe she was Tycho's sister. Sondra, was it?"

"Sophie," said Nico quietly.

"Wouldn't you like to see her again?"

Nico seemed to struggle with himself for a moment, then said harshly, "Not on this side of things."

Sarah saw Hermes stick his nose out of Nico's suit pocket. The little man pushed him back down.

"Max, spread out the folio," he barked. "Sarah, put that vial away for now."

"Harriet, you're going to love this!" cried Elizabeth. "The portal was hidden by alchemy, and only alchemy will reveal it. It's magic time."

"I assume you have the ingredients?" asked Nico.

"Removed for curatorial purposes from across the land," sang Elizabeth, pointing to the pile of boxes. "The hardest to find was a sixteenth-century Venezuelan fruit fly preserved in amber. A favorite ingredient of Philippine's. That was hidden, if you please, in a galleon inside the British Museum."

"That's what was in the galleon?" Sarah swung around. "I got high off a *fruit fly*?"

"What on earth are you talking about?"

"The cannon in the secret compartment in the galleon. I got blasted with it."

Elizabeth smiled.

"Oh, that. That was just a wee something Philippine stored for Rudolf. A nice little seventeenth-century tonic for the vagus nerve. Not important. If you had popped off the head of the emperor figure on the ship, you would've found the fruit fly. Not that you would've known what to do with it. Anyway, thanks ever so for returning the galleon. I decamped from Vienna so quickly, I didn't have time to dispose of it. And I always cover my tracks. So. Let's begin. Nico, read out the instructions."

Sarah watched as Elizabeth sprinkled various powders and liquids and objects at precise points in the room. A lifetime's worth—no, several lifetimes' worth—of collected ingredients. The feather of a dodo. A meteorite from the asteroid Vesta. Tears of an elephant shed during sorrow. A sparrow's egg impregnated with twins.

Elizabeth gathered powdered vials of gold, silver, and copper, and set a large hourglass in the center of the room Nico took a piece of chalk, marched off the paces, and drew celestial symbols on the terra-cotta floor tiles—the Sun, the Moon, and Venus. Elizabeth emptied the vials onto the chalk symbols.

"Iron, tin, lead, and quicksilver," said Nico. "Here, here, here, and here." He drew the symbols for Mars, Jupiter, Saturn, and Mercury. He seemed to be almost in a trance. "It's been a long time," he said. "I helped the Master draw this circle many times."

"As I assisted my stepfather," said Elizabeth. "Cardinal, mutable, fixed, calcination, congelation, fixation . . ."

"Distillation, digestion, solution," added Nico. "Sublimation, separation, creation . . ."

"Fermentation, multiplication, projection."

"Abracadabra," said Sarah. "I'm waiting here."

"Now, we do need someone to take my daughter's place in the past. I had to send Kubiš and Nepomuk back through because if someone comes out, someone must go in. Or things are out of balance." Elizabeth pointed at Harriet. "You," she said, "are going to have such a lovely trip."

"Harriet"—Max moved to her side—"you don't have to do this."

"I think it's all so fascinating," said Harriet, swaying. "Don't you?" She stumbled toward Elizabeth. "I'm ready."

"The time is right," said Nico. "We must marry the red and the white, Mercury and Sulfur."

Nico and Elizabeth began chanting something in Latin. *"Ut supra sub ratione temporis unum spatium itineris conficiendi hic spiritus flectatur dimittam . . ."*

And then the floor began to rumble.

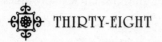 THIRTY-EIGHT

Many of the alchemists were seriously good engineers, Sarah reminded herself, as the floor began moving under her feet. The stones were rearranging themselves by some unseen force, like domino tiles. The whole building began to shake. Plaster bits fell from the ceiling, and each of them—Sarah, Elizabeth, Harriet, Max, Nico—retreated from the center of the room as the stones slid away to reveal a short flight of stairs down into darkness. Sarah lurched forward. The key around her neck was vibrating, tugging her down to her knees.

"The portal is down there," Elizabeth said. "But before you open it you must find my daughter."

"Not until Pols is safe," Sarah warned.

"I get my girl, you get yours," said Elizabeth. She dragged a large cardboard box from the corner and began slicing away the sides.

"Why don't you take the drug and see her yourself?" asked Sarah, stalling. "It's named after you."

"Hasn't the dwarf told you? It doesn't work on us. Our cells are modified in a way that makes it ineffective." She pulled the last of the box away and dragged out a . . .

An armonica. A glass armonica.

"Where did you get that?" Sarah moved forward. "It's not . . . Mesmer's armonica, is it?"

"Quiet. Now, help me bring this down the steps. Portia will still be weak and ill when she comes through the portal. I will need to keep her alive until I determine what drugs will cure her for good. I will not give her immortality in a sick body. Come, all of you. You, too, Harriet. You must be ready to enter the portal."

They descended the steps with their awkward burden. The staircase led to a small, round room.

It was the round room from her dreams. But there was only one door here, a rather innocuous-looking trapdoor in the floor. The key around her neck was jumping now. Elizabeth moved the armonica to a position a few feet from the portal.

She looked at Sarah. "Now. Find her."

"It's not that simple," Sarah snapped. "I can't just turn it on and off. And I get confused easily."

"We were here," said Elizabeth. "Upstairs." She pointed to the opening at the top of the steps. "My daughter and I were here. It was the last day in April. They opened up the palace on Walpurgis night, and we came. Portia was wearing a red cape. We stood upstairs, with the rest of the revelers, drinking hot wine."

There was a new tone to Elizabeth's voice. Plaintive.

"Look for her. She's here. It was *Čarodějnice*. Walpurgis. The emperor opened the gates of the preserve to the townspeople for the bonfire, spreading a little goodwill to counter the purges. I know you can find her."

Sarah moved back to the steps.

"Don't use your eyes. Feel her. Like music. Feel her," Elizabeth whispered.

Sarah closed her eyes. Hundreds and hundreds of people over

the centuries had wandered through the room above them. She must not get distracted. Her mind stretched out, seeking. She could smell chestnuts in the air, hear something howling in the woods outside the palace. Walpurgis in the early seventeenth century. The pagan rite that marked the end of winter. Sarah wasn't sure when the local populace had transitioned from annually burning a real live woman to burning a straw witch. Maybe not yet, she realized.

She heard voices, saw figures moving above her. She moved up the steps until she was standing in the central room.

A little girl in a red cape. Elizabeth standing next to her, wearing a black cloak like the one she wore now, looking like a child herself. The room was crowded with other figures, but they were dim compared to the hot intensity of Elizabeth's energy. The girl began coughing. Elizabeth held her tight, and the girl coughed up a spot of blood that Elizabeth wiped away with an already bloodstained handkerchief. She gave her a sip of the hot wine.

"Where is Pollina?" shouted Sarah down the steps.

"Do you see her? Do you see Portia?"

"I see her. Where is Pollina?"

In the past, Elizabeth put her hand against Portia's forehead. "Oh, my child," she said. "We must get you home."

"You're going to leave," said Sarah. "You're going to walk away. Tell me where Pollina is."

"No!" said Elizabeth. "We mustn't leave. This is the day, the day it happens. Walpurgis. The only day we were here, in the Star Summer Palace. I could feel the energy; I thought it would help her. I had tried prayer. I had tried medicines. In my desperation I was ready to try magic. I remember this. I remember the pull. I remember I was afraid. Start coming back down the stairs. She will feel your energy. She will follow it."

Sarah heard it in her voice. The sound of someone who would do anything to save the one she loved. She knew that sound. It was in her, too. She came partway down the stairs, but she could still see Elizabeth and Portia above her.

In the seventeenth century, Elizabeth was straightening Portia's cape, pulling up her hood. "We must go," Elizabeth said to Portia.

"Please," said Portia. "Just a little longer, Mama?"

"Where is Pollina?" Sarah snapped over her shoulder.

"She's here." Elizabeth's voice was cracking with emotion. "On the top floor. She's not hurt. I wouldn't hurt her. I couldn't. She's so much like Portia. Please. Please help me. I know you hate me. I've done terrible things, but only to help a sick little girl."

"In the name of love? You've perverted the whole concept."

"Maybe. But don't you see what he did to me? I was a child just like Pollina. He ruined me. And I've been alone for so long. The alchemists wanted knowledge. They wanted power. All I want is to have my child back. Please, please, help me bring Portia here. Let us be together. I didn't choose this, Sarah. Please."

"How do I do it?" asked Sarah. "The staircase is still covered up in her time. I can't drag her through the floor."

"She will come," Elizabeth whispered. "She must. I will help."

Elizabeth pressed a foot pedal on the armonica and the bowls began to spin on their treadle. Sarah thought of the woodcuts she'd seen in old alchemical books, of a musician playing near a hell portal. Music, of course. Music was the language that traversed time.

Elizabeth struck a note.

In the seventeenth century, Portia suddenly grew very still. Sarah saw the little girl's white face turn even whiter.

"Do you hear that, Mama?"

Elizabeth played a series of notes. Not a melody but a kind of calling. Summoning. Luring. Seducing.

"Music," said Portia. "It's pretty."

"It's the spirits," Elizabeth whispered. "But are they angels or demons?"

"It's working," said Sarah. "They can hear you."

"Yes. I remember. I will try to stop us. Don't let me."

In the seventeenth century, Elizabeth knelt and pressed her hand against what was, in her time, the floor. Her hand was only a foot above Sarah's face. Sarah could see the veins in Elizabeth's hand.

"Music below," Elizabeth said. "I can feel it."

"I want to try," said Portia. If the little girl put her hand down, too, Sarah thought, she could reach up and grab it.

Portia began to lean down, reaching toward the floor. Sarah reached up, but Elizabeth caught the girl's hand, pulled it away, and kissed it. "This is a bad place," said Elizabeth. She shivered. "Things happen here. Evil things."

. . .

"You won't let her come close," said Sarah. "You're afraid. She's right here." Sarah reached up her hand again, but she couldn't quite touch the little girl.

Elizabeth abandoned the armonica and raced up the stairs, holding out her hand to her daughter, and in that moment seventeenth-century Elizabeth did the same, beckoning her daughter to leave. The girl stood in the middle, two versions of her mother on either side of her, holding out their hands to her. Portia hesitated. Sarah held her breath. The little girl was looking at her, as if she could see her at last.

"But it will change things," said Max, below them. "It will change everything."

Just above them, Sarah saw Elizabeth draw her daughter close.
"You must come with me," said the woman, holding her daughter. "We must stay together."

Next to Sarah, Elizabeth was breathing rapidly.
"I remember," she said. "I remember. But we can change the past."

But the Elizabeth of the past was leading her daughter away.

"Open the portal!" Elizabeth screamed, shoving Sarah down the steps. "She will come back. She will feel it."
Sarah landed hard on the floor. The key lurched forward and she grabbed it.
"No." Sarah's head was spinning. "No. She's never going to

come through. Because you are never going to let her go. You know this."

"We can change the past!"

"No," said Sarah. "Only the future." She reached to still the key. "It won't do any good to open the portal. She won't come."

"No!" With a yell, Harriet threw herself at Sarah, grabbed at the key, and scrambled toward the portal. The chain held fast, and Sarah was dragged by her neck. They struggled together on the floor, Harriet screaming as the key burned the flesh of her hand. The magnetic pull of the key met the force of the door, and with a wrench it flew upward. Sarah closed her eyes against the brilliant flash of light. And then nothing. No scent, no sound, no light. Nothing but the pull of the portal. Sarah could feel herself sliding toward it, and then Max's hands on her shoulders, pulling her back. Harriet let go of the key around Sarah's neck.

And disappeared.

The portal door flew shut with a thunderous crack.

Light and smell and sound returned. An awful sound.

Sarah looked over to where Elizabeth was on her knees at the stairs, weeping. It was pitiful, heart wrenching.

"So close," she sobbed. "So close. Maybe. Maybe we can try again."

"No," said Nico. "Sarah is right. In the past you will never let your daughter go. This was all madness. This was a dream."

"Max," said Sarah. "Pols is here. Upstairs somewhere."

Max leapt over Elizabeth and sprinted up the stairs. Sarah, who found she could barely stand, half crawled to the crying woman.

"Bettina, Elizabeth, whatever your name is," said Sarah, "you've got to help Pols."

"I can't." She looked up at Sarah through her tears. "The drugs she's already on should have worked. There's something else. Something I can't see. I wanted to help; I did. I looked at everything. But I can't help her. I'm sorry."

"The armonica," Sarah whispered. "You said you could use it to cure your daughter."

Elizabeth shook her head. "Portia's illness could have been cured with antibiotics. Simple antibiotics. The armonica would only help the healing process. That is all. Your Pollina is going to die."

Tears of rage and despair filled Sarah's eyes. Science had failed her. Alchemy had failed her.

She forced herself to stand and look down at Elizabeth.

Why had Philippine given her the vial? Would it be helping Pols in some way, to let this suffering end?

She had no reason to show this freak, this monster, this sadist any mercy.

Pollina had talked to her once, about how Mozart's early operas had shown ambition but not compassion. Pols believed in compassion.

Sarah would not comfort this woman, but she would help her find peace at last. She looked at Nico.

"The vial?" Nico asked. "There is enough, maybe, for the both of us? I am . . . I am a small man."

Sarah looked at him. She was, she realized, crying.

How would it help Pollina, to give Nico the means to kill himself?

How could she lose him?

Nico had seen her strength, before she had seen it herself. Two summers ago he had saved her life in the tunnels under Prague Castle. He had shown her history all around her. Given her the gift of the past. He was a giant.

And now in return she was giving him what he had always sought. Death. A bitter gift. But, she knew, a welcome one. For him as for Elizabeth. As it would be for her when her time came. We live, we love, we die. Like the distant suns whose explosions sent the elements to the earth that form our bodies, we blaze and then fade, our energy repurposed to other forms. As above, so below.

"I think there is enough," she said.

Elizabeth looked up. She looked at the vial. She looked at Nico.

"Do it," said the little man. "There is nothing left for you here."

"No. There is nothing left for us here."

Elizabeth crossed herself and opened the vial. She swallowed, then handed it to Nicolas.

"Portia," she said.

And then she fell forward. Nico swiftly moved to her side and took the vial from her hand. He held fingers to her neck, then her wrist. Hermes chittered loudly.

"Gone," said Nico.

Sarah looked at him.

"Give me a kiss," said the little man. "I want to go out with the taste of a beautiful woman on my lips. Then go quickly. Don't say good-bye. No last words. Put it in your kiss."

Sarah kissed him with everything she had. Then she ran up the stairs.

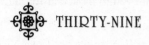

THIRTY-NINE

Max had found Pols in a small storeroom, curled up among stacks of boxes and tools. He wrapped her in his coat and was carrying her down the stairs. Pols was humming a tune under her breath. Max shook his head at Sarah. Tears were streaming down his face.

Pollina began coughing.

"It's okay," Sarah whispered. "Pols, it's okay. It's over. We'll take you home now."

"I'm sorry," Pollina whispered. "But I'm just too tired. It will be soon, I think."

Sarah looked into the girl's face. She saw it written there, what Pols had said on the phone. Pols was ready to let go. She began coughing again.

"I want to be buried with Boris," said Pols when she got her breath back. "And I've written a requiem mass. Don't let the musicians play it too slowly. And I *intended* the Lachrymosa to be humorous."

"Elizabeth?" Max asked Sarah.

"She's dead. I gave her the antidote."

"And . . . Nico?"

Sarah looked at Pols, who had her head buried in Max's chest.

"There was enough for two."

When they got to the ground floor, Sarah looked at the stairs leading down to the round room and the portal. The day crew was going to get a hell of a surprise. They could not leave Nico here. Alone. With a woman he hated.

"Stay here," she said to Max. She ran down the staircase.

Nico was lying on the ground, eyes closed. The vial was next to him. Hermes, the rat, sat on Nico's chest.

Max appeared, still carrying Pols.

"We wanted to say good-bye."

"I think we should bring him with us."

"Can you carry him?"

"I think so."

Sarah tried to scoop up Nico's small body.

"You got him?" Max asked.

"Yes. It's just . . . it's just he's actually very heavy."

"You take Pols."

"No, I've got him." Sarah tried a sort of fireman's rescue posture. Nico's pants slipped down.

"Got him?"

"Sort of. Crap. Wait."

"Oh, for fuck's sake!" Nico straightened up. "This is so undignified!"

Sarah dropped him.

Hermes the rat scampered up Nico's leg and torso to his shoulder and stared at them, nose twitching. The rat appeared to be laughing.

"You're . . ." Max said.

"Still here," said Nico, standing up and brushing off his suit. "Yes. Don't read too much into it. I prepaid for a year of Pilates."

He scooped the vial off the floor and put it in his pocket, then walked forward and held out his arms. Max leaned down and gave him Pols. The little girl looked big in the little man's arms.

"I'm maybe not quite done," Nico whispered into her ear. "And maybe neither are you. There is still music to be played. The opera isn't finished."

And that's when Sarah heard it. She heard it in her mind the way she sometimes heard Beethoven's voice. The way she had heard Philippine speak to her. The way—ever so faintly—she could sometimes remember the sound of her father calling her name, asking her to play him something.

She heard the five notes of Pollina's opera.

"Pols," said Sarah, "I want to try something. Will you trust me?"

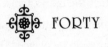 FORTY

$\mathcal{S}$arah looked at all of them. Pollina, her thin shoulders hunched forward, her fair hair falling in strands about her face. Max, whitely tense and still beside her, expectant. Nicolas, with the rat Hermes scrabbling to stay on his shoulder, nodding at her. They had covered Elizabeth Weston's body with her cloak.

Sarah had never really believed in Max's Golden Fleece with its wonderfull and awfull truth. The wisdom and magic of the alchemists. Edward Kelley's potions. Tycho Brahe's meddling and the resulting immortality of Nicolas Pertusato. She couldn't believe what she had seen tonight. Chalk symbols on the floor of a star-shaped palace in the Czech Republic. Powders and potions and chanted Latin. Hell portal doors. You strung a bunch of big-sounding words together and drew some nifty pictures and dressed up in robes and expected ... what? God? Your dead daughter? Dracula? The white rabbit? The cure to everything? Keanu Reeves in *The Matrix*?

You could swallow a drug that allowed you to expand your brain's narrow perceptions of time and see the past by following the emotional energy people left behind them.

Or you could merely think that you had. And maybe that was enough.

Dreams? Chanting? Drumming? Prayer? Visions?

Using belief to affect the body.

Using music.

Sarah could feel it within her, a kind of shuddering warmth, a loss of gravity in her bones, a humming in her blood. Everything in her life had led her to this point. Everything she had seen was just preparation for what was to come.

"Max," Sarah said, "You're going to have to help me. You too, Nico."

She must not hold back. She must not hold on. She could only go further and further. Perhaps for one time only in her life would she have—not the courage to fight—but the will to surrender.

She moved to the armonica.

"Watch," she said. "It's five notes. E, B, C, A, G. I'll show you." She pressed the treadle of the instrument and the glasses began spinning. She showed Max how to touch the rims, and which ones he should use to get the proper notes. Nico joined them.

"I'll press the pedal," he said. "Max, you just concentrate on the notes."

Max was not asking her why she wanted him to do this. He heard the certainty in her voice and he trusted it. Because he loved her, as she loved him.

"Just play," she said. "Just keep playing."

The notes filled the room. The theme from Pols's opera. Pols had said Sarah would understand. And now she did.

Sarah gave herself to the sound. She scooped up the girl in her arms. Pollina was so light, so fragile. Sarah wrapped the girl's long legs around her waist and Pollina snaked her arms around Sarah's neck. Sarah held Pols tightly to her chest.

E, B, C, A, G.

Sarah moved deeper into the music. Deeper into the trance.

Music filled the room, filled her brain, her breath, her blood.

Sarah looked at the body of the woman in the corner.

Elizabeth Weston was standing now, clad in golden armor, her face set in a mask of resolution, a long golden sword at her side.

She looked at Nico and Max. Nico's shadow on the floor, monstrously long and broad now. A giant. And Max's wings were playing the armonica. Yes, wings. A dragon and a giant. She had dreamed this. She had dreamed this.

She looked down at her own hand, which was veined with gold. She was the knight from Klimt's *Beethoven Frieze*.

She looked at Pols, who was holding Elizabeth's hourglass in her hand.

E, B, C, A, G.

"It's time," she said to Pols.

Pollina raised the hourglass and threw it to the stone floor, where it shattered, the sands spilling in a mound at her feet.

"Hold on tight," she whispered to Pollina. She felt the muscles of the thin arms and legs contract. Sarah listened. She heard Pollina's heartbeat, faint but distinguishable.

Max touched the glass for E.

The sand of the hourglass began snaking across the floor, streaming into lines and patterns. A repeated series of perfect squares each containing a six-pointed star. The sands rose and fell, swooped and glided. Fully formed, the squares formed a kind of labyrinth, which led to a central and larger square. Sarah walked the path carefully until she reached the center. She took the last step into the center of the star.

In an instant, cold blackness enveloped her. No breath. The

blackness was heavy, dense. There was nothing to equal this density. No air. Her lungs were crushed. Sarah felt them splintering into needle shards.

And then nothing. She was part of the heaviness, of the cold blackness. She could not move her hand because in this airless smothering void there could be no movement. But she could hear Pollina's heartbeat, feel her arms and legs around her, and because of that she could think of her own hand, of the space where she used to have a hand. Which still existed somewhere, surely.

And from out of the darkness and the cold and the heaviness, the sound of the second glass: B.

Now there was light in the dark. A golden thread that floated and twisted and coiled in a sinuous dance. The thread was alive. Nearly alive. Now truly alive. The thread grew thicker, began to pulse. Features began to form on its surface, onyx eyes, a flickering ruby tongue. A snake. A snake with a white-gold tail. It floated before them, waiting. Breathing. Watching.

I am not afraid, thought Sarah. *I am not afraid.*

The snake opened its mouth and sang the third note. C.

The most beautiful C. The C at the center of all things. The snake swung its tail up and brought it to its mouth. It turned one black jeweled and lidless eye toward Sarah, then swallowed its tail, creating a perfect ring. An *ouroboros*. Sarah found that she could move, or at least imagine herself moving. She could float into the circle of the snake. Sarah, with Pols, moved into the *ouroboros* and as she did so she reached out her hand and stroked the golden skin of the snake, which rang.

The fourth note: A.

The snake released its tail and stretched, expanded. The golden scales fell away and Sarah could see veins with blood, glowing blue, then dark red. It was a column, a river of blood.

Branches shot out of the river like tree limbs, reaching out, groping, feeling. Sarah could hear them singing to one another. Pols's heartbeat was growing louder now, but Sarah no longer felt the girl around her.

She was inside. Sarah was inside Pollina. Like Nina had described the nanotubes, going inside her veins, her blood. And the blood was getting darker and closer and heavier. And the song of the tree limbs became harsh and discordant. Sarah felt as if she were in a tunnel now, and the tunnel was getting smaller and smaller until it was so narrow that Sarah could not move forward any more. The blood slowed, then stopped. She could not go forward. She could not turn around and go back. She could not move.

But the heartbeat was still there.

One more note.

The fifth note.

Please, Max.

Yes, there it was. G.

The tunnel immediately began to expand, fusing and forming a ladder that twisted and turned. The ladder ribboned around her, seemingly without end or beginning.

A double helix.

Somewhere in this chain was the thing that was killing Pollina.

So they needed to go beyond that. They needed to go farther.

Sarah took a deep breath; and as the last vibration of the last note faded into silence, the chain shattered.

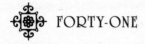 FORTY-ONE

They had arrived back at the Star Summer Palace. Sarah stood in the center of the star, in a round white room.

A round white room with five doors. Exactly as in her dream. Pure white, polished to a high shine. Max and Nico and Elizabeth had all vanished. Sarah became aware of Pollina against her chest, grown suddenly very heavy. Sarah looked down at her and the girl drew back her head and raised her face toward Sarah.

Pollina's eyes were open. They were almost all white, all iris, the pupils almost swallowed by the white. Pollina shut her eyes.

"Where are we?" the girl asked. Sarah set her gently on her feet and Pollina stretched out her hands.

"We're at the Star Summer Palace, but it's a little different. It's all white now. I mean, empty. And we have five doors."

Four of the doors had keyholes and looked quite ordinary.

The fifth door was different.

Sarah took a step away from it.

They should not open that door. It was not a hell portal. It was something else.

Pols snapped her fingers and they listened to the sound, which was not at all commensurate with the space. Pols might just as well have snapped her fingers in the Colosseum.

"Big room," commented the girl.

"What do you think we should do?"

"It's a classic scenario." Pols shrugged. "The whole thing seems a bit obvious. Room-with-doors as metaphor. We must be in *your* brain, not mine."

"I'm not sure about that," said Sarah. "There is no color. Anyway, we have four choices."

Technically they had five choices, but every cell in her body was telling her not to touch that fifth door.

Pollina was swaying. Sarah caught her just before she crashed to the floor. The girl's lips were dry and cracked, but her forehead was beaded with perspiration.

"Sarah," the girl whispered. "I think you should . . . hurry."

Sarah took off her jacket and cradled it under Pollina's head. The girl curled up in a ball, coughing weakly.

Sarah moved to the nearest door and sank to her knees, peering through the iron keyhole.

She saw a stream and a cluster of moss-covered rocks. The air was misty, and Sarah caught the scent of fir trees. The figure of a man sat on the largest of the rocks, singing in a flat, deep voice. *Da-da-da,* he rumbled, then paused. He tootled experimentally, like a trumpet, then honked a series of minor notes. Then sang again: Da-da-da . . . *Pa! Pa! PA!* He turned his head, keeping time in the air, as if he were conducting the water before him.

Beethoven. Of course it was he. In a large hat crammed low over his forehead, stained breeches, and a long coat. Ludwig van Beethoven. Luigi's hair was streaked with white and his face was lined. Beethoven in his fifties, near the end of his life. Sarah didn't recognize the work he was singing. A little something he would discard in midcomposition? A last sonata?

Was she hearing the rough beginnings of what would have been—had he lived long enough—the Tenth Symphony?

Sarah, who didn't believe in God, whispered, *Oh, God, God, God.* To sit next to Beethoven by a stream, in nature, the place that had always replenished this genius's perturbed spirit? To hear him compose? Maybe she had died, after all. One thing she knew for certain now, if she were to open this door and enter it, it wouldn't be as a ghost. Beethoven might not be able to hear her, but he would see her. He would talk to her, and she to him. *Luigi, it's beautiful. Sarah, do you think so?* Oh, God, God, God.

Pollina, behind her, coughed again. Beethoven would die soon. Pollina even sooner. Beethoven was already dead. Pols was still alive.

She moved to the next door and peered through the keyhole.

A bedroom lit by hundreds of candles. Sarah could see the full moon through a small casement window. And the wasted figure of a woman on a low bed. A man stooping over her.

"My darling," said the man. "My love. My love, you must try."

It was Ferdinand. And the woman on the bed was Philippine. She was dying. Sarah could feel it in her own body. The pain, and the fatigue.

"I can feel the moon on my face," said Philippine. "I can feel the pull."

Ferdinand crossed to the window and drew a curtain across it.

"No," he said. "*No.* You must tell me how to help you. Your medicines—"

"There is no medicine for this—"

"There is one medicine," said Ferdinand, heavily. "And you

cast it upon stones. But I know you remember. You could tell me . . . you could tell me and I could make it . . . "

Yes, thought Sarah. Tell him. She could listen. She could make the elixir of life for Pols. So what if it was a curse? She could keep Pollina with her for a little longer.

She would go through this door. She would join her body with Philippine's and she would know how to make the cure for Pollina. Or she would force Philippine to help her. To help her truly this time. Philippine would not refuse her.

"But it is my time," she heard Philippine say. "It is simply my time. I am ready. I have had my last dream."

"What was it?" Ferdinand curled his large frame around his wife's, and pulled her head onto his chest. "Tell me your dream."

"A mother's wish was denied, but she suffers no more," said Philippine. "A giant has been given a choice. And now someone who is loved can be helped. But the journey to that is not finished. I have no answers for her. She must find them herself."

"Ah, my dear . . . I don't understand."

But I do, thought Sarah, slumping against the door, the strength going out of her limbs. She had to crawl toward the next door. Drag herself up to look through the keyhole.

Sarah cried out.
It was her father.

She thought she had forgotten what he really looked like; that the original had long been replaced by photographs in her memory; that she could not really recall his particular scent, or the feel of his arms, or his laugh, or the color of his eyes.

But she could. It was too painful to remember. And too dear to forget.

Her dad was seated in the old green tweed armchair that had been "his" chair in their old house, the house they had sold after his death. On the table next to him was a bowl of walnuts, a cup of tea, and a transistor radio, the one he carried about with him in the garage, tuned to the classical station. He was listening now to Itzhak Perlman playing Beethoven. Dad loved walnuts, loved the violin, loved Beethoven, loved that green chair. If he was sitting in that green chair then it meant he had finished work for the day, which meant it was late, because he worked so hard, all day, and his hands were so callused, and he never got enough rest, enough sleep, enough of the pleasures in life, because he was working, and saving, saving for her, for her music lessons, and her education, saving for a day in his future when he could sit in his green chair and maybe listen to Sarah on the radio, and that day would never come because he had been killed in a car crash and all the music had stopped for him on that day. And somewhere in her, too, the music had stopped. Not the music of others, but her own music. She had never stopped studying music but she had stopped wanting to perform it, or write it. For whom would she write, if not for her father?

Sarah, kneeling by the keyhole, drew in a ragged sob. She could open this door, and she could kneel at her father's feet and feel his rough hands in her hair. She could hear him say that he loved her, but, more important, she could say it to him.

I love you, Dad. Dad, I love you.

If she opened the door now, would she be a child again? Would she be able to change time? Stop him from driving on February fifth, when the roads were so icy? Save him?

Everything would be different. Everything.

"Sarah?"

It was Pollina. Pollina who was struggling to sit up, to stand.

For a moment, Sarah could only watch her. How could she leave her father? How could she make this choice? And then Pollina stretched out a hand, feebly, and moved blindly toward her, flailing and unsteady.

Sarah knew Pollina would not say "Help me."

And so Sarah staggered to her feet and grabbed Pollina by the hand and crashed through the fourth door.

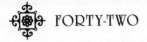

FORTY-TWO

They stood in a garden, at twilight. A large and formal garden, laid out in the Rococo style with paths of low and perfectly tended shrubberies, ornamental trees, and languid flowers, statues of tastefully draped nymphs and fauns and benign deities. In the center, a fountain splashed gently into a large, round marble basin. Sarah turned, and the door they had entered was gone. All she could see was a gazebo on a low hill.

Sarah looked at Pollina, who seemed to be dressed now in a pink and dark blue striped dress, caught up like an opera curtain in front and showing a frill of petticoats. Her hair hung in limp ringlets. Sarah raised her hands to her own head, which felt oddly heavy. She discovered she was wearing lemon-colored gloves, and some kind of plumed hat, perched up high on a tower of her hair, which was itself piled over some kind of cushion. The pins were sticking into her scalp. The tips of her gloves came away from her hair with traces of white powder. The bodice of her gown was cut low, although covered demurely with a froth of chiffon. She was wearing a corset, and something around her hips, which padded out her gown to the sides.

A gentle glissando of musical notes caught her ear. An

armonica. Sarah took Pollina by the hand and followed the sound, down a swept gravel path through a grove of yew trees. This was what she had in her desperation hoped for when she had taken them through the fourth door. This was the garden of Landstrasse number 261—"a miniature Versailles" on the banks of the Danube—the home of Franz Anton Mesmer.

Vienna, and, judging from the clothing, Vienna somewhere around 1780.

Pollina, silent, clutched Sarah's hand very hard. Her breathing was shallow and she was trembling.

As they neared the mansion, a footman in a powdered wig approached them on the path. Although he seemed somewhat startled to find them there, when Sarah gestured to Pols and inquired if Herr Mesmer might be disturbed—a matter of some urgency—he nodded and, after a quick but searching look at the shivering girl, invited them to follow him to the house.

Halfway down the path, Pollina, who had pressed herself against Sarah's skirts and was taking small steps, began to shake so badly she could no longer walk, and Sarah, fighting the stiffness of her garments, tried to pick her up.

"Please," she begged the footman. "Please, we must hurry."

The footman nodded and swiftly scooped Pollina, too weak to protest, into his own arms. They began to half run, the footman shouting out an order to a housemaid as they entered the mansion. To Sarah's intense relief, the footman led them toward the sound of the armonica, eventually calling to another footman, who threw open the doors of a large room.

In a blur, Sarah took in a frieze of plasterwork on a ceiling above delicately tinted paintings of garden scenes, enormous gilt mirrors, a central glass chandelier, and a series of wall sconces; small carved chairs and loveseats padded in rose and green velvet; a pianoforte, and yes, an armonica, and a man leaning over it. The footman set Pollina gently onto a settee, although once there the girl seemed to revive and sat up very straight, though still trembling.

Franz Anton Mesmer came forward, moving with deliberation. Clearly they were not the first visitors to simply appear on the doorstep, asking for the doctor's help. Mesmer listened with great attention to Sarah's garbled introductions.

"We've come from . . . from Prague," Sarah said. "I need . . . I beg you . . . to look at . . . at my daughter. She is very ill."

Mesmer dismissed the footman and—moving with almost irritating slowness—drew a chair near to the settee where Pollina perched. He took the girl's hand and studied her intently. His own hands, large and steady, felt Pollina's pulse, tested the movement of her joints, tilted the girl's chin up and down, and then lifted her eyelids. Pollina sat back and covered her eyes protectively, pushing Mesmer away.

"Don't touch them," she hissed.

Mesmer sat back and considered her for several minutes.

"No," he said at last. "I will not."

"It's *not* my eyes," said Pols. "It is something else. I am taking medicine. But I can't make it work."

Again Mesmer seemed to consider this for a long time before he spoke.

"Why?" he asked. "Why can't you?"

Pols shook her head. She began to cry. Mesmer began to stroke the tears from her face, then lightly touched her neck, her narrow chest, her arms and hands, her legs.

"The thing that is wrong. It is everywhere," he said.

"Yes," Pollina said. "It is everywhere."

"Do you wish it to be gone?"

"Of course."

"Truly?"

"I can't," said Pollina. "It is a part of me now."

"You are afraid"—Mesmer pressed his hand against her heart—"that if you let this medicine work upon you, you will lose your blindness. And you will see."

Sarah drew in her breath. She had not realized Pollina had been thinking this.

"I don't want to see," Pollina said.

"You do not want to see the stars?"

"I will lose their music."

"You do not know this."

"I feel it," said Pols. "I am afraid."

"I understand."

"I would rather die," said Pols, starting to shake again. "I would rather die." Her body bent forward, wrenched with a terrible fit of coughing.

Of course, thought Sarah. Pollina was not afraid of dying. She was afraid of living and losing her music. Music was her vision.

No one had been able to understand why the medicine that should have stopped her disease had failed. Especially when Pols was so strong, had such an iron will.

An iron will strong enough to stop the medicine.

Mesmer began stroking the air above the girl, and when Pols at last ceased coughing, he began taking very deep breaths.

"Follow my breath," he said.

"I can't," she gasped. "I can't breathe that way. It's too deep."

"Listen to me," said Mesmer. "You will never see in this world. That will never change. But the rest can change. The rest *will* change. You must let it. You must know it. Come. Listen."

He rose from his chair and took Pollina's hands, guiding her to a position in front of the armonica. And then he began to play, touching the glasses softly while looking at the girl.

He played for a long time. Sarah, whose eyes were at first also intently focused on Pollina, began to feel herself sliding into a kind of lucid dream. She saw the little girl before her and did not see her. She saw Mesmer playing, and she did not see him. She saw Philippine Welser, and Beethoven, and her father. She saw Max, and Nico.

I, too, have to let myself change.

For a moment, Sarah saw herself. As she had been, as she was, as she could be.

Mesmer stopped playing.

Was it over? Was Pollina cured?

The girl coughed and Sarah felt her heart plunge.

But then Pollina smiled. She touched her chest, proudly. The door to the salon opened. Sarah saw a young man with powdered hair tied in a ribbon stride into the room.

Mozart.

He was a little older than when Sarah had seen him at the *Schloss* in Innsbruck, but still crackling with energy, still alight with life and music and dreams of what was still before him.

Pollina turned to the young man and began speaking to him. Mozart laughed and gestured to the piano. Mozart and Pollina sat themselves on the bench. Pollina touched the keys. She began to play the beginning of Mozart's Piano Concerto no. 9.

"It's *very* good," Pollina said, patting Mozart on the arm.

"Thank you," said Mozart.

Pollina's hands hovered above the keyboard for a moment and then she smiled. She improvised for a few minutes. Sarah recognized a playful rendition of the overture from Mozart's opera *The*

Magic Flute. An opera Mozart wouldn't begin writing until near the end of his short life, still a decade away.

"I like that," said Mozart, when she finished. "Is it your own composition?"

Pollina shrugged.

"You can have it," she said solemnly. "Clean it up a bit. I am working on something else. An opera."

"Ah," said Mozart. "I would like to hear it. When you are finished."

Pollina smiled.

"Okay," she said, in English. "Cool." This made Mozart giggle. They shook hands.

"Sarah," said Pols, "we can go now." She held out her hands and Sarah moved forward and took them.

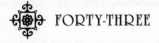 FORTY-THREE

$\mathcal{S}$arah opened her eyes. She was standing with Pollina in the Star Summer Palace. Elizabeth Weston was once again a cloaked corpse in the corner. Max and Nico had stopped playing the armonica. They appeared to be frozen. Sarah looked down. The sands of the hourglass were sinking into the stone floor.

"I think we have a few minutes," Pollina said. "If you want to talk."

"How are you feeling?"

"Well, I'm not going to start shouting 'I am going to live! Live, I tell you!'" Pols snorted. "But I'm hungry."

"Did that all just really happen?"

"I think so."

"That was nice of you," said Sarah. "To give Mozart *The Magic Flute*."

"I borrow from him all the time," said Pols. "It seemed fair." She waved a hand toward where Elizabeth lay. "I'm not sorry she's dead. But I will pray for her."

"I suppose the security guard will wake up in a few hours and think she broke in and killed herself. Which she did. I'm glad Nico's still here, though."

"I think it will change things for him." Pols smiled. "Having the choice to live or not. It's very powerful."

"Also, he has an immortal friend now," said Sarah. "Wait till you meet Hermes."

"If Nico sticks around," Pols said grandly, "I shall dedicate my opera to him."

"You might want to include Max in the dedication. He'll probably be the one paying for it."

"Max will be disappointed we didn't find the Fleece," said Pollina.

Sarah thought of the fifth door. She knew what was behind it. And why Philippine had made Ferdinand put it there. "Maybe not."

"Maybe not," agreed Pollina.

"I think I'm going to switch career paths. Something happened to me, too, back with Mesmer. I saw myself . . . I saw what I could be. I'll have to go back to school."

"You're not thinking of becoming a doctor like Mesmer, are you?" Pols frowned. "Your nose is too sensitive. You'd spend half the time puking."

"Not a doctor," Sarah promised. "Music, of course."

"Music? Play professionally, you mean?" Pols smiled. "I can tell you right now that you understand music better than anyone else I know but you are only a very fine violinist and a really good pianist. There *are* better out there. Maybe you could get work in a decent orchestra. I might be able to find you a job."

"Not play professionally exactly."

"Let's have it."

"You know what I mean. You're just teasing me."

"I want," Pols said, "to hear you say it."

"There really," Sarah said, feeling almost shy, "aren't enough women conductors. Of orchestras, I mean."

"Well, I assumed you didn't mean trains."

"Is it in my stars, do you think?"

The last of the sand slipped away into the stone floor and Max and Nico turned, blinking, to where Sarah and Pollina stood.

"Yes," whispered Pols. "Brava, Sarah. Brava."

 FORTY-FOUR

It was a white Christmas in Prague. Sarah looked out the window of Lobkowicz Palace and watched as snow silently blanketed the red roofs of the city. The black tongue of the Vltava was barely visible, tram lines erased, cars buried. Nothing moved in the streets below her. The twenty-first century had been brought to a halt in its tracks, and the world she gazed upon was the same world seen from this window over the centuries.

She could see a lot if she wanted to. But mostly she was practicing controlling her ability to see the past. Especially when the future was so interesting.

Sarah finally shut her laptop and picked up her hot mug of *svařené víno*, having fired off the last of her applications for music conductor internships. She was considering some intriguing places, though she had decided against Vienna. Berlin, though. Also Paris, Siena, and London. An interesting new program in Istanbul. Well, wherever she ended up, she knew that standing in front of an orchestra, hearing each instrument individually and at the same time as part of a whole that was so much greater than the sum of its parts—that was where she was meant to be.

But right now she was meant to be here. The museum was

closed for the day, and Max had set a long table in the Balcony Room, where they had gathered to eat, drink, and watch the storm. He had rolled the piano in from the Music Room, and Pollina was alternating between the *Messiah* and hilariously elaborate renditions of "Frosty the Snowman." Beneath the piano, a puppy—a rescue from the shelter on Pujmanové who might grow up to be a large terrier or, Jose joked, a grizzly bear—batted a tennis ball at Pols's feet. Pollina tapped it back to her. She had named her Natasha, in honor of Boris.

Nico, in an apron embroidered with the alchemical symbol for poison, was refusing Jose's offer of help in removing a giant roast goose from the oven. "I wanted the more traditional swan," he teased, surveying it for doneness, "but at the public gardens Moritz wasn't quick enough. Pass the powdered bezoar, would you—I want to give this bird some zing."

To spare the delicate sensibilities of the mortals' feelings on rats-in-the-kitchen, Hermes remained hidden in Nico's apron pocket, fortified by a peppermint drop.

Oksana was mashing the potatoes and talking about arranging a troika ride for later in the day. Sarah had no idea where they would get three horses, not to mention a troika, but had no doubt it would happen, if Oksana were in charge.

Harriet Hunter had not reappeared. She was perhaps celebrating Christmas with Charles Dickens or Napoléon. Or her mother.

Bettina Müller's body had been transported back to Austria and buried in Vienna's Central Cemetery not far from that of Ludwig Boltzmann, a Viennese physicist who'd studied the visible properties of matter, also a suicide. The city's cafés were full of gossip about the deadly love triangle she had been part of. Her lab was now occupied by a delightful chemist, Alessandro reported.

Sarah was fairly sure what "delightful" was a euphemism for, and that Alessandro was not having a solo *buon Natale*.

She'd had a postcard of Apollo from Renato and Thomas, who were spending the holidays together at a beach house on the Greek island of Symi.

Marie-Franz's card said she had begun her book on Mesmer and was looking forward to the ball season getting into full swing. She did not plan to have fat injected into her soles in order to waltz all night: *Strauss will keep me dancing on air,* she wrote.

The grave of Elizabeth Weston remained empty, as it had been for four hundred years.

The von Hohenlohe brothers' castle had been seized by the state as part of a criminal investigation into corporate espionage and afterward would be undergoing renovations. Archduke Ferdinand's *Kunstkammer* was scheduled to open in the summer to the general public. The newly restored castle would no doubt be one of Innsbruck's most fascinating attractions. Philippine Welser's *De re coquinaria* had been moved to the Austrian National Library in Vienna, where scholars would have easy access to it. Gottfried von Hohenlohe had confessed to stealing Bettina Müller's laptop on behalf of his brother, Heinrich. Heinrich's company denied all knowledge of Heinrich's activities. His role in the deaths of Nina Fischer, Gerhard Schmitt, and Felix Dorfmeister was under quiet investigation, but he had been jailed and publicly excoriated for setting fire to the stables of the Spanish Riding School. For saving the horses, Gottfried had been pardoned of all crimes. A recent Internet poll had named him "Austria's Sexiest Man Alive."

On an anonymous tip, the police had raided a house just outside of Kutná Hora and found a trove of stolen objects, most of them dusty old apothecaries' jars that, having been returned to the museums whence they'd come, were once more interred on basement shelves. Since the museums' curators hadn't actually noticed they were missing, they also didn't notice that some of them were not returned.

Moritz, gnawing on a bone under the table, had to move as Sarah's and Max's ankles entwined.

After dinner, Pollina played the overture of her new opera, *The Golden Fleece*. It was a story of ambition and compassion and heroism and sacrifice. Transgression and redemption. Wisdom and folly. And love. And death.

It was a story of life.